'*Thegn* is a meticulously researched and compelling tale of the Norman Conquest as we follow the fate of Edgar, the embattled protagonist. With universal themes of love and loss, heroism and treachery, conquest and resistance, this is one for fans of Rosemary Sutcliffe and Ken Follett alike. I cannot wait for the next in the series.'
Bill Rogers

Thegn

Patrick Maloney

Copyright © 2020 Patrick Maloney

All rights reserved.

ISBN: 979-8-63-197183-7

This book is a work of fiction and except in the case of historical events and characters, any resemblance to actual events or persons, living or dead, is purely coincidental.

No part of this publication may be reproduced, stored in a retrieval system, or transmitted, in any form or by any means without the prior written permission of the publisher, nor be otherwise circulated in any form of binding or cover other than that in which it is published and without a similar condition being imposed on the subsequent purchaser.

For Marie and Terry Maloney, my parents.

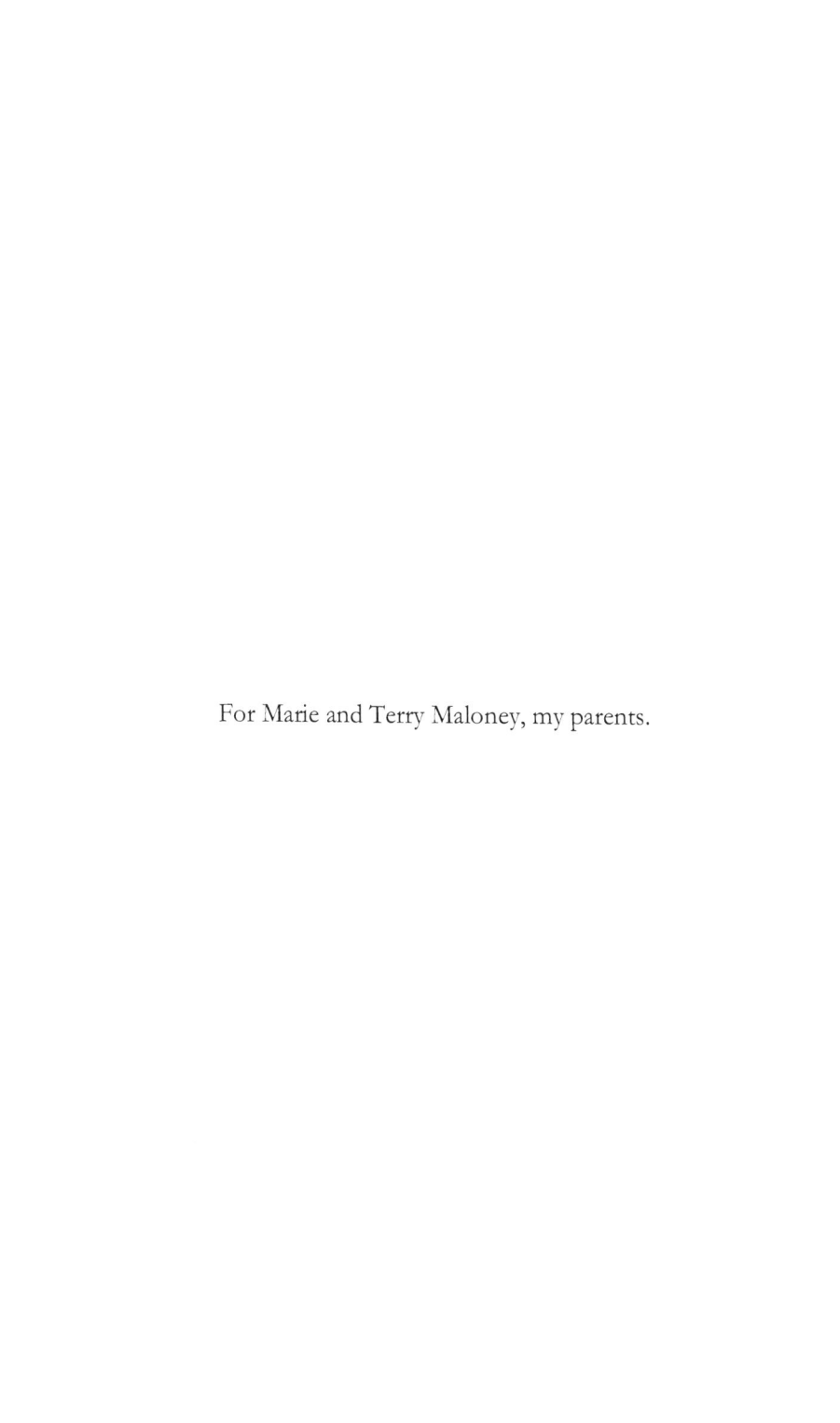

1
The Mead Hall

September 1066

'When I saw you yesterday, I couldn't understand why you wouldn't speak to me. Then I realised. That wasn't your face I saw before me – I was talking to a pig's arse!'

Two men faced each other across the width of the mead hall. Every face in the hall was turned towards Guthrum. Nobody dared utter a word. A tense silence filled the hall.

Outside, a blackbird loudly and defiantly sang his evening refrain, daring any other bird to invade his territory.

Everyone present held their breath, waiting to hear what Guthrum's reply would be to this grievous insult.

Guthrum narrowed his eyes. The wide leather belt around his waist creaked as he leaned back slightly.

The rider leaned forward into the neck of his horse. He could hear the breathing of the beast, just beginning to sound laboured as it thundered on into the gathering gloom. His thighs ached and his eyes watered from the constant rush of cold air in his face.

Even the young servants, boys and girls, usually busily carrying great plates of meat and flagons of ale stood wide-eyed and silent as they watched the two warriors. The silence in the mead hall was thickening with tension, fuelled by the collective stillness and rapt attention of a room full of people.

Barely daring to breathe, the assembled men of Rapendun waited to hear Guthrum's reply.

'You are mistaken, my friend,' said Guthrum, mildly. 'That was not a pig's arse.' He paused, casting a sidelong glance along the feasting table. 'It was your mother!'

The mead hall erupted into a cacophony of cheers and jeers. Those sitting around the long table slapped the palms of their hands on the bench in approval. Ale slopped from the drinking vessels held by the men and dripped unnoticed off the edge of the table.

Eric stared at his opponent as they stood up to each other across the hall.

He placed his hands on his hips.

'If that pig's arse had been my mother, she would have shat right in your face!'

Another wave of approbation rose from the table.

'How would I tell the difference from her normal speech?' yelled Guthrum.

'And how could we tell that you had been shat on?' replied Eric instantly.

The hall was in uproar. More ale was spilled from beaker and horn. The men around the table laughed and yelled their encouragement to the opponents.

At the top table, Thegn Wulfmaer rose swiftly to his feet, holding his large drinking horn in his right hand. He held it high for silence. The clamour died down, with just a few lingering laughs. The two opponents turned to face the Thegn. He was a man of middle build, clearly once solid and strong but now in his decline.

Every face in the hall was fixed on his. The revellers waited in respectful silence and keen anticipation for the verdict of their Thegn. Bets had been laid, winners and losers were about to discover their fate.

Wulfmaer looked keenly at each of the combatants. His grey eyes glistened in the candlelight and the skin at their corners creased in deliberation. His unruly white hair formed a halo round his lined face. A long, noble moustache of white hairs, yellowed round the mouth, hung down to his clean-shaven chin.

After a long pause, he thrust his drinking horn towards Eric.

'Eric wins! Fetch the bowl!'

A young girl, no more than ten years old, with flaxen pigtails and eager smile, walked from the far end of the hall. In her hands she held a wide bowl, filled with ale almost to its brim. She walked carefully, watching the surface of the ale, making sure none spilled on the rush-strewn, beaten-earth floor.

The men along the feasting table began beating their cups on the table, at first in time with her steps, then increasing the frequency, encouraging the girl to walk ever faster.

She speeded up in time with their promptings, her face creased in concentration. She reached Eric without spilling any ale, and the men at the tables loudly cheered her efforts.

She lifted the bowl towards Eric and dipped her head in a polite bow, smiling in her small triumph.

Eric grinned at her and returned the bow. He took the bowl, and as everyone in the hall chanted 'Down, down, down, down!', he drained it. It was far too wide to be used as a serious drinking vessel, and to everyone's delight, ale tipped out of the sides, pouring down Eric's leather tunic.

As he finished, he held the bowl up in triumph, to cheers.

'I now invite Guthrum to drink!' he shouted.

The girl took the bowl from Eric and passed it to Guthrum, picking up a jar of ale from the table and refilling it.

Again to the chant of 'Down, down, down, down!' Guthrum messily poured the ale into his mouth and down the front of his jerkin.

The horse's breath was beginning to sound ragged, yet still it pounded on. Foamy sweat streaked back from its deep, powerful neck. The rider held on grimly. He was tired, and he shared the fatigue of his horse. Not long now...

The hall resounded to the sound of palms slapping the table and voices raised in cheers and shouts of admiration of the fine *flyting* – the insulting competition they had all just been treated to. The girl with the pigtails walked along the top table, filling the beakers with ale. She filled Wulfmaer's horn first.

At Wulfmaer's left hand sat his grandson, Edgar, a handsome, athletic young man with short-cropped, light brown hair and the grey eyes of his grandfather. The girl filled Edgar's beaker. She then filled the beakers of the two guests who sat on Wulfmaer's right side; a short, balding man with a pleasant face and a younger, quietly demure man who sat silently beside him, intent on the food he was eating. Finally, she topped up the cups of the three well-dressed village headmen who had been able to attend the evening's celebration.

This night was one of the highlights of the year. The harvest had been good and finished in short order. The Thegn had thrown this magnificent and generous feast as a reward for his hard-working farmers here in the mead hall, the very heart of social and community life in Rapendun.

Three benches stood in the hall, two along the length of the building and one across the top, slightly raised above the other two and separated from them to allow the servants to pass freely between the tables. At the top table sat Thegn Wulfmaer, Edgar and their guests. On the benches on either side sat around forty men, some in soiled work clothes, others displaying more finery. In the centre of the long hall was a rectangular pit, which in the cold months of winter was home to a hearty fire, though now it was clean and clear of ashes. Bundled stakes stood ready to be lit.

Along each side of the building stood solid wooden posts, each one the trunk of a mature tree, twelve to each side. Connecting the posts of one side to those on the other were wooden beams sculpted with heroes and fabulous beasts, intertwined with finely carved foliage. From the beams hung large bundles of herbs, drying in the warm air of the hall.

Leaving the top table, the girl scuttled across the rush-strewn floor to the long feasting tables and poured both contestants fresh ale into the beakers that the two men now held out eagerly. They raised their beakers to each other and to their Thegn, and swallowed down the ale in a single draught, then held them out again for refilling. The small girl obliged and the two men sat down.

A smile flickered round Edgar's full mouth. He wore a moustache in the same style as his grandfather, though his was light brown, almost golden, and thinner than the old Thegn's. He leaned forward slightly over the table and turned towards Guthrum.

'Tell me, Guthrum, did you ever meet Eric's mother?'

'Never to my knowledge, Master Edgar.'

Eric leaned over the table towards them.

'It's a good job too, old man, she would have eaten you alive!'

Guthrum laughed. 'As ever, child, you underestimate me. My prowess is legendary! No woman can resist the lure of Guthrum's meat!'

He paused, a look of alarm spreading across his hard features. 'Tell me. What was your mother's name? May God forgive me; I could be your father!'

The comment drew more appreciative laughter from all the seated men and even Eric's face broke into a wide smile.

Eric and Guthrum were Thegn Wulfmaer's chief housecarls, and although they habitually referred to each other as 'old man' and 'child', there was barely ten years between them.

Guthrum grimaced. 'Actually, I'm sorry I said that; I should have used it at the next flyting!'

'No more contest tonight!' called Edgar. He pushed himself to his feet and banged loudly on the table with a beaker. The chatter and laughter around the hall subsided and everyone turned to face Edgar.

'Tonight, we drink!' he began. 'We have a fine crop

from the fields, thanks to the ceaseless labours of our excellent ceorls.'

The farmers and labourers cheered. Wulfmaer slapped him on the back, nodding his head and smiling in agreement.

'And tonight, we celebrate their great hard work, tonight we give ale and food beyond compare!' Another great cheer, in a night of great cheers, arose from the long table. Edgar's voice dropped a tone. 'This year has had its share of setbacks. The death of Gethwyn,' he nodded towards a farmer in a crumpled tunic, sitting with a couple of friends at the end of the hall. His wife Gethwyn had collapsed and died during the first days of spring, and Edgar had arranged for a decent burial for her. The farmer nodded; grief still etched in the deep lines of his face.

'Within Rapendun we lost three infants, at God's will. We have also had successes, seven healthy infants in Rapendun, two in Osmundestun and one in Willetun. We also have from our fields the best crop that we have seen in many long years, and this is all down to you. So now we thank you, with meat, ale and mead!' He lifted his beaker of ale high above his head. '*Waes thu hael!*'

The men in the hall all raised their cups, beakers and horns and returned Edgar's toast with gusto.

'*Waes hael!*'

Edgar sat down, and next to him Thegn Wulfmaer regarded his grandson proudly.

Wulfmaer's son – Edgar's father – had died when Edgar was just two years old, and Edgar's mother had succumbed to a pestilence the following winter, weakened by her grief. Wulfmaer and his wife, Hilde, had taken Edgar into their home and raised him as their own.

Wulfmaer began to turn in his chair and then stopped, a furrow creasing his brow. He had been turning to speak to Hilde, having just for the moment forgotten that she, too, was now dead, and cold in her grave. He missed her company and her wisdom and her smile every moment of every day. On the rare occasions when he forgot she was dead, he braced himself for the wave of grief that rocked him as he remembered and lived the terrible moment once again. It always felt like the first time.

He had sat by Hilde's bedside for three days and held her hand, whispering inconsequential words to her as she lay dying.

Finally, she had turned her head slightly towards him and whispered 'It is time, my love.'

Her hand had gone limp in his and she was gone.

Wulfmaer often thought of that moment. A tiny instant of time that dropped an impenetrable iron gate between himself and his beloved wife. He closed his eyes, feeling the sting of unformed tears in his eyes.

He shook his head slightly and returned to the present. Edgar was joking with the housecarls and heaping praise on his tenant farmers. Wulfmaer smiled slightly. The lad was a credit to his grandparents. He was popular and respected. He spoke with authority and yet could still talk on equal terms with a ceorl farmer. He would make a fine thegn one day, once Wulfmaer was reunited with his precious Hilde. Not too long now, my love, he thought to himself.

Another great cheer arose from around the mead hall tables as the serving girls and boys walked in with huge plates of roasted meats. A whole hog, coated in honey and spit-roasted over an open fire was placed in the centre of the table, where it steamed enticingly along with plates of roast goose, duck, sheep and goat.

Almost as a man, the collected menfolk of the settlement drew out their seaxes, the single-edged knives that were the only blades they were allowed to bring to the mead hall, and began to carve away at the meat. Edgar sliced a large piece from the hog's rump and held it up on his knife in front of Eric's face.

'Is this your mother?' he said.

Wulfmaer laughed out loud. 'Well said, Edgar. You can have some ale too!' He signalled to the little fair-haired girl, who ran forward, almost staggering under the weight of the huge jug full of ale that she carried.

She carefully filled all of the men's drinking vessels, being especially careful to fill almost to overflowing the rough beaker of one of the ceorl farmers; her father. The man ruffled the girl's pigtails affectionately as she hurried on to fill the next beaker.

The road was becoming better defined now, signs of greater use. This showed the rider that he was getting closer to his destination. A thin, low hanging branch whipped across his face, leaving a stinging red welt. Flecks of froth from the horse's sweat-soaked neck flew back and spattered his face.

The noise in the mead hall grew steadily. Good food and good ale were having their warming and relaxing effect on all those present. For most, it was rare to eat such good food and in such great quantities. The celebration was a precious time, a time in which to renew the bonds of friendship with neighbours and to give thanks for the generosity of the Thegn.

Most of the food had been reduced to bones, and at one

end of the table, a few of the men started stamping their feet, an action that was soon picked up by all present. The stamping got faster and faster until it just became a solid wall of noise.

Wulfmaer stood up once more and held his hands up for silence, to little effect. Eric and Guthrum stood up and started shouting at the gathering to shut up. Eric punched a particularly noisy individual on the shoulder, nearly spinning him off his stool. The noise abated into small scufflings and laughs.

Wulfmaer spoke. 'I hope you've all had enough to eat because there isn't any more.'

His words were met with loud approval and great shouts of thanks. Wulfmaer held up his hands once more. 'Very well. There is of course still plenty more ale and mead…' his next words were drowned out by even louder roars of approval.

'And also, we have with us tonight Alduin of Lincolia, a travelling bard whom I have heard before, and I can promise you that he will be spinning some pretty tales for us.' There was another outburst of clapping and cheering. 'Now shut up, drink and listen!'

The clapping died down as the small, balding man who had been sitting beside Wulfmaer stood up and walked past the tables to the far end of the hall. He carried a lyre lightly in his left hand. The strings spread over the sounding board and up to the arch of the instrument like a fan. The arms of the arch were delicately carved to resemble two horses' heads, nose to nose. Following him was the younger, quiet man in a simple tunic. He sat against one of the great supporting upright wooden posts, apparently taking no part in the bard's performance.

Alduin pulled a three-legged stool from the side of the hall, withdrew a cloth from his scrip and very conspicuously wiped down the stool before he sat on it. The hall erupted with laughter. The bard sat down, settling his stringed instrument at an angle across his body. He strummed the lyre a few times, sending little ripples of sound around the hall. The men smiled with glee. It was rare indeed to hear a musical instrument being played.

He played the chorus line from a popular drinking song, making the last note sound flat. This raised another laugh. He pulled a comically puzzled face and looked down at his instrument. He played the line again. This time the last note was sharp. Now he looked really puzzled and tried another well-known tune. Again, the final note went flat and then sharp. He looked up at his audience, holding his hands out, palm up, as if suggesting that he didn't know what to do. Rumbling laughter rolled round the hall.

Suddenly, the bard's face lit up in comic alertness as though he had just had a brilliant idea. He held one finger up and his face broke into a huge smile. He pulled out his cloth, stood up, placed the instrument on the stool and quickly cleaned the patch of hard-packed earth floor immediately in front of the stool. Then he knelt and held his palms together as if in prayer. The hall erupted in laughter and hands slapped the top of the table in appreciation. The bard crossed himself, returned to his stool and once more took up the instrument. He cautiously picked out the notes of the drinking tune again, this time perfectly. Cheers rose from the audience and the bard stood, spreading his arms in appreciation of their applause, bowing deeply.

The horse crashed into a clearing. Yes, the rider remembered, this would be the first of the outlying farms. The small house of the farmer would be just ahead, to the right of the road, near the tree line. One more push, Boy, he willed his horse to carry on. Panting now, the horse showed no signs of slowing. One more push…

Alduin the bard had started his recital with the tale of Saint Oswald, the good Christian King of Northumbria. As the tale swept towards the saintly King's encounter with the pagan King Penda of Mercia on the battlefield, so the music swelled in volume and complexity. In between sung verses, the bard's fingers flew across the strings so quickly that no one in the hall could follow them. The excitement was palpable. Men sat open-mouthed, their drinks forgotten as they listened intently to every word the bard sang, and every note he played so brilliantly. Each man held his breath as the song reached the dramatic climax. Alduin sang of the sword of the heathen Penda cleaving Oswald's mail coat and reaching deep inside, to find the pumping heart and extinguish its life.

Bright Blade, Blessed Hand
He raised his eyes to God in heaven
And fell, fell from his steed
Onto the blood-red ground.

Alduin stopped for a moment, allowing the tragedy of the situation to sink into the hearts and minds of his audience. The last chord he had struck faded away as if following the saintly King into death. He began singing again, the music discordant and uneven as he described how Penda dismembered the body of the holy King.

At heaven's command, a raven swooped
Tears in its fierce eyes
As it fell to the ground
The ground now so holy with the Bright Blade's blood
In its claws it grasped
The King's blessed arm, still warm from its saintly life
But the arm would not be parted from its God-beloved host
And fell, fell as from heaven itself, it fell to the foul Earth
Now all the more wicked for the loss of the sacred King
And where it fell, there sprang a gush of holy water,
Water so sweet and good that to this very day
It heals the ills of all around, the blessed water
Of the Bright Blade and Blessed Hand.

Alduin played on, a tune of such sadness and melancholy that not a man in the mead hall remained unmoved. The music softened and gently faded away.

As the last notes fell to silence, the bard's voice lifted softly again, barely more than a murmur. The men around the tables strained to catch the words as they slipped like tears to the earthen floor.

Time of goodness is past
The King beloved of God walks with us no more
Glorious champion of good
Shining ring-giver; there is a hole in the hearts of men
Nevermore his goodly gifts to receive
Nevermore his mighty arms to shield
Shadows stalk the land
Dark men in the pay of the wicked one
The one who took our lord
Sliced him like a butcher

Now walk in his holy footprints
Befouls the ways of our land
Our blessed King is gone
We are left in the shadow
God has turned his back on us.
Men groan under the cruel rule
Women weep and children cry out loud;
What is become of our land?
What is become of us?

Alduin strummed his lyre very gently, plucking out a melancholy final tune. His lyre fell to silence.

After a few moments of absolute quiet, the mead hall erupted into the most vigorous applause of the evening, with cheers and shouts for more.

The bard accepted the adulation modestly, beaming at the young girl as she brought him a large drinking horn, filled to the brim with fine brown ale. With a theatrical flourish, he downed the ale in one, adding to the appreciation shown by his audience. He resumed his seat and motioned with one finger to the man who had been sitting quietly beneath the great wooden post during his performance. Nobody knew the man, but as he approached the bard, he pulled a reed whistle from out of his belt. It was notched at one end and had six small holes equally spaced along its length. He stood next to Alduin and waited for silence.

Alduin spoke for the first time. 'This is Tula, he will assist me for the next tune.'

Tula blew down his whistle and produced the same drinking tune as Alduin had done before. The last note was flat. Everyone laughed again. Tula made a quick sign of the

Thegn

cross and looked upwards. He mouthed the words 'I'm with him,' as he pointed at Alduin. He tried the tune again. This time it came out right. He received his own cheer and bowed, a huge smile on his face.

Alduin started playing a slow, rhythmic tune, tinged with sadness. The whistle player joined in, playing a high, fluting melody above Alduin's strings, following Alduin's lead at one time, drifting away in little harmonies of his own at another.

The men at the table were entranced. Nobody had ever heard anything like this before. The tunes being played were different, and yet they worked together to make a melody that was infinitely finer than either of the two individual tunes that made it up. The audience watched spellbound as the bards' fingers flitted across their instruments; Alduin's crabbed hand stilling the strings he wished silenced, his other hand plucking and strumming. The fingers of Tula's right hand danced over the holes in his small reed whistle, producing the most extraordinary top notes over Alduin's more bass, persistent melody.

The tune came to an end. There was silence. Alduin looked quizzically at his partner; had they played badly? Tula returned a slightly puzzled look. Then suddenly everyone was clapping, half the men got to their feet and cheered and whistled. Everyone was stamping their feet on the solid earthen floor.

The two men bowed and placed their instruments on the stool, indicating that they had not finished. They walked back to their places beside Wulfmaer.

Edgar stood up, nodded to the two minstrels and whispered in his grandfather's ear. Wulfmaer nodded briefly and patted his grandson on the forearm. Edgar walked across the hall to the door, centrally placed in the wall.

As he stepped outside, a rush of cool air enveloped him. The food and the ale were resting none too lightly in his stomach, and he breathed deeply of the refreshing evening air. He looked across from the hall's door towards the line of trees that stood some hundreds of yards away to the west and north. The sky was bright where the Sun had recently dipped below the horizon. No stars were yet visible but to the east, the sky was darkening.

Despite the heaviness in his stomach, Edgar felt at peace. At nineteen years of age, he was at the dawn of his full manhood. The careful instructions and training given to him by his grandfather and grandmother ensured that he was prepared to take over as thegn when the time came, though he was far from eager to do that for it could only happen on the death of his grandfather.

Since he could first walk and carry a wooden sword, his grandfather's housecarls had trained him in the use of the sword, the single-handed and the double-handed battleaxe. He had had three tutors, the first two now dead, the last one Guthrum, who was perhaps the best of them all, so patient was he, possessed of an inner calm and stillness that was the envy of all who knew him. Edgar exhaled explosively, releasing a cloud of vapour that drifted very slowly away from him. The evening was chill, a sign of the cold months ahead. The thought of the cold nights brought with it another, not unrelated, thought. His grandfather had been dropping hints, none too subtly, about Edgar's future, specifically his need to choose a bride.

Wulfmaer had spurned his own father's wishes that he marry a daughter of a noble family. He had secretly married Hilde, the daughter of a farmer. The match had, however, been well made, and Wulfmaer's father eventually admitted that Wulfmaer could not have chosen a better bride, though he regretted the missed opportunity to forge a useful alliance with a neighbouring thegnly family.

Despite this, Wulfmaer was trying to persuade Edgar to marry for alliance. Edgar had detected some sympathy from his grandfather when he suggested that he should, perhaps, marry for love, as Wulfmaer had done. Edgar, however, was not in love and had never fallen for a farmer's daughter, and so he idly began considering the daughters of nearby thegnly houses.

He walked slowly down the path leading from the mead hall and across a small cobbled area and out of the open gate that allowed entry to the ditched and palisaded enclosure in which the most important buildings of Rapendun stood.

He strolled down to the fence round a cattle field. The cows were munching grass contentedly, but one of them looked up at him as he stood there. It bent down to get more grass, but then looked up again. A second cow started contemplating him. Edgar smiled. The cows were such curious creatures. He knew that if he stood here long enough, the whole herd would come to him, pressing against the wattle fence beside which he stood. He doubted the fence could take it, and so moved slowly off along the fence line.

He paused again; a noise had caught his attention. Faint and far away, but yes, he could definitely hear it. It sounded like hoof beats, and they were getting closer. He moved away from the cattle fence and back across the ditched defences to wait to see who was coming.

A few moments later, the horse and rider came into

view, racing towards him along the road. The horse careened through the enclosure gate.

'Whoa! Whoa boy!' the rider called to his horse, which skidded to a halt just feet from Edgar. The horse looked exhausted, Edgar noted, its chest heaving as it panted noisily, foam falling from its open mouth in huge drops to the ground by its front hooves. The rider rolled off his mount and almost fell to the ground. He staggered a little with weariness and Edgar moved forward to catch him by the elbow. He steadied himself and stood upright.

'I am Coel, from the household of Earl Edwin. I have grave tidings and must speak with Thegn Wulfmaer at once.'

Edgar nodded. 'The Thegn's in the mead hall. I'd better fetch him. It's full and noisy in there.' He turned and ran back up the path to the hall.

He entered and walked swiftly over to his grandfather, who was deeply involved in a conversation with Alduin. Edgar ignored the bard and spoke into Wulfmaer's ear.

'There's a messenger from Earl Edwin outside, he says he has grave news.'

Wulfmaer was instantly attentive. He snapped his fingers at Eric and Guthrum and together, the four of them strode out of the mead hall. When a messenger from the Earl of Mercia himself arrived, he demanded instant attention. Edgar called to one of the less inebriated of the ceorls sitting at the end of the table and indicated that he should follow them.

They all stepped outside, the ceorl looking puzzled and worried. Edgar held him by the upper arm. 'Occa, that horse is close to collapse. See to it.'

Occa looked at the horse. 'Aye, Master Edgar,' he said, and led the horse away to stables where he could get water for it to drink and with which to wash it and cool it.

'You are from the Earl?' said Wulfmaer as he strode up to the messenger.

'Aye, my lord. I am one of many messengers who have ridden all night and all day from Eoforwic, sent from the Earl, stopping at each great hall on the way.' He paused to catch his breath.

'A large force of Norsemen, under the leadership of Harald Sigurdson-king has landed on the east coast of Northumbria. A coastal fishing town, Scardeburg, has been sacked and burned and Heldernesse has been devastated. The Earls Edwin and Morcar are raising an army in Northumbria to meet the Norsemen. Earl Edwin instructs that an army be raised in his earldom of Mercia and that it marches to Eoforwic. He requires you to supply the men that you are bound to. Faster messengers than me have been dispatched south to inform Harold-king of the invasion. The Earl expects that the King will march north, gathering fyrd and burwarran as he goes.'

The four men looked at each other. Wulfmaer spoke first. 'This is bad. Eric, Guthrum, get back in there and quieten everyone down. I will speak to them.'

Eric and Guthrum turned to do their master's bidding.

'How many fyrdmen do you have, my lord?' asked the messenger.

'There are seventeen within my lands, but I myself am too old now to be of use. Estate duties will require one of my men. I will appoint the oldest to that task. We will therefore provide the Earl with fifteen. To that, I can add forty burwarran.'

'That is good, my lord, every sword, spear and axe that we can raise will be needed.'

'How large is the Norse army?' asked Edgar.

'Five, maybe six thousand. It is said that three hundred ships made land and that Tostig Godwinson was with them.'

'Tostig!' Wulfmaer spat.

Just one year ago, the Northumbrians had risen in revolt against the severe rule of their Earl, Tostig. Old Edward-king had deposed the Earl and sent him into exile, on the advice of none other than Harold Godwinson, Tostig's brother and now Edward's successor as King of England. Now it seemed Tostig was back for his revenge. 'I knew we hadn't heard the last of him!'

The messenger swayed slightly. 'My lord, I beg that I might impose on your hospitality tonight, I have been riding all day and I am weary.'

'Of course, I'll have a pallet laid out for you in the hall. Come, we must speak to our men.'

Most of the guests filed out of the mead hall, a mood of sombre determination replacing the careless jollity. Although not Northumbrians themselves, but Mercians, the name of Tostig had animated the men. The rebellion raised against Tostig's rule had spread far into Mercia.

The following day the fyrd and burwarran would gather in the morning, and begin the three-day march to Eoforwic to meet the Earl's forces.

A small party of women remained behind to clear up the mess left by the feasting men. Amongst them was the young girl who had served the ale so enthusiastically at the feast. She looked tired as she carried the large platters, now stripped of their fine food. Some of the men remained behind in the hall, mostly waiting for wives and daughters to finish their duties so that they could walk back home together.

Thegn Wulfmaer, Edgar, Guthrum and Eric sat quietly with the Earl's messenger, Coel. They sipped ale and discussed plans for the coming march.

As the girl returned empty-handed to clear more dishes from the top table, Thegn Wulfmaer stood and called across the hall to her.

'You girl! Come here!'

She stopped, like a startled hare. Her face registered fear and indecision. She looked across to the side of the hall, where her father sat in the shadows waiting for her to be released for the night. He nodded cautiously at her, then stood up and approached the Thegn a few paces behind his daughter. She stopped at the head of the table, where the Thegn sat.

'What is your name, child?' he asked.

'Edda, my lord,' she replied.

'And this is your father is it?' He indicated the man behind her with a dismissive flick of his finger.

'It is, my lord,' replied the girl.

'I've been watching you tonight,' said the Thegn. 'How old are you?'

The girl looked uncertain. She turned her head to look inquisitively at her father. Wulfmaer raised his eyebrows to the man in a gesture that gave him permission to speak.

'This is her eleventh summer, my lord,' he said.

'And your name?'

'Thorgils, my lord.'

'Are you of the burwarran?' asked Wulfmaer.

'I am, my lord,' replied Thorgils with evident pride.

'Good, good.' He paused for a moment, looking at

Edda.

'You have worked very hard tonight, Edda. Your father will be rightly pleased with you. So am I.'

He withdrew his hand from within his tunic and held up a beautiful, shiny, black shale bangle. Edda's eyes opened wide. He passed the precious object to her and her mouth opened in astonishment as she ran her fingers over its silky-smooth burnished surface.

She looked up at Wulfmaer with wonder and joy in her eyes. 'Thank you, my lord,' she managed.

Behind her, Thorgils looked on with pride. He nodded his thanks to the Thegn.

Wulfmaer smiled at them. 'Go home now, both of you. We will see you, Thorgils, in the morning.'

2

The Road to Eoforwic

The following morning the levy of Rapendun gathered on the cobbled courtyard in front of the mead hall. The participants in last night's festivities had travelled home by way of their neighbour's houses, visiting those who had not been at the hall, informing them of the news and of the fact that the Thegn had called for the levy to assemble the following morning.

Long before sunrise, the bell in the church tower had begun tolling its mournful message across the fields to any who did not yet know. Three rings of the bell, repeated over and over. The message was clear; everyone knew what the three bell-ring meant.

In the east the sky was daylight bright, heralding the imminent sunrise. A dozen or so mounted men sat together on their horses a little way from the centre of the crowd. They stood out not simply because of their horses, but also because of the quality of their clothing. None was wearing his mail armour this far removed from an actual battle, but their tunics, leggings and capes were made of fine, rich material, with intricate patterns stitched into them. These were the fyrdmen, professional warriors, from the wealthier levels of society. During times of peace, these men were the Thegn's supervisors and administrators, but each kept up with weapons practice at all times and were ready for war at very short notice. They chatted and laughed casually amongst themselves, displaying none of the nerves and anxieties being displayed by the men of the burwarran.

The men of the burwarran, men who normally ploughed and reaped, stood in leather jackets padded to withstand casual weapon strokes, if not a concerted attack. Most had the jackets open at the front, as it was a warm morning, still and humid. Thick leather caps sat on many of their heads, the straps hanging unfastened. Some of the more fortunate ones had steel helmets, some inherited from earlier generations of burwarran, some taken from the field of battle. Wives tutted and fussed around the fyrdmen and burwarran, balancing in equal quantities pride and anxiety.

To the rear of the party stood two more horses, each riderless but carrying large quantities of provisions for the journey.

Not only the levy and their families were gathered; most of the rest of the population of the local farmsteads stood around, variously gossiping excitedly and standing in nervous silence. Old men gave last-minute advice to sons and grandsons who were about to march off to war. Amongst the gathered crowd, Alfgaer, the priest who presided over Rapendun's fine stone-built church, in his brown habit and sandals, wandered around amongst the gathering, offering words of comfort and encouragement.

Within the mead hall, Edgar, Guthrum and Eric stood with bundles at their feet containing their mail shirts, helms and shields. Each had an axe hanging from his belt.

Thegn Wulfmaer walked out of his private chamber and strode up to Edgar.

'Before you go, Edgar, I have something for you,' he said.

He held out his hands, in which was the most beautifully crafted scabbard Edgar had ever seen. Long, thin, twisted animal shapes coiled and writhed in silver along the length of the rich red leather of the scabbard. Protruding from the scabbard was the hilt of a sword, the grip bound tightly in some black material. The pommel was shaped like a large almond in gold, set with a large, deep red garnet and with a protruding tang, square in section but tapering, not quite to a point.

The housecarls gasped as Wulfmaer withdrew the blade. It was exquisitely made, mirror-like steel, with razor-sharp edges.

'This blade was won by my grandfather, Alfhaere, when he marched with Earl Byrhtnoth against the Viking Olaf Tryggvason at Maldon seventy years ago.'

He passed the sword and its scabbard to his grandson. 'If you look at it in the right light, there is some writing at the top of the blade, near the hilt,' he said.

Edgar was left almost speechless by his grandfather's gift.

'Thank you, Grandfather,' he stammered. 'It's exquisite. I will do my best to honour your name with it, and that of your grandfather.'

'What does the writing say, my lord?' asked Guthrum

with a keen interest.

'I think you've probably guessed, Guthrum,' smiled Wulfmaer. 'Between two crosses is the word "Ulfberht".'

Guthrum and Eric gaped at the sword.

'It's an Ulfberht!' whispered Guthrum, in awe.

'It's not quite that, Grandfather,' said Edgar. 'Look, the second cross lies between the h and the t.'

Wulfmaer looked carefully at the blade where his grandson was pointing.

'So it does,' he murmured.

'You all seem to know about these swords,' said Edgar. 'What is an Ulfberht?' His eyes were drinking in the loveliness of the sword as he turned and twisted it in his hand.

'It's a Norse blade,' explained Guthrum, 'those with the word "Ulfberht" on the blade are the very finest swords anywhere in the world. That blade will almost slice through the iron of a normal blade. It's probably worth more than our yearly income. They aren't made any more, haven't been for many, many years. Maybe Ulfberht and all his apprentices are now dead.'

'It was made by Ulfberht?' asked Edgar.

'Or his family or assistants. There never was a sword like an Ulfberht, they are legendary. I have only ever seen one once before and that was many years ago, I was not much more than a boy. Use it well, lad.' Guthrum beamed at Edgar.

Edgar turned to his grandfather and made a shallow bow towards him.

'I will treasure it, Grandfather.'

Wulfmaer slapped his grandson on the shoulder, 'Keep it honed and clean, use it well in battle, and I will be well pleased.'

Edgar slipped the wondrous blade back into its beautiful scabbard.

'Come, it is time to go,' said Wulfmaer.

The housecarls led the way out of the hall, but at the threshold, Wulfmaer took hold of Edgar by the arm and held him back.

'Edgar, you are the leader of this expedition, but Guthrum has a great deal of experience. You should rely on his wisdom, and not be too keen to command at any price. Listen to him, trust him.'

'I would never presume to go against any advice that Guthrum chose to give,' replied Edgar. 'Apart from yourself, I trust nobody more than I trust him. He's been my teacher and counsellor for many years. Have no fear on that account.'

Wulfmaer squeezed Edgar's arm.

'Good lad,' he said, leading him out of the hall.

Outside the hall, a young boy in a short, belted tunic was leading three horses, ready saddled and provisioned, across the cobbles towards them. Edgar, Guthrum and Eric swiftly mounted their steeds as four more horsemen walked slowly up to them. Edgar nodded in greeting to the horsemen. He knew them well; he had grown up with them. They had played together as boys and were bound together in firm friendship.

One of the horsemen barked a word of command and the men started falling into a loose column. There was a final flurry of hugging as the men took their leave of their families. One or two of the women stood aside, weeping, whilst most simply stood in silence.

Silence fell as Wulfmaer raised his voice. 'This is not the first time that the levy has been raised from our lands, nor do I imagine that it will be the last. As some of you may know, a Norse army has landed far to our north, near Eoforwic. Our Earl Edwin and his brother Morcar, Earl of Northumbria, have raised an army to oppose them, and it is to that army that I am now sending you. You may think that such a small force as you are can do little to help in great affairs of state, but be assured that all over the kingdom, small bands like you are gathering and marching towards Eoforwic. When you are all together, the small bands will make a huge army, and under Earl Edwin's leadership, you will undoubtedly flush out this Norse rabble and send them packing back where they came from. They are the aggressors, so we can be confident that God is with us. May He be with all of you.'

A ragged cheer rose from the column.

Wulfmaer continued 'When you have done your job, be assured that there will be a warm welcome for you all in my mead hall. Go now and make those of us who must stay behind proud!'

The men cheered again. The priest walked up to stand beside Wulfmaer and the noise died down again. The priest raised his right hand in benediction and the men bowed their heads. He blessed the men using Latin words that few of them understood, but the meaning was crystal clear to them. The priest finished his blessing and made a sign of the cross with his raised hand. When he stopped speaking, the men all muttered 'Amen.'

The horses were walked to the head of the column, and once there, Edgar raised his hand vertically in the air. There was a moment of absolute silence as the men and all the gathered villagers waited for the command to advance. Edgar dropped his hand, and the column began to move out of the courtyard and towards the road.

The road from Rapendun wove northward towards the town of Deorby, a major centre of the former Danelaw. Rapendun had been the capital of the old kingdom of Mercia, but when the Vikings invaded a couple of centuries earlier and England had been split into English-controlled and Danish-controlled areas, Rapendun had diminished in importance. Its northern neighbour Deorby had, however, risen in prominence to become the most important town in the region. This area of Mercia was still heavily populated with people of Viking extraction. Two out of every three who lived here had some Danish or Norse ancestry, and English and Danish were spoken fluently by almost everyone.

The road passed through cleared and cultivated land, much of the first part under the authority of Wulfmaer. Men and women working in the fields by the side of the road stopped their labours to wave at the passing levy. Friends called out greetings to each other as they passed.

The day was fulfilling its early promise, and the heat increased as the sun climbed from the east towards its culmination in the south. In less than half an hour, the company was bearing down on the town of Deorby and they could see the defensive ditch and palisade that ringed the settlement.

As they got nearer, a small party of men moved into position in the open gateway of the town.

Edgar got down from his horse and approached the group of men. At their head was a huge bear of a man, his arms folded across his wide chest. He wore a brown belted tunic. Edgar approached him.

'Thegn Godric, greetings,' he said.

'Young Edgar,' the big man rumbled. 'I take it you're on your way to meet the Earl at Eoforwic.'

'Yes, my lord.'

'How many men do you have?'

'Barely fifty-five, but every axe will count.'

'Indeed. I'm in the process of raising my own levy. I can raise two hundred, maybe two hundred and fifty. I'll be marching later this afternoon. Hopefully, we will meet at Eoforwic.'

Godric signalled to his men and they stepped out of the way of Edgar and his men. Edgar bowed slightly to Godric and climbed back up onto his saddle. He gave the signal and his men continued marching forward, through the wooden gateway and along the road that passed right through Deorby.

The street through the centre of the small town was dusty in the heat, and the sound of industry and commerce surrounded them. They passed a smithy, and they could see the sparks flying as the smith pounded a strip of brightly-glowing iron. The smith never looked up from his task, his sweat-soaked face always towards his work.

Most people out and about in the main street stopped and stared at the company as they walked through. Little children waved at the men and were quickly gathered up by protective mothers. Nevertheless, the men waved back cheerfully.

They crossed the river Derwent at the narrow bridge to the north of the town and joined the Roman road, the Icknield Way, which would take them almost halfway to

Thegn

Eoforwic. On their right was the ancient Roman fort of Derventio, mostly demolished, the stone of the walls and internal building having been carted away to make new buildings and walls.

North of Deorby were more open fields, the workers more distant now, and none waved. Ahead of them was a line of trees, the end of Deorby's pasturelands.

As they reached the first of the trees, Edgar called a halt, and the men threw themselves down gratefully onto the sides of the road. Most of the men brought out their waterskins and drank from them.

'We'll stop for a short while, just long enough for the men to recover their breath,' said Edgar. 'If we're to make Eoforwic in three days, we can't afford to stop for long breaks.'

Eric and Guthrum sat with their backs against the trees and their faces towards Deorby, now quite distant but discernible by the thin smoke columns rising into the clear, still air.

'It may be some time before we see this again,' said Eric.

'Don't be pessimistic, lad,' replied Guthrum. 'We'll be back within the month. Three days to Eoforwic, one day to slaughter the Norse, two days to celebrate, four days back, ten days in all.'

'Four days to celebrate,' said Eric.

'Aye, alright then,' conceded Guthrum.

They sat in companionable silence for a few moments until Edgar sat down next to them.

'We reckon two weeks,' said Eric.

'Let's pray it's so,' said Edgar.

'Of course, we're allowing four days for celebrating our victory,' added Guthrum. 'Though I think the boy will need one of those days to get over his headache.'

Eric slapped Guthrum's head. 'Any time, old man, any time.'

Edgar smiled and took a draught from his water-skin. He closed his eyes and allowed himself a moment for the water to soothe his parched throat and to enjoy the simple pleasure of feeling the sun on his face and the silent company of his two friends. Just for a brief time, he could forget that he was marching himself and his men to a battle in which some or all of them might die.

The moment was soon past, and he opened his eyes again.

'Alright, let's move on,' he said, getting to his feet. Seeing their leader stand, all the other men also stood, those with horses mounting them and getting back into their loose formation.

Edgar turned to one of the mounted men. He had known Modbert since he was a child. They had grown up together in the household of Thegn Wulfmaer and had been close friends, sharing many of the experiences of growing boys.

'We'll be in the woods for several miles now. I don't expect any brigands to attack a column of armed men, but for form's sake, I'd like you and Halfdene to form a rearguard.'

'Aye, Master Edgar,' replied Modbert and signalled Halfdene to follow him.

They set off into the woods, the old road cutting a swathe through the trees. At least under the shade of the trees it was cooler, and the walking more comfortable.

'How much farther do we need to travel today, Guthrum?' asked Edgar.

Thegn

'I reckon we've covered about ten miles so far, maybe another twelve or fifteen to Cestrefeld. We should stop there for the night.'

'Very good. We'll need to form a detail to hunt some food for us, and find water, too.'

'Water will be no problem. There's a good clean river at Cestrefeld.'

And so it proved. Cestrefeld was a small scattering of farmsteads. There was a mead hall, though it was smaller than that at Rapendun. Edgar and his housecarls walked up to the hall to pay their respects to the local Thegn, an old man with long white hair and a walking stick. He gave them food for their men and invited Edgar to sleep within his hall, an invitation which Edgar declined politely, preferring to share the hardships of the road with his men.

They camped at the edge of a wood beside one of the old Thegn's fields. Branches and withies were quickly gathered and made into shelters, packed with bracken and covered with sheets of waxed leather.

They ate bread provided by the old Thegn and hares caught by the food hunting party that had set to work as soon as they arrived at Cestrefeld, the hares being boiled in the large iron cauldrons carried by the pack horses.

After eating, the men retired to their shelters. Edgar, Guthrum and Eric sat around the dying cooking fire in silence, listening to the fading sound of the men muttering to each other, small scatterings of laughter and, ultimately, snoring.

'We've made good time today,' began Edgar.

'It's been a long march, though,' said Guthrum. 'The

men will find tomorrow difficult. The road has been in good repair so far. It's in a far worse state further on. We may lose it completely before we get to Donecastre. There's not much in the way of hospitality at Donecastre, so I've heard. It's a pitiful collection of hovels.'

'We'll send the hunting party out at first light. We'll need more meat for the journey tomorrow,' said Edgar.

The following day dawned ominously, with thick rolling clouds moving in steadily from the north. The hunting detail returned with a roe deer and eight hares, enough for the day ahead. The men fed on dry bread, cheese and water, and quickly and efficiently prepared themselves for the day's march.

After only a single hour's marching, the first drops of rain began to fall. Heavy, fat drops that could be felt hitting the top of the head. The rain was warm and it quickly increased from a light shower to a heavy downpour. The men grumbled but pressed on.

Another hour and the rain showed no sign of easing. The clouds thickened and sagged ever lower in the sky, close and claustrophobic.

As Guthrum had predicted, the condition of the road rapidly deteriorated so far from settlements. 'Nobody to maintain it,' said Guthrum.

The road, where it was visible at all, was pitted with deep holes. There were long stretches where it was completely impassable. Tracks left the original course of the road and spread out into the neighbouring land, sometimes as a deep, narrow track whilst elsewhere the road seemed to flare out to a hundred feet or more across where multiple paths, avoiding multiple obstacles, had merged over the years.

Modbert, who now rode in the vanguard, rode back hurriedly towards Edgar.

'Problem ahead,' he said. 'The bridge over the river has gone. The river here is deep and fast. We'll either have to search up- or down-river for another bridge or we'll have to devise another way of crossing it here.'

Edgar cursed and turned to Guthrum. 'Is there another bridge reasonably close?' he asked.

Guthrum shrugged. 'I don't know, I've always passed this way. That bridge has always looked a little weak to me, I'm not really surprised that it's gone, especially after last autumn's heavy rains. I think we'll have to arrange for an alternative crossing at this point. Obviously, we can't build another bridge in the time we've got. We'll have to cast a rope across and use that.'

'Bugger,' said Edgar. 'Do we have any strong swimmers with us?'

'We can but ask, Master Edgar,' said Guthrum calmly. 'Myself, I like to steer clear of water altogether.'

'Great,' muttered Edgar. He turned his horse round and held up his hand to halt the column of men behind him. The men stopped marching and looked at Edgar.

'We need a strong swimmer. Do we have a strong swimmer amongst us?' he called.

Reluctantly, one man lifted his hand in the air.

'Yes, you, come forward,' called Edgar.

The man walked to the front of the column.

'What's your name?' demanded Edgar.

'The lads call me Tanner, sir.'

'Well, Tanner, it would seem that there's a bridge out over the river ahead of us. It's deep and swift. Do you think you could take a rope across to the other side?'

'I'd have to see the river for myself before I answer that, Master Edgar,' replied the man.

'Of course. Follow Modbert, he'll take you there.'

'Yes, sir.'

The man followed Modbert, who led him the quarter of a mile to where the flimsy remains of the bridge jutted out barely twenty feet across the river, which churned and surged where the bridge should have crossed.

Modbert dismounted his horse and stood with Tanner.

'Do you think you can do it?' he asked.

'It doesn't look easy, though I won't know till I try. Do you have the rope?'

Modbert opened a saddle-bag and passed a coiled rope to Tanner, who unwound it and passed one end to Modbert. He then took off his shoes and stripped off his tunic and leggings.

'Keep these dry for me,' he said, tying the rope around his waist.

Modbert looked down at the pile of sodden clothes and laughed.

'And keep tight hold of this end of the rope. If I look like I'm drowning, you pull me back, got it?'

Modbert nodded. 'Got it,' he confirmed.

Edgar, Guthrum and Eric drew their horses up alongside Modbert. They watched as Tanner stepped carefully into the fast-flowing river, cautiously feeling his way forward and holding on to rocks that protruded from the water, each with its upstream white foam and its downstream whorls and eddies. As he moved further across the river, the water got deeper. Suddenly, he plunged into what was obviously a deep pool, his head momentarily disappearing beneath the waters.

'Modbert, keep hold!' called Edgar.

'It's alright, I've got him,' replied Modbert, pulling on the rope to make sure that he had.

Tanner's head appeared above the water. He spluttered and wiped his face with his hand, seemingly unperturbed by his dowsing. He continued across the river, swimming strongly through the deceptively calm central stretches of the flow. He was being washed downstream, and Modbert kept a tight hold on the rope to prevent him drifting too far. Tanner's stroke suddenly faltered, and he stood up, now only chest-deep in the water. He struggled against the pull of the river, grabbing hold of rocks at the far side to help him complete the crossing.

On the far side of the river, the bridge had been even more thoroughly washed away, and only three or four pilings still stood to mark the placement of the bridge. Tanner waded ashore, ever more easily, and once out of the water walked back upstream to the bridge pilings. He grasped one piling with both hands and pulled it backwards and forwards. It moved too much. Rejecting it, he tried a second one. It remained firm and so he lashed the rope to it.

He raised his arms above his head, and with each hand gave a thumbs-up signal to the horsemen on the opposite shore.

'He's done it!' cried Edgar. 'Extra rations for that man tonight!'

Tanner was pulling hard on the rope to make sure it was sound, as Modbert tied his end of the rope to the remains of the bridge on the near side of the river. Once he had finished, he called across the river to Tanner, who re-entered the water and dragged himself across the flow by pulling hand over hand on the rope. Back on the near shore, he pulled on his clothes.

'Don't know why I bothered taking these off,' he grumbled.

'Alright, everyone, listen to me,' called Edgar above the hiss of the rain and the rushing of the river. 'Now I know this isn't going to be fun, but we have to get across this river, and we have to do it now. We'll cross just one at a time so as not to put too much weight on the rope. The horses will have to swim it. I need volunteers to ride the baggage horses across. Yes, you and you,' he pointed at two men who had put their hands up.

'One thing, sir,' said Tanner behind Edgar's back.

'Yes, what's that?'

'Boots, sir. The men should take their boots off. It's much harder to move in the water with boots on, and if anyone should lose their grip on the rope then the boots will be too heavy and will pull them under.'

'Right, did you hear that? Boots off, everyone. We'll put them all on one of the baggage horses.'

The men began dragging off their boots, muttering under their breath.

'Oh, come on, it's not that bad,' cajoled Edgar. 'It won't do you any harm at all to give those feet a wash, the Norsemen can probably smell us coming from here!'

Scattered laughter broke out. 'He means you Aella!' called one of the men, to more appreciative laughter.

The first man approached the river, looking dubiously at the rope. 'Are you sure, sir?' he asked.

'Look, Tanner just went across there without the use of the rope. If he can do that, I'm sure you can pull yourself across.'

The man waded out to the end of the bridge and took hold of the rope with both hands, letting himself get into ever-deeper water. The current pulled at him and the rope tightened. He started dragging himself across. About two-thirds of the way across, there appeared to be a submerged rock that caused a large swell in the water. At this point the water flowed even faster, and the man struggled to keep hold of the rope. Once past the obstacle, however, he speeded up and quickly gained the far bank, to ragged cheers from his comrades.

The second man stepped forward, looking dubiously at the river. He stepped back a pace, nervously.

'Come on man, you can't get any wetter!' called Modbert.

The man visibly pulled himself together and was soon making his way across the river with relative ease.

The rain, though it did not seem possible, was getting even heavier. The river level was slowly rising, and the force of the current getting ever greater as the men pulled themselves across one by one.

Once all the foot soldiers had crossed, Edgar ordered the housecarls to begin swimming their horses across the river. They removed their boots, in case they were swept from their horses, and added them to the baggage train.

Modbert was first to cross. His horse was a strong swimmer, and though the current was now faster than ever, he made the other side with little difficulty.

The other housecarls then followed until only Guthrum and Edgar and the two volunteers to ride the baggage horses across remained on the near bank.

'Right, first baggage horse. It had better be the one

that's carrying the men's boots,' said Edgar. The volunteer climbed up onto the back of the horse. There was no saddle, so the man had to position his legs as comfortably as he could between the bags and panniers that had been strapped to the horse.

He urged the horse forward, but as the horse began to wade into the river, Edgar called 'Whoa! Wait!'

The rider hurriedly stopped the horse and turned round to see what Edgar wanted. Edgar pointed upstream, and the rider saw a large tangle of branches sweeping down the river towards their position. He waved his thanks to Edgar and waited while the branches whipped past, right along the centre of the stream.

'Looks like some grief's come to a tree somewhere upstream,' commented Guthrum. 'We'd better beware, there may be more where that came from.'

Once the raft of branches had passed, the rider rode the horse back into the water. It gushed and raced around him as the horse walked further into the flow. When it got deep enough in the water to float, the horse began to drift downstream and the eddies around it smoothed away. Only when the horse's hooves once again made contact with the river bed did the water again begin to swirl violently about the horse. It staggered slightly until its flanks were out of the water. It then pulled itself out of the water with evident relief.

'Alright, next horse,' said Edgar and the second rider walked his horse down to the water's edge. The horse strode confidently into the river and soon was swimming strongly towards the middle of the stream.

'Edgar, look!' cried Guthrum. He pointed upstream, where more fallen wood was rushing towards them.

Edgar called out to the rider in midstream, who turned and looked at the approaching debris.

'Christ! It's not just branches this time, it's the whole bloody tree!' cried Guthrum.

Edgar looked again. It was indeed the trunk of a tree or at least a large part of one. It was crashing over rocks and hurtling towards the rider.

'Keep moving man!' called Edgar.

The horse was struggling against the current, being somewhat more loaded than the first horse. When it reached the submerged obstacle that was causing the large hump in the stream, it began to panic. The rider pulled at the reins to keep the animal's mouth and nose above the turbulent water, but the horse had stopped moving forward. Edgar watched in horror as the tree trunk smashed over one last rock, almost lifting itself above the water as it bore down on the struggling horse and rider.

'Jump!' shouted Edgar as loudly as he could, but it was too late. The snapped end of the tree trunk smashed into the horse, pinning the rider's leg to the horse's flank and pushing them violently downstream.

The rider was immediately unseated and disappeared beneath the horse. The horse was in a full panic and was screaming in terror and pain. Its useless thrashing about in the water no longer carried it against the current, and it started drifting downstream, the tree trunk still pushing it along. The water around the horse was turning red.

'The broken end of the tree must have impaled the horse,' said Edgar in horror. There was no sign of the rider, and Edgar feared that he had gone under the horse and into its thrashing hooves. The men on the far side of the river were running along the bank, trying to keep up with the horse. Many still did not have their boots on.

'Come on, Guthrum, we have to get across,' called Edgar, urging his horse into the stream.

Guthrum looked nervously upriver, but there was no sign of any more parts of the tree. He followed Edgar into the river, and soon both men were across and galloping down the far bank in pursuit of the flailing horse.

The horse was weakening quickly. Its head kept dipping down into the water only to be pulled out again, less strongly each time. It was now free of the tree trunk, which bumped along past it as it fought to gain the far bank. A stout lower branch, however, managed to entangle the horse's legs and the animal was dragged under the water as the tree trunk rolled.

The horse remained underwater for a long time, and when it reappeared, only its back was above water, the head hanging lifeless beneath the torrent. The horse snagged on a bush that jutted out across the water, and several men dived back into the river to pull the carcase to shore.

'Get your boots on!' ordered Edgar. 'Get downstream and find the rider.'

He turned to Guthrum. 'Christ, I don't even know the poor bastard's name.'

'Tufa,' said Guthrum simply. 'Shepherd from Willetun.'

'Shit,' muttered Edgar. 'Shit, shit, shit!'

Men were running past them now, in their search for Tufa the shepherd.

Edgar ordered the remaining men to redistribute the baggage from the dead horse amongst the housecarls' horses. He then ordered a break for food, early though it was. Cold meat was passed out amongst the men and given to each man as he returned from the search for Tufa. No one had seen any sign of him.

Edgar wandered over to the river bank and stared across in silence.

Guthrum appeared at his elbow. 'He's gone. We've lost him.'

'I know,' said Edgar.

'We need to move,' said Guthrum firmly.

'I know that, too. Give the order, we move on.'

The rain eased during the night. The men had woken to find the promise of a clear, dry day. Their clothes steamed gently in the morning sunlight. The mood in the camp was subdued. The loss of Tufa hit hard. They hadn't even reached the battlefield, and already they were a man down. Their failure to find his body and give it a decent burial added insult to injury. It put a sheen of misery over everything.

The road was clean and well maintained here, so at least they did not have to contend with a great deal of mud, but the chatter of the previous days was almost completely absent.

Around midday, a rider was spotted ahead of them, galloping at full speed. Modbert and Halfdene pulled ahead of the column to meet him, their hands resting loosely on the hafts of their axes.

He pulled up a few paces short of them. His face was covered in the hood of a heavy, waxed cloak. He threw it back to reveal his face, red with exertion and dripping with sweat, which plastered the hair across his forehead.

'Rest easy, friends. I am an envoy of Harold-king. I must speak with your leader.'

Modbert nodded and twitched his horse round. He

escorted the messenger to the front of the column, where Edgar rode.

Edgar and the messenger led their horses off the road to allow the column to pass as they spoke.

'My name is Alfric, envoy of Harold Godwinson-king,' began the messenger. 'Where have you come from and where are you going?'

'We are the levy from Rapendun in Mercia,' replied Edgar. 'We're travelling to Eoforwic to meet with Earl Edwin's forces.'

The messenger nodded quickly, understanding.

'Two days ago, an army led by the Earls Edwin and Morcar met with the Norse army at a place well-named the Foul Ford, near Eoforwic. There the army of the Earls met with a devastating defeat. Thousands of men lie dead. What remains of the Earls' army is regrouping at Tatecastre, ten miles this side of Eoforwic where they will meet with an army under Harold-king, who will be marching north as we speak, raising the fyrd as he goes. The army gathered at Tatecastre will be of a very considerable size. You should go there and wait for the King, and join with his army.'

Edgar nodded. 'Very well, that will shorten tomorrow's march at least. Are you headed south to meet the King?'

'I am, and I have little time. I will bid you good luck and good fighting.'

With that, the messenger pulled his horse's reins and the horse leaped back onto the road, barely missing the men in Edgar's column.

Modbert and Halfdene had been sitting on their horses just out of earshot. They now joined Edgar. He repeated the message to them.

'With God's grace, we will outnumber the invader. His

army will be reeling from their last battle, and though the King's men will be tired from the march, at least they will not be bloodied.'

Halfdene ran his fingers over the smooth end of the axe-haft that protruded from a harness over his horse's shoulders and back under the warrior's calf. 'They will regret coming here, I think. They don't have a chance.'

'Overconfidence is not a worthy attribute for a warrior, Halfdene,' said Edgar.

'How so? Christ is surely with us.'

'I have no doubt that the Northmen also believe that Christ is with them, and judging by their successes so far, they may be right.'

Modbert chuckled. 'Listen to you two! You should believe as I do; that my axe is with me, my shield is with me, and if God is with me, I will live and be victorious. If He isn't then I shall die and join my ancestors in perpetual feasting. What's to worry about?' He laughed cheerily and kicked his horse's sides to send it off in pursuit of the retreating column.

'Is he right?' asked Halfdene, looking perplexed. 'Should we not be concerned if Christ is with us or not?'

Edgar sighed. 'I know of no sure way to know whether Christ is with us, Halfdene, but Modbert's attitude does seem to inspire him more than worrying about something we cannot know the answer to. Come on.'

They turned their horses and followed Modbert.

The final day of the march was drawing to its close. They had followed the road up a hill. It had not been steep, but seemed interminable, and even the hardiest of them had fallen silent before the end. Over the top, they had at last spied the first of the small farmsteads that made up Tatecastre. Another half mile and they could see, spread out in the fields around the small village, the camp of the English army. Those lucky enough to have tents had pitched them in ordered rows and smoke rose gently from a multitude of campfires into the still air of the early evening.

As they neared the camp, they were approached by a small official-looking party. The leader of them held up his hand in a command to stop. They halted, and the man approached Edgar. He asked where they were from and how many they were. Edgar told him and they were quickly directed to a corner of the camp where a young man who called himself Ulf met them. He showed them to the piece of land they could use for sleeping, and informed the horsemen that feed was available for the horses a short way away.

The camp stood on the west bank of the River Wharf, where the river widened to a deep pool after a run of rapids. The pool was filled with cavorting men, swimming around and splashing each other. To the south of the camp stood a church, beside which was the road bridge, now guarded by a sizeable force of fully-armoured men.

Edgar turned to face his men. 'All right, lads. We've arrived. See if you can gather some branches and ferns. Get the leather sheets from the baggage horses and make shelters. Build fires and eat your food. After that, you can join in the fun, if you like.' He indicated the loudly splashing men in the pool. 'See if you can catch us some nice fish whilst you're at it.'

Edgar and the fourteen horsemen walked their horses towards the stabling area, where food and water had been supplied for them.

The men stripped the riding tackle from their horses and walked back to where the men of the burwarran were busy setting up shelters and starting campfires.

'What now?' asked Modbert as they walked.

'Now we spend a little time recovering from the march,' said Edgar. 'Gather our strength and await the arrival of the King.'

3

Battle at Stanford

25th September 1066

The King and his army arrived the following afternoon. Edgar ordered his men to eat well and go to bed early. It seemed that the call to march would come the next morning.

That evening, as they prepared to turn in for the night, messengers walked all round the camp, passing on the King's orders for the following day.

'This morning, the invading army marched beneath the walls of Eoforwic,' said one of the messengers to Edgar, Guthrum and Eric. 'The citizens of the town surrendered immediately. Can't really blame them, I suppose, they didn't know how close our army was. The King rode out to Eoforwic with a small force this evening, and the town straight away withdrew its surrender to the Norse. Our King spoke with the leading burghers of the town and was told that they had agreed with Harald Sigurdson to send him fifty hostages as insurance of their loyalty. The invaders will be at Stanford in the morning to receive the hostages. It's there that our army will meet them. You are to have your men ready to march at dawn.'

Edgar acknowledged the order and the messenger moved on to the next group.

'It seems like Sigurdson is going to get a nasty shock,' said Guthrum.

'Oh yes,' agreed Eric. 'This is actually really good news. I think the advantage has just moved another notch to our side.'

'Let's hope so,' said Edgar. 'Now, to bed. We should try and get as much sleep as possible.'

Harold-king rode at the front of the column, his armour glittering in the early morning sun. He was a large, broad-shouldered man, his strong legs gripping the sides of his horse with solid surety. He was not wearing his helmet for the journey, and his fair hair blew around his head, his short beard twitching beneath his chin in the breeze. Around him were the earls and the king's thegns, barely less magnificent. Banners fluttered above them, red, blue and gold, proclaiming the presence of the kingdom's noble earls and above all, two huge banners, streaming out to their tapered ends, one displaying a golden wyvern with a coiled tail, rearing up against a red field, the other also red, this time with an embroidered figure of a man bearing a shield and a spear in glittering golden thread. The great banners of Wessex and the Armed Man declared the presence of Harold Godwinson, King of the English.

The road was dry, and a cloud of dust accompanied the army as it tramped relentlessly forward. The road out of

Eoforwic rose slightly, passing through rich pasture land. Peasant farmers ceased in their labours to watch the great host pass by.

Two miles before the meeting place at Stanford stood a small settlement, Elmeslac. Before reaching it, the King ordered a scouting party forward to seek out any advance guards that the Norwegians may have placed on the approach road.

The scouts slipped off their horses, pulled peasant cloaks on top of their armour and approached the settlement on foot. Sure enough, as they neared Elmeslac, two Norsemen stepped out of the cover on the side of the road and stopped them. The scouts immediately threw off their cloaks, drew their axes and dispatched the two Norsemen as quickly and quietly as possible. They dragged the corpses off the road and signalled back to the King that the road was clear. They replaced the peasant cloaks and continued along the road, walking casually but with keen eyes for any further ambush until the bridge at Stanford was in view ahead of them.

The Norse army was busy at the bridge. They were split, half on the north side of the river, half on the south. All were eagerly collecting cattle and sheep belonging to the local populace and herding them together to be returned to their main camp, further along the river at Richale.

Harold-king looked down the shallow incline of the road towards his enemy. He leaned slightly in his saddle and called to the king's thegn who rode beside him.

'Am I seeing right?' he asked. 'They are so confident that they are not even wearing their mail?'

The Thegn squinted into the distance. The men gathering up the cows and sheep wore helmets and had their swords and axes slung on belts around their middles, and a pile of round shields stood nearby, but none of them was wearing his mail coat.

'Aye, my lord,' replied the Thegn, 'but in all fairness, it is an uncommonly warm day. Harald Sigurdson clearly has his men's best interests at heart.'

The King laughed. 'He will learn a hard lesson this day,' he said.

Ahead of them, less than half a mile away now, the warriors of the Norse host were beginning to take notice of the dust cloud approaching them.

'They seem very slow,' mused the Thegn.

'They are expecting the hostages. It will dawn on them soon enough that it does not take five thousand armed men to deliver fifty hostages. Prepare to charge, we cannot waste an opportunity like this,' replied the King.

The Thegn quickly turned and galloped to the section commanders, preparing them for a charge. At last, the penny seemed to drop with the Norse when the English were just a few hundred yards from them. Those on the bank closest to the English ran for their shields, abandoning the cows and sheep they had been rustling.

Harold-king gave a great cry, 'Forward!' and the mounted men of the English host leaped forward. Edgar felt a great rush of adrenalin as he brought his shield up to protect his body and lowered his spear towards the Norse invaders, who were now forming themselves into a ragged defensive shield-wall.

Ahead of him, Edgar saw the lead horses of the English smash into the shield-wall. It buckled and gave way, but a well-aimed Norse axe dug deeply into one of the lead horses, and it fell, screaming and kicking, to the ground. The horses around it shied away and the momentum of the charge was lost. The horsemen wheeled around and began circling the shield-wall, which had now contracted into an efficient circular bulwark. Edgar held his spear firmly, thrusting it forward whenever he caught sight of any part of a Norseman that remained exposed.

Guthrum's horse trotted beside Edgar's. 'This is easy,' rumbled Guthrum, leaning over to jab his spear between a gap in the shields, and then pulling back sharply as an axe slashed out in retaliation.

'They may be unarmoured, but they can still sting,' replied Edgar.

The English horsemen continued their relentless circling, and one by one the Norse fell to their spears. Bowmen had followed the horsemen and occasionally the horses would pull back, allowing a deadly rain of arrows to fall mercilessly amongst the Norsemen.

Across the river, Harald Sigurdson-king watched in impotent fury as the English horsemen continued to wear down the Norsemen.

'Reinforcements!' he cried, pointing at the bridge with his battleaxe. 'Get more men across there now!'

His section leaders jumped to obey and ordered more of their men to cross the bridge.

Seeing the danger, a company of English axemen raced forward to the bridge, obstructing the Norsemen's route to the battle. The bridge was narrow, and although not without losses, the English had little difficulty in preventing the Norsemen from crossing.

The shield-wall was weakening by the minute. Many men had fallen, and the formation was becoming untenable. One man, with a cry of despair, threw down his shield and axe and began to run for the river. Before he had run twenty yards, a heavy arrow thudded into his back and he fell forwards to the ground. Panic now took hold of many of the Norsemen, and the wall collapsed as they broke and fled. The horsemen, with a cry of victory, thundered after them, cutting them down as they ran.

On the far side of the river, Harald Sigurdson-king watched in growing horror at the massacre. He turned to see that his men who were trying to cross the bridge had failed and were falling in large numbers.

'Get back!' he yelled. 'Off the bridge! Regroup!'

His men began to retreat across the bridge, the English axemen jeering after them.

'Quickly!' shouted Harald. 'Three runners to the ships, bring the rest of the army here as fast as possible!'

Three men threw down their arms and helmets and set off at a run back to the Norsemen's base camp at Richale.

By now, the slaughter on the north bank was over, and Edgar and his fyrdmen galloped back to join the main body of the army. The English infantry had formed a deep shield wall facing the Norse across the river. Slowly and rhythmically, the English were beating their swords and axes against their round shields, shouting 'Out! Out! Out! Out!' in time with the rhythm.

About a dozen of the English axemen by the bridge began to walk cautiously, shields raised, across the narrow wooden bridge, but as they did so, a giant Norseman ran across to the centre of the bridge and stood before them, blocking their way. The Englishmen approached him cautiously, but his reach was far greater than theirs, and his axe was immensely long.

A single great swing decapitated the first of the English

warriors, and in a lightning-fast switch, the Norseman reversed the swing of his huge axe and took another English axeman in the chest. Before the others could react, the giant took three steps forward and dispatched another two with a second stroke of his mighty axe.

There was a hearty cheer from the Norse host as they watched their hero stop the English in their tracks. Three more Englishmen approached the giant, one attempting to distract him as the other two thrust spears at him. He swatted the spears away with his axe, dragging them from the fingers of the Englishmen and sending them spinning uselessly into the river below. The back-swing continued and the axe embedded itself deeply in the side of the man who thought he could distract this giant.

The two spearmen began to back away, but before they had taken three paces, the giant stepped forward and swung again, slicing one of the spearmen's arms off just above the elbow. He screamed and blood pumped from the severed limb. The other spearman took his cue and retreated at full pelt back to the end of the bridge.

'Any more?' yelled the Norse giant, to great cheers from the army behind him. The opposing forces appeared to be at a stalemate. Neither could get to the other. This was working to the Norsemen's advantage; every minute they could stall would bring reinforcements closer.

On the right flank of the English shield wall, Edgar and his carls sat on their horses watching the events unfold. Edgar turned to speak to Modbert, who was beside him.

'Modbert, do you remember how we tormented the cows as they crossed the bridge at Rapendun?'

Modbert turned to Edgar. 'Aye, I do.' A big smile creased his face. As children, the young nobles of the village had played together, and one of the things they used to do was to hide beneath the small clatter-bridge over the river at Rapendun and poke their little swords up at the feet of the cows as the farmers herded them across. At least, until the farmer had caught them and beaten them. The boys had complained to Wulfmaer, but he had refused to support them, and in fact had had them beaten again. They had learned several valuable lessons that day, now perhaps a new lesson blossomed from their past.

'Say no more,' grinned Modbert. He and Edgar galloped to the rear of the English lines and left their horses in the care of a baggage boy. They ran behind the English host until they were round a bend of the river. There they quickly ripped some branches from a tree and bound them together with withies that Edgar hacked down with his axe. Within a few minutes, they had a workable raft. Modbert took off his mail and left his axe, shield and helmet on the bank. He lay face down on the raft, which sank enough for him to be half submerged. Edgar passed him his spear and then covered him with wet leaves and soggy material from the river bank. When he had finished, the raft looked like any clump of detritus that had been gathered in the calm stretches of the river upstream of them. Edgar waded out, pushing the raft until he was almost halfway across the river. He patted the mound of flotsam about where Modbert's shoulder would be.

'Good luck! Don't let the big bad cowherd catch you!' he called quietly. Then he let go of the raft and it floated down the river, carrying Modbert towards the bridge.

Edgar gathered up Modbert's equipment and headed back to the shield wall. He walked past the backs of the English soldiers and out at the other, downstream end. He turned and looked back at the bridge. The huge Norseman still stood there, holding his axe threateningly over his right shoulder. A few more bodies lay piled up before him, and the bridge was dripping with English blood.

Looking back behind the English ranks, Edgar caught sight of Harold-king deep in discussion with one of his thegns. They were clearly trying to work out a strategy to get past the Norseman.

Not long now, my lord King, thought Edgar.

Barely daring to breathe, Modbert looked up slightly to see where he was going. The bridge loomed ahead of him. The posts holding the bridge up were tall in the middle, as the banks here were quite steep. Modbert reflected that this also was to his advantage, because nobody could see down to the water unless they were right on the edge of the river bank, and at this moment, the Norse host was holding well back. The raft nudged gently against one of the great wooden uprights supporting the bridge. Modbert cautiously moved his position until he was kneeling on the raft. He slowly and carefully raised himself until he was vertical, and he gripped his spear carefully, turning the point upright. The giant was slightly forward on the bridge from where Modbert had ended up, so he drew himself along under the bridge using the pilings as handholds. The going was not easy, as the raft was anything but stable, but using care and a well-honed sense of balance, Modbert managed to position himself immediately underneath the huge Norseman. Blood dripped onto Modbert's face from between the slats of the bridge walkway. Slowly and carefully, he positioned his spear so that the tip just rested between two slats immediately beneath the Norseman's body. He estimated the length of push required and positioned the spear in his hands to give himself maximum reach. He looked up to where the Norseman stood as solid as a statue. Modbert took two deep breaths and then pushed his spear upwards with all of his strength. He felt the tip bite and be deflected, then it thudded heavily into something that gave. Suddenly Modbert's hands were slick with blood and he knew he had hit his target. He twisted his spear savagely and the tugged it down with so much force that he fell off the raft and into the river.

Edgar's keen eyes were focused on the Norseman, and his heart skipped a beat as he saw the man flinch, his eyes bulging. His body jerked slightly and a low moan escaped from his lips as he fell like a great oak tree onto the bridge beneath him. Modbert had done it! Magnificent!

Puzzlement swept through both armies as they watched the giant topple. Then a wave of understanding followed, the English crying out in victory, the Norsemen moaning with sorrow. Harold-king, standing up in his stirrups, strained to see what had happened. At that moment, fifty yards downstream, he spotted Modbert clambering out of the river onto the steep bank of the river. He was covered in wet vegetation and still held his spear, which he thrust upwards in victory.

A huge smile creased the King's face. 'A hogshead of mead for that man!' he bellowed.

On his command, the English swept forward over the bridge and formed up on the far side of the river in another deep, wide shield-wall. The Norse drew back, and retrenched a hundred yards from the English, shouting their defiance and clashing their weapons on their shields.

They stood facing each other for some time, neither

side committing to an all-out attack. A group of twelve horsemen broke from the English ranks at a gentle trot and approached the Norse shield wall under a flag of parley.

Harald Sigurdson looked over at the party approaching his lines. 'Looks like they want to talk,' he said.

He turned to his ally, Tostig Godwinson, who sat on his horse beside the King.

'Go and see what they have to say, then send them packing,' he said.

'Aye, my lord.'

Earl Tostig signalled for some men to follow him and he slowly walked his horse towards the English emissaries.

Harald Sigurdson-king, tired and leaning heavily on the pommel of his horse's saddle, spurred his horse gently forward, but as it moved, it stumbled, and the King, tired as he was, lost his grip on the reins. Slowly, and with a horrible inevitability, he fell forward, catching ineffectively at the horse's neck, and tumbled to the ground. The men around him gasped. This was an ill omen. The King quickly leaped to his feet.

'A fall forebodes a good journey,' he proclaimed in a loud voice, but the men around him looked worried. The interpretation of the omen all too clear in their eyes.

Amongst the Englishmen, Harold-king turned to his colleagues. 'I think his luck has left him.'

They all nodded agreement; such an omen was open to only one interpretation.

Harald climbed back into the saddle and watched as Tostig and his guards approached the English. When the two parties were about thirty feet apart, they stopped.

Harold-king of the English raised his voice. 'It would seem the day does not go well for you, Tostig.'

Thegn

Tostig spat on the ground. Incautiously, he walked his horse forward towards his brother. The horsemen around Harold bristled, but the King held up his hand to still them.

Tostig drew up in front of Harold. 'It goes well enough,' he said, 'There are enough of us left to make raven food of all of you.'

'We will accept your surrender, Tostig. You can be reunited with your own people. I promise that your earldom shall be restored to you, and more. Come back to us. Your men can go home.'

'You offer me back my earldom?'

'I do, and as I said, even more. You will be the most favoured at court, as you should be.'

'That is not how you spoke last year when you advised Edward-king to depose me and exile me away from his court, his kingdom, and my lands.'

'You know as well as I do that we had no choice at all in the matter. The whole of the kingdom north of the Thames was in open revolt. If you had not been banished, we would have lost the throne itself to Morcar and Edwin. Would you have preferred that?'

Tostig stared sullenly at his brother but made no reply.

'Let's put all this behind us,' said Harold. 'As king, I am prepared to forgive. I am willing to do that. I entreat you to come back.'

Tostig paused, looking squarely at Harold.

'And what of Harald-king? What will you give him?'

Harold snorted gently.

'I shall give him seven feet of good English earth,' he looked across at where Harald stood, just out of earshot. 'Or as he is uncommonly tall, maybe as much more as he requires. Come home Tostig.'

Tostig spat again. 'Your actions of the past belie your words of today. I am loyal to my king, and my king is Harald Sigurdson. Prepare for battle, brother.'

He swung his horse away and trotted back to Haraldking.

'Who was that you parleyed with?' demanded Harald.

'That was my brother Harold, King of the English.'

Harald looked angry. 'Why did you not let me know? I could have had him shot as you spoke!'

For a second a look of anger swept across Tostig's face.

'That would not have been honourable, my King.'

The two men spurred their horses on, followed by their guards.

Harold watched as they departed, knowing that he had probably just had the last conversation he would ever have with his younger brother. He wheeled his horse round and returned to the English lines.

Harold turned to his Thegn beside him. 'As these men are unarmoured, I think we can use the horses again, don't you?'

The Thegn looked across at the Norsemen. English armies normally fought on foot, and an engagement on horseback felt alien.

The Thegn nodded. 'In the unusual circumstances, I believe you are right, my lord.'

The King looked back at his mounted men. With a single word, he ordered the battle to recommence.

'Forward!'

The English horsemen advanced again, and as they approached, the Norse line contracted into a hard, solid wall, curving round to deflect the horsemen and their spears. The fight was not an easy one for the English, the

Norsemen had seen the first half of the battle and had adapted their tactics. Now, although the English horsemen had the advantage of height, the Norsemen all had spears and could attack the English on their unarmoured horses almost as easily as the English could attack them.

Harold now ordered the footmen forward. The great host of the English, their mail chinking, their swords and axes clanking, their spears and helms glinting in the sunlight, began to move forward towards the enemy. Suddenly, with a great shout, they hurled themselves at the Norse shield wall. An immense shoving fight began, each side trying to push the enemy back whilst simultaneously hacking at them with their axes.

Some of the Norsemen at the back of the host now unleashed a volley of arrows. Edgar swung his shield round to protect his head and body from the deadly shower. One arrow thudded into his shield, whilst another pierced his horse's throat. The animal reared in shock and pain. Edgar was thrown heavily to the ground, and he felt his left shoulder pull out of place. He cried out in pain, and in an instant, Eric was on the ground beside him.

'Where does it hurt?' he demanded.

'Left shoulder,' replied Edgar, 'just displaced, I think.'

Eric took hold of Edgar's shoulder and gently manipulated it, feeling for the injury.

'Yes, you're right. There may be more damage but I'll pull it back into place. This is going to hurt like fuck, hang on.'

Eric placed the sole of his booted foot in Edgar's left armpit, took hold of his wrist and then pulled sharply. Edgar howled and cursed.

Eric grinned. 'It's back. Maybe you should retire? Your

shield arm will be greatly weakened.'

'No, no. I'll join the shield wall. You get back on your horse.'

Eric jumped back on his horse and Edgar struggled back to the lines of infantrymen.

The battle continued for several hours. Every twenty or thirty minutes, Edgar dropped back from his place on the front line, to be replaced by fresher men from the rear. After thirty minutes of relative ease in the rear, the rested men would return to the front line. Fighting was heavy work, and the Norsemen were employing the same tactic. One sure way to victory was to prevent as many of the enemy as possible from getting their rest periods. The front line of the battle was gradually being pushed back by the superior English numbers, and now stood almost a mile from the bridge where it had all started.

The Norsemen were falling back ever more quickly, and the field of battle was littered with the mangled bodies of the dead and dying. The Norsemen's actions were becoming desperate. The English, on the other hand, were settled into a steady rhythm of advancing; chopping and hacking as they went. The ground beneath Edgar's feet was slick with blood. Victory now seemed assured, and the English were making a final push into the weakened Norse lines.

Obeying a command issued from behind him, Edgar dropped back to the rear of the English lines. He groaned to himself as he swung his axe loosely in his right hand, trying to loosen the tight, tired muscles.

Suddenly from Edgar's right, there came a huge howl of rage from many throats. Along a ridge of slightly higher ground, the remainder of the Norse army had arrived from their camp at Richale, and although they must have run much of the way in full armour, the sight of them provided a much-needed boost to the exhausted Norsemen.

The new Norse contingent crashed into the English lines. In front of Edgar, a small man, gasping for breath, swung his axe at him. Edgar lifted his shield, deflecting the axe blow with ease. He swung his own axe down on the Norseman's helmet, and the man dropped instantly. Edgar swung back from the momentum of the blow found himself facing a huge, sweating Norseman wielding a vicious looking battleaxe. Edgar could see the man's face beneath his helmet. Blond hair was plastered with sweat onto a face florid with exertion. The man raised his battleaxe, bringing it crashing down towards Edgar's head. Instinctively, Edgar raised his shield to block the blow, but his shoulder betrayed him. His shield barely got to shoulder height as the Viking's axe smashed down onto Edgar's helmet.

Edgar felt pain such as he had never felt before, the whole side of his head exploded in white-hot agony. He felt the pain for less than a heartbeat, and then everything went black.

4

Aftermath

The main residence at Scarpenbec was a comfortable place. Ingui, the headman of the village, was an aspiring thegn. His residence was not sufficiently grand for him to be entitled to the rank yet, but slowly he was improving his home so that he might petition the Earl for the title. He had built a gate and a small church which stood within its own enclosure next to his home. His current project was a bell tower. The first dozen or so courses of stone, up to the height of a man's shoulder, stood a few yards away from the church, awaiting the addition of the timber upper levels. These buildings were all essential for any headman who aspired to the rank of thegn to have at his residence.

Scarpenbec was a quiet, small and undistinguished place, hidden from the main roads and only accessible down narrow, leafy lanes, all but impassable in wet weather. Today the headman's residence was humming with the sound of quietly efficient industry. Items of worth had been removed from the house and placed in stone-lined pits, scattered around the property hundreds of yards away. The pits were sealed with stone caps and clay and covered with earth, safe from the plundering of an invading army; safe from the plundering of a defending army.

The men of the village were assembled in the courtyard outside Ingui's house. They each had farm implements; bill hooks, scythes, wood axes, just in case any marauders should attempt anything.

The women and the children stood to the side, looking apprehensive as they waited.

They all looked nervously along the muddy lane that ran through the village towards the road known locally as the Dolegate. It connected with the Roman road that led to Stanford, where the men knew a great battle was taking place.

As they watched, they saw a young man running across the fields, cutting the corner to get to Scarpenbec as fast as possible. As he approached, he was recognised as one of the village lads, and the men relaxed.

The lad ran into the courtyard, his face red with exertion. He came to a halt, panting, and gasped 'It's over. The battle has finished!'

Ingui stepped forward and held the lad by the elbow.

'Who is the victor?' he demanded.

'The men from Eoforwic won. There was a wave of reinforcements to the invaders, but they were too few and too late. The Eoforwic men fought them to a standstill. The invader's leader is dead, and the headman from Eoforwic is talking to whatever leaders the invaders have left.'

There was a collective gasp of relief.

A young woman appeared at Ingui's elbow. She had

long dark hair, held at the back with a silver ring, so her hair fell in a pony-tail down to the middle of her back. Her eyes were large, almond-shaped and a deep grey in colour. Her mouth was wide and danced with the hint of a smile.

'Godgifu,' said Ingui to his daughter.

'We should go, Father,' she said.

'Yes. Yes, we should.'

Ingui called his people to order and they set off for the battlefield, each man and woman carrying empty bags and baskets. Two carts followed behind drawn by slow, plodding oxen.

A battle on the doorstep was not only extremely dangerous, flooding the area with bloodthirsty warriors, but it also provided unparalleled opportunities for plunder for the locals, who could pick over the battlefield for any choice booty.

As the party from Scarpenbec approached the site of the battle, Ingui called them to a halt and sent four men on ahead to scout.

They returned after half an hour to report to Ingui.

'The invaders have all gone back to wherever they came from and the victors are heading back to Eoforwic. There are some warriors picking through the battlefield, but we should be safe now.'

Ingui ordered the plunder party forward and soon they came to the battle site. It was worse than any of them had imagined. There was barely anywhere were you could place your foot without stepping on a corpse. The whole field was slick with blood and the river itself ran red downstream as far as the eye could see.

Ingui looked on in horror. Drawing himself up, he addressed his people; 'Much evil has happened here today.

Thegn

Come on, we have a job to do. Spread out and gather anything valuable. Be careful, everyone.'

Godgifu walked out among the mutilated bodies. Her shoes and the hem of her dress were soon soaked black with blood, and she felt with icy terror the cold blood oozing into her shoes and slapping against her lower legs.

A glint caught her eye. A man with his right arm missing had a thick gold chain round his neck. She stooped down and deftly pulled it off over his head, muttering a silent prayer for the man's soul as she did, and dropping it into the bag she wore over her shoulder. Beside him, another man wore a silver ring studded with garnets on his left hand. She bent over to pull the ring from the man's finger, but it was stuck. She reflected that he had probably worn it for years, never having taken it off. The ring was beautiful, but she could not move it no matter how hard she pulled. One of the villagers walked up beside her.

'Here,' he grunted, pulling out a pair of sheep shears. He deftly placed the man's finger between the blades and squeezed, grunting with effort. The blades snapped together and the finger came off. The man slipped the ring off the severed end of the finger and handed it to Godgifu.

She took it numbly and dropped into her bag. She prayed for the man's soul and for his forgiveness for the violation.

A few yards away, she heard a groan. Looking up from the severed finger which now lay in the mud beside its former owner, she saw a man lying on his back, his face covered in blood. His chest was heaving as he caught short breaths. She hurried over to him. His eyes were open and he was staring up into the sky. Blood trickled from his mouth and nose. There was a deep gash above his right eye.

She dropped to her knees beside him. His breaths were shallow gasps. She slipped her hand under his head and lifted it gently, pulling a cloth from her bag. She wiped away some of the gore from his face, but it was being constantly replaced by the blood flowing from his forehead, nose and mouth. His eyes gradually shifted from the sky to Godgifu's face. Blood spat from his lips as he gasped. He tried to lift his right hand, but the effort was too much. His eyes fixed on Godgifu's and he appeared to be straining. He coughed sharply, sending a new rush of blood from his mouth. Godgifu placed her hand gently on his chest. It came away slick. Blood was flowing freely from a wound there. She could hear his lung bubbling as the man drowned in his own blood. The man still stared into her eyes, and she found she could not look away. He gasped again and tried to speak.

'Are...' he gasped.

She bent closer to him, still not taking her eyes from his.

'Are... you...'

Suddenly the heaving and gasping stopped, and she saw his eyes glaze. All the small tremblings ceased instantly.

Godgifu placed his head gently back on the ground and closed his still staring eyes with tender fingers. A small sob escaped from her. She bowed her head and prayed intensely to God for a few minutes. She had never actually witnessed a soul departing the body before.

The man wore a thin leather thong around his neck with a small, crudely made iron cross hanging from it. She reached behind his head and slipped it over his head. Carefully and deliberately, she placed it around her own neck. She looked at the man's face, peaceful now, one last time. Then she stood up and moved further into the battlefield.

Close to her, some soldiers were gathering weapons and mail from the fallen and piling them into a handcart. They stood beside a deep pile of bodies. This appeared to be a part of the field where particularly intense fighting had taken place. Bodies were piled on bodies. The soldiers began pulling the corpses off the pile, stripping them of their accoutrements and slinging them onto another pile.

Godgifu moved on, not wanting to risk annoying the soldiers. Ahead of her, three wounded men were searching the faces of the dead, looking for a fallen friend, she assumed.

She heard a shout behind her 'Hey! This one's alive!'

She ran back. Half buried under dead bodies lay a young man, his head unrecognisable beneath the blood that covered it.

'Get him out,' she ordered the soldiers. They looked at her, but obeyed, dragging the man by his arms out of the pile of bodies and depositing him a few yards away.

'Actually no,' said the soldier, 'I thought he was alive, but he can't be, can he?' He indicated the massive wound to the left side of the man's head. His cheekbone protruded from the bloody mess, clearly badly broken. His jaw, too, was broken and the jagged edges of the bone jutted out, pearly white amid the blood. The wounds seemed to have been imposed by a single extremely powerful blow.

'Here, look at this!' called the soldier who had pulled him out. 'I guess this must be his.'

He tossed a shattered helmet towards Godgifu and it clanked as it rolled up against the young man's body. Godgifu picked it up. The helmet had had cheek flaps and a screen of mail across the lower face. The left side of the helmet was shattered, just a small sliver hanging down where the armoured cheek guard should have been. The mail across the face was twisted and several rings had been bent and were falling apart.

One of the wounded men who had been searching for something walked over to see. He stood above Godgifu, his right arm hanging uselessly by his side, blood dripping slowly from his middle finger.

He bent over and squinted at the young man's shattered face. He gasped. Standing up straight, he bellowed to his colleagues, 'Eric! Halfdene!'

The two men hurried over, one limping heavily. They looked down at the body. 'Oh, sweet Jesus,' whispered one of them.

The handcart trundled into the courtyard at Ingui's house, pulled by Eric and Halfdene. Guthrum's broken arm prevented him from helping. Halfdene had a deep cut to his thigh, but Eric had bound it with rags, and the bleeding had slowed to safer levels.

'Inga! Nessa! Cwenburgh!' called Godgifu as they arrived. Three women came to the door of Ingui's house, then ran across the courtyard when they saw the load the cart bore. The severely wounded young man, whom Godgifu had learned was called Edgar, lay on the cart, motionless.

'Come on, we have to treat this man's wounds now! Inga, fetch water! Cwenburgh, get a pallet put up in the main hall and bring me a needle and thread! Nessa, fetch skins!'

The three women rushed to do as they were bid. Halfdene bent over Edgar, his face creased with anxiety. Godgifu pushed him out of the way unceremoniously.

'You two,' she addressed Halfdene and Eric, 'strip him,

we need to know if there are any wounds we haven't seen.'

Obediently, Eric and Halfdene began to strip Edgar, pulling off his boots and leggings, his mail surcoat, padded leather jacket and tunic. Edgar lay now in just his loincloth, stained and wet with the contents of his bladder.

Eric looked questioningly at Godgifu. She sighed. 'It will have to come off, too. He needs to be washed and dried. First let me examine him for further wounds.'

She bent over Edgar and felt his body all over with gently probing fingers, ignoring the stink of sweat, blood and piss. She found no further puncture wounds, but there was more damage. 'He has two broken ribs on his left side, his left shoulder is broken and there is considerable bruising.'

Nessa ran out of the house with an armful of large animal skins and placed them on the handcart by Edgar's head.

Godgifu spoke to Halfdene without pausing in her examination of Edgar's wounds. 'Look, just get it off. Cover his modesty with a skin for now, we can clean his body of the sweat and piss once we've dealt with the wounds. Look away, Nessa.'

Nessa and Godgifu turned their backs as Halfdene swiftly stripped off Edgar's loincloth and placed a bearskin over his midriff. 'Alright,' he said.

'Is there any damage there?' asked Godgifu, her gaze still averted.

'No,' said Halfdene.

Godgifu turned back and immediately began feeling at the shattered side of his face. The damage was severe. His left cheekbone and lower jaw were badly broken, and the flesh was pulled away from his left eye, which was swollen shut and black with bruising.

Inga returned to the courtyard, carrying a large pot of water. She also held a fistful of clean rags.

'Well done, Inga,' said Godgifu as the girl approached.

Inga smiled with pleasure at her mistress's praise. 'Cwenburgh has some water on the boil, I'll go and get some hot.' She turned to go and Eric followed her.

Godgifu dipped a rag in the pot of cold water and began carefully wiping away the blood on Edgar's face.

'The blood is flowing more slowly,' observed Guthrum, 'that's good, isn't it?'

'His heart is slowing. He is near death. No, it is not good. Here, hold this.' She guided Guthrum's hand to the wet cloth on Edgar's face.

'Hold it firmly. You can't hurt him while he's like this.'

Guthrum pressed down, wincing as he felt Edgar's bones against his fingertips.

Eric and Nessa re-emerged from the house, each carrying a pot of steaming water, their hands insulated by thick cloths. Cwenburgh was with them, holding a small wooden box which she opened towards Godgifu.

Godgifu flicked impatiently at Guthrum's hand. 'Away,' she ordered.

She felt carefully at the broken bones and manipulated the flesh around the breaks until she was happy that the bones were in the best possible alignment.

'You,' she said to Halfdene, 'hand me a hot rag.'

Halfdene took a rag from Nessa and wetting it in the pot of hot water held by Eric, passed it to her. She tutted angrily, wringing it out without looking at him. The water fell onto the cobbles with a surprisingly loud splattering sound. She wiped away the last of the gore from Edgar's wound, pulling back the flaps of flesh and cleaned inside them.

'Another,' she commanded, dropping the first hot rag to the floor. Halfdene repeated the procedure, this time wringing out the cloth himself.

Again, Godgifu performed the excruciating task on Edgar's face.

'And another,' she said. This time Halfdene was ready before she asked.

'You learn quickly,' Godgifu said as she wiped away the trickle of blood from the shattered jaw. To Halfdene's horror, she pushed her fingers into the wounds, manipulating the bone ends so that they lined up as best they could. He winced as he heard the broken ends of the bone grinding against each other. She turned to the box presented to her by Cwenburgh. Deftly, she removed a needle and thread and turned back to Edgar. With swift precision, she began to sew the flaps of flesh back into place over the traumatised bone.

'I am not very experienced with this,' she said as she sewed, her slim fingers nimbly pushed the needle through Edgar's flesh and pulled each stitch tight. 'I have stitched arms and legs in the past, but never a face, and never anything as damaged as this. Your friend will not be pretty after this, I'm afraid.'

Once done she picked a small pot out of the box held by Cwenburgh. She pulled off the cloth that covered it and stuck two fingers in, smearing the white contents over the stitching and all over the damaged part of Edgar's face.

'What's that?' asked Eric.

'It's mostly beeswax, but there are other things in it, like honey and yarrow. It will aid the healing process.' Eric nodded. 'If there is to be any,' she added.

She pulled some long strips of cloth from the wooden box and began wrapping Edgar's head. She placed extra padding and some more of the waxy poultice on the closed and bruised eye.

'I don't know how damaged his eye is. He might lose it. I'll keep watch on it, but if it starts to go bad, I will have to cut it out, or it will kill him. There.' She stepped back from the cart, feeling suddenly very tired. The adrenalin rush had kept her focused and alert, but now tiredness swept over her like a wave.

'Take him into the house – carefully! Cwenburgh, did you make up the pallet?'

'Yes.'

'Alright, put him on it and cover him with skins. Then you two come back out here. You both need my attention, too.'

Halfdene and Guthrum nodded and with Eric, they carefully lifted Edgar and walked slowly into the house with him.

That evening, Halfdene, Guthrum and Eric sat round the fire in the centre of Ingui's hall. Godgifu had stitched Halfdene's thigh and covered it with the same poultice she had used on Edgar's face, and Guthrum's right arm was now wrapped tightly, bound with strips of cloth to two sturdy lengths of wood. Edgar lay unmoving, his pallet a few feet from the fire.

At long last, the participants in the day's dramas introduced each other.

'Godgifu?' said Guthrum as she introduced herself. '"God's gift". You are well-named, my lady.'

Thegn

'Indeed she is,' said Ingui. 'The last gift of my wife, God rest her. She died giving birth to Godgifu, after we had been childless for seven years of marriage.'

Godgifu stood. 'I'll bring more ale,' she said, as the jugs that had been brought earlier in the evening were now dry.

Eric leaped to his feet. 'No, my lady. Tonight, you shall be waited on. You have saved the life of our lord's grandson and our friend, you have healed Halfdene's limp, and set the bones of my ancient comrade here,' he indicated Guthrum, 'I will fetch the ale.'

Godgifu bowed politely at Eric, who stomped off in search of a barrel of ale.

'My lady,' began Halfdene, 'where did you learn such skill as you have?'

Ingui answered for her. 'My sister was a great healer, with much knowledge passed to her from our mother and grandmother. The women in our family have always been healers, and the skills are passed down between them. One day, Godgifu's daughter will also be a healer, God willing.'

Godgifu smiled. 'My aunt was a gifted teacher. I can remember her very words and the way in which she spoke them as she taught me. I hear them in my head as I work. I miss her.'

Eric returned with a large pitcher filled to the brim with ale. He bowed slightly to Godgifu and filled her beaker before moving on to fill the men's.

Godgifu spoke, 'I need you to know, Eric, that I have not yet saved the life of your friend,' she nodded to Edgar, lying on his pallet. 'He has a long and difficult road ahead of him, and that road is still full of potentially fatal pitfalls.'

'Nonetheless, my lady,' replied Eric, gravely, 'without your intervention today, Edgar would now be gone from us, standing before St Peter at the gates of Heaven, and we would be the poorer for it. I give you my thanks and offer you my eternal gratitude.'

'Aye!' chorused Halfdene and Guthrum, raising their beakers of ale in salute.

'I see you have started building a bell tower for your church,' said Guthrum to Ingui. 'Do I take it that you are preparing for an elevation in status?'

Ingui nodded. 'Indeed, once the tower is completed, I can begin my petition to Earl Morcar to be counted a thegn.'

'Then whilst we are here awaiting Edgar's recovery, will you accept the three of us as willing workmen on the building?' He indicated his broken arm. 'I won't be able to do much building myself, but at least I can shout at these two.'

Ingui laughed. 'I think that would be most acceptable, Guthrum.'

Guthrum raised his ale in salute to Ingui.

Eric drained his beaker, and as he refilled it, he said 'Right! Now that's done. Guthrum, have I ever told you that your face is like a pig's arse?'

5

Recovery

The pain seared through his face and head. All he had known for all his existence was pain. He was in darkness. He could see nothing, hear nothing, touch nothing. His mouth was dry, and the dryness roared through his body. He could not move, and he was glad of it.

Godgifu watched attentively over Edgar. She even had a cot placed next to his pallet in the mead hall so that she could sleep beside him lest his condition change during the night. He was deathly still for two days, and then on the third day, he started to move slightly. His head shook slowly from side to side, and small gasps and groans escaped from his lips. Godgifu leaned over him and felt his brow. Even through the wrappings she had put on his head she could feel the heat. His face was slick with sweat.

Godgifu sat back, worried. The fever had come on him quickly. She knew that now was the most dangerous time, the time when he walked hand in hand with Death. If only she could persuade him to walk back towards the land of the living. She bent back towards him and placed her lips close to his ear.

'Stay with me, Edgar. Stay with the living. Your friends are here, they pray for you. Eric, Guthrum and Halfdene. My name is Godgifu, I am your watcher. Stay with me Edgar, for I long to hear your voice.'

He stilled his movements, though there was no other sign that he had heard her.

'That's good, Edgar, stay peaceful. You must walk this path alone, though I'm not far away, and will be here when you need me.'

To add to the pain, he now felt himself to be on fire. He could feel the flesh curling away from the bone as it blackened and crisped. I am dead, he thought, and I am in Hell. The fires of Hell are splitting the flesh from my bones. And yet the flesh did not leave his bones, it simply remained constantly being stripped from them. As he writhed in agony, it seemed to him that a voice carried across the gulf, down, down, down to where he lay in torment. The voice was cool, and it soothed, though he could not understand the words.

'He looks terrible,' said Guthrum.

'The fever began last night,' said Godgifu, 'I need you to know that this is the most dangerous time. If he is going to die, it will probably be within the next two or three days. If the fever breaks, then he will most likely live, though what sort of life he will be able to live with such injuries I do not know. There is also another danger that we have not discussed yet.'

'I know. His head. I have seen lesser head injuries than this cause a man to become an idiot, rambling and unable to understand the simplest thing.'

'Most of the damage was to his cheek and jaw. I'm hoping that he will remain himself, even with this,' she indicated his bandaged head.

'And if he does wake up not… himself?'

Godgifu sighed. 'He is your friend. You must decide what is best for him.'

'It would be better if he'd died on the field than for that to happen,' whispered Guthrum.

'Let's not be hasty. Time will tell.'

More voices were falling from Heaven to his tortured ears. Again, he could not understand what was being said, the voices drifted in and out, faint at best, inaudible otherwise. Another voice had joined the cool one. He didn't know why, but the new voice brought him pleasure, some dim, half-remembered thing. The voice was strength, and he drank from it.

Halfdene walked up to Guthrum as he stood outside the mead hall, breathing in the autumnal air.

'Guthrum, I've been thinking. One of us needs to go back to Rapendun. Wulfmaer needs to know what's happened to Edgar. He must be beside himself with worry. Our levy will be arriving home tomorrow, probably, and if none of us are with them, Wulfmaer will surely think us all killed.'

Guthrum nodded. 'Yes, you're right. But which one of us would leave now? Edgar stands on the very brink of death. Surely it's better for Wulfmaer to know for certain whether his grandson is alive or dead? Better to leave it just another three days. Then we'll know which way he's gone.'

'Very well. I'll prepare to leave in three days, as long as

we know by then. You and Eric should stay.'

Shards of piercing light lanced into his eyes. It had been dark for so long, so very long. Light again, painful, dazzling light. Something moved, a large shadow across his line of sight. There was something wrong, this was not how he remembered seeing. The view was too bright, he couldn't focus. There was a great physical blackness on his left side. Blind, he thought, I've lost an eye. As he crawled up from the depths of his darkness and pain, the voice came to him again. This time it had words; this time it called his name.

'Edgar?'

He did not know the voice, yet it was somehow familiar. Comforting. Yes! Yes, that was it. It was the cool voice that floated down to him from on high. Now it was speaking his name.

'Edgar, can you hear me?'

He fought with the pain in his face and in his jaw. His throat felt harsh and dry and he struggled to recall how to use it to make a sound. What sound? How could he reply?

Edgar made a weak sound as Godgifu placed her ear to his lips. He gasped with the pain of trying to move his jaw. She took his hand in hers.

He felt something. A long way away, there was a familiar pressure. He knew what this was, he knew, he knew. He groped for understanding. His hand. It was his hand. He remembered the feeling now; yes, it is somebody holding his hand.

Thegn

'Edgar, don't try to speak, just squeeze my hand if you can hear me.'

He remembered how to squeeze his hand. If only he could get his body to do his bidding. It was an effort, but he felt the squeeze travelling through his hand. He squeezed with all his might.

Godgifu felt a twitch in the hand she held. 'Good, Edgar, that's good!' She placed a hand on his forehead. It was sweaty but cool. 'Don't try to move, Edgar. Just lie there for now. Here, try a sip of water.'

She picked up a cup of cold water that was sitting beside the pallet. She dipped a clean square of cloth into it and pressed it gently to Edgar's lips. She squeezed it slightly and a small trickle flowed into Edgar's mouth and he coughed feebly but swallowed.

'Good. Very good. I need to renew your dressings. I'm afraid this might hurt a little.'

Edgar gave a tiny grunt. Godgifu gently pulled the pins out of the bindings round Edgar's head. Slowly unwinding them, she checked carefully how her stitching was holding up. The wounds appeared clean. His left eye was still closed, the heavily bruised flesh around it forcing it shut. She knew that the eye was not destroyed, as there was no seepage of the fluid from it, but she would not know whether the sight remained in it until Edgar could tell her himself.

She stood up and walked out of the mead hall. The three housecarls were across the courtyard, assisting Ingui's men as they raised long wooden beams up to the top of the bell tower's growing walls. They all turned towards her as she approached.

'He's waking up,' she said.

Instantly they were alert. Eric leaped down from the ladder he was on.

'Can we see him now?' he asked.

'Not yet. He's just stirring and beginning to respond to my voice, but we won't know for a while how full his recovery will be.' She looked at Guthrum in a meaningful way. He nodded.

'You mean we don't know whether he will still be… Edgar.'

'That's right. We should know soon, though.'

Edgar slept the rest of that day, and all through the night. Godgifu kept her vigilant watch on him and slept next to him again. The following morning, she woke to find him lying on his right side looking at her with his one open eye.

'Good morning, Edgar,' she smiled.

His eye narrowed. He opened his mouth, but only a small croak emerged. Godgifu reached for the water jug, poured a little into a cup and put it to his mouth. He swallowed, painfully.

'Who…' he tried swallowing again, and Godgifu pressed the cup to his lips again.

'Who are you?' he whispered.

'My name is Godgifu. You are in the hall of my father, Ingui. You have been wounded. Do you remember what happened?'

'Fight. I was in a battle at… at…' he closed his eye. 'I can't remember,' he whispered.

'It's alright. It will come back to you. What else do you remember? Can you tell me who you are and where you come from?'

He whispered without moving his jaw, barely even

moving his lips.

'My name is… Edgar. My home is Rap… Rap… Rap-something. My grandfather is Wulfmaer. Yes, Wulfmaer. He is thegn. My friends… where are my friends?'

'They are here. Would you like to see them?'

'Yes, yes I would.'

Godgifu went outside to fetch the housecarls. They nearly fell over each other in their haste to see Edgar.

'Gently now, boys,' cautioned Godgifu. 'He's very weak. Don't over-face him.'

'Edgar!' said Guthrum, his face cracked wide open in a joyous grin.

Edgar looked slightly confused, then gave a tiny smile. 'Guthrum,' he replied, and turning to the other men greeted them in turn, 'Halfdene, Eric.'

They returned his greeting joyfully.

'Did we win?' he asked, barely moving his jaw.

'Aye, lad. We won. Sent the Norsemen packing, what few of them remained. Harald Sigurdson and Earl Tostig lie rotting as we speak.'

Edgar's small smile slipped. 'Someone missing. Where is… where is…?' He closed his eye tight shut and then opened it again. 'Modbert? Where is Modbert?'

The three men's smiles fell.

'We lost him,' said Halfdene, 'in the battle; we don't know where he is. We haven't seen him since the battle. We searched the field but didn't find his body. There were a lot of bodies, and many were unrecognisable. We don't know. We haven't got drunk for him yet, though.'

Edgar smiled, then winced at the pain. 'Good. I should like to be there for his remembrance, should one be called for,' he smiled again. 'He…' he made small upwards thrusting motions with his hand.

'Yes! That was brilliant!' laughed Halfdene, 'put paid to that great Norseman once and for all. He's a hero, wherever he may be.'

Two days later, Edgar was sitting at the long table in the mead hall, eating a bowl of pottage hungrily but carefully, mopping the bowl out with a hunk of fresh bread. He sucked at the bread until it broke, not being able to chew. He looked up at Godgifu, who sat opposite him, watching him eat.

'Stanford,' he said. 'The battle was at Stanford.'

'Very good, Edgar, it seems that your memories are returning quickly.'

'I still don't know where I am.'

'This is the hall of my father, Ingui. I told you that,' she said gently.

'Did you? And where exactly is Ingui's hall?'

'Scarpenbec, about two miles from the battlefield.'

'Scarpen…?'

'…bec.'

'Never heard of it.'

'Hardly surprising,' she replied, 'I've never heard of Rap…?'

'Rapendun. Ah!' he smiled at her.

'I think we can have no more fears about your memory. Come, you need to exercise.'

She led him out of the mead hall into the bright morning. A chill had settled, clearing the mugginess of the previous week. Dark clouds threatened on the western horizon.

They walked out across the courtyard and onto the

Thegn

rutted, dusty road that passed through the village. Edgar's legs felt weak, and he held onto Godgifu's arm to support himself as he walked. They walked slowly on in silence, Edgar occasionally gripping Godgifu's arm more firmly as he felt some weakness come over him. They walked a little way from the settlement and came to a small copse by the roadside.

'Here, let's sit for a while. I like it here,' said Godgifu.

'It's very peaceful,' said Edgar.

They sat quietly for a while, listening to the birds and watching the first red and yellow leaves begin to drop, twisting and spinning from the branches.

'Godgifu,' began Edgar. 'I want you to know how grateful I am to you and your father. You've spent a great deal of time and effort to see me right. It shall not go unrewarded.'

She looked at him, wrapping her arms round her knees and flattening out her skirt over them.

'Seeing you up again is reward enough. To be honest, though, I welcome the opportunity to put the teachings of my aunt to good use. I must admit that I'm pleased with the results of my work.'

'Me too,' he said.

She laughed. It was a pretty laugh, clear, bright and uninhibited. He liked the sound of it.

'You should laugh more often,' he ventured.

'I've had little to laugh at whilst looking after you. I laugh enough otherwise.'

'I'm glad.' He paused for a while, simply enjoying sitting with her.

'I'm getting tired,' he admitted.

She stood up, slapping the loose vegetation from the

back of her skirt, and held out her hand to help him up. He took it and stood, wearily.

She carefully unbound the wrappings round Edgar's head. Guthrum, Eric and Halfdene looked on anxiously. The wound was visibly healing, but the flesh was still badly bruised and swollen. The stitches still held the flesh together, though they now seemed to be pulling slightly.

His face was still extremely tender, and he admitted that it was giving him a lot of pain. She moved to the thick wad of padding that she had secured over his left eye.

'I'm going to take the eye wrappings off, be ready.'

'Alright,' he said.

She slowly pulled the padding away.

'Oh!' exclaimed Edgar.

'Sorry,' she said, 'did that hurt?'

'No, well, yes, but that's not what I cried out for. I can see a little bit through it. It's very bright.'

Godgifu peered hard at the swollen mass that covered his eye. It was slightly reduced, and the bottom of the eye was beginning to emerge, bloodshot and bleary. She could see that the flesh around the bottom corner of the eye was pulling down, a result of the healing of the flesh beneath her stitching. The eye was weeping slightly, and she wiped away the gunk with a clean rag dipped in water.

'Can you make out shapes or just a brightness?' she asked.

He put his hand across his good eye. 'It's just bright at the moment, but there are some shadows. There!'

'That's my hand. You may regain some or all of the sight, I'm not sure yet. Most of your eye is still behind the swelling. However, it all seems to be healing well. There's no sign of it going bad, which was a great danger.'

'Thanks to you.'

'Thanks to God, and maybe a little to me,' she said.

A week later, Ingui laid on a fine meal for invited inhabitants of the village. The bell tower had been completed and a roof fitted. All that remained now was for the bell itself to be installed. Ingui had been to Eoforwic and paid a bell maker for his services. The bell was due to be cast the next week.

Edgar had slept through the afternoon and now seemed full of energy. Two villagers entertained them with their playing of reed whistles. Good, but not in the league of Alduin the bard, Edgar thought. This was a poorer settlement than Rapendun, but their generosity was unequalled.

Ingui stood up as the meal came to a close. He held up his hands for silence.

'My friends, I hope you have enjoyed our plain fare,' he began. There were shouts of approval and one or two men banged their cups on the table.

'You will all have noticed that we have some guests with us. These brave men came here to fight with Harold-king to repel the Norse invaders. Thanks to their efforts, we are safe from invasion, and we can all get on with our lives.'

There was a chorus of approval.

'And they have helped us well with our bell tower, which thanks to the extra hands is now complete.'

More cheering and cup-banging followed.

'I have been informed today that of the three hundred ships that arrived carrying the invading force, just four and twenty sailed away with the pitiful remnants of that force.

We know that their King, Harald Sigurdson, lies dead. By his side lies our former Earl, the treacherous Tostig Godwinson. Our King was generous in his victory. He allowed the surviving Norsemen, including their King's son, Olaf, to leave the battleground unmolested.'

There were murmurs of approval of this kingly magnanimity in victory.

'The threat is over; we are at peace once again. Long may it remain so. *Waes thu hael!*'

The hall erupted with cries of '*Waes hael!*', as the men drank down their cups of ale and the freshly produced mead of the season.

Ingui sat and turned to his right, where Edgar sat with a cup of mead.

'Well, Edgar, although I've enjoyed your company, I'm sure that you are keen to return home, as soon as my daughter declares you fit to do so.'

'Father!' exclaimed Godgifu, on Ingui's left.

'Now, now, Godgifu, this is an important question. Edgar must be getting back to his home and duties as soon as he can. His grandfather will be anxious for him, and I understand that as Wulfmaer is not a young man, Edgar takes on many of the burdens of his position. Is that not so, Edgar?'

'Yes, it is, though my grandfather has many capable men in his employ, who can manage the duties without even knowing that I'm not there, I'm sure. Halfdene will be back with my grandfather by now, so at least he knows that I still walk amongst the living and will return to him in due course.'

Godgifu was not placated. 'Edgar is still some way from being fit to travel any distance. The bones in his face are not yet knit, and I need to keep watch on that eye.'

'Of course, my dear. I wasn't suggesting that he leaves right away.'

'A good thing too,' she retorted, glancing at Edgar, who was grinning at her. She smiled back, a little coyly.

Ingui caught the look and cast his eyes down at his cup. That wouldn't be so bad, he thought.

Edgar's health and strength improved steadily over the following days and weeks. Ingui's generosity and hospitality seemed boundless, and Edgar promised himself that he would repay the man's beneficence in some way. Meanwhile, he was spending more time with Godgifu and enjoying every minute of it. She was beautiful, wise, generous and marvellously clever. She showed him flowers and herbs in the woods, and explained what each could be used for, which ones added sweetness to food, which spice. She could tell him which plants to use for healing various wounds and sicknesses.

'Here,' she said on one of their woodland walks. She stooped to a small plant with bright green, serrated leaves. 'This plant is called eyebright. It's more obvious in spring and summer when it has small white flowers with yellow centres. I mix it with marshmallow root to make the eye bath for you.'

Edgar looked in wonder at the insignificant-looking plant which Godgifu plucked from the ground.

'It just looks like a weed to me,' said Edgar, 'yet the eye bath is very soothing.'

'Well, it is a weed, but weeds can be very useful and restorative.'

'You're a marvel,' he said.

'I'm not, nature is. God, if you will.'

He laughed at her natural modesty. He placed his arm round her waist and they walked on. He no longer needed her support to walk, but they had continued to link arms and hold on to each other nonetheless.

After a short walk, they arrived at a clearing with a fallen tree lying to one side of it. They sat on it.

'How long will it be before I can go home?' he asked her.

Her face fell slightly. 'Not long. A week, maybe. The bones are knitting well and since I took the stitches out of your face the wound has shrunk considerably. Apart from your poor eye.'

She held her hand up to his face and very gently touched the area beside his eye where the flesh was pulled downwards away from the eye. He held her hand and kissed the palm.

'I have fleeting memories of when I was unconscious,' he said. 'Amid eternal agony and darkness, I thought I heard a voice, falling towards me as if from heaven. It was soothing and gentle, and it promised an end to the torment and of happier times to come. Then when I first woke, my sight landed on what seemed to me an angel, dispensing comfort and removing pain. I do not want to go, my angel, but I must.'

He put his hand behind her head and drew it towards himself. He kissed her tenderly on the forehead and wrapped his arms tightly round her shoulders.

Godgifu was making her final inspection of Edgar's wounds. The bindings were off now. The wound still looked appalling, with shiny puckered skin stretching from his left eye to his lower jawbone. On either side of the scar, along its entire length, were red spots marking where Godgifu's stitches had held the wound together as it healed. The cheekbone had set slightly awkwardly, giving his cheek a lumpy look, and the skin was pulled away from the lower corner of his left eye, revealing more of the white of the eye than would normally be visible. It also made the eye appear to droop slightly.

The ribs and shoulder had set normally and caused him no more than the occasional twinge.

'Well,' she said, 'I must declare you fit to travel. You may go home, Edgar.' She turned away from him and started gathering up her medical supplies.

'Gifu,' he murmured, but she did not turn. 'Gifu,' he repeated, slightly louder.

She turned, her eyes liquid with unshed tears. 'There's nothing left to say,' she said.

'There is. There is everything left to say. Please sit.'

'You are going, Edgar, that's all there is to it. I know you have to go, but I don't have to be happy about it.'

'I'm not happy about it, either, Gifu, but I could be a lot happier, if only you'll listen to what I have to say to you.'

Godgifu sat reluctantly down on a stool beside Edgar.

'Very well. Say what you have to.'

'I'm going home. I have to, we both know that. I don't want to leave you, Gifu, God knows I don't.' He paused.

'But you are going to, Edgar.'

'I don't have to. You can come with me.'

She whipped her head up and stared fiercely at him. 'You would take me home as some trophy of war?' she asked, icily.

'No, Gifu. I would take you home as my wife.'

'What? Wife? You would need my father's permission. You probably need your grandfather's permission, too, you being a thegn-in-waiting and all, and me not being the daughter of a thegn. Well, not yet anyway, though Father is convinced that it's only a matter of time.'

'I'm sure he's right, and I can speak to him, I'm confident he would agree. He's not so blind as you think him. As for my grandfather, well, he was married for a long time to a woman he really loved. She was just a peasant girl, and his father did not approve, but Wulfmaer's arguments eventually won him round, and Hilde became my grandfather's wife. She was a formidable woman, but wise and kind, and a huge source of strength for Grandfather and his parents through some very difficult times. Wulfmaer's father soon admitted that he'd been wrong to resist the match in the first place. Indeed, for the rest of his life he called her "daughter", and pride shone in his eyes as he looked at her, so Wulfmaer tells me. This all left Wulfmaer with a somewhat kinder view on marriage than many people have. "My lad," he's said to me many times, "when you find her, grab her with both hands and don't ever let go. You'll know her when you find her, and you will have my blessing." So, I am not concerned about Grandfather. He'll welcome you with open arms and a huge heart.'

'Do you really think that it could be?'

Edgar smiled broadly, wincing a little as the skin on his face tightened. 'I am certain of it, my angel. Let me speak with your father.'

Silent tears began to drip down Godgifu's face. 'Yes,' she nodded, 'yes, do that. Do it now.' She wrapped her arms around his neck and hugged him. Edgar gasped as she accidentally brushed against his battered face. She drew away quickly. 'Oh, my love, I'm sorry. I'll never hurt you again, I promise.'

He laughed again. 'Don't make promises you can't keep. Let me go to Ingui. I'll be back as soon as I can.'

He walked across the courtyard to Ingui's private residence, an impressive two-storied building, stone-built on the ground floor with an upper storey of timber. He was surprised to discover that he found the walk very difficult indeed. His heart felt like it was in his mouth, and was beating very hard. His legs seemed to veer away from the house's door of their own accord. He gritted his teeth, sending shafts of pain through his healing cheek and jaw. The main door was wide open and he strode in purposefully. He walked into the main living area, to find Ingui sitting on a wooden settle, a large beaker of ale in his hand. Cwenburgh stood protectively beside him.

Ingui looked up as Edgar walked in. 'Edgar,' he said, 'join me in an ale before you go. Sit, please,' he indicated another settle next to his and at right angles to it. 'Cwenburgh, a jug of ale please, my sweet.'

Edgar noticed the term of endearment and the way Cwenburgh looked at Ingui as she left. The suspicion had grown within him over the past few weeks and now he was sure of it. They were lovers.

He sat. 'Ingui, I have…'

Ingui held up his hand. 'First, ale!' he declared.

Cwenburgh walked back in with a large brown glazed jug and another beaker. She handed the beaker to Edgar, who held it whilst she filled it with brown ale. He thanked her and took a drink. It was good.

'My private supply. Cwenburgh makes this herself,'

Ingui said proudly.

Edgar raised his beaker to Cwenburgh. 'This is fine ale, indeed, Cwenburgh, I salute you.'

She bowed politely to him and then sat down on the settle next to Ingui. An unusual move for a servant.

'To your safe journey home, Edgar,' said Ingui.

'To your very generous hospitality, Ingui,' replied Edgar.

They drank silently for a few moments.

Edgar cleared his throat. 'Ingui, I have something to ask you, something very important, and I would have you hear me out before replying.'

'Ah,' said Ingui, 'would this have anything to do with that?' he pointed across the room where several bags and boxes sat on the flagged floor.

'Er... what is it?' asked Edgar, confused.

Cwenburgh spoke up. 'It's Godgifu's dowry,' she said.

Edgar's jaw dropped, sending more pain through his face. He winced and closed his mouth again.

'We've all been pretending that each of us is blind to what's going on,' said Ingui, 'I know what's been developing between Godgifu and you, and I think you know what is going on here.' He looked pointedly at Cwenburgh.

Edgar let out a sigh of relief. 'Yes, I think so,' he said.

'Well thank the gods for that,' exclaimed Cwenburgh, pulling a third beaker from within her clothing and pouring herself a cupful of ale.

Edgar laughed and saluted Cwenburgh with his cup again. 'My lady,' he said, bowing his head to her.

'Not yet, I think, but maybe soon. *Waes hael!*'

They all drank deeply and refilled their beakers from the jug.

Thegn

'So, do you have plans to marry?' asked Edgar.

'It seems we have a wedding to attend in any event,' said Cwenburgh.

'Aye, I hope so, if the bride's father gives his consent,' mumbled Edgar through his ale.

'Given. You must, of course, marry here. Our church is newly built and has not yet celebrated its first nuptials. Our priest visits every month from the great minster church at Eoforwic. I'll speak to the priest tomorrow; I have business in town to attend to. I might as well attend to this at the same time.'

'Seems a shame to make two bookings for weddings. You'll have to donate twice as much to the priest's drinking fund,' said Cwenburgh.

'An excellent point, my sweet,' said Ingui, happily. 'Will you marry me?'

'Of course I will, you fool,' she snapped, and kissed him on the end of his nose.

They finished the jug of ale and Cwenburgh went to refill it. Once she was out of hearing, Edgar looked at Ingui.

'Does Godgifu know about you and Cwenburgh?' he asked.

Ingui puffed out his cheeks. 'Has she said anything to you?'

'No, but she's very protective of you.'

'Hmm. I don't know. She lives in this house, and she is an intelligent young woman, so I would tend to believe that she does know,' suddenly he looked doubtful. 'I hope she knows, otherwise I may be in trouble.'

Edgar laughed and held out his beaker as Cwenburgh returned and filled all three again.

Godgifu was still sitting on her stool when Edgar weaved his way back into the mead hall. He sat down heavily on the stool beside her.

She looked at him and sniffed. 'Edgar, are you drunk?'

'No. Well, maybe a little. Yes.' He grinned happily at her. 'I have been drinking with my soon-to-be father-in-law.'

'He said yes?'

'He said yes!'

'Oh Edgar!' she threw her arms around him again, being careful not to touch his tormented face this time.

'Cwenburgh was there, too,' he began, clumsily. 'She… she… er…'

'She's my father's lover. Yes, I know.'

'Do you approve?'

'Cwenburgh is a good woman, I see how she looks at my father when she thinks I'm not looking. Of course I approve.'

'Oh, that's good. Because we're having a double wedding.'

It was Godgifu's turn to laugh. She threw her head back and laughed that laugh that Edgar had first heard on their first walk out together. He felt his heart melt. 'Come on, let's join the happy couple,' he said.

They walked out of the mead hall to see Ingui and Cwenburgh walking out of Ingui's house. Cwenburgh and Godgifu stopped and stared at each other. Then they started walking across the cobbled yard towards each other, increasing pace until they were both running. They threw themselves into each other's arms and stood there, hugging each other and sobbing.

6

Return

November 1066

Ingui gave Edgar a waxed, wide-brimmed leather hat to keep the worst of the rain and weather from his face. It retained its waterproofing for the whole journey, and as the small party approached the thegnly residence of Rapendun, the rain dripped from the brim, seeping down Edgar's back. His face, however, remained dry, a fact for which he was very grateful.

Godgifu looked in admiration at the stone-built church which rose above the wooden palisade.

'My father could only dream of building a church like that,' she said.

'It was once part of a monastery, when Rapendun was the capital of Mercia. That was when Mercia was still a kingdom,' replied Edgar. 'Mercian kings lie still within its crypt. The crypt also once held the sacred bones of St Wystan, a martyr, but they were removed some time before

I was born.'

'Where is the monastery?' asked Godgifu, looking around.

'It was destroyed by a great Danish army a couple of hundred years ago. They also built the huge bank that the palisade is built on. Notice how the church is built into the defensive bank?'

'Yes, it seems to form part of the defences.'

'It does. The Danes used it as a fortified gatehouse.'

Godgifu was shocked. 'A church? The heathen barbarians!'

Edgar smiled and shrugged, then suddenly drew his breath in sharply and his hand shot to his cheek.

'Ow,' he muttered, grinning sheepishly at Godgifu.

'It's just healing, that's all,' she said, smiling back.

Godgifu had carefully rubbed her healing creams onto his wounds three times a day. The treatment was working well. The wounds were now mostly healed, and the skin over them was red, shiny and tight, but Godgifu knew that the skin would relax in time.

They passed through the gate and into Wulfmaer's residence. Small children ran towards the riders, squealing with excitement. Across the courtyard, Halfdene looked up from the stakes he was sharpening to replace rotten ones in the palisade and grinned. He stood up and strode across to greet the riders. Behind him, Wulfmaer stepped out of the door of the mead hall. He looked old and troubled, but his face lit up as he recognised Edgar. He half-ran as fast as his old legs could take him, arriving at the horses just as Halfdene was helping Edgar down from his mount.

Wulfmaer waded through the gaggle of excited children and grasped his grandson by the shoulders. The smile dropped from his face as he saw the extent of Edgar's wounds.

Edgar noticed the change in his grandfather's look. 'It's not as bad as it looks,' he said, smiling his now-lopsided smile.

Wulfmaer looked anxiously at his grandson's face. Then his face split into a broad grin. 'How could it possibly be as bad as it looks?'

They both laughed and hugged each other tightly. Behind them, Halfdene helped Godgifu down from her horse.

Edgar turned to her. 'Grandfather,' he said. 'This is Godgifu. She is the angel who saved my life and healed my wounds. I'm sure that Halfdene will have told you about her and the wonderful care she has taken of me.'

Halfdene smiled and nodded.

'She is now also my wife.'

Halfdene laughed delightedly and Wulfmaer raised his eyebrows. He looked wonderingly at Edgar and then back at his lovely new bride. He stepped forward and threw his arms around Godgifu.

'Welcome to my house, Daughter,' he said. 'Edgar, you have much to tell me about, and you two!' he pointed at Guthrum and Eric, still sitting on their horses, 'get off those beasts and organise a feast!' He put one arm round Edgar's shoulders and the other around Godgifu's shoulders and walked them back across the courtyard and into the mead hall.

Within minutes, Wulfmaer, Edgar and Godgifu were seated with the housecarls at the long table in the mead hall. A large jug of ale had been placed on the table and they had each been given a cup. Wulfmaer poured the beer and looked questioningly at Edgar.

'Halfdene has told me what he knows, but you must clarify for me, how came you by those terrible wounds?'

'I can't remember much of it. Our shield wall was holding fast, and theirs was breaking. They were starting to scatter and fail, but I remember a great shout to my right. A contingent of reinforcements had arrived from their ships. They slammed into the right flank of our shield wall, where I was, and we began to fall back. I can't remember beyond that, but obviously, someone got a good whack in. The next thing I can remember, but hazily, is drifting in and out of consciousness, and being tended by a heaven-sent angel.' He smiled and held Godgifu's hand on the table.

'I think it's an axe wound,' said Godgifu. 'It was delivered with immense strength. One of those big, shaggy Vikings, no doubt. Edgar's cheek and jaw were both broken, but I managed to get the bones roughly back where they should be before the bone started knitting again. I did a better job on the jaw than I did on the cheek, I'm afraid.'

Wulfmaer reached out with a finger and gently felt at Edgar's cheek.

'It is a bit lumpy,' he agreed. 'It will be a proud badge for the rest of his life. You did very well, Daughter, I owe you great thanks.'

Godgifu lowered her eyes to the table and took a drink of her ale.

Wulfmaer's face became serious.

'I don't know how much you know of recent events in the kingdom since your battle,' he began.

Edgar grinned. 'Scarpenbec is a small, remote place, well away from the main routes of the king's messengers.

Thegn

You may safely assume that we know nothing.'

Wulfmaer glanced at Halfdene, whose face was set in a stony mask. Edgar followed his grandfather's glance and saw Halfdene's expression.

'What?' he said. 'What is it? What's happened?'

'Whilst Harold-king was still north, in Eoforwic, after your battle, a second invasion fleet landed. This time on the south coast of Wessex.'

'A second fleet? From the Norse lands?'

'In a way. Not from the Norse lands themselves, but from the south. From the Vikings' great conquest, Normandy. It was led by William, their bastard duke. Harold-king marched swiftly south, probably whilst you were still lying unconscious. There was another great battle.'

Wulfmaer paused, his eyes falling to the table in front of him, where his hands lay, the fingers picking nervously at each other.

'Harold-king was killed. As were most of the southern Saxon nobles and nearly all the royal housecarls.'

Edgar gasped. Guthrum and Eric sat, stunned, and stared at Wulfmaer.

'Now this Duke William is consolidating his position. Lundenburg and Westmynster have opened their gates to him and he sits comfortably there.'

'What of the Witan?' asked Edgar.

'The Witan has elected young Edgar Atheling as king. Though he is barely more than a boy, as Edward-king's great-nephew and grandson of Edmund-king, he has the best claim to the throne of any man alive. I don't know where he is, but he or his thegns will surely be gathering forces to resist the Norman invader. William is already calling himself King of England. We have heard that more of his earls and knights are arriving almost daily on the south shore.'

'This is very bad,' said Edgar. 'Is it possible, do you think, that the attack in the north and the attack in the south were co-ordinated? It seems too much of a coincidence that the King should have to face two large armies at opposite ends of his kingdom at almost the same time.'

'It seems that the King was aware that the Normans were poised to attack from earlier in the summer. The attack on Northumbria does look like a diversion.'

'One that cost its perpetrators very dearly,' said Guthrum.

'And yet one that ultimately succeeded,' said Wulfmaer grimly. 'For William so far has been successful.'

'So what do we do now?' asked Eric.

'I don't think that there is anything that we can do,' replied Wulfmaer. 'Eventually, I hope that the call will come to join the Atheling's army. Then we can become part of the fight back. Until then, we must simply carry on as before. We have had violent changes of king before. We weathered the storms then, and we can weather them now. Halfdene?'

Wulfmaer looked at Halfdene.

'I am overseeing the repair of the palisade. It's well overdue, and we may have use of it in the weeks to come, depending on how William intends to extend his rule. If it's to be accepted by the Witan and in line with our traditions and laws, then all very well. If he chooses a more direct approach, then we'll be ready to defend ourselves.'

'Good,' said Edgar. 'We can all get involved in that.'

The wet autumn turned into a cold, frozen winter, which in turn gave way to a warm, wet spring. The repairs

Thegn

to the palisade were finished, and life continued as it always had in Rapendun.

One morning in mid-April, Eric and Halfdene were patrolling the palisade. They walked in opposite directions, and met every half-hour or so at the gate. As they approached each other, Halfdene stopped, tilting his head to one side. He held up a hand to Eric, signalling him to listen. Eric stopped and listened. Riders. Not in any hurry, but getting nearer. Halfdene and Eric hurried towards the gate. Within minutes, an armed band came into view.

'Get the Thegn,' said Eric.

Halfdene climbed down the ladders at the gate and ran across the courtyard to the mead hall, where the Thegn was ruling on a boundary dispute between two of his farmers.

Wulfmaer looked up sharply as Halfdene burst into the hall.

'Riders, my lord,' said Halfdene.

Wulfmaer immediately stood up and strode across the hall to the door. He stepped outside.

'Edgar, Guthrum!' he called at the top of his voice.

Behind the mead hall, Edgar and Guthrum were practising their archery at the butts. Both came running to Wulfmaer's call.

'We have visitors,' explained Wulfmaer.

Together the four men walked across to the palisade and climbed the ladders up to the top of the gate.

A column of about two dozen mounted men was approaching the gate. With them were half a dozen or so unarmed men, including one who looked to be a monk.

The column stopped short of the closed gate. One of the unarmed men rode forward a few more paces. When he stopped, he looked up at the men on the gate and called out to them.

'His lordship the Baron Roger de Barentin would speak with Thegn…' he looked down and consulted a small book in his lap. 'Wulfmaer.' His voice was unfamiliarly accented, and he mangled the pronunciation of Wulfmaer's name, but his meaning was clear.

Wulfmaer stepped forward.

'I am Wulfmaer. What business does the Baron have with me?' he called down.

'The King's business. Open your gates.'

Wulfmaer looked at Edgar and his housecarls. Halfdene already had his hand on his axe shaft.

'Alright. There's no point in antagonising them. Open the gate.'

'My lord?' said Halfdene. 'This is the enemy; we cannot just open the gate!'

'They may not be the enemy. I will not bring down the wrath of the Normans on the people of Rapendun without at least knowing what it is they want of me. Open the gate.'

Halfdene dropped his eyes. 'Yes, my lord.' He said, and slid down the ladder to open the gate.

Across the courtyard, Edgar noticed Alfgaer the priest stopping short as he stepped out of the church door. Edgar held his hand up as a signal for the priest to come no closer.

The Norman party walked in through the gate and spread out until the courtyard was ringed by the mounted men. Their leader, a large man with curly brown hair and a pockmarked face, sat on his horse in the centre of the ring of men with one unarmed man on either side of him. For the first time, Edgar saw that a huge dog with coarse grey hair followed the Baron's horse, keeping close to its back legs. It sat and regarded the Englishmen with open suspicion as they climbed down from the walls.

Edgar was immediately aware of their disadvantage. They were standing on the ground, whilst the Normans were astride their horses. Edgar studied the Baron's horse. It was a truly magnificent animal, a deep chestnut brown with a white blaze between its eyes. The man seated on it was hardly less impressive. Although clearly carrying too much weight, he had the look of a man barely restraining his own fury. His arms and legs were massive and powerful, and a richly embroidered tunic stretched across his broad, barrel-like chest. Around his shoulders was a heavy animal fur cloak. Probably a bear, thought Edgar. The man's fingers were encrusted with gold rings, and a large gold chain hung prominently across his chest.

'How may I be of assistance to you, Baron?' asked Wulfmaer in a clear voice.

The Baron leaned slightly towards one of his unarmed escort, who whispered something to him. The Baron looked down at Wulfmaer and spoke. None of the Englishmen could understand what he said in his barbarous tongue, but the translator began talking in a high-pitched voice even before the Baron had finished speaking.

'His Lordship is here to inform you of your liability to pay tax to the King. The Baron will be responsible for the collection of the tax.'

'I have always paid my taxes to the King. I will continue to do so,' replied Wulfmaer cautiously.

The translator spoke to the Baron, who replied in a sneer-laden voice.

'The Baron commends you. You will also have to pay a lease for the land which you are occupying.'

Wulfmaer bristled. 'I pay no lease for this land. It is my

property, granted to my grandfather by Aethelred-king.'

'Do you have documents to confirm this, signed by that King?'

'Of course we don't have documents! The land was granted over eighty years ago!'

'Then if you cannot prove that you own it, the land is legally the property of King William. You must lease it from him or you will be evicted.'

'What is this? Are you aware of the law of this land that you have invaded? You cannot…'

'King William is the law now. You will obey him or suffer the consequences.'

The Baron turned to his other unarmed companion and gave him a curt order. The man pulled a roll of parchment from a large bag that hung around his neck. He unrolled it and made a show of reading it slowly and carefully. He spoke quietly to the Baron and handed the roll to him. The Baron grunted at his translator.

'This document is the demand for tax and for the lease. You will take it now and prepare the funds. The tax and lease both become due in three months. You will have to pay the full amount then or you will be evicted.'

The Baron leaned forward in his saddle and extended the roll of paper to Wulfmaer. Wulfmaer stepped forward to take it. As he did, the Baron dropped the paper to the ground. He laughed, and his men joined in.

With a bark of command, de Barentin wheeled his horse around and made his way out of the palisade. His dog and his men fell in line behind him and followed him out.

'Close the gate,' snarled Wulfmaer, scooping the roll of parchment from the ground. 'Edgar, Guthrum, with me.' He strode into the mead hall, the parchment screwed up in his clenched fist.

Edgar had never seen his grandfather so angry. His face was bright red, his breath ragged and his hands shook with fury. He slammed the parchment down on a table and spread it out.

'Sweet Jesus, Mary and all the saints!' he exclaimed.

'Grandfather…' began Edgar, hoping to calm the Thegn.

'They want sixty pounds from me! Sixty pounds!'

Guthrum gasped. 'Dear God!' he sat down heavily. 'How are we to raise that much?'

'Grandfather,' said Edgar insistently. 'Sit down, please.'

Wulfmaer continued to pace across the hall.

'Grandfather, please!'

'What? Yes, yes, alright.' Wulfmaer strode to a stool and sat on it, still staring at the Norman tax demand. 'Last year,' he said, shaking the document in Edgar's face, 'we were taxed fifteen pounds. That was reasonable, it was fair, it was achievable.' He looked again at the parchment.

'Sixty pounds!'

'All right!' shouted Edgar. 'Sixty pounds, I heard you! Now let's all calm down and think about how we can raise it.'

Wulfmaer fumed. He threw the parchment to the floor.

'The lad's right, Wulfmaer,' said Guthrum.

Wulfmaer looked up. Guthrum rarely called his Thegn by his given name, and when he did, the divisions of rank between them somehow dissolved. Guthrum was not only Wulfmaer's principal housecarl, he was also his closest and most faithful friend.

'The law is gone,' said Guthrum calmly. 'These invaders now rule. The only way we can survive, for now, is to do as they say. Maybe later we can expel them from our lands, but for now, we must pay their geld; as the Norsemen had to be paid, so must their offspring. Think of it as a modern-day Danegeld. It's a tax, it's a bribe, it's an extortion. Call it what you will. Whatever it is, we must pay. We can raise this money, it's not beyond our means.'

Wulfmaer rubbed his hand across his face and snorted.

'Guthrum's right, Grandfather. We have no other choice at the moment. We can do this.'

Wulfmaer's ragged breathing slowly calmed. After a short while, in which Edgar and Guthrum remained silent, he spoke. 'Yes. You're right, both of you. Of course you are.'

Guthrum and Edgar looked briefly at each other. The Thegn picked the parchment up again and placed it on the table. He flattened out the creases absent-mindedly as he spoke. 'We can raise this. If we use what we already have in the coffers and supplement it with an extraordinary tax on our carls and ceorls, we should be able to meet their demands, but it will take every day of the time they have given us. We must start today.'

Wulfmaer led Edgar and Guthrum out of the hall and across to his private house, separated from the hall by a cobbled courtyard populated by quietly clucking hens.

An examination of the Thegn's money chest revealed that he already had over half the required amount. He needed to raise twenty-five pounds of silver from his tenants in three months. That represented a four-fold increase in taxation from the previous year.

'Guthrum, organise the carls. We need to inform everyone that this extra tax is necessary. Make sure that the word is spread that it is not of my doing and that I shall endeavour to make some reimbursement if and when I am capable of doing so.'

Guthrum bowed shallowly and left to arrange the tax-gathering.

'Edgar,' said Wulfmaer as he watched the door close behind Guthrum, 'We will not be alone in this. Our neighbouring estates will no doubt also be at the receiving end of outrageous tax demands. I would like you to visit our neighbours. Speak to the thegns, maybe we can form some sort of policy between us. Tell them that I would like to convene a meeting of local thegns here in one month's time. Take Eric and Halfdene with you. Be prepared to ride out tomorrow morning.'

Edgar's tour of the neighbouring estates had produced only a lacklustre response. There was much confusion amongst the thegns, and few of them saw eye-to-eye on the idea of a joint policy. Nevertheless, on the allotted day, seven thegns arrived at Rapendun to talk.

The meeting had begun informally with the thegns standing together in the hall, being served with fresh ale by Godgifu and the ladies of the kitchen. This had been Wulfmaer's idea; to put the thegns at their ease before they began talking about their shared problem.

Wulfmaer greeted all his guests cordially. Many were old friends; some he did not know so well. He greeted one with particular fondness. Sigewode, Wulfmaer's immediate neighbour to the west, was the oldest thegn present at the gathering. He had a distinguished look, tall and stooped with long flowing moustaches and an aquiline nose. His hair was braided at the back and fell down to his belt. After greeting Wulfmaer, he drew him aside inconspicuously.

'Before any of us say anything else, may I inject a note of caution?'

Wulfmaer nodded, 'Of course, old friend. What's your concern?'

'It seems to me that many alternatives may be considered at this meeting.'

'That was the idea, it's why we're here.'

'Be careful what you say. Not everyone here may share your concerns with the Bastard's tax demands. Some may well be regarding it as an opportunity. Remember that if we cannot pay, we will be evicted. Someone here may well see such an event as an opportunity to gain new lands.'

Wulfmaer shook his head. 'The Bastard has enough cronies to fill any vacant estates,' he said.

'Of course, but you're thinking rationally. Look to those who have a reputation for greed. Someone who does not get on particularly well with his neighbours. Someone who has conspicuously enough wealth to pay not only his own tax but maybe that of several others as well.'

His eyes slid across the room and back again. Wulfmaer looked around nonchalantly. His eyes fell on one of the thegns that he did not know so well. He knew him only as Dudda, but thought that that was just a nickname. Dudda was dressed well, an embroidered maroon tunic with fur trimmings was held at his ample girth by a thick leather belt fastened with a large, intricately decorated gold buckle.

'Dudda?' whispered Wulfmaer.

Sigewode nodded imperceptibly. 'He's been sniffing around my estate already, his words full of sympathy, but his little piggy eyes glittering with avarice as he asks quite openly whether I can afford to pay.'

'You think he might betray us?'

'He can only do that if we do or say something that could be considered treasonable.'

'Thank you Sigewode, your advice is well taken.'

'Just be aware, Dudda may not be the only one.'

After half an hour, Wulfmaer invited his guests to sit around one of the long tables. More jugs of ale were provided. Wulfmaer and Edgar did not take their accustomed places at the high table but sat on one side of the long table with their guests. All were equal here.

Wulfmaer rapped his beaker on the table, and the thegns settled down into silence to hear his opening remarks.

'Gentlemen, neighbours and friends. I thank you for coming here today to discuss our mutual concerns. We all have a similar problem, I believe. Here at Rapendun we have received a tax bill four times what it was last year. I understand that you have all received equally huge demands.'

There was a muttering of agreement from around the table.

'Very well. We should therefore address certain issues that will be of great importance to all of us. Can we all pay the demand? If we can't pay, can we send representation to this new Norman King and seek some agreement with him? Is there anything we can do collectively to raise the necessary geld?'

He paused to draw breath, and as he did so he looked very intently into the faces of those thegns that he knew well and trusted.

'Of course, we must pay. The alternative is to be evicted. The new King has set his levy, and we are bound to pay it.'

Several of his friends looked slightly askance at him. Confusion crossed some faces, but Godric of Deorby spoke up.

'None of us expected this. If we do pay, and I suspect that we all *can* actually pay it, reluctantly or not, will we be setting a precedent? If we pay now, will this so-called king expect a similar amount next year and the year after? Will he expect more?'

Agreement rippled round the table.

Wulfmaer again spoke, looking directly at Godric and speaking slightly more slowly than he would normally do.

'Whether we like it or not, William now sits on the throne of England. He wears the crown of Edward-king. He carries his sceptre, but he also carries his sword. Failure to pay carries its penalty. Either we pay or we are forced out. Any other course of action may be considered an act of treason by… some people.'

Wulfmaer saw understanding followed by alarm flash across Godric's features. Looking round the table, he saw understanding on enough other faces to be sure that he had got his message across.

'Well then,' replied Godric, 'as that is the case, let us discuss matters of mutual benefit for the raising of the tax.'

Predictably, the meeting came to no firm conclusions. It was evident as the thegns left one by one, that they had understood Wulfmaer's warning. That was the main message that they took back to their own mead halls that evening.

When all others had gone, Wulfmaer and Edgar sat down with Godric and Sigewode in Wulfmaer's private rooms in the hall.

'It appears that the Bastard is really getting his claws into us thegns,' said Godric.

'Divide et impera,' said Sigewode.

Godric looked at him quizzically. 'It's a Roman military maxim: "Divide and rule".'

'Ah.'

'He's certainly doing that,' mused Wulfmaer. 'We've never been very good at getting along together, but now the Bastard has given what seem to be huge incentives to any thegn willing to stab another in the back.'

'Seem to be incentives, but actually aren't,' said Sigewode. 'As you said before, the Bastard has enough hangers-on to fill any vacancies caused by non-payment of tax. He has to reward them somehow for their help at Senlac and afterwards. All he has to do is sit back and let our own greed do the dirty work for him.'

Silence filled the small room as they all contemplated Sigewode's words.

'We're stuffed, aren't we?' grunted Godric.

'I don't know. There may yet be an organised rebellion against the Normans. All we can do is wait for the word. What of the Atheling, for example?'

'I've heard nothing,' said Sigewode.

'Once the thegns and the earls realise what's going on, I think rebellion will be inevitable,' said Godric. 'It's clear that the Norman seeks to clear out all the present ruling class and replace it with one that owes him their loyalty.'

'When the call comes,' said Edgar, 'we must all be ready.'

They drank to that, then lapsed again into silence.

7

Disaster

July 1067

The horses' hooves dragged lazily along the gritty road. Flies buzzed around the horses, occasionally being swatted away by the men on the horses' backs. The summer sun was at its most intense. Edgar, Eric and Guthrum sat upright in their saddles as the horses trudged slowly on. The landscape around them had been growing more familiar with every hour. Now they were close to Rapendun, and the desire to finish their long journey caused them to hurry their horses on a little. The horses picked up the pace from a walk to a canter.

They crossed the river Trent at the little settlement of Burtone, close by the great abbey of St Mary, the final river crossing they would have to make before reaching Rapendun.

The carls held back whilst Edgar chivvied his horse across the bridge. Its hooves clattered on the rough wooden planking. He had always seen this bridge as the edge of his personal stamping ground. Beyond this bridge was The South, though as a young boy he had had no concept of just how far south the roads went.

He and the housecarls had been travelling beyond the boundaries of their immediate neighbours, trying to determine the mood of the people, and in particular the will to resist and fight demonstrated by the thegns of central England.

Edgar felt disheartened by what he had found. The mood was certainly rebellious, but nobody was taking the lead. They had learned that William had returned to his duchy of Normandy, taking the most important English leaders with him; Earls Edwin and Morcar, Archbishop Stigand of Canterbury and even Edgar Atheling himself, who had apparently surrendered to William. In short, there was nobody left around whom to foment an organized rebellion. Edgar had spoken with many thegns over the past two weeks of his travels. The story was always the same. Anger and resentment at the huge tax burden and the Normans' blatant attempts, often successful, to evict the rightful landowners.

Despite all this, the views of almost everyone he had spoken with remained depressingly parochial. The thegns were concerned only with their own selfish stakes. They wanted to retain their land, and would probably fight when the Normans came to evict them, but there was no interest in helping others in the same situation. They would probably have rallied under a rightful English claimant to the throne, or even under a powerful earl, but William held all the potential leaders of rebellion.

Small, localised pockets of resistance had sprung up,

but they were uncoordinated and disorganised. They were clearly causing the new King some aggravation, however. Disturbing reports had reached them as they travelled across the heartland of England. Marauding Norman knights were said to have been terrorising settlements up and down the land, reputedly on the orders of William himself. The man was said to be furious at the resistance of those he considered to be his rightful subjects.

Eric and Guthrum followed Edgar across the bridge and pulled alongside him. The river beneath the bridge was low and moved sluggishly. Large areas of black stinking mud were revealed that would normally lie beneath the water. It was turning out to be a hot, dry summer, and many feared a poor harvest. Rain was desperately needed, yet there had been none for seven weeks. A man stood in a field to their left. He was worriedly inspecting the harvest in the field. By now the wheat should be grown to his midriff. It barely reached his knees. He did not even look up at the sound of approaching horsemen, feeling the cracked earth with careful fingers.

Edgar tapped his horse's flanks with his heels, and the animal walked on, Guthrum and Eric following. They rode through more parched fields until they arrived at the first of the Rapendun farms. The picture was much the same, stunted crops stood miserably in the fields, promising a lean winter. After some distance, Edgar pulled up his horse and sat in the saddle staring over yet another poor yielding field. The housecarls joined him, one to either side. The horses whickered softly. The field in front of them had the familiar underdeveloped crops, but it had been disturbed. The tracks of several horses could be seen entering at one side of the field, crossing to near the centre, where there was a large flattened area, and then the trails led out of the field on the other side.

'Something's wrong,' said Edgar quietly. 'You two stay here.'

He climbed down from his horse and walked through the thin crop.

He heard the flies first. He stepped out of the crops into the disturbed area in the middle of the field. The cereal had been flattened by the hooves of several horses. Edgar couldn't tell how many horses had been here, but the trails leading into and out of the disturbed area indicated at least a dozen. To one edge of the clearing were two piles of rags. With a sinking feeling, Edgar approached them.

As he had feared, he saw that the rags were the clothing on two dead bodies. He recognised the two men as having been present in the mead hall during last year's harvest celebration when the messenger had arrived to tell of the arrival of the Vikings in the north. The men had been hacked brutally. The blood had soaked into their clothes and dried black and pungent. One of the men had had his right arm hacked off before he died, and the other's head was held on only by some sinew at the front of his neck. He had been attacked from behind. Flies infested the area, and Edgar swatted them away from his face.

Although no expert, Edgar guessed they had been dead for a few days. The bodies had begun to bloat, and the smell was appalling.

He returned to the housecarls, who were waiting anxiously.

'There's been trouble here. Two men killed – ours. At least a dozen horses involved. Let's get back to the hall as quickly as we can.' He sprang up onto the back of his horse and kicked it into a gallop.

They sped on through the fields, spotting other signs of trouble. A barn stood half-collapsed, one side of it seemingly burnt away. Sheep fences had been broken down, and the animals were scattered far out of their paddocks.

The three men galloped into the courtyard outside the mead hall and pulled their horses to a stop in shock. The roof of the hall was gone, the beams blackened and charred, protruding from the hall like the ribs of some sacrificed animal.

A man ran across the courtyard towards them. 'Master Edgar! Master Edgar! Thank the Lord you're back!' he shouted. Edgar climbed down from his horse and grasped the man by the shoulders.

'What's happened here?'

'Raiders, Master Edgar. Big men on big horses. Two days since. All in ring armour they were, with plate helmets. The leader shouted for the Thegn to come out, and when he did the raider said that taxes were due and that if the Thegn would not or could not pay then he was to be forcibly removed from this land. Lord Wulfmaer said that they were a month early and that he had another month in which to pay. Their leader said that if the money was not paid immediately then he was taking the land and would pay the tax himself.'

The man paused for breath, sobbing. 'Oh, Master Edgar, Lord Wulfmaer said that *he* was Thegn of this land, *sake* and *soke*, and that it could not be snatched by a gang of raiders who claimed to be from the King, even if he *was* king. The leader looked down on Lord Wulfmaer from his huge horse. The horse was skittish and it was dancing under him. He signalled one of his party, and this other man came forward and struck Wulfmaer to the ground with his shield. Well, some other of our men came out and started shouting at the raiders, and threatening them with whatever came to hand; sticks, scythes, a few axes. The raiders went berserk, they killed three of our men and the rest ran away. Then they set fire to the mead hall.'

'And my grandfather, where is he?' demanded Edgar.

'He's in his house, Master Edgar, but sir…'

'What?'

'They hadn't finished with him.'

'I see, take me to him now.'

The terrified man led Edgar into his grandfather's house, where Edgar found the old man lying amid a pile of furs next to a large open fire. Edgar swept over to where he lay and knelt beside him. The old man lay on his back, his face and head covered with sweat, his pallor grey and pasty. His eyes were closed, but he was breathing still, albeit shallowly.

Edgar placed his hand on Wulfmaer's shoulder. 'Grandfather?'

His grandfather made no move.

Edgar shook his shoulder gently. 'Grandfather? It's Edgar, I've returned.'

Wulfmaer sighed and his eyes opened slightly, though remained slits.

'Edgar?'

'Yes, Grandfather, I'm here.'

'Oh Edgar, look what they've done. They came before they said they would. They gave me three months, you were there, you heard them.'

'I was, I remember. We can rebuild. It won't take long.'

'No, they will be back, Edgar. The Bastard's Normans

will be all over the kingdom by now, claiming the ancient estates for themselves.'

'Then we must work with them. If we co-operate, we will be able to remain here.'

'I don't know, Edgar. I just don't know. I needed the extra month, then I could have paid. Not now, not now.'

The old man closed his eyes and slipped back into sleep. Edgar stood up and turned to the man who had met him.

'How bad is he?' he asked.

The man stepped forward and peeled back some of the skins from Wulfmaer's sweating body. He had been dressed in a long shift, but Edgar could see the masses of bandages around his Grandfather's body and arms. Many were seeping blood.

'Will he…?' began Edgar, but couldn't finish.

The man cast his eyes to the floor and shook his head slightly. 'The wounds are deep and numerous. In a younger man, then maybe, but at his age…'

Edgar looked down at his dying grandfather, then knelt and pulled the skins back across his wounded body.

He stood. 'Where is my wife?'

The man looked panic-stricken. 'Master Edgar, that's another thing. She was taken by the raiders!'

'What?' Edgar grabbed hold of the man and held him tight. 'Why didn't you mention this before?'

'I am so full of fear for Lord Wulfmaer that all else diminishes in my head.' The little man squirmed in Edgar's grip.

Edgar thrust him away. 'Who were they? Where did they go?' he demanded.

'I think he said his name was Roger. Roger something, I couldn't understand him. I don't know where he went.'

'Roger de Barentin.'

'That's it! That was the name!'

'Who else witnessed this attack?'

'The priest, Alfgaer, he was there at the time. He tried to stop them.'

'Is Alfgaer still here?'

'He was in the church earlier; he may still be there.'

Edgar ran out of the house, calling Guthrum and Eric to him.

'Wulfmaer is near death,' he said curtly. 'Godgifu has been taken by the raiders. I need to find out more, then we follow them.'

As they stood together, a lone horseman turned into the courtyard. He was wearing mail armour and was dusty and dirty, his horse limping slightly on its front left hoof.

The rider climbed down from his horse and patted the worst of the dust from his legs and arms. He walked up to the three men, removing his helmet as he came.

'Halfdene!' exclaimed Edgar.

Halfdene looked exhausted. 'I tried to follow them, Edgar. I tracked them for a day, but my horse fell lame and I had to return.'

'Which way did they go?'

'North, though I think they didn't get past the walls at Deorby.'

'How did they get in here?' demanded Edgar, looking at the open palisade gate.

'I don't know. The gates were closed earlier in the day, but I wasn't here at the time the raiders arrived.'

'Who was manning the gate that day?'

'The rota was drawn up by one of the estate managers, I could find out.'

'No, not now, we have more urgent matters to attend to.'

He was interrupted by a shout from the direction of the church. Alfgaer the priest hurried across the courtyard, hitching his cassock to his knees so he could run faster.

Reaching Edgar, took him by the elbows. There was a large cut above his left eye that had been inexpertly treated.

'Edgar, thank God you're back!' he gasped.

'Did they really take Godgifu?' demanded Edgar, without preamble.

'Yes, I saw her being hauled up onto the back of one of the soldiers' horses.'

'I must find her. The leader of the raiders, was it Roger de Barentin himself?'

'Yes, the big surly fellow who brought the tax demand two months ago. He had that same grey dog with him.'

'Is there anything else you can tell me that might help?'

The priest shook his head. 'There were about a dozen of them, but they were all heavily armed and armoured. They rode huge, powerful horses. Will you follow them?'

'I have to. Pray for me Alfgaer.'

'I have been doing, and I will continue to do so. Your grandfather…' Alfgaer faltered.

'I know,' said Edgar quietly. 'There is nothing I can do for him. When the time comes, he is to be buried with all the dignity accorded to a thegn of Rapendun. Even if I am not present.'

'Yes. Yes, of course. I will see to it when necessary.'

'Thank you Alfgaer. Now, we must eat before we follow the bandits.'

Edgar led the three housecarls across to the settlement's bakehouse. The bakers had managed to make some bread,

Thegn

and one of them ran out to fetch meat from the hall's kitchens. When he returned, he had barely enough food for the four men, but they accepted it gratefully anyway.

'It's not much, but it will do for now. We have some hard riding ahead of us, I think,' said Guthrum, around a mouthful of bread.

'With luck, they won't be expecting anyone to follow them,' said Eric.

'I think you're right,' added Halfdene, 'They've been careless about covering their tracks. They don't seem to care.'

'Overconfident,' muttered Edgar. 'We'll have the bastards yet.'

They finished their food and stood to leave.

'I must pay my final respects to my grandfather,' said Edgar.

Edgar walked out of the bakehouse and back to his grandfather's house. Guthrum, Eric and Halfdene followed a respectful distance behind him.

Once inside the Thegn's house, Edgar knelt once more by the heap of skins. He took his grandfather's hand in both of his. The Thegn's eyes fluttered slightly.

'Hilde?' he murmured.

'It's Edgar, Grandfather,' Edgar said softly, his face only inches from Wulfmaer's.

'Edgar. I thought you were… but no. Not yet,' he smiled weakly. 'Soon, though. I can feel myself slipping, lad. It's not so bad.'

'I'm going after the raiders, Grandfather.'

'Ah, good lad. You be careful, though. They are brutes, and…' his eyes lost focus and his attention drifted away for a few moments. 'What was I saying?' he said.

'It's alright Grandfather. I will avenge what has been done here.'

'Vengeance. From where I'm lying, that seems a poor excuse to get yourself killed. Those Normans will kill you, son. They'll kill all of us.'

Edgar was about to tell his grandfather that the raiders had taken Godgifu, but held his tongue. The old man was dying, there was no need to add worry and anxiety to his final moments. Wulfmaer had utterly doted on Godgifu since Edgar had brought her back from Scarpenbec just seven short months ago. He had treated her with the utmost respect and soon she told Edgar that she had started to think of him as a true father figure. The love they held for each other was clear to all who saw them.

'You have the sword I gave you?' asked Wulfmaer in a husky voice.

'I have it,' replied Edgar.

'It's a fine sword. Use it well. Did I ever tell you…' his eyes rolled upwards, he gasped slightly and was still.

'Grandfather?' Edgar rubbed Wulfmaer's hand between his.

Guthrum stepped forward. He knelt beside Edgar and placed his fingers on the left side of the old Thegn's neck, just behind the jawbone.

He withdrew his hand and sat back on his heels. 'He's gone, lad.'

Guthrum stood up and looked at Eric, his face grim. Eric cast his eyes down. Guthrum grasped Edgar's shoulder briefly, then followed Eric out of the house.

Edgar remained where he was, looking down at the body that no longer was his grandfather. He felt nothing. The man he loved most in the world had just died before his eyes and yet all he felt was emptiness. He rubbed Wulfmaer's hand one more time and then slipped it beneath the skins. He looked carefully at his grandfather's face, as if wishing to sear every crease and age spot right into his mind, though he knew that he didn't need to. Wulfmaer's face would always be there in his mind to smile at him.

He leaned over and gently kissed Wulfmaer's forehead. He closed his grandfather's eyes and carefully drew the skins up over the dead man's head.

He stood and walked out of the house without looking back. Alfgaer stood outside the house with Guthrum and Eric, who had rejoined Halfdene in the courtyard. Edgar nodded to Alfgaer, and he went inside to perform the last rites over the body.

Edgar looked at his three housecarls.

'Deorby,' he said.

The four men walked over to their horses, mounted them and set off at a gallop towards the north road.

8

The Search Begins

Edgar and his three comrades stopped their horses and dismounted as they approached the wooden gates of Deorby. A guard looked over the parapet. 'Who are you, and what do you want?'

'It looks like our Norman friends have been here before us,' muttered Guthrum.

Edgar took a few paces forward and stood directly below the guard. 'I am Edgar of Rapendun, friend of Godric, Thegn of Deorby.'

The guards head disappeared from view. A moment later, the hugely bearded head of Thegn Godric appeared in its place.

'Edgar, is that you?' he called.

'It's me, Godric,' Edgar replied in a flat, emotionless voice. 'Rapendun has been ravaged by the Normans. They have burned our mead hall. They have killed Wulfmaer. They have taken Godgifu.'

Godric turned his head and shouted an order to someone beneath him. Slowly, the gates began to swing open, the wooden hinges creaking and groaning in protest.

Edgar and the housecarls led their horses through the gate and stopped where Godric stood to greet them.

'The bastards have been through here, too,' said Godric. 'There weren't many of them, and they couldn't get in here, but they've burned and sacked the villages around. Come, we can talk inside.'

He led them into a stone-built structure, like a small mead hall, nestled in close by the inside of the palisade wall. Godric indicated stools around a long table and called for ale.

They sat in silence as a middle-aged woman smartly set cups before them and filled each with ale from a large jug. She placed the jug on the table and went back to her duties.

'Wulfmaer dead, you say?' growled Godric.

Edgar nodded. 'I've arranged a proper burial for him. I would remain for it, but I must find Godgifu.'

'Of course, of course. I grieve for the loss of Wulfmaer. He was a fine man, a fine thegn and, in his day, a fine warrior. He was a good friend to me. He will be sorely missed. Ah!' He shook his shaggy head as if to throw off the sorrowful thoughts as a dog throws off water from his coat.

'So, your wife; you're sure these Normans took her?'

'Alfgaer, our priest, says so.'

'When they arrived here, shouting their mouths off about being the new lords of the land, there were maybe two dozen of them.'

'That's more than the number that attacked Rapendun. There may be many bands about, splitting and rejoining each other as they go.'

Godric nodded and stared at his cup. 'They had a sort of baggage train with them,' he said at last.

Edgar looked up, and the three housecarls stilled in attention.

'The baggage train was some way from us, being held back, I think. There were a couple of waggons, one covered. It's possible that Godgifu was in that one. I'm very sorry for you, Edgar. You will need to exercise great caution in retrieving your wife. These men are worse than animals. They care nothing for life or property.'

'And yet I must follow them,' replied Edgar.

'I know, I know.' He paused, looking at the cupped palms of his large, knurled hands. 'There is something else you must now consider.'

He sat in silence for a few moments more. 'With Wulfmaer's death, you are now thegn.'

'I know,' whispered Edgar.

'With that title goes great responsibility. You are no longer responsible only for the welfare and good health of your family, but also for all the men, women and children of whom you are now lord. In these times especially, they will be looking to you for protection.'

'I cannot abandon Godgifu,' he said.

'I know. I'm not asking you to. I just want you to be clear about all your responsibilities. It is no easy thing to be a thegn, not a good one at least.'

'I have to find her, Godric. I have to.'

'I agree. And to that end, I will spare you some of my housecarls. I fear that you will need them before this is through.'

'Thank you, Godric. Your help is greatly appreciated.'

'I was a comrade-in-arms with your grandfather, lad. I

owe him at least that.'

With that, Godric called out and the same woman came into the small hall again. 'My lord?' she asked.

'Send that lad out who's always hanging round the kitchen. Tell him to fetch Sebbi, Osfrid, Enni and Hunwald.'

'Yes, my lord,' and she was gone.

Godric refilled everyone's beer cups, emptying the jug in the process. He lifted his beaker and held it towards Edgar. 'Maybe this isn't the best time to do this, but let us drink to the memory of Thegn Wulfmaer and to the good fortune of Thegn Edgar. *Waes thu hael!*'

Guthrum, Eric and Halfdene raised their cups in response, '*Waes hael!*' they called, as one.

Without any prompting from Godric, the serving woman brought out a dish of cold meat. Edgar shook his head.

'We ate just before we set off,' he said.

'You'll need it, lad,' said Godric. 'God alone knows what privations await you on the road. Eat.'

As Edgar and his companions ate, four men entered the hall and walked over to the table. One of the men stepped forward. He was tall and sallow, with sunken cheeks and drab, lank, blond hair. There was a large shiny spot on his chin that he had obviously been scratching. He approached Thegn Godric. 'You asked for us, my lord?'

'Yes, Sebbi. Sit down, all of you,' he indicated stools around the table. The four men sat. 'Edgar, these are Sebbi, Osfrid, Enni and Hunwald. Lads, this is Thegn Edgar of Rapendun, you're going to help him with a little problem he has.'

The four men nodded in greeting. Sebbi frowned. 'Rapendun? What of Thegn Wulfmaer?'

'Dead,' replied Edgar.

The four men muttered expressions of shock and sorrow.

Edgar acknowledged them. 'I am his heir, and his death is related to my problem. The Normans who visited you recently have done extensive damage in Rapendun and the outlying districts. Men killed, including Wulfmaer, the mead hall destroyed, buildings burned and crops trampled into the dirt. They have also taken my wife, Godgifu. I intend to get her back. Your help would be most welcome.'

The four men looked at each other. The one called Hunwald, a short, stocky man with a completely bald head but a long flowing moustache, slapped his palm on the table. 'I'd love to have a crack at those bastards. We need to smack 'em hard and soon, send 'em back where they came from.'

The other three voiced their approval.

Godric grunted. His eyes glittered beneath his bushy eyebrows. 'I admire your spirit, lads. But these Normans are not like anything we've ever dealt with before. They have something of the Devil about them. I fear for the future, I really do. They're working their way into the very land, like the roots of a tree. It will take a great deal of effort to uproot them, especially with our earls submitting to them like frightened women.'

There was a chorus of aggrieved approval from around the table.

Edgar spoke up. 'We don't yet know what game the earls are playing. They could be biding their time, waiting for the right moment to strike back, maybe when sufficient forces have been raised, the earls can act as one.'

Thegn

'The earls will never act as one. Not even at a time like this. They're too busy scoring points off each other, and no doubt they're ingratiating themselves with the Bastard as we speak. No, I'm sorry Edgar, but if there is to be a popular uprising against the Normans, it must come from us, the thegns. It will never come from the earls.'

There was muttered agreement around the table. Even Edgar had to agree that Godric's appraisal of the situation was probably accurate.

'But for now,' Godric slapped his fingers on the table, 'we must concentrate on the job in hand. Securing the release of Godgifu. Lads,' he turned to his four housecarls. 'I want you to follow Edgar as you would follow me. He may be young, but he's got a good head on his shoulders, and good men with him. Now gather what you need and meet us by the gate as soon as you're ready.'

The four carls rose and left the building.

Godric turned to Edgar. 'This will not be easy, lad,' he said. 'I said there was something of the Devil about these Normans and I meant it. There's evil there. They won't just give her back to you. They may accept gold for her, they seem mercenary enough for that. Then again, you may have to fight for her, and that is where the greatest danger lies. I fear that they will have no qualms about killing her if they think that they are going to lose their prize.'

'I agree,' said Guthrum, speaking up for the first time since they arrived in Deorby. 'We will have to proceed with the greatest caution.'

'Very well,' said Edgar, placing his hands on the table and pushing himself up. 'Let's be going, then.'

They headed eastwards, in the direction that Godric had

seen the Normans leave after their abortive attempt to enter Deorby. The Normans had made no effort to hide their trail, or even to disguise it. The hoof-prints were deep and fresh, and where the trail was at its clearest, the eight riders followed at a gallop, slowing down only where the trail ran across stony ground. Halfdene was a good tracker, but Godric's man Sebbi was superb. Between them, Sebbi and Halfdene kept up a relentless pace, never pausing for more than a moment to study even the faintest spoor of the enemy.

They passed through several more devastated villages. At each one, crops had been trampled and sometimes burnt. Men lay dead by the side of the road, but the riders did not have time to stop and perform the necessary acts. They passed by a small, walled cemetery on the outskirts of one village. It was filled with weeping women and children, and grim-faced men. Edgar saw six freshly cut graves, burly men placing linen-wrapped bodies into each one. Edgar paused, and his men stopped in turn. The mourners looked up at the riders, fear in their eyes. To the untrained eye there was little to distinguish an English warrior from a Norman one. One of the gravediggers, an elderly, grizzled man in an earth-stained tunic walked towards them. His eye caught the preference the warriors had for axes over swords. They saw him relax slightly. He said nothing, just pointed up the road in the direction that the Norman raiders had passed. Edgar nodded to him and wheeled his horse round in the direction the man had pointed. He spurred his horse, and all eight riders galloped away.

As the sun dipped below the horizon, the temperature began to fall quickly. Edgar called his men to a halt, and they

Thegn

walked their horses off the road and a little way into a small patch of forest to their right.

'We'll rest here for the night,' he said. 'We'll put up the tents and build a small fire. Eric, Enni, can you gather up some meat?'

Eric and Enni took their small hunting bows and loped off into the forest. The remaining men threw up the tents, no more than leather sheets thrown over low branches and pegged into the ground. Each tent would sleep two men, providing basic shelter from the elements.

Eric and Enni returned within the hour with three hares and a pair of grouse. Guthrum built a spit over the fire with small branches he had collected from the forest floor.

The catch provided plenty food for the eight men, and they retired to their tents ready for sleep. Eric and Osfrid took the first watch, squatting thirty feet or so away from the camp. They whispered almost inaudibly to each other, occasionally dropping to silence to listen carefully to the noises of the night. The night was quiet. Long spells of absolute silence were broken only by the gentle rustle of the trees when the light breeze summoned up enough energy to cause a ripple amongst the leaves, the quiet scrabblings of small animals and the distant call of a brown owl.

Osfrid whispered, almost making no noise above his breathing. 'I slightly knew Thegn Wulfmaer. He was a good man. I am sorry that he has met his end this way.'

'He took me in when I was orphaned,' said Eric in a low voice. 'My parents were killed in a flood when I was about five years old. I had no other family. Thegn Wulfmaer brought me into his household and had me raised with a load of other brats.' Eric smiled at the memory. 'We were holy terrors. I was selected for weapons training. Well, we all were, but it was taken more seriously for some of us if we showed an aptitude from an early age. When I was thirteen, I met Guthrum there,' he waved an arm at the tents. 'Guthrum was ten years older, already an experienced warrior, and well versed in all matters important to a housecarl. His skill with an axe and a sword were phenomenal, still are. For some reason that I still can't explain, he took a shine to me, taught me as much as he could. I could never best him, never will, but I'm a far better warrior now because of him.'

Osfrid sat silently, not responding. He knew he didn't need to.

'But if you ever tell him I told you so, I will deny it with every fibre of my body. And then I'll cut your legs off.'

Osfrid chuckled quietly. 'Your secret's safe with me, Eric.' He looked up towards the sky, looking south where the waning gibbous moon cast its silvery light down through the leaves.

'Moon's at its height. Our shift's over. You wake Halfdene and I'll wake Sebbi.' He began to stand up when Eric grabbed his arm.

'Wait!' he hissed.

Immediately, Osfrid dropped back to his guard stance in silence.

Eric pointed with his finger ahead of them. Osfrid strained his ears. Yes, there was a noise that did not belong with the quiet sounds of the forest night. A slight sloughing noise away toward the road, not quite regular, but odd enough to raise the suspicions of the two men. Eric glanced towards the tents and was pleased to see that the small fire had died away, leaving not so much as a glowing ember. The smell of burnt wood was more discernible, though there was little he could do about it. The noise came again; an uncertain shuffling, as though someone was walking very carefully and hesitantly towards them. Eric flicked his fingers to his right and to his left, indicating that he and Osfrid should split up and approach the target from opposite sides. The men rose and began their glacially slow pincer movement around the target.

The moon slid behind a cloud and the forest was plunged into near absolute blackness.

Eric keenly felt the absence of his mail but also was thankful as it was almost impossible to walk silently in it. He held tightly to the handle of his seax, the long, single-edged knife that all free men kept in a sheath at the front of their belts. Eric's seax was longer than the traditional blade, something he held in common with many carls and warriors he knew. He had noticed that Osfrid, too, had a long-bladed seax, and was glad of it.

The quiet scuffing came again, this time more to his right than immediately ahead. He began to close in and prayed that Osfrid was doing the same from his side. Eric walked stealthily but steadily, keeping the trunk of a large tree between himself and the intruder, if intruder it was. He was suddenly gripped with fear. What if it was a wild boar? A boar could easily kill both him and Osfrid. Their eyesight was poor, and in the dark they were as good as blind, but their senses of smell and of hearing far surpassed that of Eric himself, and were quite sufficient to pinpoint a man in complete darkness. The sound was there again, but a little quieter this time. No, this could not be a boar, the rhythm was definitely that of two feet, not of four. Besides, a boar would be far noisier. They had no reason to be stealthy. The slight shuffling was there again, and a tiny snap of a twig. The intruder was very near to Eric now, he must redouble his efforts to be silent. He strained his ears, as he knew his quarry must also be doing. Was that…? Yes! He could hear faint breathing. His man was immediately behind the tree that Eric was hiding beside. Listen, make sure. Yes, an almost inaudible creak of leather, right ahead of him. Eric held his breath and stepped out from behind the tree, pulling his seax from its sheath as he did so.

'Don't move,' he muttered. Although quiet, the words shattered the silence. The moon was passing behind some scudding clouds, and Eric strained to see anything, but he heard the man in front of him involuntarily draw breath. He sensed him turning, taking advantage of the darkness to make a quick escape.

'I wouldn't, Friend,' said a voice, and at that moment the moon came out from behind the cloud and revealed Osfrid standing immediately in front of the man, his seax drawn and pressed to the stranger's throat. His eyes glittered with excitement and determination. By the Christ, thought Eric, this man is fast! I never heard a thing.

The intruder slumped visibly and dropped something to the ground. It glinted in the moonlight. A long, double-edged dagger. Moving so quickly that Eric couldn't catch quite what happened, Osfrid brought his seax up and forward, there was a thud and the man fell to the ground.

'Christ, what have you done?' gasped Eric.

Osfrid grinned and held up his seax. The pommel was augmented with a large lump of iron. It glistened blackly in the moonlight. Blood.

'He'll have a headache when he wakes up,' smiled Osfrid.

Guthrum splashed a cup of cold water into the man's face. He spluttered and opened his eyes. They closed again immediately, responding to the blinding pain in his head. He struggled but gave up quickly when he felt that his hands and feet were bound. Edgar and the housecarls stood around him in a semicircle, looking at him impassively. He looked up. He was tied to a tree.

Edgar stepped forward and spoke to him.

'Why were you spying on us?' he asked.

The man squinted up at him. He shook his head as if trying to clear foggy thoughts. His eyes closed again and his head slumped down onto his chest. Guthrum grunted and passed the cup to Eric. 'More water,' he growled.

Eric refilled the cup and handed it back to Guthrum.

'Pick his head up,' said Guthrum.

Eric grabbed the man by his brown mop of curly hair and held it up. Guthrum threw the water into his exposed face.

His eyes opened again and he shook his head to disperse the water. He looked up at them.

'Why were you spying on us?' repeated Edgar.

The man smiled. 'Why, because I am a spy, my lord,' he said.

His voice was melodious and clear. The English was good, but he was betrayed by a hint of an accent unfamiliar to his captors.

Edgar stepped back. Halfdene half pulled his axe from his belt. 'He's a bloody Norman!'

'Hold!' commanded Edgar. 'We need information from him.'

'He can't be trusted, he'll just lie.'

'That's as maybe, but we must still try.'

He approached the bound spy and squatted in front of him.

'What is your name?' he intoned slowly.

'My name is Alaric,' he replied, distinctly, in his lightly accented English.

'Who is your master?'

'Whoever pays me.'

'And who is currently paying you?'

'My present master is Guillaum de Caen, a knight in the service of the King of England.'

The housecarls behind Edgar bristled, but Edgar ignored them.

'Why were you spying on us?'

'I am a… a…' he fished for the right word, '…scout.'

'There is a band of marauding Normans passing through these parts. Are you with them?'

'I believe they consider themselves to be the rightful inheritors of this land.'

'They are not. Are you with them?'

The man licked his lips. He frowned and then clearly decided that honesty was the best choice.

'I believe I am attached to the party you mean.'

'They have a woman with them, they took her from Rapendun three days ago.'

'They have many women with them. That is one of the things they do. They kill, they steal, they take women.'

'What do they want with the women?'

The man shrugged as best he could with his hands tied behind a tree. 'You do not need me to tell you what they want women for.'

'Where are they now?'

Thegn

'I don't know, my job is to fall behind the main party and ensure that nobody is following. At least, nobody worth worrying about.'

Edgar straightened up and turned to face his colleagues. 'It seems the Normans are being more careful than we thought.'

'Not careful enough,' growled Halfdene.

Edgar caught the dangerous look on Halfdene's face. 'We need this man. He will be far more useful to us alive than as a corpse.'

Halfdene stared down at the helpless spy, then slowly nodded.

Edgar turned back to the man. He squatted down in front of him. 'My wife is one of the captured women. You are going to help us get her back.'

'It seems I have little choice,' he replied. 'I'm sure that if I refuse you will kill me, and what good will that do anyone?'

Edgar stood again and faced the housecarls. 'Guthrum, you and I will take over guard duty until dawn. The rest of you get some sleep.'

The following morning dawned overcast and misty. The Norman spy was tied to the saddle of his horse, which Guthrum had retrieved from the far side of the road at first light. The horse, in turn, was connected by a rope to Eric's horse. The spy's hair was matted with blood by his left temple, but the wound seemed to be slight. Enni, who appeared to be experienced at healing, had inspected the wound briefly and washed it with a little water. He had declared it superficial, and was admiring of Osfrid's skilful clubbing. 'Exactly enough force to stun without any serious damage. Nice.' Osfrid had grinned and bowed slightly to Enni.

They had eaten their breakfast of cold hare meat without giving any to their prisoner. Edgar had quizzed the man again as soon as they had finished eating. The spy had revealed that the band was travelling north and west, claiming land in the name of William of Normandy. Their leader was one of the Bastard's barons, a man called Roger de Barentin.

'We've met,' said Edgar. 'I will have his head before I'm done.'

Their prisoner remained calm and conformed with all their requests. He seemed to be little troubled by his predicament. They followed the route indicated by Alaric, but apart from an occasional trampled field, they saw few signs of their quarry's progress.

Late in the afternoon, they came to a fork in the road. The ground was heavily disturbed, and it seemed that the party they were following had split up. Sebbi grunted. 'The ground is too churned up here for any clear picture of what happened. I'm not sure which way we should go.'

'There's a village just ahead, let's go there and see if anyone can help us,' suggested Enni. They rode on about quarter of a mile until they arrived in a small village comprised of poor, rough huts and at one end, a larger, hall-like building, most likely the village's moot house.

Behind the houses were pasture fields, in which stood a few thin cows and a dozen or so healthy-looking pigs.

They dismounted from their horses and walked towards the larger building. As they approached, a pair of broad-shouldered men stepped out and walked towards them, cautiously. Their hands were prominently on the handles of their sheathed seaxes.

The two men stopped short and waited, their eyes watching for any sign of treachery. Edgar motioned the carls to remain where they were. He approached the two men alone. He held his hands well away from his sword and axe, which swung loosely as he approached them. He stopped ten feet from them, still holding his hands away from his sides.

'I am Edgar, Thegn of Rapendun. These are my carls. We are in pursuit of a band of Norman raiders whom we believe have passed this way. We mean no harm to your people or your property.'

The two men gave each other sidelong glances but did not move.

'From your stance, I would guess that the raiders have been here and have done you some harm. They have done us harm too, and we would take payment from them for that.'

One of the men slowly moved his hand away from the handle of his seax. He stepped forward slightly.

'I am Osric, headman here at Windeham. The men you speak of did pass through here, just yesterday. They were in a great hurry, it would seem, for they forgot to kill any of us. They were not the first Normans we have encountered here; the others did not forget. Forgive our caution, my lord.'

He held his hand out to Edgar, who grasped it. The second man let go of his seax, but he still looked nervously around him, licking his lips. The tension in the air had not completely gone.

Edgar quickly made an appraisal of the second man. He was squat and powerfully built, with bulging shoulder muscles. His hands were scarred. He wore a leather apron covered in small burnt holes. A blacksmith, then.

'May my men approach?' asked Edgar.

Osric nodded his acquiescence and Edgar signalled for the seven housecarls to approach. They dismounted and walked forward and stood behind Edgar.

'What's this then?' asked the headman, looking at Alaric, bound at the wrist and now with a rope round his neck, the other end of which was in Eric's hands.

'This is a Norman scout. We captured him last night spying on our camp. He is with the raiding party we are hunting. He is helping us.'

The headman walked up to Alaric and squinted at him, looking over his features. The headman towered over Alaric, who stood, calm and unbowed in the face of the big man. The headman snorted and turned away, showing no more interest in the spy.

'How can we be of help to you, my lord?' he said bluntly. 'We have no spare food to give you unless you intend to take it from us.'

'We have no such intention. I said we meant no harm to you. I did not lie.'

The headman grunted. 'Then how can we, pitiful as we are, help you?'

'The trail left by the Normans leads into this village, but there seem to be two sets of trails leaving it, at the fork in the road back there. Did the party split?'

'Aye, they did as it happens,' said the headman rubbing at the grey stubble on his chin. 'They came racing up the road, then the leader wheeled round and shouted some commands in his heathen tongue, I don't know what he said, but half the party set off on the Snotingeham road and the rest headed north towards Hochenale.'

'They had captives with them, possibly in a covered waggon. Which way did they go?'

'No waggons with them, sir. As I said, they appeared to be in a hurry.'

Edgar turned and looked at his carls.

'There was no sign of waggons turning off before we got here,' said Halfdene, and Sebbi nodded his agreement.

'How could we have passed them?' demanded Edgar.

'We didn't,' replied Guthrum.

'Then where are they?'

Guthrum could only look back blankly at Edgar.

'I'm sorry we can't help you, sir, but I think you'd better go elsewhere in your search.'

Edgar turned back towards his men. Guthrum blinked slowly.

'Let's carry on, we'll decide which tracks to follow.'

'Should we not split, my lord?' asked Sebbi.

Edgar did not answer directly. 'Back to the horses,' he ordered.

The men walked back to the horses; Alaric being shoved unceremoniously onto his. As he walked back, Guthrum stared intently at the ground.

They mounted and turned their backs on the village and headed back along the road the way they had come. Once back at the fork in the road, Guthrum turned in his saddle and spoke to Edgar.

'They're hiding something.'

Edgar nodded. 'The headman was unfriendly, he wanted us to leave just a little too much. The other man was very nervous. He kept looking towards the houses. What's going on do you think?'

'The ground in the village was badly churned up, just

like here,' he indicated the road under them, 'it didn't look right. It looked... deliberate.'

Edgar agreed. 'We mustn't let them know that we suspect anything. Halfdene,' he said, still looking at the mud beneath his horse's hooves, 'are we being watched?'

Halfdene lifted his head slightly as if speaking to Guthrum. He dropped his head immediately and pointed at a piece of the road near Edgar's horse's front hooves. 'Yes,' he said. 'It's the second man, the blacksmith. He's hiding behind a tree at the edge of the village, but he's not very good at hiding.'

'Very well. We must be seen to make a decision, let's take the route that won't take us back through the village.'

He spurred his horse and the eight men and their prisoner set off on the road that the village headman had said led to Snotingeham.

A mile down the road, Edgar called a halt and they all stopped.

'We'll wait here for nightfall. Set a camp in the woods over there. No fires tonight.'

9

Attempted Rescue

Edgar and Guthrum lay flat on their stomachs, peering into the dwindling light of the late evening. The buildings of Windeham were getting hard to distinguish in the gloom, but they could still see some movement as a few people walked home from the fields to their shabby little cottages. They were working late, Edgar thought, a sign of the poor harvest, and possibly of crop ruination by Norman raiders. What were these Normans thinking? Did they hope to starve the kingdom into submission? There were surely much simpler and more productive ways to rule. Not for the first time, Edgar realised that this was an indication of the Norman way of thinking. They did things differently. There was no obligation to protect their dependents as there was in English society.

The last farmer had now gone home and the village fell quiet. An occasional raised voice could be heard from within the cottages, but no more. It was now quite dark, though with his improving night vision, Edgar could still make out the cottages, especially where flickers of candlelight seeped around ill-fitting wooden doors.

Edgar and Guthrum had left the remainder of their party behind in the woods, ensuring that Alaric the scout had been well gagged to prevent him from shouting any warning, though the little man seemed strangely content to sit in silence.

The two men remained still and silent, patiently watching the village from across a narrow field. They lay in an unruly hedgerow, brambles prickling through their clothing. As they watched, the door of the moot house opened, allowing dim candlelight to silhouette the figures of two men leaving the building. Edgar tensed as he watched the two men. There was no doubt, they were wearing helmets. Soldiers.

Edgar gently squeezed Guthrum's wrist. 'I see them,' whispered Guthrum.

'Get the others. I'll keep watching,' said Edgar in a low voice.

As Guthrum crept away, making very little noise, Edgar screwed his eyes up and tried to keep track of the two men, who had separated and were walking away from each other. One went out of sight behind the moot house whilst the other walked slowly down the village street. Faintly, Edgar could hear a metallic clinking noise. So, the soldiers were in mail, then. They would be fully armed. The presence of two Norman sentries could only mean one thing. The rest of the raiding party was here, hiding for some reason, within the moot house, and possibly also amongst the villagers' cottages. Edgar found himself clinging onto the hope that the hostages were also here, including Godgifu. He badly wanted to see her. He had to know that she was safe and had come to no harm at the hands of these barbarous animals.

He was roused from his reverie by a gentle touch on his arm. Guthrum had returned, and the others were with him, squatting low behind the hedgerow.

'We must all get closer, then send in Eric and Osfrid. That man is as silent as any I've ever met, fast, too.'

Guthrum patted Edgar's shoulder in acknowledgement of the order and slipped back to the others.

Keeping low to the ground to prevent their figures being visible against the sky, which was still slightly lighter than the surrounding trees, the eight men crept through the hedgerow and into the narrow field separating them from the village. Spreading out along the hedge, they slowly moved forwards, each man holding tightly onto his mail shirt, preventing it from making any giveaway sounds.

They reached the top of the field and began closing in on the village. A small croft now lay between them and the village street. Edgar clicked his tongue quietly and the men came to a stop. Straining against the dark, Edgar searched the shadows for any sign of the two men. The first he had not seen since he disappeared behind the moot house and the second had dropped out of sight as they turned the corner of the field and started to approach the village. Now the croft provided low fences, made of wicker, behind which the men crouched.

From the black rectangle of a cottage wall, a smaller shadow separated itself. Eric, squatting right beside Edgar, tapped him on the arm to indicate that he too had seen the soldier. He tapped again and pointed to Edgar's left, where the second soldier was just visible as a slowly moving shadow along the village street. Edgar placed his hand on Eric's shoulder and gave the slightest indication of a push. Go.

Eric crouched low and headed remarkably quickly towards the first soldier, whilst Osfrid sped silently towards the soldier on the road. Eric approached his quarry without making a single sound. His hand went to his seax and he withdrew it in one swift motion from its sheath.

The soldier turned towards Eric, who stopped instantly and remained motionless. Against the darkness he was quite invisible, and the soldier turned once again towards the moot house. Being at the side of one of the cottages, he could not be seen by his colleague further down the lane. Eric knew he had to strike quickly or his man would become visible. He sped up and when just a couple of feet from the soldier, he leaped, grabbing the man's throat in the crook of his arm and squeezing as tightly as he could. A surprised gurgle issued from the man's mouth, not loud enough to alert the other soldier. Eric felt his victim shift his weight, putting it all on his right leg as he freed his left leg for a backwards kick. Eric quickly brought up his right hand, holding the seax, and drove it hard into the struggling man's throat. He made another gurgle, began struggling wildly, but Eric held tight, his hand now pressed firmly against the soldier's mouth. Very quickly all strength left the man, and Eric felt him falling towards the ground. Still, he held on firmly to the man's mouth and prevented him from falling. After a minute, once he was sure that the man was dead, Eric lowered him carefully to the ground. From the field across the road, he heard a pig grunting contentedly.

Meanwhile, Osfrid ran silently towards his quarry. The guard was strolling nonchalantly back up the street. Osfrid held up his seax and brought the heavy pommel down precisely where the man's helmet stopped and his neck was unprotected. The man gave a short grunt and began to fall. Osfrid deftly caught hold of him, and before he had any chance to regain consciousness, drove the blade of his seax hard up just behind the helmet's chinstrap. The blade pierced to the centre of the man's head, and Osfrid quickly dragged the body to the side of the street where he deposited it in the roadside ditch.

Eric gave a low whistle, like the distant call of a brown owl, and Edgar and his companions ran carefully and quietly across the field to join him.

They could hear the sound of voices coming from the moot hall. 'I guess the rest of them are in there,' said Edgar. 'Round the back.'

They separated into two groups and cautiously made their way round the sides of the moot hall to the back. A large midden heap, reeking, filled much of the land behind the hall. Outbuildings surrounded the plot; a kitchen, a brew-house and a smithy. The brew-house and smithy were dark and silent, but from within the kitchen, they could hear voices and see light around the door.

Edgar sized up the situation. 'All of you, round here now,' he hissed.

They moved round beside him, to the side of the smithy hidden from the kitchen. Just as they got to him, the kitchen door opened and a large woman backed out of the door into the night. In her hands was a large platter containing hot food. She turned and walked past the midden and into the moot hall by a small back door. A few moments later, she emerged and returned to the kitchen, wiping her hands on her apron.

'Come on,' said Edgar.

They silently drew swords and axes and crept towards the small door. Edgar carefully opened the door slightly and pressed his eye to the crack. A hanging blocked the view, it would have to be drawn back before they could get in. He slipped quietly through and slowly pulled back the hanging. He saw eight, no, nine men seated at a long table with their backs to him. Standing beside the table were the headman and the blacksmith with whom he had spoken earlier. The seated men were eating from the pile of steaming vegetables that had just been brought in. A large fire burned in the centre of the room, filling the upper part of the building with woodsmoke. The men seemed to be at their ease. Stripped of their mail, they were dressed only in leggings and jerkins. Their weapons, however, remained on their belts.

Edgar backed out and reported back to his men.

'Surprise, quick and strong,' said Sebbi, to whispered agreement.

'Remember, we need to interrogate them, so leave some alive,' warned Edgar. They nodded solemnly.

'Right.' Edgar led his band through the small door, and they silently gathered behind the hanging. Immediately, Edgar walked out from behind the hanging and thrust his sword point into the neck of the man closest to him. The sword pushed in hard enough to draw blood, but not to do any damage. The man immediately twisted, swiping his arm behind him to knock the sword away. He was not expecting the razor-sharp edge of the Ulfberht sword, however, and the blade sank into the muscle of his forearm. He cursed and pulled his bleeding arm back. By this time the others had entered the hall and were covering all the other men at the table.

'Remain seated, all of you!' commanded Edgar.

One of the Normans, the leader, Edgar presumed, snapped out an order in French, and the men, in the process of standing, sat down again.

'Remove your belts and let your weapons drop to the floor.'

Again, the leader spoke a few words.

Belts undone, the swords fell to the floor, and the Englishmen kicked them out of reach.

'You!' Edgar called to the headman and the blacksmith. 'In front of the table, now! Lie face down with your hands behind your necks. Do it!'

The two men, ashen with shock, hurried to obey.

Edgar swept his eyes across the faces of the Normans at the table. The heavy, jowly face of Roger de Barentin was not amongst them

Edgar addressed all the assembled men. 'Where is Roger de Barentin?'

The demand was met with stony silence.

'Again, where is Roger de Barentin?' demanded Edgar.

The one Edgar had marked as their leader, now covered by Enni's sword, cleared his throat.

'Yes?' demanded Edgar.

In halting English, the man spoke. 'Roger de Barentin. He is… not here.'

A cold chill ran through Edgar. Maybe the other Normans were somewhere else in the village, maybe even now closing in on the moot hall.

'Who are you, and where is de Barentin?' he asked.

'I am Guillaum de Caen, er… esquire to Roger de Barentin. He is, er… gone nord,' he indicated north with a wave of his hand.

'Why are you here?'

'This land is now the… property of Roger de Barentin. The… previous lord could not pay the tax imposed by our lord the King. Roger has paid it and is now lord. It is the law.'

Edgar's teeth were grinding together. He recalled the tax demand received by his grandfather, over four times the rate paid for the previous ten years. This was the method by which the Bastard was placing a thin veneer of legality on his massive land grab.

The Norman muttered a few words in French under his breath. Enni, standing behind him, pressed his sword a little harder into the man's neck. The man leaned a little forward, as if to relieve the pressure, but suddenly ducked low, and scooping a knife from where it had lain hidden beside a bowl on the table, he leaped to his feet and brought the knife down with lightning speed into Enni's face. Enni collapsed, the knife embedded up to its handle in his left eye. The Norman grabbed Enni's sword as it fell from his grasp, and as he did so, all the other Normans jumped up and round.

The Englishmen's reactions were no slower, Edgar thrust his sword forward as his man moved, and a great gout of blood spurted from the jugular vein, just below his ear. Turning, Edgar faced the next man, covered by Halfdene. Halfdene had taken a small step backwards to give him better clearance. The man had drawn a short sword from somewhere, presumably on a different belt from his main sword. It was flashing up towards Halfdene and struck him in the midriff. Halfdene went down with a grunt and Edgar thrust his sword into the Norman's unprotected side. The

Norman screamed and fell.

Meanwhile, the leader of the Normans was thrashing wildly at Sebbi with his knife in one hand and Enni's sword, in the other. Sebbi held up his arm and sword to deflect the blows, but several made clear contact with his arm. Osfrid, having just dispatched his man, swiftly turned, and smashed the flat of his sword into the Norman leader's head. The side of his face crumpled as the cheekbone smashed, and the man went down.

Sebbi, recovering fast, switched his sword to his left hand and slashed at the Norman who was laying into Guthrum with a broken chair leg. Guthrum's helmet had been knocked off. The Norman staggered under Sebbi's assault, and Guthrum strode forward and brought his sword down on the man's head. It glanced off and embedded itself in his shoulder. The man screamed and staggered again but astonishingly did not go down. Sebbi stepped in again and thrust his sword into the man's back.

The man Eric was marking had leaped over the table and grabbed a sword from where it had been kicked, he had pulled it from the scabbard and was now attacking Eric with considerable ferocity and skill. Eric was backing slowly away. Hunwald, having killed two, picked up a stool and flung it at the man, hitting him hard on the shoulder. Eric dived forward, slashing at the man's sword arm. Everyone in the hall heard the arm break. The sword fell from his hand, and the man backed off, gasping and holding his arm close to him. Eric advanced, but the man knelt and held his unbroken arm up in token of surrender. Eric kicked him hard in the midriff, and he rolled over, groaning.

Edgar slid his sword back into its scabbard and looked round. Seven dead Normans, two still alive.

'Pick up the breathers, and tie them securely to the posts.' He ordered.

He walked swiftly over to where Sebbi knelt next to Enni. As Edgar approached, Sebbi looked up and shook his head.

Edgar helped him pick Enni up and place him on the table where so recently the Normans had been feasting. He carefully withdrew the knife from Enni's eye, and it came out with a gout of blood that stopped flowing immediately.

'Halfdene!' called Edgar, 'Tie up our two hosts.' The headman and the blacksmith lay in a state of terror where Edgar had ordered them to lie not five minutes before.

Halfdene tied the two men to an upright post, their hands behind their backs and the rope tightly round their necks.

'My lord…' choked the headman.

'Shut it,' growled Halfdene.

The back door of the hall flew open, knocking the hanging aside, and an elderly man and the woman they had seen earlier fell into the room. Seeing the carnage, the woman threw her hands to her mouth and gasped. The old man stood very still.

'Get in, shut the door,' commanded Hunwald, who stood nearest to them. They obeyed silently.

'Are there any more out there?' demanded Hunwald. The old man shook his head. The two newcomers stood to one side of the hall, their eyes darting around as they tried to work out just what had happened here. Seven dead Normans were strewn across the hall, and a dead Englishman lay on the table. The headman and his deputy, the blacksmith, were tied to a post and nearly choking, and two seriously wounded Normans were tied to another, albeit in a sitting position.

Edgar picked up a pitcher of water, which had miraculously remained untoppled on the table. He threw the contents across the face of the Norman leader. He then kicked his feet.

'Wake up you Norman filth!'

The leader stirred. His face was a mass of seeping blood and was beginning to swell. He looked up groggily at Edgar.

'Can you hear me?' asked Edgar.

The man nodded.

'Do you understand me?'

Again, a slight nod.

'I am Thegn Edgar of Rapendun. During your criminal raid on that town, you killed the previous thegn, Wulfmaer, my grandfather. You will die soon for that act. The method of your death depends very much on how you answer me now. Do you understand?'

A haunted look passed across the man's face. He nodded again.

'Whilst in Rapendun, you took a prisoner, a woman by the name of Godgifu. Do you remember doing that?'

He coughed and spat a bloodied tooth to the floor. 'I did not know her name.' His voice was thick and unclear, and it obviously pained him a great deal to speak.

'But you took her?'

'Yes.'

'Where is she now?'

'She will have travelled nord with Baron de Barentin. He likes to have women with him.'

Edgar closed his mind to the implications.

'Where are they going?'

'As I said, nord. The Baron is part of the King's tax-gathering operation. He is headed for Eoforwic.'

'Killing and plundering as he goes?'

De Caen shrugged. 'Of course.'

'Why did you remain here?'

'We were due to return to Londres. De Barentin is meeting up with other tax-gathering parties tomorrow at a place called Mammesfeld. They are waiting for him there.'

Edgar looked over at Guthrum. 'Mammesfeld,' he said, 'how far is that?'

'Maybe twelve, fifteen miles,' replied Guthrum, 'We can't make it there tonight.'

Edgar nodded. He walked away from de Caen.

'Eric, Guthrum.' The two men hurried over to him. 'At first light take those two criminals out and hang them.'

'Yes, my lord.'

Edgar turned to the headman and the blacksmith, both sweating heavily.

'You seemed to be getting on well with our Norman raiders,' he said softly.

'My lord,' began the headman, swallowing noisily. 'They have our women captive. They are locked in the smithy. We had no choice; I beg you to believe me.'

Edgar stared at him, expressionlessly.

'My lord,' the old man from the kitchen stood forward. 'Begging your pardon my lord, but he speaks the truth. My daughter was the only one they let free, as she is the cook for the moot hall.'

'Eric, Guthrum, Halfdene. Go out to the smithy and see what's there. Be wary.'

The three carls walked out of the hall, Halfdene taking a torch from a sconce on an upright post as he passed. They crossed the yard to the smithy. It remained dark and silent.

Halfdene held the torch so that the light fell on the door. Guthrum hammered his fist on the door, the old fittings creaking as he did so.

'Is anyone in there?' he called.

There was a scrabbling from within, faint, but distinct.

'Who's there? You've nothing to fear from me.'

'Help us!' a frightened voice squealed and was quickly hushed.

'Stand back from the door, I'm coming in,' called Guthrum.

The men examined the lock. A short iron bar slid into a slot in the wooden doorpost. It was held in place by a simple wedge and pin. He pulled the wedge out and slid the bolt back. Halfdene followed him in with the torch.

The inside was fusty with the smell of unwashed bodies and urine. The roof of the smithy was held up by two stout poles along the central axis of the building. Tied to these were perhaps a dozen women of all ages, dishevelled and frightened. They backed away from the light held by Halfdene. Guthrum immediately took off his helmet and crouched down beside the middle-aged woman nearest to him.

'Have no fear, I'm going to release you.'

He pulled his seax from his belt, and the woman drew back as far as she could.

'I need it to cut the ropes,' he said, gently, holding the knife on the flat of his hand. 'See, I'm not going to hurt you, any of you.'

He began to saw at the woman's bonds, and soon she was free, standing up and rubbing her wrists where the ropes had chafed. Still she did not speak.

'How long have you been in here?' asked Guthrum.

'Two days,' she said finally. 'Where are the strangers? Have they gone?'

Guthrum continued cutting ropes from the other women as he replied. 'The strangers who put you in here are dead, or soon will be. Their bodies lie still in your moot hall, though we will clear them out before you eat there again.'

'What of Osric?' asked the woman.

'The headman?' asked Guthrum.

'My husband, yes.'

'Ah, he's being held by my lord, Edgar, in the moot hall. He seems to have been consorting with the enemy.'

'No! Not Osric! We were hostages, he was only trying to save us.'

'That remains to be seen.' Guthrum stood up. 'Have you had any food in the past two days?'

'No,' she said, 'Only water, and none too much of that.'

'Right,' said Guthrum. He addressed all the women. 'Pay attention to me. All of you. The men who tied you up in here are dead. Your headman and the blacksmith still have some questions to answer, but for now you should all return to your homes. Have no fear, you are free.'

'Please, I need to see my husband,' said the middle-aged woman to Guthrum.

'Not now. If all is well, we'll send him back to you in due course.'

She opened her mouth to answer back, but thought better of it, nodded, and led the women out of the smithy and back into the village.

The three carls walked back to the moot hall. The headman and the blacksmith were still tied to the post, but their neck ties had been loosened slightly.

'Well?' demanded Edgar.

'He told the truth. There were a dozen women tied up in there. One of them says she is his wife,' he nodded towards the headman. 'She says they've been there for two days with no food.'

'It is true, my lord. I beg that I may see my wife.'

'Your wife is well. She's a strong woman,' said Guthrum.

The headman relaxed visibly. 'Aye, she is that.'

'Why were the Normans here?' asked Edgar.

'I don't know, my lord. That one,' he nodded his head slightly towards the Norman leader, still tied to the next upright. 'He said that his master was joining forces with more Normans in Mammesfeld. They are extorting tax from thegns and headmen who can't pay and grabbing land in payment. He said that his little band was returning to meet with some others. I don't know why.'

'Where are their horses?'

'In the stable, my lord, out of the front door and a couple of hundred yards to your right.'

Edgar walked away from the man, rubbing the coarse stubble on his chin where three days of unshorn beard was making its presence felt.

He spoke to Hunwald. 'Alright, cut them down.'

Hunwald drew his seax and cut the two men free of their ropes.

'Thank you, my lord,' said the headman. The blacksmith just muttered and rubbed his neck where the rope had bitten in.

'Hunwald, Eric; go to the stables. Check the Normans' horses and tack, we may need to change horses here. See if they were carrying anything, check the tack very carefully.'

Hunwald and Eric hurried out.

'The rest of you, get these bodies outside. Search them and strip them.'

The remaining carls hurried to obey Edgar's command and soon the bodies had been cleared from the moot hall. Only the two surviving Normans remained, tied to their post. The leader had lapsed into unconsciousness whilst the second one had never woken up.

The following morning Eric and Guthrum tied ropes to a large tree growing in a field beside the village. Two stout branches had been selected. Guillaum de Caen and his comrade were made to stand on a handcart piled high with hay bales. Rough hoods were thrown over their heads. Guthrum quickly pulled the nooses over their heads and tightened them, then he jumped down off the handcart and stood beside it waiting for Edgar's order. After a few moments' reflection, Edgar nodded to Guthrum and Eric, who pushed the handcart away. The Normans fell from the cart, being pulled up about four feet from the ground. They twitched and struggled, legs kicking out uselessly. Edgar walked up to them.

'That's enough,' he said to Guthrum, 'We needn't prolong this any more than necessary.'

He grabbed hold of one of the Norman leader's legs, just above the knee. Guthrum caught hold of the other knee. Together, they lifted themselves off the ground, and a noise somewhere between a pop and a crack was heard from the man's neck. He stopped twitching immediately. Edgar and Guthrum moved on to the other man and performed the same merciful service for him.

Guthrum walked back to the dead leader and looked

carefully at him.

'What is it Guthrum?' asked Edgar.

'I'm not sure, something about…' he reached up and felt the man's midriff. He felt a sturdy belt around his waist. Hurriedly, Guthrum reached up and unbuckled the belt.

'Horse turds! This belt is heavy!' He pulled out his seax and began unpicking the coarse stitching on the back of the belt. The first dozen threads unpicked, he poked his finger inside and pulled out the end of a tube of thin material. It was packed with silver pennies.

'Meeting with another party? Taking the first fruits of the raiding parties' efforts.'

Guthrum tugged at the tube of material and it came free from the leather belt.

'There must be two pounds of silver here,' marvelled Guthrum.

Edgar looked at it. 'Well, it's ours now. Keep hold of it, Guthrum, we may well have need of it before we're done.'

'You are merciful my lord,' said the headman as Edgar returned.

'I am not merciful. Those men were guilty of murder and pillage. They deserved to die, but I will not tolerate unnecessary suffering, not even for these animals.'

He turned and started walking back to the village. 'Come, we ride for Mammesfeld,' he called behind him. Osric ran and caught up with him. Edgar gave him a sidelong glance.

'You will see to it that our comrade is given a decent burial befitting his status. His name was Enni, housecarl of Deorby.'

'Yes, my lord.'

'We will be back here some day, and we will wish to visit his grave. May the good Christ help you if you have not done all that is fitting.'

'It will be done, my lord.'

Edgar strode up to his horse and made a show of tightening some of the harness straps. The other warriors did the same and began mounting.

'My lord,' began the headman.

Edgar paused.

'What shall we do with the other bodies?'

Edgar looked around the village to the fields beyond, where the pigs and cattle contentedly stood, eating.

'Feed them to your pigs,' he replied.

10

Chase

The trail of the remaining Norman raiders was soon lost in the deeply churned surface of the road to Mammesfeld. The road was too much used even for trackers like Halfdene and Sebbi.

Their prisoner, Alaric the spy, remained tied to his saddle. When he had been informed that his master had been hanged, he merely shrugged. His attitude puzzled and concerned Edgar. The man seemed to have no connection with his colleagues at all. He clearly was not distressed in any way by the death of his former master, nor by the manner of it. The man remained unnaturally calm and unperturbed by his circumstances. Edgar began to suspect that there was more to the man Alaric than met the eye, possibly far more. He made a mental note to speak more closely with him at the first opportunity.

The road north continued to be rough and muddy. There was no chance that a trail could have been followed, even if that had been needed.

Towards the middle of their second day riding north, they approached a wide tract of forest. Guthrum grunted. 'The Great Forest,' he said. 'I've heard of it but never seen it before. Last time we came north, before the battle, we travelled too far east to see it. It covers a wide expanse of land right through the middle of England here, and somewhere in there is the border between Mercia and Northumbria.'

The forest spread out before them, a blanket of green overlying the land. In places it was thinly spread, and in others it was very dense. The road led down the side of a gentle valley, sparsely dotted with thin, white-barked birch trees. The day was bright and clear, and the sun shone from out of a deep blue sky.

As they travelled on, the road led them into deeper sections of the woodland, intermittently relieved by open fields and glades, often with one or two farmsteads. The trees soon became more mixed, with areas of oak and beech along with the frequent stands of birch. Low, scrubby alders squatted around reedy ponds in which hunchbacked, stick-like herons strutted, eyes ever watchful for the flash of fishy scales beneath the surface, their long beaks poised like daggers.

Darkness fell faster here in the denser regions of the woodland, and shortly after sunset, Edgar called a halt and commanded his men to set camp for the night. They stopped at a small glade, opening up to their left. A ditch separated the glade from the road and they led their horses cautiously over it. Hunwald and Osfrid collected branches from the forest floor, initially for tent posts and then to build a fire. Eric and Guthrum headed off with hunting bows and returned half an hour later with six hares and five grouse.

'Water's getting down,' said Halfdene, as he inspected the men's canteens. 'I can hear a stream; I'll go and refill all our skins.'

He walked off towards the north, where Edgar could also hear the sound of a stream, as if it was pouring over a small waterfall.

Hunwald and Osfrid had erected the tents with little fuss, and Guthrum had set about constructing the fire. He started small with a loose collection of dried grass, over which he used his flint and striker to send sparks into the grasses. Smoke began to spiral from the small bundle, which he still held in his hands, blowing gently on it until finally, a flame flickered forth. He put the burning grass down beneath a fist-sized pyramid of thin, dry twigs, and soon they too were alight. He added slightly larger twigs and so on until there was a fire of small logs burning away. Carefully, he placed some large stones at the edge of the fire, then built a containing circle of stones around it all.

Halfdene had half-filled the iron cooking pot with water from the stream. Once the stones in the fire were hot enough, Eric wrapped a thick piece of leather around his hand and fished them out, tossing them into the water in the pot, then placed the pot onto the fire. The water was soon boiling and Eric skinned and gutted the hares, cut them into good-sized pieces and threw them into the pot.

After eating, the seven men sat in silence on the ground around the fire in the deepening darkness.

Edgar cleared his throat. He had been thinking as he had ridden that day and had realised that Enni's death had not been mentioned by any of the men, though surely it was necessary to do so.

'I didn't know Enni very well,' he started. 'I only met him a few days ago. What I did know, though, was that he made no demur at all at being volunteered to travel with me on this journey we are all undertaking. He followed willingly. I noted his skill in healing and the casual ease with which he assessed wounds and their potential for future problems. I am sorry that I did not get to know him better, but would like to hear more of him now, if any of you would care to speak.' He looked questioningly at Hunwald, Sebbi and Osfrid.

Hunwald spoke up, the firelight gleaming on his bald pate and his heroic moustaches swaying as he spoke.

'Enni and I grew up in the same village. He was a quiet child, studious and quick to learn. He took to healing from a very young age and learned all he could of the craft from those skilled in it in our village. Some years ago, he married Aedyth, a farmer's daughter, again from our village. She was a year older than him. Plain to the eye of a young stud, maybe, but kind of heart and clever, very clever. A year and a half later, Aedyth died in childbirth, as did the child, Enni's son. He was deeply distressed by the loss, of course, but I think that by now he had come to accept it, if not gladly, and not without the occasional pangs of bitter regret. His life continued, however. He was always willing to help anyone in any kind of trouble. I truly believe, Lord Edgar, that if he had not been volunteered for this task but had heard of your plight anyway, he would still have come, of his own volition, Lord Godric permitting.'

Here Osfrid and Sebbi both nodded and muttered in agreement.

'I will miss Enni, he was a lifelong friend. But he will

always remain alive to me,' he placed his fist above his heart, 'here, where all the loved ones who have been taken from us shall always live.'

They sat in silence; each man lost in his own thoughts as they stared into the flames. A burned-through branch broke under the weight of the cooking pot and sent a bright constellation of red sparks streaking up towards heaven.

After a few moments of quiet reflection, Edgar leaned over to the cooking pot. There was still some food left in the bottom, so he spooned it out onto his wooden bowl. Walking carefully, he went over to where Alaric sat, his hands tied round the trunk of a young tree. Edgar crouched down beside him.

'I am sorry for the loss of your friend,' said Alaric.

'Yes? Why? It was your people who killed him.'

'It was de Caen's men who killed him, de Barentin's men, King William's men.'

'Are they not your men, Norman? Are you not de Caen's man, de Barentin's man, the Bastard's man?'

'De Caen was my paymaster. Now, it would seem, he is not. I don't owe him anything.'

The scout shrugged easily, as if to indicate that he cared nothing for his former employer.

Edgar held the bowl up. 'I have brought you food.'

'That is kind.'

He used the spoon to feed Alaric, who ate hungrily. This was the first proper meal he had had for nearly three days. Once he had finished, Edgar brought him water in a wooden beaker, which he drank down in one.

'Thank you, my lord,' he said in a satisfied voice.

'Your lack of interest in your countrymen concerns me, Alaric,' said Edgar, sitting down beside the trussed-up spy.

'Why is that, my lord?' he asked.

'If any man of mine were to speak of me the way you speak of de Caen, he would not be a companion of mine any longer. Without loyalty there is nothing.'

'Maybe you inspire greater loyalty than my former employer did, my lord.'

'You owe him your loyalty.'

'No. No, I do not. De Caen was a stupid, violent man. De Barentin is worse, not only is he vicious, but he enjoys it. He will never choose the easy way out for an opponent, even if that opponent is helpless. As for William himself, he is… well, he's a bastard.'

Edgar was taken aback. 'These are your superiors, your masters, how can you speak of them in such a way?'

Alaric just shrugged his careless shrug again. 'I simply speak the truth, my lord. You have seen the results of these people's raids yourself. Did you see any justice, any fairness in the way they dealt with their opponents? Have you not seen the rotting corpses of unarmed men and women in your pursuit of them? Was your own grandfather not slain totally unnecessarily? I speak from the heart, my lord. Men such as these do not earn much loyalty, nor do they deserve it. For a short while, de Caen paid my wage. Now he does not. That is all there is to it.'

'Do you not support the Bastard's claim to the English throne? Do you not believe that he is right to pursue that claim, which he says is legal, to the very limit of his ability?'

'The rights of kings are far above my simple thoughts, my lord. Whether William is acting lawfully and thus in accordance with God's wishes, I cannot say, nor is it my place to say. All I can report is what I see with my own eyes. The actions of William and his henchmen, such as de

Barentin, are, from what I have seen first-hand, unnecessarily brutal. The innocent are being slain. It seems to me that if William follows his present course of action, he will win the kingdom, but there will be no one left within it to rule. That does not strike me as the approach of an intelligent, enlightened ruler. He seeks to replace the entire aristocracy of England with his own murderous bunch of followers. An intelligent ruler would surely simply have persuaded your Witan that having defeated King Harold, he was the natural leader of the country, left the present aristocracy in place and then dealt harshly with the rebellions that would inevitably follow, but would in time die out. Is that not so? However, that is not William's way. Nor is it the way of his followers. This does not look, to a simple man such as myself, like the lawful expression of one man's right to the throne, but more like a simple land seizure of huge proportions. Your country is being raped and pillaged. I cannot give loyalty, real loyalty as opposed to paid-for loyalty, to a man who behaves so.'

Edgar stared at the scout. He was astonished to hear such an eloquent outpouring of anger, calmly argued as it had been, from the Norman. He sounded like he wasn't even truly a Norman. No countryman of William's would have spoken thus about him. Edgar began to wonder.

'Your attitude seems very odd for a Norman,' he observed.

Alaric simply shrugged his shoulders.

'Maybe you're not a Norman? What are you, Alaric?'

'I am what I am. A spy, a scout, a man for hire. That is all.'

'How did you come to be with the invaders?'

'They needed spies and scouts. They seemed to think

that I could fulfil that role for them. Obviously, I couldn't, or I wouldn't be tied up here.'

'Why would they think that you would make a good spy?'

Alaric smiled and snorted softly. 'I did not say that they thought I would be a *good* spy, merely that they thought I could fulfil the role of a spy.'

'What does that mean?'

'William pressed hundreds of men into spying for him. He doesn't really care how good they are. If they are captured or killed, it doesn't matter. He has so many spies that some are bound to succeed and give him information that he might not have had in any other way.'

'Why you?'

Alaric shrugged again. 'I was in the wrong place at the wrong time. I was pressed along with all the others.'

'Very well,' said Edgar, picking up the bowl and cup and standing up. He returned to the camp-fire, deep in thought. He was sure that Alaric was not actually lying, but he was also sure that the vague, evasive answers were hiding a deeper truth. A truth that Edgar was determined to discover. Their lives might depend on a clear understanding of this strange, ambiguous little man.

Guthrum reported when he got back, 'Halfdene and Osfrid have taken first guard duty, Hunwald and I will take second shift. We're turning in for the night now.'

Edgar muttered his consent and crawled into his tent, still much puzzled by Alaric's outburst and subsequent evasiveness.

Edgar woke the following morning, Guthrum gently shaking him.

'Morning, Edgar,' he said cheerfully.

'Good morning, Guthrum,' replied Edgar, rubbing the sleep from his eyes. 'How went the night?'

'Very quiet. No traffic along the road and there doesn't seem to be any inhabitation in this part of the woods. I snatched another hare to add to our larder.'

'Good. Are we ready to pack up?'

'Yes, as soon as we've eaten. Here,' he handed Edgar his wooden bowl with a pile of dried black berries in it. 'Eric had the foresight to bring some bags of dried fruit with him from Rapendun.' He playfully patted Edgar on the feet and backed out of the tent. Edgar sat and munched the berries. They were certainly very good, and he ate every last one before sliding out from under the leather tent.

The morning was bright and clear, and although the sun was not yet above the horizon, the sky was a rich blue and to the east, the imminent arrival of the sun was heralded by a clear brilliance.

Edgar looked around him at his men. Under Guthrum's supervision Sebbi, Hunwald and Osfrid were taking down the tents and stowing them for the onward journey.

As Edgar took a step forward, he heard a solid thump on the ground in front of his feet. He looked down to see the shaft of an arrow, still quivering from its impact, sticking out of the ground just in front of his left foot. He looked quickly up, to see that every man in the clearing had also stopped. Before each man was a shaking arrow, each arrow fitted with identical white flights.

Edgar held up his hand in a signal to his men. 'Hold!' he called, 'Nobody move!'

The precision of the archers who could drop seven arrows at exactly the same time in front of seven different men was frightening, and yet it was obvious that whoever had shot the arrows did not intend to kill them, at least not immediately. The message was plain, simple and perfectly clear.

All seven warriors stood still, glancing round to see if they could catch any sight of the archers. There must be at least seven archers to loose seven arrows at seven targets at the same time.

A voice called from somewhere within the woods. 'Drop your weapons. Axes, swords, seaxes, bows. Drop them all, drop them now!'

'Do it,' Edgar added.

The men unbuckled their belts and an array of weaponry fell to the grassy ground.

'Walk towards my voice,' commanded the speaker.

Edgar caught the eye of his men and nodded. There was no point in defying the speaker, nor of resisting in any way. It was obvious that he had it in his power to kill any one – or all – of them.

After thirty paces, the voice called out again, 'That's far enough. Lie down on your faces with your arms stretched out away from your bodies.' They complied.

From the trees all around the glade emerged a collection of strangely garbed men. They were all dressed in ragged tunics of green and brown, and some sported foliage as part of their costume. Some wore helmets that had clearly been darkened by soot from a fire and were now a deep, matte black instead of shining steel. Edgar noticed immediately how they seemed to blend into the background of trees, shrubs and leaves.

One of the green-clad men stepped forward and stood over Edgar's head.

'You appear to be the leader,' he said.

'I am,' replied Edgar, giving nothing away.

'You may consider yourselves prisoners of the Wildmen. What are you doing here?'

'We are travelling north, to Mammesfeld.'

'Mammesfeld? Why there?'

Edgar thought desperately. Who were these men, what was their purpose in taking him and his men prisoner? Were they allied with the Normans? With de Barentin?

'We have an appointment.'

'With whom?'

'With Roger de Barentin.'

Edgar heard the swift withdrawal of a sword from its scabbard, and the cold pricking of a blade on the back of his neck.

'What business do you have with Roger de Barentin?' hissed the voice, seething with hatred and venom.

Got you, thought Edgar.

'I am going to kill him,' he said.

The blade trembled slightly against Edgar's neck.

'Why?'

'He killed my grandfather, the Thegn of Rapendun. He killed many in my town and in other towns and villages between Rapendun and here. He has my wife hostage.'

The pressure from the blade on the back of his neck eased slightly.

'Name?'

'I am Edgar,' he replied.

The blade was withdrawn, and Edgar heard it sliding back into its scabbard.

'Stand, Edgar of Rapendun.'

Edgar slowly and deliberately stood up to face his

captor, holding his arms away from his body.

The man standing before him was broad and of middle height. On his head was a blackened helmet. He wore a drab, brown tunic with similarly coloured leggings and boots. At his side hung a large sword, and in his left hand was a strong-looking longbow. Over his right shoulder was the strap for a quiver of arrows which hung by his left hip. Each arrow was fitted with white feather flights.

'You may be going the wrong way,' said the man. 'Our scouts noted that half of de Barentin's party headed south a couple of days ago.'

'They are dead. De Barentin was not amongst them,' Edgar replied casually.

The man looked at him with renewed respect. 'You killed twelve Normans?'

'Not without loss. One of our men died with them. Did you say twelve? We killed eleven.'

'Maybe you missed one.'

'No, we got them all.'

The man nodded and looked across at his colleagues. 'Let them up,' he said. Slowly, Edgar's men stood up, each looking in wonderment at the motley collection of ruffians who had bested them so easily. Guthrum looked round to see that their weapons had all been collected.

'You must come with us,' said the leader of the ruffians who called themselves the Wildmen.

'Why?' asked Edgar.

'Because we have your weapons, because if you try to escape you will be killed. And…' he paused. 'And because we make common purpose, and your ends may well be best served by coming with us.'

Edgar turned to Guthrum. 'Finish packing up, make

sure we leave no trace. We're going with these men.'

'Yes, my lord,' said Guthrum, emphatically. He pointed at carls individually and then to items that needed stowing or clearing away. Within minutes the campsite was cleared, with only the remains of the campfire visible.

The leader of the Wildmen looked at the blackened, charred patch of earth with distaste.

'There is nothing we can do about this. You must learn not to leave such obvious traces,' he said. Then he turned and began walking back towards the trees.

'Wait!' called Edgar. The leader stopped and turned, a quizzical expression on his face. 'There is one more in our party, over there,' he pointed, 'He's our prisoner.'

'The one you tied to a tree?' asked the man.

'He's our prisoner,' repeated Edgar.

'Not any more, he's not. He made off during the night. Silent little bugger that one.'

Edgar felt a cold sweat prickle his head and neck. If Alaric was gone where would he go? Surely straight back to Roger de Barentin to report on everything that he had learned about the pursuers. Alaric's words of discontent, even contempt for the Normans sounded very fine to English ears, but one thing he had certainly learned about Alaric was that he was above all practically-minded. He may well hate de Barentin, but de Barentin would offer him some form of protection, and probably a stipend as well. Was all to be undone by this morally flexible spy?

'He's a Norman spy. We need to recapture him. He knows we're in pursuit of de Barentin, he knows we killed the other party. He knows where we're from and where we're going.'

The leader shrugged. 'He knows where you *were* going.

Your plans have just changed. Come, our men will pick him up, have no fear. My name is Godwin, by the way.'

Edgar turned to look at their horses.

'Don't worry,' said Godwin, 'my men will bring your horses.'

Edgar turned reluctantly and followed him into the woods.

They wandered for some time along a very slight path, made by deer, Edgar assumed, until they came to a claustrophobic little clearing in which several horses stood patiently eating grass. The leader gave a low, three-toned whistle, and two more green-clad men, whom Edgar had not seen at all, dropped out of the lower branches of two of the trees surrounding the clearing.

'You can mount your horses now,' Godwin said to Edgar. 'We still have some way to go. May I rely on your men not to try to escape? There really is nowhere for them to go, and we are your best hope for the future.'

Edgar turned and gathered his men about him.

'Listen. We are technically prisoners here, we have no weapons, we are seriously outnumbered, and this man, Godwin, has made an interesting proposition. I want to go along with it for now. I must ask that each of you bide your time. I don't think we're going to come to any harm. They certainly aren't Normans. This may turn out to be a lucky break for us. Do I have your word?' He looked at each of them in turn and received assent from each.

'You have our word,' he said to Godwin.

'Very good, wise choice. Come, ride with me at the front.' He climbed up into his saddle, and Edgar climbed into his.

Godwin rode onwards, slowly and carefully picking his

way through the tangle of undergrowth along paths that were barely visible, so narrow were they. They rode in silence, the profound stillness of the forest affecting all of them. Small animals occasionally scurried out of their way, and at one point, Edgar spotted half a dozen roe deer in a clearing dramatically illuminated by a ray of golden sunlight. The deer looked up as the party of horsemen passed, but they were far enough away to feel relatively safe and remained where they were.

The peace and tranquillity of the forest began to seep into Edgar's senses. He started to relax, feeling that here was a safe place. Although he was a prisoner, he did not feel any real danger from his captors, only a shared hostility towards the Normans and perhaps a promise of help. That help, he realised, would be mutual. His captors, or new comrades, whatever they turned out to be, would expect service from him in exchange for whatever it was that they were going to offer. He thought back to the words of Thegn Godric in Deorby, that he, Edgar, was now Thegn of Rapendun and had a duty of care to his people there. In that, he had already failed them, by being absent when the Norman raiders attacked. He had not stayed long enough to discover the extent of the damage, nor how many of his people had been killed or injured. The only thing that had mattered to him, and he admitted, still mattered to him, was the safety of Godgifu.

He looked about him. The woods were heavier here, large, gnarled oak trees so close together that their outer branches met and twisted together far above the riders' heads. There was no sky to be seen, just a huge, over-arching of leaves. Last autumn's fallen leaves lay curled and crisp, crunching beneath the horses' hooves.

Godwin held up one arm and the horsemen came to a stop. Godwin cupped his hands to his mouth and make a cry that to Edgar's ears was astonishingly like that of a grouse.

They sat quietly for a moment; Edgar strained to hear whatever response might come. He could hear the gentle creaking of leather harnesses and saddles, the quiet clink of mail as one of his men twisted his head round to look about him, some soft bird-calls and a slight patter of falling detritus from the trees all around him.

From a stand of holly trees a few tens of yards ahead of them, a bird was making slight cluck-clucking noises as it grubbed for food.

Godwin nodded to himself and signalled the horsemen to proceed. Only then did Edgar realise that the clucking noise had been the response to Godwin's grouse call. The sound had been subtle and so natural sounding that under normal circumstances, Edgar would never have paid any heed to it. Indeed, he might not even have heard it.

Godwin's horse entered a densely-packed hedge of hawthorn, turning right between closely pressed branches. Edgar was astonished to notice that the thorns of the bush had been carefully removed along the virtually invisible path that the horses followed. After twenty or thirty yards of passing through the high, apparently impenetrable bush, round twists and turns, they emerged into an open space maybe fifty yards across and surrounded by the prickly hawthorns. He could see that the clearing was man-made, the bushes having been cleared at ground level, leaving a huge open space in the centre of a truly vast accumulation of hawthorn, blackthorn and elder bushes.

Within the open space, several more horses stood,

Thegn

contentedly grazing and paying little attention to the newcomers. With them were a few more raggedy men, each armed with a longbow and with a single-handed battleaxe hanging from his belt.

'Godwin,' called one of them. 'You have brought us visitors.'

'I have, I must call the council, we need to discuss what we have here.'

'Very well.'

'Dismount,' commanded Godwin.

Edgar and his men climbed down from their horses, which were led away by some of Godwin's men, who had also dismounted. The ragged men who had been in the clearing when they arrived approached cautiously, their hands visibly on their weapons.

Godwin pointed to an area where several felled tree trunks lay, stripped of their branches and with the uppermost surfaces flattened to provide seating.

'Sit over there, and please make no attempt to move. You cannot get out of here. If any one of your men makes any sudden move, you will all be slain, and I do not want that.'

He nodded to one of the men surrounding them, and they all immediately withdrew arrows from their quarrels and nocked them to their bowstrings. They stood in a loose circle around Edgar and his men, far enough away to be completely out of reach and yet easily close enough to plunge an arrow into any one of them within a couple of seconds.

'You heard the man, lads. Let's sit down and enjoy the sunshine.'

Godwin set off at a lope towards the surrounding

bushes and disappeared through what Edgar presumed was another carefully prepared and de-thorned path through the thicket.

Edgar and his six housecarls sat down. The sun was indeed shining. Here in the clearing there were no overhanging branches and the mid-morning sunlight streamed unobstructed onto them. The sky was mostly blue, but some small clouds drifted lazily from west to east. Within the shelter of the hedge, there was very little breeze and the day felt pleasantly warm. Bees droned around the flowers strewn amongst the grass, and swallows darted acrobatically a few inches above the top of the grass, grabbing flying insects as they went.

After a few minutes – Edgar wasn't sure how long, he had surprised himself by beginning to doze in the balmy sunshine – a party of men emerged from the hedge where Godwin had passed through. Their leader was a man of middle height, with a girth that spoke of a well-fed but active life. His face was rounded, almost cherubic, with eyes that glittered above rounded, pink cheeks. Contrary to the fashion amongst most men, he wore a full beard, wide and bushy, streaked with grey. His greying black hair was combed back severely.

He approached Edgar, who stood, as did his men.

'Edgar of Rapendun,' said the man; a statement, not a question.

'I am he. Might I ask who you are, presumably on whose authority we have been taken prisoner?' Edgar stuck his thumbs into his belt and waited for an answer.

'Prisoner? No, no, no. You are our guests. Your weapons have been removed for your own safety. During your journey here to our Paddock, there were several

Thegn

occasions on which you passed through guard points where our sentries would have slain you had you been armed.'

Edgar must have looked surprised.

'You didn't notice them, did you? Nor should you. We are the Wildmen, these woods are ours and only those whom we allow to pass freely do so. Sit, please,' he indicated the tree trunks with his left hand. Behind him, the men who had accompanied him into what he called the Paddock seated themselves facing Edgar and his carls.

'You asked me my name, I shall give it. I am Alfweald, formerly reeve of Warwic.'

'You're a king's reeve?' asked Edgar, astonished.

'I was. The price of retaining my position was beyond my reach, and I was replaced by a Norman. He also replaced me in my home and in my bed.'

Edgar's jaw dropped slightly and he struggled for words.

'Your story is far from unique, Edgar of Rapendun. I understand that a certain Norman noble,' he paused, 'though the word seems strangely misplaced when applied to those most base of men, has made off with your wife. You are not alone. I have over two hundred men here, ranging from thegns to simple farmers. All have tales of murder, rape and dispossession to tell. For most of them, the opportunity to right any wrongs is long gone, and only vengeance remains. For some, there is yet hope that some semblance of normality can be restored. You are lucky in that respect; we may be able to… er… retrieve your wife.'

'I would be very grateful for any help in that regard,' began Edgar.

'Your gratitude would not be sought. Your service and loyalty would.' Beneath Alfweald's cherubic smile, there was a flash of hard flint. This man was no soft-bellied time-server in a cushy king's position. He was a fighter; Edgar could see that clearly.

'What do you propose, Reeve?'

Alfweald raised his voice so all Edgar's men could hear him clearly. 'I am demanding the fealty of your lord, Edgar. That means your loyalty, too. We will guarantee that every attempt will be made to retrieve your lord's wife, though the timing and the method of those attempts will be at the discretion of our council here, and at no other. You will obey my orders and protect the safety and secrecy of this place and the people who live here. I ask nothing of you that your lord would not ask.'

'Three of the housecarls who travel with me are not of my household,' said Edgar. 'Stand up, lads.' The three remaining Deorby housecarls stood as instructed. 'Sebbi, Hunwald and Osfrid are excellent men, but I am not their lord, they are of the household of Godric, Thegn of Deorby. He lent me their services to assist in my search for my wife.'

'Then they too must swear fealty either to you now, or directly to me. I should say that if they choose the latter option, they may be here longer than you. If they swear to you, they shall be released with you from that obligation.'

'Do you swear fealty to me under those terms, lads?' Edgar swung round to face the three standing men.

'Sebbi?'

'I do my lord, saving that I will do nothing against the interests of my lord Godric.'

'Acceptable?' asked Edgar.

Alfweald paused a moment and then nodded. 'Yes. Acceptable.'

'Then I so swear, my lord,' said Sebbi.

Hunwald and Osfrid also assented.

Edgar stood. 'Then before these witnesses, I accept your fealty and declare to all that you are now under my protection,' he turned back to Alfweald, 'Under these same conditions, I hereby swear fealty to Alfweald, former reeve of Warwic, and become his man.'

Alfweald stood and grinned. 'Well done, lad. A wise move.' He turned to face the men behind him. 'These men are now under my protection. Welcome them as brother Wildmen.'

A quiet cheer rose from the assembled Wildmen, who un-nocked their arrows and returned them to their quivers. Alfweald turned to Edgar. 'We do nothing loudly here. Come, you all have much to learn.'

11

Wildmen

September 1067

Over the next few weeks, Edgar and the housecarls were taught the ways of the Wildmen. They were given tunics and leggings of green and brown and their helmets were roughened and coated with a sort of paint made from soot. They learned the arts of travelling silently through woodland paths and of leaving no trace of themselves behind so that even the most skilled tracker would be unable to follow them for more than a few yards through the woodland that they were ever more beginning to think of as their home.

They were taught how to track and trap animals to a level of skill that far surpassed what any of them could do before, and they learned the value of trapping even insignificant small birds and animals when larger game was hard to come by.

Edgar and the carls soon came to realise how large the settlement within the woods was, even though to the

Thegn

untrained eye it was for the most part completely invisible. Men lived in burrows with entrances concealed beneath bushes. The burrows were small but snug, reinforced with solid stone walls and wooden roofs. Chimneys were constructed that cunningly diverted the smoke from cooking and warming fires away from the settlement itself, and even when the dens were brightly lit, no trace of the light could be seen from the outside.

Nor was it only men who inhabited the settlement. Many men had brought their wives and children with them. All were trained in the way of the wild woods, and all could pass unseen and unheard wherever they wished to go.

Deep in the wildwood, this small community was flourishing, though it was not without constant fear of discovery, and of a brutal Norman crushing.

The hub of the entire community was the Paddock. Not only was this the place where the horses were kept, but many people, including Edgar and his men, lived within its protective hedge in tents and light shelters. Here, too, the Wildmen's council sat. The council comprised a leader, Alfweald, and several other men – Godwin included – mostly former thegns dispossessed by the Normans.

Edgar learned that the Wildmen were highly organised into small units, which could harry Norman patrols in and around the whole of the forest.

'It was as well that we diverted you from your journey to Mammesfeld when we did,' said Alfweald to Edgar one afternoon after an intense bout of sword training.

'Oh yes?' replied Edgar, wiping down the blade of his Ulfberht sword.

Alfweald was running a leather rag up and down the blade of his sword, checking the edge for sharpness and rubbing at stains.

'I believe you were aware that de Barentin's party was going to meet with other "tax-collecting" bands?'

'That's what Alaric told us,' Edgar replied.

'It seems that your Alaric failed to mention just how many others would be there. Our scouts estimate that over six hundred mounted Normans descended on Mammesfeld, all at about the time you would have arrived there.'

'Six hundred? Sweet Christ!'

'You wouldn't have stood a chance.'

'Why would six hundred troops gather at Mammesfeld? What did they want there?'

'We gather it was just a meeting to compare results before scattering off into the four corners of the kingdom for more extortion. It seems the leaders of the raiders stayed at the king's manor in the town. I went there once, with old Edward-king. Good hunting.'

'I suppose they killed everyone there?'

Alfweald shook his head and concentrated his cleaning on a stubborn stain on his blade. 'Apparently not. They took most of the available food, of course, but apart from that, they seem to have left everyone more or less as they were.'

'I don't suppose your scouts have any clue where de Barentin went? And if my wife is still with him?'

'I'm sorry, Edgar. Have heart, though. We have many eyes and ears throughout the area. The more the Normans upset the local people, the more eyes and ears we have, and the more people are willing to join our cause.'

Edgar inspected his blade carefully, and satisfied with the cleaning, he slid it back into its scabbard.

'Are there other groups that you know of, like us?' he asked.

Thegn

'There is certainly a great deal of resistance to the north, in Northumbria. I expect that the Bastard's men are not having an easy time of it anywhere at the moment.' He spat on a particularly tough stain and rubbed intently at the spot. Pulling away the leather rag, he smiled at the results and put the sword down on the ground by the side of the wooden stool he was sitting on.

'Resistance will grow, I'm sure. I am still in contact, albeit infrequently, with some of my former colleagues in the southern part of Mercia. I understand that a request for help has been sent to Sweyn of Denmark, and overtures are to be made to the Emperor in Germania. Of course, these great magnates will have to decide what's in it for themselves before committing. Frankly, I can't see why the German Emperor would be interested, unless he has a particular quarrel with the Bastard himself, and I don't know about that. Sweyn-king may respond, but I can't see him helping unless he can see himself on the throne of England. Still, better a Dane than a Norman, eh?'

Edgar agreed. Coming from within the Danelaw of old, he and most of the people he knew were of joint English and Danish descent. The difference was indistinguishable to him.

'I would fight for Sweyn, as long as it was against the Bastard,' he said with feeling.

'Good lad. I'm sure that those feelings are echoed by a good many Englishmen. But you mustn't forget that personal ambition amongst the aristocracy here may thwart any attempts. There's more than one earl who must now be seeing visions of himself sitting on Harold's throne. They will split the resistance. We must move with caution.'

Edgar was surprised to hear a former king's reeve speak

so disrespectfully of the kingdom's earls. Alfweald saw the consternation on Edgar's face.

'Don't forget, lad, I knew these people. I worked with, aye, and against, these men for nearly twenty years. You can't survive in royal circles without knowing your friends intimately, and your enemies better.' He slapped Edgar on the knee. 'Come on, it's time we ate.'

As they sat within the Paddock, eating from their wooden bowls, Edgar was approached by a large man with powerful arms and close-shaved head.

'We have not met,' began the man, in a deep, rumbling voice, looking down on Edgar as he finished his food. 'My name is Bjarn, I am the Wildmen's blacksmith.'

Edgar stood and took the man's proffered hand. 'I wasn't aware that we had a smithy,' said Edgar.

'We don't,' smiled the man. 'Not here, at least. I come in from Redford, a village a few miles away, where I have a smithy and can undertake any work that's needed. A smithy is a very loud and visible place, not the sort of thing you'd want in a secret community.'

Edgar sat down again and invited the man to sit next to him.

'So, what can I do for you, Bjarn?' he asked.

'If you don't mind, I would like to have a look at your sword,' said Bjarn.

Edgar hesitated a moment, then removed the scabbard from his belt and handed it over to Bjarn. 'Of course,' he said.

'Thank you,' replied Bjarn. He held the sword within its scabbard reverently in his big, scarred hands, inspecting every ornamentation and device on the sheath carefully.

Thegn

'The scabbard is exquisite,' he said, 'I've rarely seen such workmanship. See how the animals flow into one another and how if you turn it this way,' he turned the scabbard through ninety degrees, 'All that foliage becomes a mass of human faces. Wonderful, truly wonderful.'

A couple of nearby Wildmen had started listening in to the conversation, and now they stood and walked over to see what the smith was looking at. The smith looked up and smiled at them. 'See this,' he said to them, holding the scabbard slightly away from his body and towards them. The men murmured in appreciation, and one of them turned round and whistled softly. Several other nearby Wildmen now walked over to see the wondrous weapon.

Bjarn ran his fingers now over the handle of the sword itself. It was covered in a very dark, almost black, skin of some type, held in place with intricate windings of gold wire.

'Marvellous,' he mused to himself, 'See how the grip is smooth this way,' he ran his hand down the handle towards the blade, 'And extremely rough this way,' he ran his hand back up the handle, his hand skipping and catching as it went.

'It is some sort of animal skin, I fancy,' said Edgar, 'but I have never seen the like before, grasping the handle at the right point is very easy, but then the sword will never slip out of your hand, it's so difficult to pull your hand against the grain.'

Bjarn nodded approvingly, still stroking the handle. 'It is the skin of a fish, my lord.'

'A fish? What fish has such tough skin as that?' asked Edgar incredulously.

'I once lived out on the coast, in a little fishing village. The fishermen there told tales of a huge fish, as big as a man, with rows of hideous barbed teeth with which it could tear a man to shreds in just moments. Sometimes they managed to catch one; a smaller one, that is. They called the fish 'shark', and this, my lord, is the skin of a shark, and from a large one, too, I would say, judging by the strength of it. When the skin is still on the beast, this direction,' he pointed towards the blade of the sword, 'is the direction away from which the animal's head would be. The smoothness of the skin in this direction allows the fish to slip easily through the water.'

'A fish that can tear a man to shreds?' asked one of the Wildmen in astonishment. 'Surely you're mistaken, Bjarn?'

'No,' he shook his great head, 'no doubt about it. The fishermen lived in fear of the fish, and I saw the smaller ones myself. I can vouch for the number and sharpness of the teeth. Beware the sea, my friend, for it is dangerous, and full of teeth.'

The Wildmen chuckled.

Bjarn inspected the rest of the hilt. The pommel was made of gold with a huge garnet within it. Bjarn held the pommel to his eye and peered at the sky through it, muttering with approval. He ran his fingers over the crossbar, iron, and polished to a high sheen. Coloured stones were fitted into the bar at its ends.

'The hilt is not original to the sword. It is far too expensive and highly decorated. This hilt has been fitted…' he squinted at the join between the blade and the hilt. 'And very well fitted, by a master craftsman. It is an exquisite thing. I suspect that the scabbard was made at the same time as the hilt. See how the designs match and flow into one another? This is work that was done for a very important and very rich man. Maybe even a king.'

Bjarn held the scabbard with one hand and the handle of the sword with the other. He looked at Edgar. 'With your permission, my lord?'

Edgar nodded. 'Yes, of course.'

Slowly and carefully, Bjarn withdrew the blade from its protective sheath. There were gasps from the assembled Wildmen. Bjarn looked lovingly at the blade. 'This is what it's all for,' he rumbled quietly, 'all the finery and decoration. It's all about this.'

The blade flashed brilliantly, like a mirror. Bjarn ran the tips of his fingers up and down the flat of the blade. It was so smooth it took his breath away.

'If only I had a tenth of the skill of the smith who made this blade,' he said as if to himself.

'You are a fine smith, Bjarn,' said a voice from within the gathering. It was echoed by those around.

'Thank you, but what I say is true. I may be a fine smith, but the man who made this was far, far more skilled than I ever could hope to be.'

Beneath his fingers, he felt the irregularities in the blade where the maker's name was inscribed. He looked carefully along the blade and smiled, nodding.

'Ulfberht. I knew I would see that name,' he said.

'You have seen one before?' asked Edgar.

'Yes, my lord, but only once. When I was just a lad, beginning my apprenticeship, I was shown one of these by a Danish lord. "One day," he said, "you may make swords like this."' Bjarn laughed and shook his head. 'Though his was by no means as highly decorated as this one. Quite plain by comparison.'

'Do you know anything of Ulfberht himself?' asked Edgar.

'No. He must have been the master of all smiths, but I believe all the swords which bear his name were made long ago, before living memory. You are fortunate indeed to have such a thing. May I ask how you got it?'

'It was given to me by my grandfather, Wulfmaer, Thegn of Rapendun, and he had it from his own grandfather, a man named Alfhaere. He served with Earl Byrhtnoth, and won the sword in that Earl's great battle against the Viking invaders.'

'There, you see? Your grandfather's grandfather won it maybe a hundred years ago. Like I said, these swords are all old.'

He cautiously tested the blade against his thumb, placing very little pressure on the blade. His thumb came away apparently unscathed. He held it up, and a thin red line appeared where he had touched the edge of the blade. He sucked at the thumb.

'These blades can hold their edge like no other. Given a really good swing, this blade should be able to slice clean through a lesser sword blade.'

'So I have been told, though I haven't had chance to test that yet.'

'No,' Bjarn shook his head, 'probably best not to. It would work, but you may damage the blade beyond most smiths' ability to mend – including mine.'

He carefully slipped the blade back into the scabbard and held the sword in both hands as he returned it reverently to Edgar.

'Thank you, my lord, you have made a smith very happy, and yet made him feel quite inadequate at the same time.'

Thegn

It was a cold night in the woods. Stars sparkled frostily overhead as a runner from the sentries entered the Paddock, expertly threading his way through the defensive bushes even in the dark. Edgar watched as he hastened across the open area to where Alfweald sat with two of his deputies. The runner spoke rapidly to Alfweald, and although he could make out none of the words being spoken, he could tell from Alfweald's stiffening posture that the runner brought news of considerable import. Alfweald stood and strode over to Edgar.

'Edgar, you must come with us. It seems your Norman spy is back. My men have captured him about quarter of a mile from here. If he knows where we are, then I have no doubt that his masters do too. We need to interrogate him, and then I fear that we must kill him.'

Edgar frowned but was forced to concede. 'He certainly seems a slippery character. I agree that if there's any chance at all that he could give away our location to the Normans then we cannot allow him to live. But first, let me speak to him.'

'Very well. You must find out as much as you can from him. I know he escaped from you once before, but we have ways of ensuring that he doesn't do so again. You must take whatever time you need.'

At that moment, two sentries entered the Paddock, with Alaric, wrists bound behind his back with a rope that also encircled his neck, and hobbled with a short length of rope between his ankles. One of the guards shoved him in the back and he fell to the ground, unable to prevent the fall, his hands being tied behind his back, his face hit the dirt with some force.

Edgar walked over to him, with Alfweald following a

pace behind. He stood over the prone man.

'Alaric, we meet again,' he said.

Alaric lifted his head and rolled over onto his side. Edgar could see that his nose was bleeding.

'My lord Edgar, how nice to see you,' he said in his lyrical voice.

Alfweald looked at the two guards. 'Pick him up, bring him over by the fire.'

The two men lifted Alaric roughly by the armpits and the five of them walked across the Paddock back to where Alfweald had been sitting with his deputies when the messenger had arrived. Close by were a series of stout wooden poles, used for holding archery targets and swordsmanship practice. Alaric was tied to one of these in such a way that he could not sit down. One of the guards punched him in the stomach once he was tied in place.

'That's enough!' barked Alfweald. 'Get back to your posts.'

The two men retreated, casting vicious backwards glances at Alaric as they went.

'Feelings run high,' said Alfweald to Edgar. 'Many men here have lost friends and family to the Normans.'

Edgar approached Alaric. 'Have you been sent to spy on me again, Alaric?'

'No, my lord,' he replied, between gasps. 'I came of my own free will. I wished to speak to you.'

'*You* wished to speak to *me*?'

'Indeed, my lord.'

'So why were you creeping about, only to be captured by two of our sentries?'

Alaric looked insulted. 'I was not "creeping about", I was heading here openly and deliberately. I surrendered to those two oafs as soon as I saw them.'

'Why would you do that?'

'As I say, I wanted to speak to you.'

'What did you want to say?' asked Edgar.

'Careful, Edgar. He's bargaining for his life,' said Alfweald.

Alaric did not react to the news that he was bargaining for his life. He was not stupid, Edgar thought, he already knew what was at stake.

'Well?' said Edgar.

'I have located your wife.'

'What?'

'Roger de Barentin is currently overseeing the building of a fort at Redford. He is staying at the king's hunting lodge. He has with him a group of women. He keeps them locked up and out of sight.'

'How would you know this? Are you now working for de Barentin? You want me and my colleagues to attempt a rescue, yes? A rescue attempt that is fully expected by de Barentin's men. We will all be killed or captured, right?'

'No, no that's not right at all. I do not work for de Barentin.'

'That's right, your master was Guillaume de Caen, was it not?'

'He paid for my services in the past, it is true, but you know what I think of him from our past… conversations.'

Alaric stopped to spit some blood from his mouth. His nose was still bleeding and it dribbled into his mouth as he spoke.

'So now you report directly to de Barentin?' asked Edgar.

'I would never take that man's pay. He is a brute, and

God will surely punish him for it.'

'So will I, if I get to him before God does.'

'I can help you, my lord. I am known amongst the Normans. I wouldn't say they trust me, but at least I can travel unhindered amongst them.'

'Why would you want to help me? How could I possibly ever trust you? You're a Norman, for Jesus' sake!'

'No, my lord, I am not.'

Alfweald stepped forward. 'What do you mean you're not a Norman? It's as plain as the nose on your face that you're a Norman! You ride with them, you speak like them, you dress like them.'

'Nevertheless, sir,' Alaric turned his head to face Alfweald, 'I am not a Norman.'

'Then what the devil are you?' demanded Alfweald.

Alaric paused. He looked across the Paddock for a moment, and then said 'My master, my true master, is Duke Robert of Burgundy.'

'Burgundy? What has he to do with all this?'

'My master is a powerful man. On the face of things, he has not objected to the Bastard's invasion of England. From his point of view, it distracts a turbulent near-neighbour from causing trouble closer to home. It is well that he is aware of everything that the Bastard does. I am one of his agents. I and others have infiltrated the ranks of the Bastard's army, we report back to our master, and also we make small ripples. We upset plans when and where we can.'

'Edgar,' Alfweald pulled gently on Edgar's shoulder, and together the two men walked back to the small fire and sat down.

'Do you believe him?' asked Alfweald.

'I don't know. It sounds possible. I have spoken with

him before, and I believe that he truly does hold the Normans in contempt.'

'If what he says is true, and I do mean "if", then this man could be a huge asset to us.'

'I know. What he says about passing freely amongst the Normans is true. Also, if he has any real information on the whereabouts of my wife then I must get that information from him.'

'Yes, I see that, but we must always bear in mind the fact that he may be lying. Maybe he really is a Norman, and he plans on leading the Norman soldiers right here to our sanctuary.'

'That can't be allowed to happen, I know.'

Alfweald nodded, 'Right. For now, we treat him with caution. We'll let him have his say about the location of your wife, but he remains tied up until we're absolutely sure.'

'Agreed,' said Edgar.

The two men stood and returned to Alaric.

'Very well, Alaric, we will continue our discussions on the basis that you are not, in fact, a Norman. That does not mean that we think of you as a friend or an ally, or even as a neutral party. You are still, in our eyes, the enemy, and you will be treated as such.'

'As you wish,' said Alaric. 'However, I will prove myself to you somehow.'

'You do that, Alaric. Tell me one thing. Why did you escape from us? If you wished to "upset" some of the Norman's plans, why not stay with us? Why return to the Normans if not to report our whereabouts and purpose?'

'You would have killed me,' said Alaric. 'Oh, not you, my lord, not personally, but some of your men. They looked at me with hungry eyes.'

Edgar knew the truth of the statement. He had himself feared that one morning he would wake to find Alaric mysteriously dead.

'I did not report your purpose or whereabouts to de Barentin. Instead, I reported that I had followed you, as I had been ordered to, but that you had given up the chase and returned the way you had come.'

'Nobody is looking for us?'

'No, my lord.'

'How did you know where you would find me?'

'I have been here before.'

'What?' roared Alfweald. 'When have you been here before?'

'When I escaped from you last time, my lord, I did not go far. Your Wildmen are good, sir,' he looked at Alfweald, 'but I am better. They did not find me when they captured my former captors. Neither did they nor any of the sentries they passed see me as I followed them here. Please do not be hard on your men, sir. I am very, very good. I could have killed many of your men and led the Normans right here, but I did not.'

Alfweald grunted and rubbed his chin thoughtfully. 'So why did you allow yourself to be captured tonight?'

'If I had made my way here in secret, sir, I could not be sure, I mean absolutely sure, of my success. I am, as I say without boasting, very, very good. And yet I was not so confident that I could outwit all your men here. A useful skill for a spy is that of recognising a worthy adversary, and modifying one's methods accordingly.'

Alfweald grunted again, but the grunt sounded more mollified this time. 'You modified your methods accordingly. Are your methods still modified? Are you allowing us to think in a certain way about you, a way that might be entirely false?'

'The method I have chosen to deal with you, sir, is honesty. Total truth. It is the best method to use when the plan is to convert an adversary into an ally.'

Alfweald backed away and stared thoughtfully at him. He turned back towards the small fire. He gave a low whistle and one of his men trotted across to him.

'Double the sentries tonight and until further notice. I know this will be hard on the men and reduce their sleeping time, but our safety is at stake. Make sure everyone knows to be doubly alert for the next few days.'

'Yes sir,' answered the man, bobbing his head. He hurried off in the direction of the hidden passage through the hedge.

Alfweald returned to Alaric. 'Alright Edgar,' he said. 'Let's give him a little slack. Loosen his bonds just so that he can sit down. The next few days will show whether he is genuine or not.'

Edgar loosened the rope around Alaric's neck.

'Thank you, Lord Edgar. You will not regret this, I promise.'

'I had better not.'

Edgar slept comfortably that night. Despite his reservations about Alaric, he found that he could not help liking the man, and hoped fervently that he was telling the truth. It would make such a difference in his search for Godgifu. If Alaric really did know where she was, and he was able to pass freely amongst the Normans, the task of securing Godgifu's escape was made many times easier, and with the skills and courage of Alfweald and his Wildmen, it could now only be a matter of time before they were reunited.

He was woken by Guthrum, returning from his early morning sentry duty.

'Morning, Edgar,' he grunted as he shook Edgar's shoulder. 'What's this we have tied to a post outside?'

Edgar roused himself and smiled mysteriously at Guthrum. 'Alaric has returned to us, Guthrum. He says voluntarily. Whether that is true or not, we have yet to ascertain.'

'I can think of some men who won't be happy at his reappearance.'

'Their personal feelings are not important. I want you to make it very plain, Guthrum, that Alaric is for now under the personal protection of both myself and Reeve Alfweald. If anyone, and I mean *anyone* so much as looks at Alaric askance, I will have their hide, do you understand me?'

Guthrum looked slightly wounded. 'Yes, my lord, of course. I shall make sure that our men understand completely.'

Edgar softened his tone. 'He says he knows where Godgifu is. He says he can help us to get her back. If he's telling the truth then he could be the key to releasing her.'

Guthrum nodded. 'I see. Yes, I understand and I'll make sure the men understand, too.'

'Good. Thank you, Guthrum. Now, let's eat and then I wish to speak some more with our little spy.'

Alaric sat calmly, his arms still tied behind the post, and the bonds round his neck just loose enough to allow him to look around. He clumsily pushed himself to his feet as

Thegn

Edgar, Guthrum and Alfweald approached him.

They stood and looked at him in silence. He looked back, quietly and calmly. Alaric cleared his throat. 'I have a gift for you. A token of my good faith.'

'And what might that be?' grunted Alfweald.

'The tax enforcers are sending back several waggons to Lundenburg, loaded with coin and other valuables that have been taken. The King…' he stopped, acknowledging the frowns on the three men's faces with a gracious nod. 'The Bastard is back in his duchy in Normandy. In his stead, he has left his half-brother, Bishop Odo, and his cousin, William fitzOsbern in charge of matters, as regents, as it were. Each of these men is even more of a bastard than the Bastard himself. They have increased the pressure on the tax-collectors to raise more and more revenue from the incumbent landowners. You thought the Bastard was hard. These two are worse, believe me.

'In order to keep the two regents off their backs, the tax enforcers are sending back regular supplies of booty to Lundenburg. The next waggon load is due to pass through this area sometime tomorrow. I heard talk of the arrangements for guarding the hoard. A party of two dozen fully armoured horsemen was to set out from Snotingeham and meet the waggon. Now in the past, I believe the changing of the guard has always taken place somewhere called Hildeston, though I don't know exactly where that is. Maybe some of your men would know. The location is important because the party of two dozen horsemen is replacing a guard of only sixteen, so if you wish to take advantage of this, you really need to get to the waggon whilst it is still guarded only by the sixteen.'

Edgar and Guthrum looked at each other, and then at

Alfweald.

'How much loot is being transported?' asked Alfweald.

'Enough to fill at least one large waggon. Two have been sent in the past, but the further north we go, the less able people are to pay the tax demand. Unless they've been particularly successful this past week, I would expect there to be only one waggon.'

'Apart from the guard, who accompanies the waggon?'

'Usually one of de Barentin's lieutenants, a trusted accountant and a waggon driver. They will stop at several places along the way to add more collected taxes to the waggon. There will be changes of waggon drivers, too. The drivers will be locals, pressed into service. That's all.'

'This could be a trap,' said Guthrum.

'If you don't believe me, then just observe the waggon from anywhere along its route. There's no need to attack or even make yourself known. You could have one of the women sit by the side of the road and report back to you if what I say is true. That way you will know that you can trust me. De Barentin would not risk one of his treasure waggons to trap you.'

'We won't even know if it *is* a treasure waggon. It could be empty, or full of shit.'

Alaric looked disappointed. 'It is all I can do to prove myself, sir.'

'Edgar, Guthrum, come with me,' ordered Alfweald. They followed him to where the senior men were gathered eating their breakfast.

'It would seem that an opportunity has been placed in our laps,' began Alfweald without preamble. He outlined the information imparted by Alaric. 'Reactions?' he asked once he had finished.

Thegn

One hoary old veteran put his bowl on the grass by his feet. 'If this information is true and not simply given as the bait for a trap, then we *must* act on it. The possibility of disrupting the Bastard's extortion cannot be passed over. There is a twofold advantage if we are successful; the holding back of money from the Bastard's treasury, and the obtaining of it for ourselves, whatever we choose to do with it. If it is a trap, then we will be none the worse off anyway. I suggest that we see if we can find this waggon today, or tonight, and somehow ascertain if it is indeed carrying what the prisoner says it is. There are only so many places it could be if it is to be at Hildeston tomorrow.'

'You know this Hildeston?' asked Alfweald.

'Oh yes. It's not much, just a single farm, really, and it's in a remote spot, but on the main route south. Maybe we should place some men there today as well, to forestall the possibility of us being surprised there.'

'No, no,' Alfweald shook his head. 'That would be too dangerous. As it's the location of the changing of the guard, then both sets of guards would be there, a total of forty soldiers. We can't risk that. We have to make any move that we are going to make well in advance of it arriving at Hildeston.'

He paused, tapping his teeth in thought. 'That doesn't mean that we can't plan something for the second guard unit once we have disposed of the first. But that's for later. Right now, we need to find this waggon, as you say. That's a good plan. Let's talk.'

Alfweald sat down with his lieutenants and signalled Edgar and Guthrum to do likewise. After an hour, all were agreed on a course of action.

12

A Small Victory

Later that evening, the report came back to the Paddock that a waggon fitting the description given by Alaric was under guard in the village of Tilsdene, some twelve miles north of Hildeston. The Wildmen knew the region very well, and a spot had been chosen for the ambush. Seven miles from Tilsdene and still five from Hildeston, the road passed through a dense area of forest for two miles. The road was in poor condition and had not been repaired this year. Deep ruts had formed, and there were many large holes that a waggon would need to avoid. Also, close to the midpoint of this two-mile section of road, there was a sharp bend to the left, providing an even better location for an ambush.

Whilst the sky was still dark, a troop of forty mounted men left the Paddock, carefully picking their way along deer trails and the occasional woodcutter's path. It took three hours to reach the spot identified for leaving their horses. They dismounted, left their horses in the care of three men, and proceeded on foot. As they left, the three men took out shovels from the horses' panniers and began to dig a trench.

As the ambush party approached the road, the twelve men under Edgar's command selected to form the rearguard slowed and settled down, their green tunics over their mail shirts blending into the background. Alfweald had entrusted the leadership of the ambush party to Godwin, who now led twenty-five men through the forest, parallel with the road, south to beyond the sharp bend, where they too, settled into near-invisibility amongst the undergrowth. A dozen of the men climbed trees alongside the road and pulled themselves in tightly against the tree trunks.

With Edgar were his own six housecarls, each one having volunteered immediately for this duty. In fact, so many had volunteered, that a second troop was even now making its way on foot to a spot a few hundred yards ahead of the main ambush troop, as a safeguard and second strike unit, should such be needed.

Edgar settled himself into a comfortable position, sitting on a carpet of pine needles, his back against the rough, fissured bark of the tree they had fallen from. In front of him the bracken swayed gently, browning now as autumn began to bite. The bracken was dying back throughout the forest but still provided sufficient cover, though it would not do for very much longer.

Guthrum settled down on Edgar's left and Sebbi on his right. He had seen Halfdene and Eric vanish into some undergrowth but had no idea where Osfrid and Hunwald had secreted themselves. The remainder of his party had disappeared into the bracken. He gave a low call, birdlike, as he had been taught. He just about heard several quiet replies. All his men were in place and ready. He placed his bow across his knees and nocked the first arrow into place on the drawstring. He noted that Guthrum and Sebbi had already done the same.

They sat for over an hour before the first call, a jackdaw-like 'Chak-chak!'. Edgar felt his comrades tense beside him. He, too, felt a rush of excitement at the call agreed for first sight. After a few moments, a single horse came into view, being ridden by a well-dressed man in a heavy fur cloak and a felt cap. At his side walked another man, evidently a servant, carrying a large satchel that looked heavy even from where Edgar was sitting. Edgar watched him closely, but released the tension in his arms and allowed the bowstring to slacken again. The man was chastising his servant, a constant tirade of insults and complaints. The servant walking beside him showed no sign even of hearing the voice of his master.

Guthrum stirred beside Edgar. 'Do you want me to shoot him?' he breathed in Edgar's ear. Edgar smiled. The two men continued on their journey undisturbed. Edgar felt Guthrum and Sebbi relax beside him.

Only a few minutes later, the jackdaw-like call was repeated, twice. The spotter seeming to be saying that this time it was definitely the target.

'Alright,' said Edgar to his two companions. 'Nice and easy now, hold back until they're passed.'

Edgar could sense the tiny movements in the undergrowth that indicated that his men were preparing for action. There was no sound that he could hear, just a slight susurration.

The waggon lumbered slowly into view. It was

Thegn

struggling to pass along the deeply rutted and muddy road. Six horsemen rode ahead of it and six behind. Four horsemen had dismounted and were walking behind the waggon, ready to push it when next it got stuck in a rut or a hole, their horses being led by their colleagues behind them. Edgar felt himself freeze. If any of his men should give themselves away now, then the ambush would probably fail, to the great detriment of the Wildmen. The horsemen were nervous, looking around in hurried, twitchy movements. Edgar knew his men were well hidden and well trained, and he felt confident that they would not give themselves or their comrades away. His scarred face suddenly started throbbing, and he unconsciously brought the palm of his hand up to soothe it.

Guthrum glanced at him but looked away again when he saw what Edgar was doing.

The waggon slid to a stop in a rut. The four dismounted horsemen leaned into the waggon and put their shoulders to it. From where he was sitting, Edgar could hear the soldiers grunting with the effort of pushing the heavily-laden waggon. Slowly, it began to inch forwards. The waggon driver urged his horses to greater effort by use of voice and whip. The cumbersome vehicle lurched to its right and suddenly started moving again. The soldiers pushing it slipped and staggered as the waggon pulled away from them.

Edgar watched with growing impatience as the waggon continued on its sluggish way, slowly moving towards the corner around which lay Godwin and his men. It slipped again, but with harsh urging from the driver and a little push from the soldiers, it kept moving, finally disappearing around the bend. Edgar waited, for they were not certain that a second force of soldiers was not following behind in case of just such an ambush as they were planning.

'Now?' whispered Guthrum after some minutes had passed.

'Now,' replied Edgar, and gave a high-pitched whistle, unlike any bird.

Instantly, the woods around him filled with men, running lightly down to the road. They spread across it as a cordon and as a man, nocked arrows to their bowstrings and stood ready. No sooner had they taken up their positions than they could hear a commotion ahead of them from where the waggon had turned the corner. Three horsemen galloped at full speed back round the bend towards them. In seconds, all three had been hit by arrows loosed by Edgar's men. Two fell immediately to the muddy ground, but the third had only been wounded, and he pressed his horse to even greater speed as he approached the line of archers. The archers hurriedly attempted to nock further arrows to their bowstrings, and the first to do so let fly with an arrow that pierced the neck of the rider's horse. It staggered to a halt and reared, throwing its rider to the ground. He lay still, and the horse galloped off, the archers parting quickly to let the maddened beast pass. One archer, faster and more accurate than most of his comrades, let another arrow off in pursuit of the horse. The arrow hit cleanly in the back of the horse's head, and the animal collapsed to the ground in a skidding heap.

Godwin ran round the corner to see what had happened to the three who had escaped the arrows of his men, and he pulled up next to Edgar, a look of cold satisfaction on his face.

'Well done, lads,' he congratulated them. 'We got them all. Now quickly, get those three off the road and strip them

Thegn

of their armour.' He looked down the road to where the dead horse lay in a tangled mess.

'Damn! You, lad!' he pointed at one of the younger Wildmen archers.

'Yes, sir?'

'Back to our horses, bring one here, we can't be down a horse. Fast as you can now.'

'Yes, sir!'

The lad handed his bow and quiver to one of his colleagues and set off into the forest at a light run.

Edgar's men had dragged the dead bodies off the road and were busy stripping them of their mail armour and outer clothing. Six men were detailed to remove the horse from the road. It was too heavy and cumbersome to be disposed of where it was, so would need to be butchered and carried back to the Paddock as meat.

The bodies of the dead men were hastily hidden some way back from the road, and Edgar's men hurried round the corner to where Godwin's men had finished hiding and stripping their victims. The horses had been rounded up and calmed. Some of Godwin's men were stripping off their own clothes and putting on the outer garments and armour from the Norman riders. At one side of the road, three men lay trussed and gagged. As Alaric had told them there would be, there was a driver, an accountant and one of de Barentin's lieutenants.

So far, Alaric's information had been good and solid. Edgar found himself feeling pleased and more than a little relieved. Oddly, he realised that he was more pleased that Alaric would now probably survive than he was that he hadn't just walked into a trap.

Godwin's men had started unloading the waggon of its

load of money and valuables. Edgar's men joined in eagerly, carrying the boxes off the road and into the woods.

Once the waggon was emptied, twelve archers climbed into the back of the waggon and the outer covers were closed. At that very moment, the young Wildman trotted a horse onto the road and dismounted. The final disguised Englishman took the reins from the lad and mounted the horse. The rest of the disguised men mounted the Norman horses and the waggon continued on its way. No more than half an hour had passed since the ambush.

Edgar watched the waggon as it continued on its journey to Hildeston, where the unsuspecting change of the guard was about to meet an unhappy end. To the Normans, it would appear that the waggon and all its valuable load, and two complete sets of guards had completely disappeared. That was why it was vital to leave no trace whatsoever of what had happened here.

The Wildmen who remained scoured the area of the road where the ambush had taken place, removing any sign at all that there had been a scuffle, or anything more than the perfectly regular tracks of the waggon and the horses skidding and struggling their way along a poorly maintained muddy road.

A small party of Wildmen set off back into the woods to retrieve the horses. Once they returned, the bodies of the Normans were placed on the spare horses and the men then mounted and rode back into the forest, the three captives walking behind, each roped to a horse.

In the clearing where the horses had been left for the ambush, the men who had remained had finished digging a long, shallow trench, and the earth they had excavated was piled up along one edge of it. The bodies of the Normans

Thegn

were dumped unceremoniously into it. Godwin then ordered that the three captives be killed and put in the trench with their comrades. The Norman lieutenant and the accountant clearly spoke no English, and so were unmoved when the order was given, but the driver's eyes widened and his face contorted into a look of sheer terror. He was gagged, but he screamed through the gag. He started shouting and through the gag his words were plain. 'English! English!'

Godwin walked up to him. He made shushing signs with his finger against his lips.

'I'll take the gag off if you shut up. Alright?'

The man nodded rapidly, his eyes wide, sweat pouring from his brow. Slowly, Godwin removed the gag.

'I'm English!' gasped the driver. 'An Englishman like you! I'm not a Norman, I just drive a waggon. They made me drive it. Please don't kill me, I have a wife and daughter.'

'You are not an Englishman like us. We are defending our kingdom. We are fighting the invader. You are working for them. You are a traitor and deserve to die.'

'No, please no! I couldn't say no to them. They threatened my wife, my daughter. They said they would kill them, eventually, after they had used them. Please!'

Godwin replaced the gag. He signalled to two of his men behind the prisoners. The three men were forced down onto their knees facing the shallow trench which now held the bodies of their fellows. The driver continued to scream as the two Wildmen brought their axes down onto the tops of the Normans' skulls. The men died instantly and toppled into the makeshift grave amongst their former guards.

Edgar tugged at Godwin's sleeve. 'For pity's sake man! This man is no more guilty of being a collaborator than am

I! If the Normans had ordered me to drive a waggon or have my wife killed, I know what I would have done.'

Godwin took Edgar by the shoulders. 'Edgar. We have no proof of this man's story. He could be a Norman who speaks English very well. If we let him go, then there will be a witness to what has happened here, and if that tale gets back to de Barentin, then he will move Heaven and Earth to find us and kill us. Our very survival depends on this one man dying here and now.'

'Just give me a little time. Bind him, gag him, blindfold him. We'll take him back to the Paddock and get what information we can out of him. Think what he might have seen, what he might have overheard. We could be throwing away a huge advantage by killing him now. I'll take responsibility for him, and keep him constantly bound and under guard every minute of the day and night.'

The man kneeling before the trench was making loud affirmative noises as if he agreed with everything Edgar said.

'Give me your axe,' said Godwin to one of the Wildmen. The Wildman handed over the weapon. Godwin took it and felt its weight in his hand. He lined up with the driver's skull. Edgar closed his eyes and turned away in disgust. At the extremity of the back-swing, Godwin tossed the weapon in his hand so it was reversed. He brought the axe down with a crack on the driver's head.

'Edgar,' called Godwin.

Edgar turned. 'Take him, blindfold him. You've got a day to prove how useful he is. Then I use this side of the axe on him.' He held the blade up towards Edgar.

Back at the Paddock, there was great rejoicing. Alfweald came rushing out to meet them as they filed in through the secret entrance. Edgar took his still unconscious prisoner to a quiet corner and tied him, still gagged and blindfolded, to another of the many posts that dotted the interior. He told Hunwald to sit and guard him. He gave orders that if the man became troublesome, he was to be killed.

'I'll tell him,' grinned Hunwald. He sat down and picked up a length of branch from the ground. Pulling out his seax, he began whittling the stick, whistling quietly and tunelessly as he did so.

Edgar returned to Alfweald, who was busy examining the contents of the cases and boxes that had been brought back to the Paddock. He was congratulating Godwin on a job well done.

'Excellent, excellent! There has to be over a hundred pounds of silver here,' he said.

'I know, we carried it back,' grinned Godwin. 'The Bastard will not be pleased with his deputies.'

'I hope not. We must sow the seeds of discontent wherever we can. It can only help our cause. Edgar!' He turned as Edgar arrived. 'It seems that your prisoner has turned out to be honest after all. I still don't trust him, mind. He still needs to prove himself more completely.'

'Yes, sir. Though I would now like to cut him from his post, with your permission.'

Alfweald nodded. 'Yes, you may do that. There is no way that he can get out of the Paddock. I have guards posted both inside and out at the entrance. Now, Godwin tells me that you prevented him from executing a traitor.'

'Not proved to be a traitor in my eyes, sir, with all due respect to Godwin. I think we should not let the rule of law be so easily forgotten, even in these desperate times.'

Godwin laughed. 'The rule of law is over, at least for

now, at least for dealing with the Normans. But you're right, maybe we should be less hasty if there is potentially an advantage to be gained.'

He turned to Alfweald. 'He's quite persuasive, you know.'

'Yes, I know. Godwin will assist in your questioning of the man. It may loosen his tongue considerably if he knows that the man who wants to kill him is listening to his every word.'

'Yes, sir, thank you. I think that would be a great motivator.'

Godwin laughed.

'Go and release your first prisoner, then. Let him know that he will still be under the closest observation.'

Edgar bowed slightly to Alfweald and Godwin in turn and then walked over to the post where Alaric sat, his hands still tied behind the post.

'Your friends seem happy,' commented Alaric as Edgar approached.

'Your information was good.'

Alaric grinned. 'I knew it was. You really can trust me.'

'Can we? It's still possible that you're leading us on. There may be more at stake here than a quantity of tax revenue.'

'Look, de Barentin and his thugs don't even know that you people exist. Not yet, anyway. I'm sure that if you carry on the way you have been doing then you will soon come to their notice. But at this moment, de Barentin wouldn't sacrifice a single penny to find out where you are, because he has never heard of you.'

Their conversation was interrupted by a party of horsemen in Norman armour riding suddenly into the

Thegn

Paddock. Their leader threw off his helmet to be recognised. It was one of the Wildmen who had accompanied the waggon to its rendezvous with the new guard at Hildeston. Edgar hurried over, along with everyone else to greet the victorious band.

As he reached them, Godwin was gripping the now dismounted leader by the shoulders.

'We did it!' gasped the man. 'We took the Norman guard completely by surprise. Got every last one of them.'

'What did you do with the bodies?' asked Godwin, gravely.

'Nobody lives at Hildeston anymore. We found only one abandoned farmhouse. Looks like it hasn't been lived in for fifty years, but round the back was a small lake, maybe a hundred yards across. Deep, too, and steep-sided. They sank straight to the bottom with all that armour on. Of course, we kept what we could, swords, helmets and so on, but I thought it best to sacrifice some of the mail shirts to speed our secreting of the bodies. They will never be found'

Godwin slapped him on the arm. 'Good, Ingi, good! You did well.' He raised his voice so all the victorious raiding party could hear, 'Come on, all of you. There's meat and ale for all!'

The raiding party gave a cheer, but in the quiet, restrained, disciplined way that the Wildmen did these things.

The party dismounted and headed for their food and drink, and Edgar returned to Alaric.

'All the Normans who accompanied the treasure have been killed. Both parties of guards.'

Edgar spoke swiftly and watched Alaric carefully as he did so.

'Good,' said Alaric, with no trace of fear or regret. 'That is good. I'm glad none of your men were lost.'

Edgar pulled out his seax and leaned over Alaric. He sliced through the ropes behind the post. Alaric pulled his arms gingerly back round to rest in his lap.

'Ow,' he said. 'It's amazing just how stiff and sore your arms get when they've been held in the same position for a day or so.' He cautiously raised his hands across his chest to massage his upper arms. 'Ow,' he said again.

Edgar cut the bonds on Alaric's ankles and the ropes fell to the ground.

'Is that it then?' asked Alaric. 'Is that a sign that you trust me?'

'It's a sign that we trust you more than we did yesterday. It does not mean that we trust you yet. You should know that you are being watched very carefully.'

Alaric looked around him. It seemed that what Edgar said was literally true. Throughout the Paddock, he saw warriors standing still, watching him intently as he tried to rub some life back into his arms.

'Very well. I understand.'

'You will not find it possible to escape the Paddock. There are guards inside and out watching the entrance. If you make any attempt to leave, I will not be able to prevent your death. Do you understand me?'

'Yes, I understand. I will make no attempt to leave. I do not want to. I am safer in here than out there, even with these men lusting after my blood.'

'I think we'll keep you away from the men for now. You may get some credit for giving us the information about the treasure waggon, but to them you're still a nasty little Norman, and there's quite a bit of blood-lust over there for

Thegn

Normans at the moment.'

Edgar held out his hand to Alaric, who took hold of it and carefully rose to his feet.

'Sit over there,' said Edgar, pointing to a large log seat, 'I'll bring you some food.'

'Thank you, but if you don't mind, I'll stand over there rather than sit over there.'

'As you wish. Don't go anywhere else.'

'I really do understand that, my lord.'

Edgar returned with a large wooden bowl of hot vegetable broth and a wooden spoon. Alaric received it gratefully, and, still standing, began to eat, blowing on each spoonful before it went into his mouth.

'It's good,' he said.

Once finished, he finally sat down on the log seat next to Edgar.

'There is still much that I need to know,' said Edgar.

'I'll tell you what I can.'

'What is your mission? By that I mean what instructions were you given by Robert of Burgundy? What were you to achieve?'

'I do not receive my orders directly from the duke. I have never even met the man. I am hired on a job-by-job basis. I am contacted by a man called Thierry Plantin, he's a cloth merchant in Dijon, at least by day. By night, he runs the duke's international spy ring. Before you ask, I know nothing about how the spy ring works. I'm just a lowly pair of eyes and ears. Plantin told me that an invasion of England was inevitable. He also knew that the Norse would be attacking in the north at about the same time. I think there was some collusion there, though from what I hear it would not have been on the Bastard's part. He's not one for power or glory-sharing. I think the trouble was stirred up amongst the Norse and the Normans by the same agency, working against England.'

Edgar gasped.

'My lord?'

'Not against England. Against Harold Godwinson.'

'The King?'

'It can only have been… Oh sweet Jesus! What did he do?'

'I do not understand you, my lord.'

'Harold's brother, Tostig Godwinson. It must have been him. Tostig hated Harold because Harold had persuaded Edward-king to remove him from his position as earl of Northumbria.'

'Why would Harold do that? Surely having a brother in such a powerful position would be useful to him?'

'No. Tostig was cruel. He was a bad earl, and Northumbria and Mercia were in rebellion, demanding the removal of Tostig. If the King had refused, Harold would have been forced to march against them as the King's champion, splitting the country in two. No, Tostig had to go, it was necessary for the stability of the kingdom. Then when Edward died, the Witan elected Harold Godwinson as king. Tostig must have been livid. He decided to topple his brother, and regain his own power at the same time, possibly even more. So he paid visits to the Bastard in Normandy, who was already rumbling about his alleged rights to the English crown, and also to Harald Sigurdson in Norway. Harald also had a claim to the English crown. Not a very good one, but Tostig was always a smooth-tongued one, so I believe. I can't believe he would be so

Thegn

stupid!'

'Greed and lust for power can make stupid men of all of us, I think,' said Alaric.

'I was there, at Stanford, when we fought a great battle against the Norse. Tostig was there too, at Harald Sigurdson's side. At one point, he actually spoke with Harold-king. I heard their exchange. Harold offered Tostig all his own lands back, and more, if only he would come back to his brother's side. Tostig refused. Why would he do that?'

'Fear.'

'Fear of what?'

'Fear that his brother the King would find out that he had also conspired with the Duke of Normandy. Fear that the Duke was going to win. Fear that if the Duke did win, and found that Tostig had switched sides again, then he would almost certainly die a very painful death. William of Normandy is not a man to let go of a grudge. Fear of the Bastard.'

'Dear God.' Edgar stared at his feet for a long time.

'For the sake of a sibling quarrel,' he said, 'Tostig sold the kingdom and placed us in the situation we are now in. What a stupid turd.'

'It makes sense,' said Alaric thoughtfully. 'Plantin's information was that an English noble was at the Norman court and that he was discussing William's claim to the throne. I think that Plantin, and therefore the Duke of Burgundy, thought that this noble was there on behalf of the English royal council, to discuss William's election to the throne. The decision to invade would then be seen as a justified reaction to Harold's usurping the throne. It's all a bit thin, I admit, but kingdoms have been lost and gained on less.'

'Stupid, stupid, stupid. However, what's done is done, and we must carry on. Your duties then were what?'

'I was to gain employment with one of the Bastard's senior lieutenants. I told you previously that I was pressed because I was in the wrong place at the wrong time. I apologise for that deception. I was pressed because I was in the right place at the right time. The best way to get where I wanted to be and free of any suspicion was to be pressed into service, so I made sure that I was. I was given certain information that I could use to sell myself to my chosen target. I was aiming for de Barentin but was unable to get close enough to him, so I had to work my way in with one of his deputies – de Caen, whom you thoughtfully hanged for me. That has presented me with an opportunity to approach de Barentin himself, though I obviously have not been able to do so yet. Anyway, once in the trust of the target, I was simply to keep my eyes and ears open and to report back when the opportunity presented itself. Robert of Burgundy is very wary of the ambition of the Duke of Normandy, and so I was empowered to erm… introduce difficulties wherever I could safely do so.'

'And just how would you do that?'

'There are several ways. Killing key members of the lieutenant's entourage is an obvious, but very dangerous one. Passing false information, introducing light and undetectable poisonous substances to food, wine and so on. That's a good one. Nobody wants to fight a battle when they can't even get off the privy. With luck, one or two of them may even die. Nobody ever suspects that stomach cramps and the shits could be due to deliberate poisoning, especially when the victims are in a foreign land. They always blame the food.'

Edgar shook his head in amazement. 'I never dreamt there was such a world as the one you live in, Alaric.'

'I sometimes wish that there was not, my lord. I often just want to go home, find a nice girl, settle down. You know.'

'I did find a nice girl. Then de Barentin took her.'

'I know, and I'm sorry. I can help you to get her back. I really can.'

'Then I accept your help, Alaric of Burgundy, with my thanks.'

They sat in silence for a while. Then Alaric said 'I think it is a good thing that we have found each other, my lord.'

13

Mixed Messages

The waggon driver sat on a log looking at the low fire. His hands were loosely bound and his feet were hobbled with an eighteen-inch strap. He felt gingerly at the back of his head where Godwin had hit him with the haft of the axe.

'He didn't have to do that,' he moaned at Edgar.

'I think he did. We do not have guests at the Paddock, only Wildmen and their prisoners,' replied Edgar without looking up. 'Is it very sore?'

'I'll live, I think.'

'Then count yourself very lucky. You're the only person from that party who's still alive.'

'When can I go home?'

'You can't. Not yet, anyway. Don't complain. If you went back now, the Normans would undoubtedly kill you.'

'Why would they do that?'

'Come on, think about it,' Edgar looked up at the waggon driver. 'All the Bastard's treasure stolen; all the

Thegn

guards vanished. Who's going to be the chief suspect?'

The driver looked puzzled. 'How could I have done all that? I'm not even a warrior.'

'You couldn't have done it on your own, I grant you. But the information must surely have come from you. They will think that you informed your Wildmen friends about your load and your route.'

He still looked puzzled. 'I couldn't have. I didn't even know that I would be driving the waggon until this morning. I was plucked off the road without so much as a by your leave.'

'How?' asked Edgar.

'Well, this morning I was driving my waggon to Redford when I was stopped by these two soldiers. They didn't speak English but made it clear that they wanted me to get down from the waggon. Well, they had swords, so I did what they wanted. They marched me off to the old king's lodge – I thought they were going to kill me. Anyway, when we got there, there was another waggon and they pointed at it, so I got up.

'There were other soldiers, on horses – the ones you killed – one of them shouted something like 'Follow!' at me, so I did. I don't know where we were going or what was in the waggon. Treasure, you say?'

He suddenly looked aggrieved. 'And I don't know where my waggon is! They just left it there in the road! Anyone could have taken it.'

Edgar looked sharply at him, scrutinising his face for any hint of deception. Ignoring the man's complaints, he said 'So you are unknown to the Normans who remained behind?'

'Yes, my lord. They wouldn't know me from any other

Englishman or Dane.'

Edgar was quiet for a moment as he thought about the implications.

'What is your name?' he demanded.

'Folcwine, sir.'

'Do you live in Redford?'

'Close by, sir. I work an outlying farm with my brother.'

'Well, Folcwine, I think the Wildmen may have a use for you after all.'

'What?'

'We'll see, but meanwhile you'll have to stay here, and you'll have to keep those on,' he pointed at Folcwine's fetters.

'Alright,' he grumbled.

'You're happy to stay here?'

'Of course, my lord.'

'Aren't you concerned about your wife and daughter?'

A flicker of something flashed across Folcwine's face. 'Er, yes, of course, but I'll do what you say.'

Edgar stood up and walked across the Paddock to where Alfweald was sitting with Godwin. At Alfweald's invitation, he sat down with them.

'So, Edgar, what does our waggon driver have to say for himself?' asked Alfweald, a mug of mead halted halfway to his mouth.

'I think he may be of use to us, sir, though I would not go so far as to trust him. I'm getting mixed messages from him.'

'Mixed how?' the mug continued its upward journey and Alfweald took a swig from it.

'He seemed genuinely puzzled when I suggested that he was in danger from the Normans should he return home.

Thegn

He claims he was selected for the task immediately before they set off and that he had no knowledge of his load or route. I think he's telling the truth there; his puzzlement was real. Yet when I asked him about his wife and daughter, whom he invoked when Godric was about to cave his skull in,' Godric nodded happily, 'he seemed for a moment not to know who I was talking about. I think they may be made up.'

Alfweald grunted. 'A man who's facing the sharp edge of Godwin's axe may well be moved to invent a good reason for him not to use it. Under the same circumstances I may have been sorely tempted to do the same thing.'

Godwin chuckled.

'And yet, sir, it does indicate that he has within him the ability and the willingness to lie.'

Edgar paused.

'You have more?' asked Alfweald.

'The man seems an ideal candidate for information-gathering. He's a native of Redford, so is known there. He may be privy to more gossip than we could hope to hear as strangers. With your permission, I'd like to take a small trip into Redford. Just myself, Folcwine and Alaric. I don't know what we might find out, but any information we can get about the location and strength of Norman forces has to be worth having.'

'I don't like it,' said Godwin. 'You said yourself that you don't feel the man is trustworthy. How can we be sure that he won't give you away?'

'Well, we can't. Folcwine doesn't know Alaric. I intend for Alaric to follow behind us without Folcwine's knowledge. That way he can serve two purposes; he can spy on the Normans and he can also spy on Folcwine, add some meat to the bare bones of knowledge we have about him.'

'No, I think it's too risky. You'd be very exposed on your own.'

Alfweald nodded. 'I think Godwin's right. It would be poor policy to send you in without backup. However, I do like the sound of an information-gathering trip. Godwin, why don't you go with Edgar? I'm sure the two of you could fight your way out of most sticky situations, should the need arise.'

Godwin nodded. 'Yes, agreed. I'd be much happier with that.'

'It's settled, then. We should strike while the iron is hot, as Bjarn says. There will have been time by now for a messenger to have travelled back to Redford to enquire as to the whereabouts of the treasure waggon. With any luck the town will be abuzz with rumour and speculation. Tongues will be wagging freely. See if you can find a gathering place, preferably with ale. Ale always helps.'

Godwin and Edgar rose and walked back to where Folcwine was sitting miserably on his log.

'Good news, Folcwine!' called Edgar cheerfully. 'You and I are going back to Redford.'

'Oh!' he replied, a small smile cracking his face for the first time since Edgar had met him.

'And Godwin's coming with us!'

'Oh.'

Edgar and Godwin dressed in simple farmer's tunics, carrying only their seaxes on their belts. They took horses to within a mile of the settlement and walked the remainder of the way, leaving their horses tethered in a small clearing a couple of hundred yards from the road.

Thegn

It was dark as they entered Redford; the settlement seemed quiet, very few people were moving about, most having gone home for the night.

'Where do people congregate here, Folcwine?' asked Edgar.

'If there is to be any gathering, it is normally at the longhouse of Osci, the Thegn's estate manager. He leaves a couple of barrels of ale there and we can help ourselves. He's a good man, Osci.'

'Free ale? His scrip must be deeper than mine,' muttered Godwin.

'I think the Thegn shares the cost. It's always weak ale and we normally only take a cup or two each.'

'Where is the longhouse?'

'Along this road, on the right. It stands a little way from the other houses. It used to be Osci's house, but he built himself a new one about ten years ago, then he turned the old one into a communal hall.'

'Generous man.'

'Our Thegn has no sons. Osci wants to succeed him.'

They walked along the road and eventually came to a path on their right, leading to a longhouse. They followed Folcwine as he walked up the path and pulled open the door in the middle of the wall.

It was fairly well lit inside, with torches in sconces on the support pillars, and rows of cheap candles on the tables, giving off a thick, smoky, yellow light. Seven men were within. Four sitting together at one end of the long table and three at the other end.

Folcwine walked up to the group of four. One of them called out as he drew near.

'Folc! Where have you been?'

'Had some trouble with the cart. Had to leave it in a ditch halfway to Hildeston. Walked the ox home.'

'Want some help with it? I can't come tomorrow but the day after I'll be free.'

'Thanks, I'd be glad of the help,' replied Folcwine. Edgar noted that Folcwine had not paused for so much as a split second in his lying. This could either be very useful or very dangerous. He decided to err on the side of caution, and assume that the man was very dangerous.

'Who are these, then?' asked the man. 'Come on, get some ale, sit down.'

'These are two men I met on the road back, Edgar and Godwin. They've come for the market.'

'Welcome, Edgar and Godwin. Get yourselves some ale, don't be shy.'

The three men walked across to where two large barrels stood in a corner of the room. Folcwine collected three wooden cups and filled them with a ladle from the barrels. Edgar took a sip. Folcwine had been right. This was small beer, but fresh and free from the sourness that came to all ale if left too long.

They walked back to the table and sat down with the four men. As they did so, the door to the longhouse opened again, and Edgar was astonished to see Alaric, rolling in as if already in his cups, hanging from the arm of a pretty girl.

A cheer rose from the three men at the other end of the table. The girl smiled at them and led Alaric across to sit down with them. She collected some ale for both of them from the barrels and fell into animated discussions with the three men. The speed with which Alaric had found his cover and ingratiated himself into it left Edgar speechless. He looked at Godwin, who merely raised an eyebrow.

Thegn

Folcwine laughed. 'It looks like Aethelgifa has found another sucker!' he said to his friends. They all chuckled.

'She's well known, is she?' asked Edgar.

'Oh yes, matey!' chimed in one of the men, a greasy looking character with lank hair and shaving cuts. 'She'll have his purse off him before he knows it. Crafty girl is our Aethelgifa.'

Edgar was certain of one thing, and that was that young Aethelgifa was probably in for a very disappointing and unprofitable night.

Despite subtle promptings by Edgar and Godwin, it appeared that the four men had little knowledge or interest in the disposition of Norman soldiers in the region. Their conversation was filled with crops and livestock, and the prospects that the forthcoming market might provide. There was talk, however, of a new fortification being built by the Normans on the northern edge of the town. One of the men, Colbert, was complaining that workers from his farm were being rounded up every morning by Norman soldiers and forced to work on the construction site.

'Just seem to be digging a bloody great ditch,' he said. 'Maybe they're going to put a new hall inside it. Who knows?'

'Nah, they're building up a huge mound of earth inside the ditch,' replied one of his friends. 'They're going to put a fort on top of that, you mark my words.'

'They're forcing farm workers to build their fortifications?' interjected Godwin. 'Bastards!'

Edgar noted how Godwin escalated any anti-Norman sentiment that was expressed.

'Yeah, and they've made a tax demand four times higher than it was last year. They say the Thegn won't be able to pay it and he'll be kicked out by a new Norman thegn. Nothing's going to be the same from now on, I tell you. Nothing.'

They all muttered in agreement and took drinks from their cups. Colbert gathered his three friends' cups and went to the barrel to refill them.

'So how many soldiers do they have here?' asked Godwin.

Colbert's friend blew his cheeks out. He shook his head. 'I dunno,' he said, accepting a full cup of ale from Colbert. 'Seems like loads, but I reckon it's probably about a hundred. Most of them are shacked up at the old King's hunting lodge down the south road.'

'Well they would be there, wouldn't they?' sneered Colbert round his cup. 'That's where they're keeping the women.'

Edgar tensed and looked up sharply, but was stilled by Godwin's urgent hand on his arm.

'They got women?' asked Folcwine.

'Oh yeah,' said Colbert, gesticulating with his cup in the direction the king's hunting lodge lay. 'I saw 'em, couple of dozen of them, all being unloaded off a waggon and ushered in. One of them soldiers saw me watching and chased after me. I was only looking.'

'So you think these women are still in the king's lodge, then?' asked Godwin.

'Yeah, I think they will be. It was only about ten days since and I haven't seen any more waggons headed that way since then. And they have to go past my place, see, to get to the lodge.'

'Did you see the women well enough to describe them?' asked Edgar.

Thegn

'What? No. Women's women in't they? Use your 'magination.' said Colbert.

Godwin's fingers on Edgar's arm tightened. Edgar got the message and settled down.

'Are all the soldiers stationed at the lodge?' asked Godwin, casually.

'Oh, no. They're scattered all through the town. Nobody can move without explaining to at least half a dozen soldiers – none of 'em speak English – exactly what you're doing and where you're going. It's a bloody nightmare. I just hope it doesn't put too many people off coming to the market.'

'It's the same everywhere. People still need markets, I shouldn't worry too much about it if I were you,' said Edgar.

At that moment, the door flew open and a party of Normans strode in. A man in a rich red tunic came in first, followed by four armed men, hands ready on sword hilts, though the swords were not as yet drawn.

'Pay attention, all of you!' shouted the well-dressed man. His English was accented, but he was quite understandable.

'Today a valuable waggon has gone missing. It was travelling from my lord Baron de Barentin to the Regent, his Grace Bishop Odo in Londres. My lord de Barentin is most displeased with this. So much so that the Baron is offering a reward for any information regarding the whereabouts of the waggon and its contents. If anyone can tell his lordship what happened, where the material is, and who was responsible, the Baron will pay that man one pound in silver.'

There were gasps of astonishment from round the room. 'This information must lead to the recovery of the goods and also the punishment of those responsible. Conversely, anyone found to have withheld information relative to this matter will be executed without trial.'

The men in the room looked round at each other, a combination of greed and fear in their eyes.

'Anyone with such information should present himself to me at the king's lodge. Failure to recover the goods will result in serious repercussions for the people of Redford. That is all.'

He turned and strode back out of the door, followed by his guards.

He left a vacuum of silence behind him. Only after a few moments had elapsed did the conversation start up again, hesitantly and more subdued than it had been.

'Here, what about you, Folc?' asked Colbert. 'You were out south today weren't you? Didn't you see anything?'

Folcwine licked his lips and looked uncomfortable.

'You did, din't you?' insisted Colbert.

'Well, I might have seen a waggon go past when I was stuck in the ditch, but I didn't see nothing more.'

'Nothing?'

'Nothing.'

'Not even for a pound of silver? Just think what you could do with that!'

'Not even for ten pounds of silver!' exclaimed Folcwine. 'I can't report what I didn't see, can I?'

'Alright, alright. I was just asking. What do you reckon they were carrying?'

'More women,' chuckled Colbert's friend.

'More likely money,' said another, quietly. 'It'll be the Wildmen who've done it, you can be sure.'

Godwin stiffened slightly, but relaxed immediately.

'Wildmen?' he said. 'Who are they?'

'Bunch of renegades, I heard. They're trying to resist the Normans. Bloody lost cause already, I say. No good'll come of it. These Norman bleeders will kill you as soon as look at you. They'll just love to have this excuse to slaughter a few more innocents. I'm getting out of here until this has quietened down. If you've got any sense, you'll all do the same.'

'Where are you going to go?' asked Folcwine.

'Anywhere, I'll sleep under a bleeding bush rather than wait for one of those bastards to come and run me through.'

With that, he downed his ale and walked swiftly out of the longhouse.

'It's alright for him,' said Colbert. 'He doesn't have a farm to run and hungry mouths to feed. Some of us just can't up sticks like that.'

'Right,' said Folcwine, looking down the table as Alaric started retching noisily.

'Get out, get out!' the woman Aethelgifa was shouting, pushing him away from her.

Alaric got up and walked unsteadily to the door.

'Come on,' said Godwin. 'It's time we were getting to bed. Folcwine, you'll have to lead us there.'

'Right,' said Folcwine, draining his cup. '"Night, lads, see you later.'

The remaining men said goodnight and Edgar, Godwin and Folcwine left the longhouse. There was no sign of Alaric as they walked out of the door. Folcwine looked around and snorted. 'That little turd obviously can't hold his ale. He's probably rolled into a ditch somewhere. This way,' he indicated down the lane, presumably towards his home.

'We're not going with you,' said Godwin.

'What? How will I explain that?'

'You won't have to. Just go about your business. If anyone asks, you don't know where we went to, alright?'

'Alright.'

Edgar and Godwin turned away from Folcwine and headed back the way they had come. Once they were round a bend in the road, and Folcwine could no longer have seen them had he bothered to stay and watch, Alaric stepped out of the shadows beside them.

'Feeling better?' asked Godwin laconically.

'Much, thank you, sir,' replied Alaric, without any apparent trace of irony.

'I think we know where Godgifu is being held,' said Edgar.

'I think I do, too, my lord. There is talk of some women being held in Edward-king's former hunting lodge south of the town.'

'Our sources agree, then.' Edgar felt elated. This was the best news he had heard in a long time. Now, at last, he could think about her rescue.

'My sources also had information about the building of the castle in the town.'

'Yes?'

'It is to be of the motte and bailey type already common within Normandy. These castles have proved to be very difficult to assault. This is the Bastard's boot coming down on the necks of the English.'

'What can be done about it?' asked Edgar.

'Very little, I fear, sir. The guard contingent is too strong for anything but a full attack by a sizeable band of soldiers. Even then, that would simply delay the inevitable.'

'I see.'

Thegn

'There may be more that I can find out, sir. The woman with whom I was drinking in the longhouse appears to have been on intimate terms with several – many, even – of the garrison's soldiers, even with some of the higher-ups. She may be a useful, if unwitting, source of information, especially if she is adept at pillow-talk.'

Godwin grinned. 'Then maybe you should pump her for information, Alaric.'

'As you wish, sir,' replied Alaric, again without any trace of irony.

'Very well, Alaric, you return to your floozy while Edgar and I return to the Paddock. We'll expect you at first light.'

'Very good, sir,' said Alaric, dipping his head slightly. He turned on his heels and was gone into the shadows in an instant.

Godwin looked after him for a moment, unable to discern any sign of the little spy at all in the darkness. 'Either that man has no sense of humour, or he's incredibly dedicated to his duties.'

'Oh, he has a sense of humour, alright,' said Edgar. 'Come on, let's get back to the Paddock.'

Alaric walked silently back towards the longhouse. As he approached, his gait became more unsteady until he was walking the same way as he had been when he had staggered out of the drinking den earlier.

His footsteps became loud and clumsy, and he soon made out the light seeping from around the longhouse door. A shadow moved across it and he was instantly alert without changing his heavy footsteps at all.

'Is that you, Siggi?' A girl's voice called out in a hoarse whisper.

'It's only me!' he replied, far too loud. 'I feel a lot better now. Let's have some more ale!'

'Shh! Come on in, don't shout the place down like that.'

Alaric staggered into the girl's arms, nuzzling his mouth into the hair at the back of her neck.'

'Eew, get off!' she giggled, pushing him away ineffectually. 'You stink of ale!'

'Well, I've had some ale!' he exclaimed, no quieter than before. 'Actually, I've had it twice, once on the way down and then again on the way up!' He burst out into raucous laughter, let go of the girl and staggered backwards, doubled up with mirth.

'Shut up and come back in!' she hissed.

With the girl supporting him, Alaric pulled open the longhouse door and they went back inside.

Edgar woke at the break of dawn the following morning and stepped outside his tent to find Alaric preparing some porridge over a low fire.

'Good morning, Alaric. Eventful night?'

'Good morning, my lord. Most interesting. Our plan to gather intelligence appears to have worked most successfully.'

'What news?'

Alaric continued to stir the porridge as he spoke. 'My lovely lady appears to be on very favourable terms with several of the garrison's soldiers and two or three of the senior men. Their leader is Roger de Barentin, as we knew, and he has with him half a dozen lieutenants, one of whom, one Guillaume de Caen, appears to have gone missing. This had been causing some consternation with Baron de Barentin. There is some bad news there, though, I'm afraid.'

Thegn

'Oh, what's that?' asked Edgar, sitting down opposite Alaric.

'It would appear that your disposal of de Caen and his men was not as efficient as you had believed. One of them got away.'

'What? That can't be! We saw them all dead.'

'Not all, my lord. When you described your raid to me after the event, you told how your men swiftly dispatched two guards who were moving around the village.'

'That's right. They both had their throats cut. There's no way either of them survived.'

'No, they did not. The third guard did, though.'

'Third guard? We saw no third guard.'

'That is how he managed to escape, sir.'

'Shit.'

'Exactly. The man apparently discovered the bodies of his comrades while on his patrol and made his way back to the moot hall, where you had already completed your dealings with those within. The guard remained in the fields nearby and observed the executions of de Caen and his deputy. Your description is now known to the Baron, and I understand that he is to issue a proclamation declaring you a wanted murderer and outlaw.'

'I shouldn't have gone into the village last night,' said Edgar, 'I put everyone at risk. This changes everything. Soon I'll be able to go nowhere without being recognized.' He placed the flat of his hand against the ruined side of his face.

'No harm done this time, sir, but I think it would be as well to inform Lord Alfweald of these developments. It may well necessitate him changing his plans.'

'Yes. You're right. I have to report to him about last

night's jaunt anyway. We'll go to see him together straight away.'

Edgar found Alfweald sitting in his usual place at the circle of log seats that served as his council chamber. He quickly informed him of the events of the previous night, emphasising that the whereabouts of Godgifu had probably now been found.

'Sir, I must respectfully request that I now be allowed to lead a party to release my wife and all the other unfortunate women from their imprisonment. I should be able to effect a rescue using only my own housecarls, subject to a greater knowledge of the lodge and its guards.

'I must inform you of one more thing before you make your decision. Last night, Alaric here made a very significant discovery. It seems that my men and I were not as comprehensive in our disposal of Guillaume de Caen and his men as we had thought. It would seem that one of them got away and has now given my description, conspicuous as I am, to de Barentin.'

Alfweald received the disturbing news calmly and stoically.

'You're right in your appraisal, Edgar. This does change everything, but not necessarily as much as you fear. Your personal risks have increased significantly, I will not dispute that, but our location is still secure, and as long as you keep out of actions where you may be recognised, then I see no reason why you cannot continue to work with us. Your helmet renders you just as anonymous as the rest of us, so you can still fight with no problem. If you are captured, though, your life may well turn very unpleasant.'

'No capture,' said Edgar with vehemence.

Thegn

'No capture for any of us,' agreed Alfweald. 'In that, too, your position remains unchanged. Thank you for bringing this matter to my attention so quickly, and thank you, Alaric, for an excellent piece of intelligence gathering.'

Alaric bowed slightly at the compliment.

'This does mean that any attempt to rescue your wife can only be carried out by you and your men. Then if – may God forbid it – you are captured, there will be nothing to link you to the Wildmen. It will appear that you are working simply under your own personal motivation.

'Tell me, Alaric, do you think you could get close to the lodge and ascertain the strength of the garrison there, and what time of day they are at their weakest?'

'I'm sure I could, my lord. After all, I will probably be known by some of de Barentin's deputies as a hireling of de Caen. They may even be glad to see me. However, I will strive to remain unseen. The less contact I have with individuals then the less chance there is of my making a mistake in what I say. When would you like me to return to the town?'

'As soon as you've eaten. I would have you go on your own. There will be nobody to watch your back.'

'That's how I normally work, my lord.'

'Good man. We will look for you tomorrow at dawn. Edgar, subject to Alaric's report, I will approve your rescue attempt. Thank you, gentlemen, that will be all for now.'

Edgar and Alaric bowed slightly and walked away from Alfweald, who sat down, rubbing at his beard, deep in thought.

14

Darkest Hour

Edgar woke well before the sun rose. He sat up on the rough pallet on which he had slept the night before. He felt his heart pounding in his chest. It had been this that had woken him up. Today was the day. This was when all his plans finally came to fruition or failed completely. If all went well, then before this day was finished, he would have his beloved Godgifu restored to him. He lay back on the pallet, willing his heart to slow and be calm. He stared up at the beams across the tops of the walls, and the gappy straw that constituted the roof of the old abandoned farmhouse. At least it hadn't rained last night.

He glanced to his left and right, where his comrades lay silently or quietly snoring. He felt proud of them. They had performed superbly at every stage of their exile. They had followed him unswervingly, even when his decisions had perhaps not been all that they could have been.

There was a small movement from across the room. He

glanced that way and noticed that Alaric was standing by the far wall, looking through a hole in the wattle and daub, out at the dark early morning.

Edgar got up and walked across to him.

'Anything moving?' he whispered.

'No. It's as still as it should be.'

'Any idea how long until sunrise?'

'Soon. Maybe an hour.'

It was cold in the draughty old farmhouse. The walls were not terribly secure, and Edgar was glad that he would not have to spend another night in there. It had served its purpose well, though, less than two miles from where de Barentin was supervising the raising of a great mound with outer defences. Once the mound was hard packed and secure, he would order the building of a wooden keep on top of it, a symbol of the Norman's heel grinding into the English landscape.

Behind him, Edgar heard the stirrings of a man awakening. It was Eric. He sat up, rubbing his eyes.

'Is it time?' he said.

'Nearly. It might be as well to wake the others now.'

Eric stretched his arms wide and yawned hugely.

'Right,' he said. He leaned over and shook Guthrum by the shoulder. Guthrum woke immediately.

'I'm awake. Stop prodding me, whippersnapper,' he grumbled.

'It's time,' said Eric, 'I know you old men need your sleep, but maybe you can have a nap later.'

Guthrum rolled over and punched Eric in the shoulder. The exchange had woken the other light-sleeping warriors, and the room filled with the sounds of stretching, yawning and cracking knuckles.

They could not afford to light a fire, lest it be noticed and reported, so they ate a breakfast of nuts and berries with some bread that they had brought with them from the Paddock. Sebbi passed round canteens of water and they all drank their fill.

By the time the breakfast had been eaten, a little grey light was beginning to show through the holes in the roof.

The men all pulled on their peasant-smocks, covering completely their special long seaxes. A normal seax was not long enough for combat, and a sword could not be effectively covered, so the men carried their fighting seaxes. Bjarn the blacksmith had been impressed with them and had made several dozen of them over the past few months for the Wildmen.

The peasant-smocks were tattered and dirty, but with cleverly contrived tears which would allow the wearer quick access to his long seax hidden beneath.

The men stood in a circle, breath steaming from their mouths and noses in the chill pre-dawn air.

'Before we go, is there anything that anyone wishes to ask? Anything at all?' Edgar looked around at each face in the circle of his fellows. All looked certain and resolute.

'Very well. I want you to know that I am very proud of all of you. You have been the finest carls a thegn could ever wish for. Whatever happens today, that will remain true.'

The carls muttered their thanks. 'Right, let's go then,' said Edgar.

They filed out of the farmhouse, leaving their extra supplies in the back of the room. They would return for them later, or if they could not, it would not matter.

The dull grey light was just enough to see the path from the house to the road into Redford. They walked along it in

Thegn

single file, treading as quietly as they could. The walk to Redford was level and easy. They saw nobody else as they travelled, but over to their left, they saw a small light appear, as if someone had opened the door to a lit room, but it was too far away to be certain what it was.

A cock crew as they arrived at Redford. They split up and walked round the backs of the shabby wattle-and-daub buildings, walking round the sides of those buildings to mingle with the weary-looking crowd of unwilling labourers forced to work for the Normans. Edgar saw six Norman soldiers, pushing at the labourers as they shuffled past, an unnecessary show of force. One of them approached Edgar, and he felt very conscious of the long seax hanging from his left hip. He pressed his arm against it to prevent any sign of it under his tunic. The soldier shoved him in the back as he passed. Edgar kept his eyes demurely to the ground, stumbling slightly as he recovered from the shove. He knew how the sight would have incensed his men. In the normal course of events, a carl would never see his thegn be treated so without immediate retaliatory action. He prayed that they would all keep to their designated roles. He glanced surreptitiously from side to side, but there was no sign of anyone coming to his aid or to retaliate. Good. His trust in his men was well placed, as he knew it had been.

The labour gang trudged to the top end of the little town, where, on a small promontory, a huge ditch was being dug, the excavated soil being thrown into the inside of the ditch to form the great mound on which the wooden keep would stand in arrogant vigilance.

There was a large pile of equipment by the side of the road; picks, shovels and wheelbarrows. Edgar picked up a spade and walked on towards the great ditch. He could see that it was not yet a complete ring. There were three quite wide gaps of undisturbed earth, breaking the ditch. One of them was marked with wooden stakes, presumably to indicated that this gap was to be kept open for the transport of materials for the keep.

The soldiers on guard – Edgar saw that there were about thirty of them – were pointing and gesticulating to the labourers. They shouted, too, but he could make no sense of their barbarous tongue.

As if at random, Edgar's men gathered around him and they all set to work, digging the ditch in one of the gaps that had not yet been dug. The ground was hard and claggy, difficult to dig, and Edgar noticed that many of the labourers were not breaking their backs to do the Normans' will. The day was cold, but there was no wind and the sun shone intermittently and soon all the labourers were sweating with the effort, even those who weren't putting much in. As midday approached, the Normans started indicating groups of workers who should return to their homes for food. Edgar's group, which had scattered slightly, began to draw together again, and about an hour after the first group had been released, a soldier pointed at them, shouting unintelligibly at them. Edgar stood up from his digging and looked at him. The soldier opened his mouth and pointed at it.

'He wants us to go and eat, lads, come on.'

Edgar climbed out of the ditch he and his fellows had dug and dropped the shovel down by the side of the ditch. Slowly, the seven men made their way back towards the centre of town. At the opposite end of the town to where the building work was taking place stood the old King's hunting lodge, set back from the main road by a few hundred yards.

'I counted thirty-three guards up there,' said Guthrum, quietly as they walked.

'Six more in the town, they might still be there,' added Hunwald.

'We can handle the six, but not thirty-three. What we need to know is how many of them there are at the hunting lodge. Is de Barentin there?'

'I've been talking with some of the men who've been here since the Normans arrived. They say that they've only seen the big boss a couple of times. They think he left the lodge sometime last week and hasn't returned yet,' said Sebbi.

'What of his hostages?' asked Edgar.

'Nobody knows. There are rumours that there are some people being held against their will at the lodge, but it's all being kept very quiet.'

'All we can do is look.'

They stopped at the cobbled road that led to the lodge, which was not visible from the road as it was nestled in a small grove of trees. Edgar had been told by the Wildmen that it was possible to approach the lodge quite unseen through those trees. This was their biggest advantage.

They looked around them, but nobody was moving. The men who should be working in the fields had all been conscripted into building the Norman fortification, and the women and children were being kept well out of sight.

The seven men inconspicuously slipped into the woods and made their way with extreme caution towards the hunting lodge. They crouched down in the tree-line just behind the lodge.

'It all looks very quiet,' said Sebbi.

'Spread out, let's make sure that we see whatever there is to be seen.'

They crept cautiously around the lodge until they surrounded it and every aspect could be observed. After a few minutes, they crept back to where Edgar had remained.

'One sentry on the front door, and there is definitely a fire lit within the building,' said Hunwald. Alaric's intelligence had been good. The guarding of the lodge was at its weakest around midday.

'Can we take the sentry?' asked Edgar.

'Yes, I would say so. He doesn't look very alert. He didn't see any of us.'

'Good. I think we may just have to trust to luck and simply go in. Osfrid, Eric, see to the guard.'

Eric and Osfrid slipped silently towards the rear of the lodge. They flattened themselves against the side of the building and Eric threw a small stone into the trees. They heard the sound of footsteps, and the guard walked straight out towards the source of the noise. Osfrid stepped up silently behind him and with the cruel pommel of his seax delivered a swift, fatal blow to the back of his neck. Osfrid caught him as he fell and between them, they dragged the guard back to the side of the lodge. The two men quickly stripped the guard of his arms and armour, and Eric put them on and returned to the guard post.

Alaric, as had been arranged, made his way back along the path towards the road. He would stand guard there, out of sight, and give a Wildman bird-call if any soldiers were seen returning to the lodge.

Osfrid turned back towards the trees behind the lodge and gave a signal. Immediately the remaining five men ran out from their cover and joined him. Edgar peered cautiously round the corner of the building, to where Eric now stood, dressed in the Norman mail. Eric nodded at him, and he led the carls round to the front of the lodge, all with their long seaxes now drawn.

'Alright Eric, in you go,' said Edgar, nodding at the lodge door.

Eric cautiously tried the door. It was unlocked. He swung the door right open and stepped inside. The building was impressive. The door opened into a great hall, in the centre of which was a large fire, being stoked by an old man. Eric strode across to the old man and grabbed him before he could make a noise.

'What do you want?' squeaked the old man.

'You are English?' asked Eric, his arm tightening around the man's throat.

'Yes, I'm the lodge-keeper.'

'Where are the Normans?'

'Gone. Some are at the building site but most have headed north with their Baron,' he gurgled. 'You're choking me!'

'Be quiet!' hissed Eric. He turned slightly and beckoned to Edgar, who was peering through the open door. All the men came into the lodge, Sebbi closing the door behind them.

'He says there are no Normans here,' said Eric.

Edgar confronted the man, still choking slightly as Eric's arm remained tight around his neck.

'Prisoners,' said Edgar. 'Where are the prisoners?'

'Prisoners?' stammered the man.

'The women.'

'Ah, the women. Yes. They're through here. I have to keep them locked up. I have to, or they will kill me.'

'Well now if you don't unlock them, *I* will kill you,' snarled Edgar.

'I'll have to get the keys. Let me go.'

Eric looked at Edgar, who nodded his consent. The man staggered away from Eric's grip and went over to a heavily studded wooden chest which sat against the hall wall. He opened the box and drew out a large iron ring on which were hung several big keys.

'This way,' he said, and walked out of a side door deeper into the building. They emerged into a short corridor, from which several doors opened. At the end of the corridor was a particularly strong looking door.

'This was old Edward-king's strong-room,' said the old man, picking through the keys on the ring. Selecting one, he bent over and inserted it into the iron lock. The lock turned with a heavy clank, and the lodge-keeper pushed the door open. There was a rush of stale air from within. The room was windowless and ventilation was obviously very poor. Huddled against the far wall was a group of six women, blinking as the light poured in from the open door. They were dirty and underfed.

Edgar rushed into the room. 'Gifu? Gifu!'

He looked at the six women but did not see Godgifu amongst them. He searched the rest of the room, but there was nowhere anyone could hide or be out of sight. He turned to the women. 'Where is Godgifu? Was she with you?'

The women drew back even further into the wall and several of them whimpered in fear. One held her hand out towards Edgar.

'Sir?' she said, asking for his hand.

Edgar took it and lifted her gently to her feet. She was

wearing a gown that had evidently been opulent but was now ripped and stained. She was clearly a lady of substance. She steadied herself against Edgar's arm. She looked up and into Edgar's worried eyes.

'Sir, I am called Eadith, my father is Thegn in Beeston. There was a woman called Godgifu with the captured women when I was taken. Long dark brown hair and a small crucifix at her throat.'

Edgar nodded, 'That sounds like Gifu, she's my wife.'

'Then I am very sorry, sir,' the woman lowered her eyes from Edgar's.

'What? What is it?'

'She was not treated kindly, sir, none of us were. She could not bear it. She had a little bag which was fastened to her belt, here?' she placed the palm of her hand just above and behind her right hip.

'Yes, she carries a supply of herbs. She's a healer.'

'It seems she carried other things too. One night, about six weeks ago, she took some berries from her bag. I watched her. She stared at them for a long time, then ate them. By the following morning, she was dead. I am sorry, sir.'

The silence following her words roared thunderously in Edgar's ears. He felt himself slipping backwards from the world. The edges of his vision started closing in until he could see only a tiny circle in front of him.

He neither saw nor heard Eric and Guthrum rushing into the room to catch him as he started to fall. He was unaware of them carrying him out of that stinking prison and laying him on the table in the main hall.

As Edgar lay in his faint, Sebbi, Hunwald and Osfrid brought the women out of their prison. They ordered the miserable lodge-keeper to bring food and drink for them and sat them down in the great hall to eat their fill.

Edgar came round after a few minutes. He lay on the table and his eyes opened. He stared up at the roof beams. He felt unable to speak, aware only of the huge chasm that had opened up in his life. He was empty and unaware of anything except a vast ocean of limitless pain.

'Edgar,' a voice from far away called. He ignored it, it meant nothing to him.

'Edgar,' a gentle shaking of his shoulder. It did not feel like his shoulder. He felt like he was detached from his body.

'Sit up, Edgar,' the voice was more insistent now, and his eyes flicked from the roof beams to the originator of the voice. It was Guthrum, leaning over him with a look of great worry and concern.

Before Edgar's eyes, a vision of his grandfather's kindly face appeared.

'Listen to Guthrum,' his grandfather said from out of Edgar's memory. 'Trust him.'

'Sit up, lad,' insisted Guthrum. He pushed his hand under Edgar's back and began lifting. Edgar cooperated and sat up, his legs dangling off the edge of the table.

'Drink,' came the short command. A cup was pressed to his lips and he felt the wine as it entered his mouth. He swallowed, feeling the warmth of the liquid working its way down his throat.

'I'm so sorry, lad,' said Guthrum, as gently as his gruff voice would allow.

The other housecarls had kept their distance, respecting Edgar in his grief, but now Hunwald, who had been keeping watch at the door, hurried over.

'Guthrum,' he said urgently. 'There are six soldiers

Thegn

walking towards the lodge. They'll be here soon.'

'Get the women out of sight. Eric, get out there and look like a sentry. The rest of you, flat against this wall behind the door. Edgar, get up. Come on lad, we don't have time for this now.'

Edgar focused on Guthrum's face. The words penetrated slowly, but he did as he had been bidden. Sebbi hurried the women out of the great hall and strode back across the hall to join the other carls against the far wall. Guthrum virtually dragged Edgar across the hall, and just as they reached the far wall, they heard one of the approaching Normans call out a greeting to Eric in their coarse language. Eric made a non-committal grunt and raised his hand in greeting. The soldiers were much nearer now. One of them spoke to Eric. From the cadence of his voice, Eric guessed that it must be a question. Eric shrugged and walked through the door into the great hall.

There were confused mutterings amongst the soldiers, and as a group they followed Eric into the hall. As soon as they were inside, Osfrid pushed the door shut and it slammed behind them. They turned in surprise and were met with the sight of five peasants with surprisingly long knives advancing towards them. Before they had chance to react, Eric had drawn his Norman sword and killed one of them. Most of the rest died even before they had drawn their swords, so total was the advantage of surprise.

The lodge-keeper cowered in a corner, his arms over his head. He started wailing, 'They will kill me, they will surely kill me!'

Guthrum grabbed him by his tunic and dragged him across to the door through which the Normans had just come in. He opened the door and threw the wretch through it.

'You'd better run then, you useless piece of shit!' Guthrum placed his boot in the small of the man's back and shoved him so hard that he fell forward into the dirt. He quickly scrambled to his feet, and with one last look back at the hunting lodge, he ran off towards the road.

'Hunwald, get the women back, we have to get them out of here. The rest of you, burn this place to the ground,' said Guthrum.

The women were taken outside and led into the woods at the back of the lodge.

Guthrum held Edgar by the upper arm and steered him out of the lodge.

'Hurry,' said Guthrum to everyone. 'It won't take long before the smoke attracts the attention of the guards in the town and up at the building site. We have to be well clear of here by then.'

The carls helped the women, who were weak and close to exhaustion. They staggered through the woods, leaving as little trail as possible, though it was difficult with six stumbling women who were untrained in the arts of woodcraft.

To nobody's great surprise, Alaric had beaten them into the woods, having read the situation with uncanny accuracy. 'No sign of any Normans yet,' he whispered as they moved through the woods. 'But may I recommend haste?'

They staggered as quickly as they could through the woodland, the women stumbling from lack of food and their cumbersome skirts. Soon they reached the abandoned farmhouse that they had stayed at the night before. Guthrum turned round and saw that the smoke from the burning lodge was just beginning to curl above the tree-line

Thegn

behind him.

'We can't stay here. The fire will already have been noticed by now. Quick, grab the gear and go.'

With the bundles of belongings now tied around their shoulders, the carls hurried on through the woods. They needed to get to as remote a spot as possible by nightfall. The Normans could not pursue them after the fall of dark, so they could rest for a few hours before continuing their flight before dawn.

Two miles further into the woods one of the women collapsed, completely exhausted. Guthrum stopped. 'Eric, take Edgar and keep going. I'll stay here until she's fit to walk again. Leave the usual signs.'

Eric nodded and took hold of Edgar's arm. They carried on, and Guthrum sat down next to the shattered woman, who was sitting on the ground with her face in her hands, sobbing gently.

'It's alright,' said Guthrum gently. 'I'm sure we've come far enough now.'

He tentatively held out his hand and placed it between the woman's sob-racked shoulders, rubbing in a circular motion.

'My name's Guthrum,' he said. 'What's yours?'

She sniffled noisily. 'They call me Willa,' she said. Wet streaks ran through the dirt on her face.

'Well, Willa, we need to get as hidden as possible, just in case the Normans do come after us, alright?'

She nodded and sniffled again.

'We also need to be completely quiet, yes?'

She nodded again and took Guthrum's hand as he stood up.

15

Attack

All the way back from Redford, Edgar remained silent and uncommunicative. His housecarls led him forcibly through tangled brush and dense thickets, all the way back to the Paddock, where he sat down on a log bench and stared at the ground, unresponsive to any of their attempts at communication. Fortunately, there had been no incidents on the way back, and no Norman soldiers had been seen. Either they had not responded quickly enough to the burning lodge, or they simply had no idea which way the perpetrators had fled. In either event, the raiding party made its way back to the Paddock unmolested.

A couple of hours after their return, Alfweald walked over to Edgar and thrust a cup of mead at him. When he made no move to take it, or even look at it, Alfweald took Edgar's chin in his hand, tilted his head back so he was looking directly at him, and forced the cup into his hand.

'Drink this, now,' he commanded.

Edgar took the cup but made no move to drink its contents.

'I said now, Edgar. I'm not asking.'

Reluctantly, Edgar brought the cup to his lips and took a sip. Then another.

'The sweetness will do you good. It numbs the shock a little,' said Alfweald.

Edgar took a deeper draught, still staring at the ground. Alfweald sighed and strode away.

He met Guthrum coming in the other direction. 'I've given him some mead. It should help to reduce the shock a little, but he has to come out of it, Guthrum. We can't afford to have unproductive members of our group, especially not leaders.'

'No sir,' replied Guthrum. 'I have some news that might lift him a little. This woman here,' he indicated Willa, who was clinging to his arm like a lost child, 'says she knew Gifu when they were in captivity. She has a pretty tale to tell.'

Alfweald grunted. 'Anything you can do to snap him out of it would be a help. Carry on.'

He strode away and Guthrum looked down at Willa. 'Come on, then,' he said, and led her towards the immobile figure of Edgar.

'Edgar,' said Guthrum loudly.

Edgar looked into his cup and drained the last of its contents.

'Edgar,' said Guthrum again. He took the empty cup from Edgar's hand and indicated Willa. 'This is Willa. She knew Gifu. She has something to tell you.'

Edgar looked up, as if seeing Guthrum and Willa for the first time.

'Sit, Willa,' Guthrum indicated to Willa that she should

sit next to Edgar on the log. She sat down demurely.

'This is Thegn Edgar, Gifu's husband. I want you to tell him what you told me as we walked through the forest. Yes?'

Willa nodded.

'Good. I'm going to fetch more mead.' He walked away and Willa looked at the ground, unsure of how to start.

'I… I was held captive with your wife, my lord. I cannot say that I knew her well, or ever spoke much to her, but I can tell you of her last days if it would please you.'

Edgar turned to look at her. His eyes were filled with anguish, and she felt a great sorrow swelling within her. Edgar did not speak, but nodded shallowly.

'Your wife was skilled in herbs and healing, was she not?'

Edgar nodded again.

'When we were on the road, we were kept in a covered waggon, but a couple of times a day, we were let out for calls of nature. I first noticed your wife at these times. She kept herself away from the other women, she always seemed to walk near to bushes, and I often saw her picking berries from them, or stooping to pick something from the grass. I didn't realise until later what she was doing.'

She paused as Guthrum returned with a jug of mead and three cups. He filled each one and handed them out. Willa took a drink from hers before proceeding. Guthrum sat cross-legged on the ground in front of them.

'When we first arrived at the lodge – they said it had belonged to old Edward-king – the room you found us in was for some reason not ready. It had to be emptied.'

'It was a strong room,' interrupted Guthrum. 'They were probably emptying it of all the valuables to be sent back to the Bastard's brother in Lundenburg.'

'I don't know,' continued Willa. 'All I know is that for the first two days we were locked in the kitchen. I saw the lady Godgifu standing close to the cooking pots, but I didn't see what she was doing. I can only work it out now. She did something with the pots, or with the water, or something. Like I say, I never saw what. I didn't pay that close attention to her, to be honest. I was wrapped up in my own fears and sorrows.' She broke off and stared into the distance for a moment before taking a long drink of her mead.

Without being asked, Guthrum refilled her cup.

'Anyway, whatever it was she did, everyone who ate there that night was very sick the following morning. We had not been fed, so it was alright for us. We could hear many people groaning and puking. It was only afterwards that I worked out that it had been the lady Godgifu's doing. Thinking about it now, I think she must have done something to one of the large water pitchers, too. The night before, she had stood by the water containers and at one point she shook her head at one of the women who went for a drink. "Not that one," she said.

The following morning, "that one" went out with the others to soothe the puking men. It only got worse. We were told nothing, but I think that a couple of them died.'

She looked at Edgar, placing her hand tentatively on his upper arm. 'So you see, my lord. She did not go on her own. She took some of them with her.'

Edgar took hold of the hand. He squeezed it and turned to look at her. 'Thank you, Willa. That does help. It really does.'

He held out his cup and Guthrum filled it with mead. They sat in silence and drank.

Late in the afternoon of that same day, the peace of the Paddock was shattered by the arrival of two scouts. Alfweald called all his lieutenants to attend him, and the two scouts began their breathless story. A large party of Norman soldiers had been sighted leaving Redford and heading towards the forest. The story being muttered around the marketplace was that Roger de Barentin had returned that morning and had finally snapped at the repeated raids in what he saw as his territory. He was striking back at the Wildmen. The soldiers were still at least ten miles away, and would soon be camping for the night, but there was no doubt that this was the most serious threat to the Paddock's security that it had yet faced. Alfweald ordered all guard posts throughout the forest to be doubled, and for extra fighters to be battle-ready in hideouts near to the guard stations.

He issued further orders that all men were to sleep dressed in mail and green over-tunics and that their shields, swords, axes and helmets be with them at all times. Tomorrow at dawn, all fires would be extinguished and a regime of total silence was to be implemented. There was little fear that the Paddock itself would be discovered, but every precaution must be taken. Women were sent out to collect as much water as possible. There was no supply of water within the Paddock, it all had to be collected from two nearby streams. In a siege situation or if an extended period of hiding within the Paddock was necessary, then as much water as possible had to be brought within the Paddock beforehand.

Foraging parties were sent out to gather as much foodstuff as they could. Snares were set close to the

Thegn

Paddock, and wild food stockpiled.

Alfweald approached Guthrum, who was sitting with Edgar's other carls. Edgar himself sat apart from them, still staring towards a distant horizon that only he could see, occasionally speaking with Willa, and absent-mindedly rubbing his fingertips over the ruined side of his face. Willa had stayed with him and brought him food and drink as needed.

'Guthrum, a word,' said Alfweald.

Guthrum rose and followed Alfweald a few yards away from the other carls where they could speak without danger of being overheard.

'How is Edgar?'

'He grieves deeply, my lord, but I think he will recover.'

'This is important. I need a forward captain to organize the guard sections in the forest. I would like that to be Edgar. Do you think he is capable?'

'I hope so, my lord.'

'Hope is not good enough Guthrum. I need your honest and truthful opinion. Can he handle a command at this time?'

'I think it would probably be best for him, sir, and yes, I believe that he would be able to cope. He will be keen for revenge, and yet he is intelligent enough to keep those urges tight and controlled, so as not to endanger himself or others.'

'Good, good. And you will be with him at all times. On that, I insist.'

'I'll make sure it is so, my lord.'

'Good man. I'm relying on Edgar, and on you.'

Alfweald walked off towards his lieutenants. He would

get one of them to approach Edgar. It would not look good for him to do it himself after so publicly speaking with Guthrum. A leader's position within a warrior society was a fragile thing, and it would undermine the men's confidence in Edgar if Alfweald had been seen to confer publicly with Edgar's underling before approaching the man himself.

Guthrum watched as six of Alfweald's lieutenants walked away from their group in different directions. Sure enough, one walked up to Edgar, who looked up as the broad, long-haired lieutenant approached him. Edgar stood and nodded as the lieutenant passed on Alfweald's instructions.

The lieutenant walked away, and Edgar called over to his carls. Guthrum joined them as they gathered around him. He watched the grim faces of his colleagues. Eric had aged noticeably since they had left Rapendun, Guthrum thought. He no longer looked the stripling lad, despite Guthrum still thinking of him as such.

Sebbi, Osfrid and Hunwald, men he now trusted as much as any men he had ever known, listened gravely to Edgar as he informed them of their new mission. Halfdene, younger by far, the same age as Edgar in fact, still looked untroubled by events, his mop of curly light brown hair and his thin moustache still giving the impression of late boyhood. Yet Guthrum knew that within his chest beat the heart of a time-served fighter, and one day, a fine leader.

Edgar finished addressing them, and they turned to leave, gathering their weapons and provisions for the days ahead.

'Guthrum,' Edgar began. He paused and looked at Guthrum, who politely kept silent. Quietly, Edgar added 'You stay with me, Guthrum.'

'As you wish, my lord,' replied Guthrum, glad to his heart that Edgar had understood the situation. He had not seen Edgar watching Alfweald and him in conference, but he knew that Edgar must have seen and drawn the correct conclusion.

'We will gather all our belongings and provisions now, that we will be ready to leave the Paddock at dawn. We will travel on foot, and as lightly as we can. I wish to visit all the guard stations as quickly as possible tomorrow. We need to ensure that all the men are following the same rules.'

'Very good, my lord.'

As darkness fell, Edgar and his six carls wrapped themselves in animal skins and settled down round a low fire. It would die long before dawn, when one of the Wildmen would rouse them from their sleep. Willa curled up in a skin close to Edgar. Guthrum remained awake for some time after the rest had fallen asleep. His eyes fixed on the glowing embers in the fire. A small branch glowed red, its surface looking like the scaled skin of some reptile from Hell. A slight breeze blew across the Paddock, and the branch glowed brighter, orange and yellow, and then faded back to red as the breeze fell.

Guthrum's thoughts flew back to happier days at Rapendun. Thegn Wulfmaer's face appeared before his mind's eye, smiling and kind. He saw Edgar as a boy, practising with a wooden sword, his mouth tight with concentration. Then he saw Edgar just a few months ago, sharing a private joke with Godgifu. She had laughed and clutched Edgar's forearm with both her hands. He had laughed with her. Guthrum smiled slightly at his daydream. His heart felt heavy when he thought of Edgar's loss. His thoughts went back again to their first meeting with Godgifu after the battle at Stanford, when Edgar lay, his head a mass of torn flesh, blood and bone. Who could have imagined that the ultimate sorrow from that terrible battle would happen here, nearly a year after the battle, in circumstances that were completely unthinkable then? The world then had been a different place, a secure place, full of certainties and, mostly, peace. Now danger replaced security, war replaced peace, uncertainty replaced certainty. Guthrum realised that their world, and the world of everyone in the kingdom, was now changed forever. Even if the resistance pockets did eventually unite and force the cursed Normans from these shores, nothing would ever be the same again. Guthrum closed his eyes. There was no purpose in wishing for what could not be. The past was gone, the future was not yet here. All that mattered right at this moment was that he sleep. And so, he did.

Before the stars had faded the following morning, Edgar and his carls set out from the Paddock. The night had been cold, though the first frost had not yet fallen. A waning gibbous moon stood high and bright in the south, and to the south-east, the brilliant Morning Star blazed. Edgar looked at the star and recalled the words of a travelling monk who had once stayed with them at Rapendun. He had pointed to the Evening Star and asked if Edgar, still only a boy, had noticed that you could only see the Evening Star in the evening when you could not see the Morning Star in the morning, and vice versa. Edgar had admitted that, in fact, he had never noticed.

'Well, there's a lesson for you, young master. There are things happening around you in plain sight that you never notice.'

'Why can we only see one at a time?' Edgar had asked.

'When the Evening Star moves close to the Sun and gets lost in its glare,' replied the monk, 'that is the time to start looking for the Morning Star. The Morning Star grows brighter and brighter and further from the Sun until it rises very early in the morning. Then it begins to move back towards the Sun until it is again lost in its glare. Then we can start looking for the Evening Star once again. The Evening Star does exactly the same as the Morning Star, moving further from the Sun each evening until it reaches a maximum distance, at which point it sets many hours after the Sun, then it, too, begins to move back towards the Sun. Do you see?'

Inspiration had hit Edgar suddenly.

'There is only one star! The Evening Star and the Morning Star are the same star!'

'Excellent! Excellent thinking young master. The Evening Star and the Morning Star are one and the same. It is one of the Wandering Stars, that move about against the background of the more fixed stars. The Romans gave this star the name of their goddess of love – Venus.'

The enthusiasm in the monk's voice echoed in Edgar's memory. Venus, the goddess of love. There she stood, high and brilliant above the canopy of trees ahead of him. Love. Godgifu. His mind made a connection at that point that was to last the rest of his life. For him, forever more, the brilliant Venus would represent Godgifu. Somehow, she was still here, still visible to him, but in altered form. He smiled up at the dazzling star. It twinkled back in delight.

As they approached the first guard station, Edgar gave a low whistle, and two sentries immediately stepped out from hiding. They were letting off the tension from their bows. They had been just moments from firing their arrows, and Edgar had neither seen nor heard them. He needed to pay closer attention to what he was doing. No more daydreaming. Yet the incident also pleased him. The guards were clearly well prepared and alert.

Edgar identified himself to the sentries, one of whom then made a 'tuwit!' noise like a brown owl. At the signal, six further guards slipped out of their hiding places in a fifty-yard circle around the main sentry post. Edgar informed them that he was now their first-line captain, under the direct authority of Alfweald, and that he and his men would be passing between the guard stations at irregular intervals until the Normans had either given up and returned to Redford or they had been defeated and lay dead on the forest floor. The men nodded in approval. Edgar stressed the necessity for silence, even when attacking the Normans. It was likely that the Normans would split up into several hunting groups. If a group were to be eliminated, it was vital that the other groups within earshot should not know of their comrades' demise.

'Pits already dug,' grunted one of the outlying guards. 'Shallow graves fit for Norman dogs. Well hidden. Never be found.'

'Good, excellent work. If you need to contact me at any time, the sign is two jackdaw calls followed by three more, got it?'

A sentry made the call, and again Edgar found it uncanny how natural the call sounded.

'Just like that. Now, back to your posts. You will be relieved in four hours.'

The guards dissolved into the gloomy morning light and

were instantly silent. Edgar felt his confidence in the Paddock's defences growing stronger.

Edgar and his men walked cautiously from sentry post to sentry post. Alfweald had deployed almost eighty men to the first-line defences of the Paddock. Edgar was once again impressed with the Wildmen's ability to remain totally silent and hidden for long periods. He began to wonder if some, maybe many, of these men had been outlaws long before the Norman invasion. They certainly seemed to have far more experience and skill than one might expect from a group of men who had been outlaws for barely a year. He also reflected that it did not matter. Everyone here was an outlaw now. The Norman boot had kicked many landowners off their land, and there seemed little alternative than to adopt the life of an outlaw. How his grandfather would have despaired. Yet he also knew that Wulfmaer would have strongly approved of Edgar's actions and of his decision to stay with the Wildmen. 'If something is worth fighting for then fight for it with all your might, until your very last breath,' he had said to Edgar on many occasions. He had also admonished Edgar from time to time because of his inability to recognize what was truly worth fighting for, and what was just childish peevishness. Edgar's hand dropped to the handle of his Ulfberht sword, feeling the large garnet that adorned the end of the pommel. It was a tangible link with his grandfather, and he imagined that he could feel the old man's strength and resolution made solid in the handle of the weapon.

A light tap on the back from Guthrum brought Edgar back from his wool-gathering. As his focus was brought back to the present time and place, he heard it. Amongst the cacophony of the birds' dawn chorus, one voice registered with Edgar. It was the bird-call that indicated that the Normans had been sighted.

Edgar glanced round at his carls, who all strained and then pointed in the direction which they thought the call came from. The call was distant and clearly from the east. Each call was followed by an identifying chirrup. This ensured that whoever heard the call also knew who had made it. The identifier confirmed the caller as the sentry farthest east. The carls looked expectantly at Edgar. Edgar turned to Hunwald, who of all of them had proved most proficient in the Wildmen's calling technique.

'Send "Hold fast. Captain",' ordered Edgar.

Hunwald turned east and called a two-tone call followed by a three-note chirrup. The call blended in with the dawn chorus so perfectly that unless someone was specifically listening for that call, they would miss it completely.

A second call came, then a third. The Normans had been seen north of the original caller and south. They were spreading out. Hunwald sent the same message to the two callers when Edgar instructed him to do so.

'I think we need to retreat a little,' said Edgar. 'They seem to be coming this way. Back into the denser bush.'

The seven men trod carefully into the denser foliage, and as they did so, two more calls confirmed that the Normans were moving steadily into the forest.

'Send "Attack when clear" to the first three callers,' Edgar instructed Hunwald. As his calls were sent out, more calls defined more clearly the route the Normans were taking.

'They're coming this way, but they seem to be a bit

north of the line that will lead to the Paddock,' said Hunwald. Edgar nodded his agreement.

A hundred feet from them, a sentry's call warned them that the enemy was approaching their position.

'Down,' ordered Edgar.

The Normans were not subtle in their approach. They were clearly not trained as the Wildmen were. Six men in mail armour, carrying swords and shields, thumped their way through the undergrowth. With no warning, all six of them suddenly fell to the ground, a feathered arrow shaft protruding from the back of each.

'That's not fair,' said Eric. 'We never got a chance.'

As he spoke, three calls came from distant sentries, announcing that three other groups were now dealt with.

A cry suddenly went up, and two more Normans crashed through the undergrowth to look in astonishment at their dead comrades. More arrows whistled down from the trees, felling one man instantly, but the other turned just as an arrow headed for him passed. It struck his shield and stuck there, thrumming. The soldier looked in fear and wonder at the arrow as it protruded from his shield. They saw him gather his wits in an instant and open his mouth to cry out to his fellows. Just as he did, Osfrid's long seax flew from the bushes and embedded itself in the soldier's open mouth. He coughed once and fell, his legs twitching.

Osfrid crept forward and retrieved the deadly weapon, cleaning its blade on the fallen man's leggings.

More calls relayed the progress of the Norman party, but Edgar could also hear the sound of fighting. Clearly, one group at least had not been felled by the lethal arrows of the sentries, and ground-based warriors had had to engage them. This was not good; the sound would surely draw all

Normans within earshot to investigate.

'Ground troops to me,' Edgar said quickly to Hunwald, who immediately voiced a complex string of bird-calls. Edgar hurried forward, treading with the caution and care that he had been taught since joining the Wildmen. His footsteps were almost silent, yet in two minutes he was at the scene of the pitched battle. In a small clearing, a dozen Normans were beating back four of the Wildmen's ground troops.

Edgar signalled his men forward, and they rushed into the clearing. Two of the Normans spun and fell as they approached, dropped by well-placed arrows from sentries rushing in from all around.

Two of the four Wildmen fighting hand-to-hand with the Normans lay dead on the ground, and the other two were close to defeat as Edgar and his men fell on the enemy. At the same moment, another five axe-bearing Wildmen burst into the clearing. They could not prevent a third one of the four Wildmen from being killed, but within moments, all the attacking Normans lay dead on the ground, hacked mercilessly from behind.

As Edgar and the others wiped their blades and checked the Normans for any sign of life, a loud and urgent call came from behind them, the west, where the Paddock lay.

They all knew the call, but Hunwald voiced it anyway.

'Fire!'

Turning swiftly, all the Wildmen from the clearing rushed back towards the Paddock, taking less care about their footsteps than normal.

Before them, they caught sight of smoke, drifting between the trees. They could smell burning green wood.

'It's the Paddock!' called Halfdene.

Thegn

Edgar called his men to order. He now had two dozen of the ground troops with him.

'Cautiously, now! We might still be able to fall on them unexpectedly. Where are the Normans?'

A Wildman he did not know pointed to the north. 'There, sir. A party got past us somehow. Whilst we were distracted by the last lot. I don't know how, but they seemed to know where they were going.'

'Alright, with me, all of you. Quietly.'

They loped off to the north. Edgar could see that the Normans were using fire arrows, in a seemingly random fashion. The Paddock was ablaze at one corner, but some of the Normans were firing their arrows into other large bushes, and some up into the trees. Clearly, they did not know exactly what they were looking for. It was vital therefore that nobody within the Paddock let out any noise at all, and unfortunately that included the tethered horses, who could not be commanded to be silent.

'We have to stop them before they realize which way to send their arrows. Ready bows,' said Edgar.

The men brought their bows to bear and let loose a rain of arrows which fell with deadly results on the besieging Normans. One who was must have been their leader, for he had clearly refused to walk on foot through the forest, turned his horse towards the source of the arrows and galloped at them. He was on them in a moment, and his sword slashed downwards, taking two Wildmen in a single blow. The others threw themselves out of the way. Edgar drew his sword and stood up, making himself plainly visible to the mounted man as he wheeled his horse around for a second pass. Edgar threw down his shield and crooked his finger at the knight, urging him to attack. The knight needed no encouragement, he spurred his horse forward, and the huge armoured beast bore down on Edgar. Edgar watched carefully. The knight held a long sword in his right hand, and Edgar shifted to his left, giving the impression that he was preparing to engage with the mounted man's sword. The horse thundered towards him, and at the very last moment, Edgar hurled himself to the knight's left and rolled away on his blind side. As he came out of the roll, just inches from the horse's iron-clad hooves, he turned and sliced powerfully at the horse's rear legs. He felt the sword bite deeply into one of them. The horse screamed in pain and fear, falling over as its hamstrung leg gave way beneath it. The knight was thrown forwards over his animal's head. He landed heavily. The crippled horse struggled to rise, but in a flash, one of the Wildmen was on it, slashing at its throat with his seax.

The rider had landed face down, and Sebbi ran forward, his axe raised ready to finish the job. The rider did not move, and Sebbi kicked him over. His head twisted at an unnatural angle. His neck had broken.

Not wasting any time on a dead enemy, Sebbi joined the rush towards the Norman archers, who were now grouping together and drawing their swords.

The Wildmen spread out and the Normans closed together, looking nervously from one Wildman to the next. Suddenly, one of the Normans called out a warning to his fellows. Unseen, another group of English warriors was creeping up silently behind them. The Normans contracted into a circle, surrounded now by grinning Wildmen.

One of the Normans threw down his sword and started babbling at his comrades. The one next to him argued fiercely, but the man would not pick up his sword again.

Thegn

With an angry roar, the man with whom he had been arguing brought his sword down on him in a powerful blow, which cleaved the man from his shoulder to his chest. The man fell. None of the other Normans followed his lead.

Osfrid laughed. 'We could just leave them to kill each other!' he jeered.

'Ready bows!' called Edgar.

The Normans raised their shields, and only two fell to the first rain of arrows. One of the Normans, the one who had just killed one of his own, shouted an order, and the Normans abandoned their tight circle and rushed towards the Englishmen. A second volley brought all but two of them down, and the remaining ones were quickly dispatched on the ends of Wildmen swords.

'Sir!' called a Wildman about twenty yards from Edgar. He was holding an unarmed and unarmoured man by his tunic. The man was struggling and attempting to hit his captor. The Wildman smashed his armoured fist into the man's face and the struggling ceased.

Edgar crossed over and looked at the unconscious man in the Wildman's grip.

'Oh, no,' breathed Edgar.

Guthrum jogged up beside Edgar.

'My lord?' he asked, then looked at the man.

'Oh Jesus,' he gasped.

It was Folcwine.

16

Exodus

Inside the Paddock, Alfweald was directing water-carrying crews to different parts of the surrounding woodlands where the Normans' fire arrows had taken hold. In the burning corner of the Paddock itself, several women were efficiently damping down burning branches with pots of water and wet blankets. The Paddock was safe; only a small fire remained deep within the hawthorn at the damaged corner. Alaric had cleared away some of the tangle of branches and was throwing buckets of water at the flames, which were soon extinguished.

He instructed some nearby Wildmen to keep watch on it for an hour, then backed away. As he did so, Edgar and his men entered the Paddock through the hidden passageway. Alaric greeted Edgar with a wry salute.

'It seems we survived this time,' he said.

'The Norman patrol has been destroyed. The sentries have counted over two hundred of their bodies. We lost twenty-three men.'

'A good exchange. Are you sure that none got away?'

'We can't be completely sure, but we have a more pressing problem.' He indicated their prisoner, still unconscious, being dragged along by two Wildmen.

'Folcwine?'

'It would appear that this is how the Norman patrol knew where to come.'

'No.'

'I'm afraid so. He's made fools of us all, especially me.' Edgar turned to the men who were dragging Folcwine.

'Take him to the posts and secure him thoroughly.'

'Yes, my lord.'

Alfweald looked on as the prisoner was dragged away. He walked over to Edgar.

'It would appear, then, that Godwin was right,' he growled.

Edgar dropped his eyes.

'It would seem that way, my lord.'

'We need to know how many of the enemy know our whereabouts. Meanwhile, I'm going to be ordering an evacuation of the Paddock.'

'Is that necessary my lord?' asked Guthrum.

'Of course it is! How do we know that another patrol isn't on its way here right now? If that scum has given our location away, we are no longer safe here. All our work will be undone. Come with me.'

He turned on his heels and marched away, calling loudly for his lieutenants to gather around him. The scattered men came running across the interior of the Paddock at his call, and they all gathered round the circular seating area where Alfweald held his council meetings.

Barely pausing for breath, Alfweald launched into his speech.

'Our position here is compromised. We have been betrayed by Folcwine, the waggon driver we so graciously spared.'

There was a gasp from the assembled men. Surprisingly, it was Godwin who spoke up.

'Are we quite certain of that, my lord?'

'He was with the search party. The conclusion seems inescapable. Godwin, I want you to interrogate the man. We must know exactly what he has said and to how many people. That's your most important job for now, off you go.'

Godwin stood and left the meeting.

'Our priority is to pack everything we can and get out of here as fast as possible. I know that this will be a huge and difficult undertaking, but I want this place empty by this hour tomorrow.'

There were mutterings around the meeting.

'I know, I know, but our lives may well depend on it. I want the double guard regimen to continue. Every other able-bodied man, woman and child is to be pressed into gathering everything that we can and preparing for the move.'

'But where are we to go, my lord?' asked one of the lieutenants.

Alfweald sighed and closed his eyes. 'I don't know, son. It's become clear to me that concentrating our people in one place is a dangerous strategy. We must scatter. Some will remain in the forest but in smaller, more widespread groups. Others will return to the villages and farmsteads. We have friends all around who will willingly take in two or three at a time, especially if they are strong and willing workers.'

'What of the fight?' asked another.

Alfweald looked up at him, his eyes hard and glistening like cold steel.

'The fight goes on. Always, the fight goes on. We must simply reorganise and develop efficient means of communication between the separated groups. Our bird-call system is efficient but short-range. We need to expand it in some way so that messages can be sent over long distances relatively quickly. Noises only travel a certain distance, especially through the forest. We need people scattered throughout the forest who would be able to hear the call and pass it on, like the water-bucket chains we formed just now to put out the fire. The call is made and passed to the next caller, who passes it on to the next, and the next, and the next, and so on.'

'How far can a call be heard before it merges with real bird-calls?' asked a young lieutenant.

'I don't know. Why don't you find out? Take four or five men and see how far you can pass a message.'

'Yes, my lord.'

'That's a good start. You can do that as soon as we're away from here. We'll set up a dozen or so temporary camps a few miles from here. If we can set up a system of calling that can pass a message from the nearest camp to the farthest, then we may be on to something.'

'Which way shall we go, my lord?' asked Edgar.

'The densest concentration of Normans is to our east. That's where all the trouble we've had has come from. We shall therefore go west. Two miles to start with, that should be far enough to cover our tracks. Questions?'

He shot a glance at his assembled deputies. 'No? Good.

You're each responsible for your own people. Begin the preparations to leave immediately. Edgar, remain here.'

The lieutenants stood and scattered back to their own groups of people to begin the task Alfweald had set them.

'Edgar, you must not blame yourself for this.'

'It was my doing that Folcwine was released, my lord. If anyone is to carry the blame, it should be me.'

'We all agreed to the releasing of Folcwine, Edgar. In hindsight, it was the wrong thing to do, but we only get hindsight after the event. The blame is shared by all of us. I want you to join Godwin as he interrogates Folcwine. Do not interfere, but Godwin may not ask all the relevant questions before he kills him, and be assured that that is what he will do. Make sure we have answers to everything that we need. Don't let him kill him before we have those.'

'No, my lord. Thank you.'

Edgar stood and crossed to where Folcwine was strapped to the post that Alaric had formerly occupied. He signalled Guthrum to join him.

Godwin emptied a pot of dirty water over Folcwine's head. The man did not rouse. Godwin signalled to one of his men who slapped Folcwine around the face. Another pot of water was splashed in his face and he finally spluttered into consciousness. His eyes opened in fear as he saw Godwin's face close to his own.

'We meet again,' said Godwin gently.

'I… I can explain!' stammered Folcwine.

'Yes. I'm sure you can. Please do so.'

Folcwine looked desperately around him. His eyes caught those of Edgar, and momentarily he looked hopeful, but the expression on Edgar's face immediately dispelled any thoughts that salvation lay in that direction.

Thegn

'I'm waiting,' said Godwin.

Folcwine stammered, again looking around in search of succour. There was none to be found.

'They were going to kill me,' he said.

'Might have been better if they did. It would have saved me the bother of doing it.'

'I had no choice!' he cried.

'Tell me what happened,' said Godwin, his voice soft and cajoling.

'I was on my waggon, heading home from Redford. A large party of Normans were coming the other way. I… I tried to pull over to let them pass. They kill ordinary people who don't move over, you know.'

'Yes, they're horrible. We know. That's why we kill them.'

'Yes, yes, you're quite right! I agree with that!' Folcwine was sweating profusely. Godwin's calm and gentle tone was not fooling him at all. It wasn't meant to.

'Carry on,' said Godwin.

'Their leader, the big bugger on the horse, he stopped right in front of my cart. I couldn't get past him; my ox wouldn't move. He… he called back to his men, and two of them ran forward and pulled me from the waggon. They cut the ox free and tipped the waggon over into the ditch at the side of the road.' He stopped, licked his lips, short of breath. He seemed close to tears.

'They… they were going to kill me; they drew their swords. They were closing in on me…'

'So you tried to save your own miserable life by giving ours to them. Right?'

'I have only the one life, my lord.'

'So did those men of ours who died just now.'

'My lord…'

'Enough,' whispered Godwin, patting Folcwine on the cheek. He nodded to his man who stood by, ready. The man was huge, and lank blond hair framed his ruddy face. A straggly, pointed beard hung slackly from his chin. He looked to have much more Danish blood than English. Godwin turned his back on Folcwine and the other man stepped up to the post. Still wearing his armoured gloves, the man punched Folcwine four times in the face. Folcwine screamed at the first three punches but was silent for the fourth.

'Godwin,' said Edgar, 'We need to find out if anyone else knows of our location. Has he told anyone else?'

'I know, I know. Patience, Edgar.'

Folcwine hung from his ropes. His nose was flattened and blood and mucus flowed from his mouth and nose. At his feet were four teeth.

Godwin's henchman threw more water in Folcwine's face. He came round slowly, moaning. His eyes rolled.

'Now, Folcwine, my friend and yours, Edgar here, would very much like to know if you have ever spoken of this place to anyone else? Maybe another Norman who would give you some nice silver eh? A friend when you were drinking together? Maybe you had a little bit too much, eh? Maybe your adventures with the Wildmen was just too good a story to keep to yourself?'

Folcwine shook his head and gasped at the pain it caused. His voice was thick and muffled. 'No. No, I swear it, my lord.'

'Not even to some cheap whore you were boffing in your shitty little hovel?'

'No, no!'

'It would make quite a story, wouldn't it? How you were forced by the horrid Normans to carry their booty, and then you were caught up right in the middle of the Wildmen's most daring raid so far, how all the Normans were killed, but not you. Oh, no. You were far too cunning to get killed. You were taken back to the Wildmen's hideout. Yes! Yes! You know where it is! You even did some work for them. Yes, they trust you. You're an important man now. You're the Wildmen's friend. Did she like your story, your little strumpet?'

'I told no one, no one! I swear it on my life!'

'Your life is not worth swearing on.'

'I'll swear on whatever you like. I swear on the Bible! On Jesus! On God!'

'Well, that's very impressive.'

Folcwine lifted his battered face towards Edgar, imploringly.

Edgar shook his head. 'There is nothing I can do for you this time,' he said.

Godwin nodded to his man again, who punched Folcwine again in the face, then twice in the ribs. He collapsed forward, unconscious once more.

'Enough!' said Godwin. 'Well, Edgar, what do you think?'

'I think he's telling the truth. I think that nobody else knows of our whereabouts.'

'I agree. However, we must turn him over to the council for judgement.'

'Very well.'

The council was convened for the hour of sunset. Folcwine was brought before them, a heavy tree branch across his shoulders, his wrists tied to each end of it, and an eighteen-inch hobble on his ankles. He was forced to his knees, a miserable sight with his smashed face still seeping blood.

Godwin gave an account of his interrogation, concluding that the balance of probability was that he had been telling the truth when he said that he had told nobody but the Norman knight, and then only under threat of his own life.

The council huddled together to consider their verdict. After a short while, Alfweald stood before Folcwine.

'We accept that you probably have not told anyone else of our location. Of course, we cannot be sure of that. When your own life was threatened, you tried to save it by sacrificing the lives of all of us here in the Paddock. We understand that you were under the greatest threat. However, we do not consider that sufficient cause to endanger the whole movement to destroy the Normans. In light of the circumstances, we order that no more pain be inflicted on you. However, your crimes against the Wildmen are the most severe it is possible to imagine, and there is only one sentence that this council can possibly pass. Godwin, prepare a gibbet and hang this miserable creature immediately. That is all.'

Folcwine was lifted to his feet, his face a mask of horror and terror. 'My lord…' he began, looking beseechingly at Alfweald. Godwin's henchman stepped up to him and plucked him from the ground as easily as he might have picked up a small child. Folcwine's voice caught in his throat and he started sobbing as he was dragged back to his post, from where he would be able to see Godwin's men preparing the gibbet from which he had been sentenced to hang.

Alfweald raised his voice to the assembled council. 'This changes nothing. We may well be in less immediate danger than we thought we were, but the idea of spreading our people around instead of concentrating them in a single location is still a good one. The Paddock will remain but will be used only as an occasional shelter. We have much work to do. Let's see that it gets done with as much speed and as little fuss as possible.'

Edgar walked round the Paddock. The tents were still standing, but piled outside each were small bundles of possessions. Weapons, clothes and packs of food wrapped in linen cloths. It would seem that everyone was ready to move in the morning. More durable foodstuffs such as grain had been placed in large pots and buried by one edge of the Paddock, where it could be easily retrieved.

The Normans who had been killed during the day were unceremoniously bundled into the shallow graves dug throughout the forest by the Wildmen. There were too many of them, and fifty or so were dragged inside the Paddock, where a long shallow trough was dug and they were all thrown in, having been stripped of their arms and armour. The leader of the Normans, the mounted knight, was left unburied, just inside the Paddock.

The following morning dawned clear and blue-skied. Edgar emerged from his tent and rubbed at his upper arms. The exertions of yesterday's fight had left their mark in aching limbs and pulled muscles. He looked over to the makeshift gibbet where Folcwine had been hanged the previous evening. Many of the Wildmen had gathered round to watch him wriggle and squirm on the end of the rope. They jeered and spat at him, and women and children threw rotten fruit and dung at him. There had been no mercy shown to Folcwine such as Edgar had shown to the Normans he had hanged in Windeham. No merciful soul had added his weight to the hanging man to speed his passing.

Edgar had not joined in the grisly celebration. He had trusted Folcwine and had been betrayed, and yet he also wondered how differently he himself would have behaved in the same situation that Folcwine had found himself. Edgar could not help feeling some small grain of sorrow for the man. He had been dead from the moment the Norman knight had met him.

The Normans were masters at turning their enemies against each other. Edgar found himself thinking that the same sort of story must be unfolding all over the kingdom, as the Normans turned peasant against thegn, thegn against thegn, son against father, all through murder and torture. As Thegn Godric had said to him all those months ago in Deorby when he had first set out in pursuit of Godgifu's kidnappers, these invaders did indeed seem to have something of the Devil about them.

Folcwine's body had been cut down about an hour after it had stopped twitching. His tongue had been cut out and his body, along with that of the Norman knight, had been taken under cover of darkness to Redford and had been dumped unceremoniously where they would be found the following morning. The message was clear: Normans will be killed, and any who work with the Normans against the Wildmen will also be killed. Folcwine was well known in Redford, and word of his death and disfigurement would spread rapidly. The fact that he had been dumped with a dead Norman knight will leave no doubt that the two had been in collusion, no matter how unwilling that collusion had been on one side.

Edgar's main concern was that the Normans would take their vengeance on the inhabitants of Redford. That seemed to be the way they worked. They would turn the population of the local area, in fear of their own lives, against the Wildmen. Last night, emotions had been running high, and even Alfweald had agreed with the plan to dump the two bodies in a place where they would be found quickly. Perhaps it was as well that the Wildmen would be vacating their erstwhile hiding place today.

'Edgar!'

Edgar turned at the call. Godwin was waving at him from beside Alfweald's tent, which came down as Edgar turned to go to him.

Godwin greeted Edgar. 'Before we strike camp completely, we need to know that the woods around are clear of Norman patrols. Alfweald has ordered me to organize our own small patrols of three or four men each to spread out from the Paddock and ensure that we will not be observed. I'd like you to lead one group, you can choose your own men. You'll be heading eastwards, with the largest number of our men, as that's where we're most likely to meet Norman patrols, especially after what they will have found this morning.'

Godwin had been one of a very few voices that had echoed Edgar's own concerns about the results of the bloody message being left in the village.

Edgar nodded his compliance with the instruction. 'I'll take Eric and Halfdene,' he said, 'I think you'll want

Guthrum to lead another party, yes?'

'I would, but he's your man, so you must decide.'

'I'll send him over to you for his orders. What of our personal belongings, should we carry them with us?'

'No, leave them here. Alfweald and I stayed awake a long time last night deciding where everybody should go. When you return to the Paddock, we'll have a complete list and once all the patrols have returned, we'll be setting off, in staggered parties, to our various locations.'

Edgar walked back to the corner of the Paddock where his men were billeted. All their tents were now collapsed and Eric was stirring a pot of oats over a low fire for their breakfast. He sat down on a log with his men.

'We'll all be going out on patrol as soon as we've eaten,' he began. 'It's important to make sure that we're not observed as we leave. Eric and Halfdene, you're with me. Guthrum, you'll be leading a patrol. Take two of the others and report to Godwin for instructions. The remainder of you will be joining patrols as per Godwin's instructions.'

They all voiced their agreement, and Eric handed out the oat porridge in wooden bowls. They ate in silence, then rinsed their bowls and spoons with water from a nearby water pot.

'Good luck to you all. We'll meet back here at midday,' said Edgar and with that, he, Eric and Halfdene set off towards the horses. Guthrum and the others walked across the Paddock to where Godwin was handing out tasks to small groups of Wildmen.

The horses walked slowly forward as Edgar, Halfdene and Eric approached the road. The trees had started to shed, and dead leaves, dry and crisp, crunched beneath the horses' hooves. Edgar held up his hand to call a halt to their progress, as he had done every few minutes. They all stopped and listened intently. Now they were approaching the road, they needed to be aware of any approaching traffic in plenty of time to take any necessary action.

Edgar strained to hear any giveaway sounds, his ragged eye watering slightly as he did so. He impatiently wiped the offending tear from the corner of the eye. He stopped, his hand halfway back to his lap. Had he heard something? He looked keenly across at Halfdene, to find him looking straight back at him. He nodded, slowly. Edgar turned round to look at Eric, who was also straining to hear, but he too, nodded. Faintly, in the distance, was the sound of several horses, walking, not galloping.

In silence, they turned their horses round and walked them deeper into the forest to a thicket of stunted alder trees. Edgar calmed his horse with a soothing hand on its neck.

They stood there silently, the sound of the approaching horses growing more distinct by the minute. It was obvious that the horsemen were not in any hurry. As well as the sound of the horses' hooves, the three men could now make out low voices. Although the words were indistinct, they could hear by the rhythms of the speech that the riders were not speaking English or Danish.

The first of the riders came into view, a large man wearing a heavy animal fur cloak. He was bareheaded, displaying the bizarre cut of his Norman hairstyle, shaved from the back of the neck almost to the crown of the head. The hair at the front was uncut and flopped down over his forehead.

He was talking to two other men who rode with him,

each wearing a fine cloak and expensive-looking boots. They, too, were bareheaded but were not sporting the Norman hairstyle. The two men deferred to the big man in the fur cloak. Following them at a respectful distance was a party of a dozen mounted men, wearing mail coats and helmets. Each carried a cavalry shield and a long spear.

It seemed that the party was going to pass by without incident when suddenly there was a piercing squeal. A large boar burst from the undergrowth at the side of the road and started running away from the men. The three soldiers at the rear let out a cheer and turned off the road, spurring their horses into a gallop and giving chase to the startled boar. The boar zigzagged as it tried to escape, its pursuers spreading out to cover as many possible options as they could.

Edgar stirred uneasily as the boar's wild dash veered towards the alder thicket. The three men in hiding looked uncomfortably at each other. The squealing boar was fast approaching, and the Norman soldiers were closing in on it.

The boar dived into the alder thicket, startling the three horses, which whinnied and pranced as they tried to avoid the boar's lethal tusks.

The Norman in the lead pulled up his horse and shouted to his two companions, pointing at the thicket with his spear. The three Normans, spotting the Englishmen, kicked at their horses' flanks.

Edgar, Eric and Halfdene wheeled their horses round and set off at full gallop deeper into the forest. They had the advantage over the Normans, as they knew the forest well and all its little navigable animal tracks and paths, but still they would need all their knowledge and skill to evade their pursuers. Eric took the lead, spurring his horse to greater speeds as he made his way through ever deeper foliage. Halfdene was hard on his heels, ducking and dodging the low branches that whipped across the path. Edgar took up the rear position. Snatching glances behind him, he could tell that the Normans were falling behind, unable to keep up with them.

'Split!' he shouted ahead of him. Instantly, Halfdene wheeled his horse round to the right, crashing through a large spread of hazel bushes and disappearing into the foliage. Edgar turned his horse to the left and thundered down a narrow clearing, as Eric continued his drive forward. A snatched glance behind him showed the Normans in a little confusion. They circled, debating which horseman to follow, unwilling to split up themselves. Edgar rounded a bend in the clearing and his horse crashed through some heavy but flexible undergrowth that marvellously whipped closed behind him. He looked back once more. There was no sign of the Normans, though he knew that he could not stop now, or even slow down. As he turned back to face forwards, his horse took a leap over a narrow brook, and halfway across, the heavy, low branch of an ash tree caught Edgar across the forehead. He saw stars and all the strength drained from his muscles. He felt himself slipping from his horse, trying desperately to cling on, his hands and legs reacting too slowly and too weakly. He was aware of the muddy little brook seemingly rising to greet him, and then he fell into blackness

17

Healing

The first thing he became aware of was the smell. A pungent smoke was wafting all around him, filling his senses. It was earthy, woody, herbal, but thick and slightly cloying. He opened his eyes. The place he was in was illuminated by a small fire, the flickering orange light at first stabbed at his eyes, bringing a rush of pain to his head. He closed his eyes again.

He slowly became aware of his surroundings, finding himself lying on a pallet, covered in animal skins. It was warm and he was for the most part comfortable. He opened his eyes again, but quickly shut them and groaned as his head throbbed with pain. He needed sleep. He was just surrendering to the warm, comforting blackness of that sleep when he felt his head being lifted. He did not have the strength to object, and he felt the rim of a wooden bowl being pressed against his lips. He opened his mouth slightly and a warm, sweet, thick substance poured in. He coughed and spat it out.

'Shush, shush, calm now.' The rim was placed back at his lips and this time he allowed some of the thick liquid into his mouth.

'Swallow, it will ease your pain,' said the voice. He swallowed. It burned a little on the way down, but he then allowed another sip down his throat. The wooden bowl was taken away.

'Good. Well done.'

Edgar opened his eyes to slits. He saw an old woman sitting on the pallet next to him. Her white hair was long, thick and unkempt, her face furrowed with deep lines and wrinkles, her skin a weathered brown, like tanned leather. Her eyes were startling, a pale blue of such ice-like intensity that they seemed to shine out of the depths of her ancient face.

Edgar opened his mouth to speak, but she placed a twig-like finger on his lips.

'You've had a fall. You have a nasty bump on your head, but it will fade. There's no lasting damage. You're safe here. That is all you need to know for now. Sleep.'

Edgar allowed his head to be lowered back on the pallet and within moments he felt himself sliding into the womb-like embrace of sleep.

The next time he awoke, there was a change in the atmosphere. The lighting was different. The fire still crackled quietly on the floor, but it was lighter now. The air was less muggy, too, though he could still smell the odour he had noticed when he first woke up, it was much less noticeable. He pushed himself upright, wincing in advance of the throbbing head he thought he would get. His head did not throb. There was still some dull ache, but it was hugely reduced. He looked down at himself and realised that under the animal skins that covered him, he was naked. He looked about for his clothes, and found them, and his sword, within easy reach.

'Ah, you're awake,' the old woman walked in, through a curtain of animal skins that he hadn't noticed in the dim light. He could see that she was short of stature and as thin as anyone he had ever seen, yet she moved with an easy grace and lightness of foot.

'Where am I?' asked Edgar.

'This is my home. You are still in the forest, but no one will find you here.'

'You tended to me,' his eyes slid unconsciously down to his nakedness.

'You were injured. You have nothing I haven't seen before.'

'Of course. Thank you. What happened?'

She shrugged. 'I don't know, I found you lying next to a stream. You were unconscious but alive, so I brought you back here to see if I could heal you.'

Edgar looked pointedly at the slight, skinny old woman. 'You brought me here? How?'

She smiled. 'I'm stronger than I look.' She laughed lightly. 'I'd have to be!'

'What about the Normans?'

'The what?'

'The Normans.'

'What are Normans?'

Edgar blinked. 'The Normans, the followers of William the Bastard. The men who are trying to take over the kingdom.'

She shrugged. 'I know nothing of that. I am long past letting the affairs of the kingdom have any effect on me.'

'I need to get back to my men,' began Edgar, starting to rise, but stopped as a wave of nausea overcame him.

'It will be a little while yet,' said the old woman. 'You still have healing to do. I will help, but you must lie back for now. You don't need to sleep if you don't want to, though it will help.'

Edgar lay back and closed his eyes. The nausea ebbed away slowly.

'My men will be worried about me; I must get back to them.'

'They will learn the truth soon enough. Not just yet, though.'

Edgar nodded and swallowed. His throat felt dry.

'Could I have some water?' he asked.

He heard her move, heard the sound of water being poured and then felt the rim of the wooden bowl against his lips again. He swallowed. The water was good, cold and clear. Edgar allowed his head to drop back onto the pallet. Within moments he was asleep again.

He could tell this time that it was after dark. The fire was low and gave out only a feeble light. He peered into the darkness, trying to get some measure of the place he found himself in. The dim flicker from the fire did little to help, but above him, he thought he could see a roof, of sorts. It was irregular and lumpy, lower in some places than others. It seemed to be made of rock. He appeared to be in some sort of cave. He felt the floor beside his pallet. It was hard, though covered in rushes. Across the dim glow of the fire, he could see the old woman, lying under a heap of animal skins. Her face was turned towards him, and he could just see the icy glitter of her eyes. She was watching him.

'Do you need anything?' she asked.

'Answers,' he replied.

She sighed and pushed back the animal skins from her tiny, thin frame. She pulled a large woollen shawl around her shoulders and walked across on bare feet to where he lay. He watched her feet, narrow, bony and coarse-skinned. She sat down.

'I will answer what I can,' she said.

'Where am I?'

'You asked this before. You are in my home. You are safe.'

'But where is your home?'

'It is here, in the forest. Not far from where I found you. Surely you know where you were when you had your accident?'

'Yes, alright. Is this a cave?'

'I suppose you could call it that. It's part of a cave. Much larger than what you see here. The deeper parts are always wet. This part is dry. I live here.'

'Is there anyone else here? How do you survive?'

She looked into the distance. 'There is nobody else here now. My husband used to live here, too, but he has been dead many years. I live by collecting edible plants and trapping small animals and birds. How else would you expect me to survive?'

He was silent for a while. She asked 'How did you get all that damage to your face?'

Edgar involuntarily brought his hand up to his face and touched the stretched, shiny skin that had regrown over his terrible wound.

'In battle. To the north.'

'It was well looked after. Who did that?'

Edgar felt a cold dagger slipping deeper into his guts. 'I was taken from the battlefield by a young local woman. She healed me.' He bit his lip, and then added 'we got married.'

The old woman looked at him intently. 'There is much pain here. Your wife…'

'Killed. Raped and killed by the Normans who also killed my grandfather and many others in my town.'

The old woman stood in silence and walked across to a small table by her pallet. She picked up a bunch of herbs and threw them onto the fire. Immediately the fire took hold and the air was filled with a sweet smell. She took something from a small leather bag and added that to the flames. The smoke was dark and pungent. It stung Edgar's eyes.

'What is that?'

'It will help,' she said, quietly. 'You feel great anger towards these Normans, now I understand why.' She stirred the fire with a stick, releasing some sparks which flew upwards, disappearing near the roof of the cave.

'Tell me,' she said, 'do you not cry out to God for vengeance, for aid in your plight?'

'God?' he almost spat, 'What will God do for me? How will God help me if he is content to see my beautiful, clever, kind, generous wife raped by a dozen of these animals and then driven to kill herself as a result?'

'She killed herself? Then the Christians would not permit her a decent burial.'

'I don't know where she's buried. We were far apart at the time. A… witness told me what had happened.'

He paused, staring into the low fire. 'I don't know

where she's buried.'

'You sound like that's only just occurred to you.'

'It has.'

'The mortal remains are unimportant.'

There was a long silence.

'What happened to my men?' he asked.

'I don't know. I didn't see them. Only you.'

'My horse?'

'No.'

'When can I go?'

'Wait until the morning. If you feel well enough then, you can go. Here…' she stood up and walked to her herb table. 'I'll make you something to ease the pain.'

'I'm not in pain, it's gone.'

She turned to him and smiled. 'Not that pain.'

She mixed some ingredients and water in a pot beaker which she then placed in the fire. When it was steaming, she took the beaker from the fire, her hand wrapped in an old piece of leather, and poured the hot liquid into another beaker. This she passed to Edgar.

'Drink.'

He sipped at the hot brew. It was bitter and astringent, with strong earthy flavours. Not at all pleasant, but he drank it all down anyway.

'Now lie down and let it work,' she said.

He lay back and closed his eyes as the old woman drew up the animal skins over his shoulders.

Soon he drifted into sleep.

He swings his axe forward, dropping his shield a few inches as he does so. The axe makes contact with the shoulder of the Norseman in front of him. The Norseman shrieks and falls back, his arm hanging useless and gouts of blood pouring from his shoulder.

A voice behind him calls 'Back!'

He obeys, falling back to allow the row of men behind him to take their turn at the front. Edgar drops his guard as others take over the fighting and allows his shield to dangle loosely from his hand. He swings his axe around lightly to relieve the aching in his right arm.

'New attack!' someone screams. 'To your right!'

Edgar turns and sees a new host of Vikings rushing along the raised ground towards them. They are fully armed and look like they've run all the way from their ships. They drop down to the level of the fight and rush towards the flank of the English shield wall. He quickly hoists his shield back into position in front of his body, trying to ignore the stab of pain from his left shoulder and turns to face the new threat. The first man to confront him looks so exhausted that it almost doesn't seem fair to fight him. Almost. The man takes a feeble swing at Edgar, who deflects the axe easily with his shield. The man staggers, and Edgar swings his axe overarm and down onto the man's head. The axe clangs noisily against the Viking's helmet, and he drops to the ground. The momentum of the blow carries Edgar round so he is looking back into the ranks of the English. Then Edgar sees the huge Viking looming up on his left. The man is red-faced and sweat pours down his face. As he raises his huge double-bladed battleaxe, the scene seems to slow down, and everything jumps into very sharp focus. The Viking's axe rises up and up, and Edgar notices a small patch in the man's mail armour beneath his right arm where a few links are missing, and the mail is beginning to fall apart. His nostrils are assailed by the stink of the man's underarms as Edgar raises his shield to ward off the oncoming blow. As he does so, he is aware of the jostling of other men around him as they defend themselves from the new wave of attackers. Edgar can feel the pain in his shoulder, it is getting worse, and even in this slowed-down state, it very rapidly reaches screaming pitch. The massive Viking roars with effort as his axe starts its descent towards Edgar. Edgar's shoulder gives way and his shield drops a little. The axe is hurtling towards him now.

Without warning, there is a fluttering in front of Edgar's shield. From nowhere, a raven now flaps furiously between Edgar and his assailant. Edgar begins to step back, and the Viking's arm wavers, just a little. Then the raven is gone, and Edgar knows that his time has come. The Viking's battleaxe makes contact with Edgar's face, but not quite squarely. Edgar feels the rush of agony as the side of his face is crushed. He begins to fall, and all is now blackness.

The pain is gone, and Edgar feels nothing but peace and contentment. He is looking at the battlefield, at the piles of dead and dying men. The battle is over; the survivors have walked away. Nobody has yet arrived at the field to strip the dead. Edgar is puzzled. He cannot remember what has happened, but he knows that he should be in great pain, if not dead. He looks around and realises that he is standing on top of a pile of bodies. He sees that one is his own. He is undisturbed by the sight. Across the field, he can see a figure moving slowly. He wears a long cloak, to his feet, and on his head is a wide-brimmed hat. A raven sits hugely on his left shoulder, while another circles above his head. In his right hand there is a long staff, which he leans on as he walks. Edgar cannot see what he is doing, but suddenly and apparently without walking towards him, the man is standing next to him. Edgar looks into the man's face and notices that the left eye is white and blind. The other eye is grey. His long, straggly white beard flutters slightly in the breeze. The man smiles kindly, and Edgar drifts back into darkness.

Edgar woke to a much brighter day. The cave was illuminated by indirect sunlight, losing much of its previous gloomy aspect. He was immediately aware that he felt much better, and he sat up, reaching for his clothes. He pulled them on but left his sword where it was. He walked around the cave. It was small and low-roofed. The floor was well strewn with rushes and fragrant herbs that gave off pleasant scents when crushed underfoot. The old woman was nowhere to be seen, so he walked across to the heavy animal skin hanging that marked the cave exit. Pulling it aside, he saw that the skin covered the entrance to a narrow tunnel, which he had to bend almost double to pass through. The passage rose at the end and opened into a thick hazel bush, which had been ingeniously woven to provide a lightly sheltered area outside the entrance to the tunnel. To one side was an inconspicuous gap in the hazel's vertical branches, which he squeezed through, and found himself in the forest, dry leaves crunching softly underfoot. He squinted as the full sunlight caught him in the face.

A few yards away, the old woman was standing by a tangle of brambles, picking large, juicy-looking blackberries and dropping them into a bag she had hung around her neck. Edgar walked over to her. She didn't look up as he approached.

'The last of this year's crop,' she said, popping a particularly large berry into her mouth and chewing noisily. 'I must try to pick them all before the birds finish them off.'

She stretched on tiptoes to try to reach a branch heavy with fruit, but could not quite reach. Edgar reached past her and pulled the fruit off, dropping it into her bag.

'Thank you,' she said. 'There are some more high ones over there, if you don't mind.'

Edgar stepped over to the area she had indicated and began to strip the higher branches of their glistening black berries.

'What did you give me to drink last night?'

She dropped another handful of berries into her bag. 'Did it help?'

'I don't know. I had… strange dreams,' he paused and ate a berry himself.

'What did you dream of?'

'The battle – you know, I told you, where I was injured… where I got this,' he self-consciously touched the damaged side of his face with the back of his fingers. He could not explain it, but for some reason, Edgar felt embarrassed by his disfigurement in the presence of this tiny, shrivelled old woman.

'It gives you character,' she said. 'I am quite sure that you look far more interesting now than you ever did before. Wear your scars with pride; I do.' She indicated the wrinkles on her face. 'They say more about you than beauty ever could.' Her face broke into a radiant smile, and Edgar, just for a fleeting moment, caught a hint of what she must have looked like as a young woman. Regret flushed through him. How time destroys everything. Must our lives always be better yesterday than they are today?

'Tell me about your dream.'

Edgar took a breath and tried to visualise what he had seen during his dream. Getting it all in the right order was not as straightforward as he thought.

'I was in the shield wall at Stanford. We were fighting a large Norse army led by their King himself. Not all the Norsemen were on the field of battle, some had stayed behind at their ships some miles away. News must have reached them of the battle, and the ones guarding the boats ran all the way in full armour. They came at us like a wave from our right-hand side. I had just fallen back into the rear ranks of the axemen when they reached us. I was on the right flank, so although I was tired, I had to fight them as soon as they arrived. The first was a small man, he was totally exhausted, and I dropped him with no difficulty, but the second...' Edgar paused and shook his head at the memory. 'Well, he was a giant. A huge man, red-faced and sweaty. He had an enormous double-headed battleaxe. I had taken a fall earlier, and damaged my shoulder – it was later found to be broken, but I didn't know that at the time. Anyway, the shoulder gave way as I raised my shield against him, and his axe hit me here.' He pointed at his face. 'I can't really remember in any detail what happened, but in the dream I saw everything with real clarity.' He stopped and took a breath.

She popped another berry into her mouth. 'And?'

'And this is where it gets strange. As the Norseman's axe fell towards me, a raven suddenly appeared between us. I don't know where it came from or how it got there, but there it was.'

She stopped chewing and looked intently at him. 'A raven, you say? Definitely a raven? Not a common crow?'

'No, it was certainly a raven, the thing was huge, I don't even know how it fit between us, but it was there. The sudden appearance of such an unexpected apparition made me step back, or at least begin to, and it seemed to put the Norseman off his swing slightly. Then the axe hit and everything went black.'

She was still staring at him, her icy blue eyes piercing, seeming to pin him to the spot. 'Well, well. It appears that God did not abandon you on the battlefield.'

'What has this to do with God?' suddenly he was angry. Since Godgifu's death, well-meaning souls had tried to comfort him with tales of God's great plan and how He was looking after him. Looking after him by smashing his face in, leaving him nearly dead, killing his grandfather, his wife and destroying his home. That kind of looking after he felt he could do well without.

'Was there any more to this dream?' She asked, unabashed.

Edgar calmed himself. This woman had probably saved his life. No doubt divine plans were afoot for her slaughter right now.

'There was another short episode. I was floating. Close to my body on the battlefield. The battle had finished and only the dead and dying were left. There was a man, walking amongst the dead. I don't know what he was doing. He wore a long cloak and a broad-brimmed hat…'

The old woman caught her breath, and Edgar heard it. 'What?' he asked.

'Go on,' she said with an intensity he had not heard from her before. 'This man, did he have only one eye?'

'Yes,' replied Edgar, puzzled. 'And there was a raven on his shoulder and another flying above him. He came over to me and smiled at me.'

The woman slowly put down her bag and sat cross-legged on the forest floor. Edgar was confused.

'What's wrong? Are you alright?' he asked, concerned.

'Yes,' she said, faintly, distractedly. 'Yes, come and sit with me.' She patted the ground next to her. Edgar walked over and sat. The ground was cold and felt slightly damp.

'Last night, I gave you a sleeping draught. It also contained a particular mixture of certain tree barks and a small fungus. In the past this mixture has helped me see things more clearly, in my head, you know,' she tapped her forehead. 'It helps me to understand what is really happening, what things really mean. I live a very solitary life here, and sometimes when I think things are truly bad, it helps me to see that actually, they're not. Though sometimes it has opened my eyes to dangers that I had not known existed. It is powerful, and it has shown you something very important. I said that God did not abandon you on the battlefield. I did not say which god.'

'What do you mean? Surely there's only one God, that is what we're taught.'

'It is indeed. But did you not recognise this man you saw in your dream?'

'Should I have?'

'It was Woden. Old Woden One-Eye.'

'Woden? What? One of the old gods?'

'Not just one of them. Chief of them, most powerful amongst them. It is Woden who fetches the dead from here to wherever it is that the dead go.'

'But the old gods are just stories. They aren't real.'

'And this God from across the seas, this God from far distant lands and far distant people, He is real, is he? Woden is of this land, of this people. He is more real than you can imagine. And he is protecting you.'

'Why?'

'That I don't know. But if Woden is your protector, you have a purpose, maybe a purpose that only he knows, but he will protect you until your purpose is fulfilled. The ravens are always with him. They are called Huginn and Muninn, they are Thought and Memory, and represent Woden's eyes and ears.'

She stopped, feeling the ground with the palm of her hand. Her brow furrowed. 'Riders,' she said. 'We must get under cover.'

Edgar felt the ground. There was indeed a very slight pounding. They stood, and hurriedly made their way back through the hazel grove into the tunnel and the cave.

'I must watch,' said Edgar, 'I need to know who these men are.'

She nodded, 'Keep your head low and stay out of sight. I have been invisible and therefore safe for many years. I have no wish for that to change now.'

Edgar nodded and crept cautiously along the tunnel. At the end, he parted the thin branches that covered the entrance and peered out. His head was at ground level, and still deep within the hazel bush. He stopped, no one could ever see him here, and that's how he wished it to remain.

He could see surprisingly far despite his cluttered viewpoint. Before long, he caught sight of two horsemen, walking their horses slowly through the forest. They were talking softly to each other, and before long, he recognised the voices of Guthrum and Eric. He could not make out what they were saying, but the cadences were as familiar to him as his own voice. He backed up along the tunnel and turned to face the old woman.

'It is my friends. They are probably looking for me. I must go.'

She was holding his sword, which she passed to him. 'Please wait until they have passed, and then follow them some way on foot. I need to remain hidden, even from your friends.'

He saw something approaching fear enter her eyes.

'Of course.' He strapped on his sword. 'Thank you for your kindness and your hospitality. How can I repay you?'

'Repayment is not required. It seems I have done Woden's work. That is enough.'

Thegn

He looked down at her, knowing that he would not see her again.

'Here,' she said, scrabbling at the front of her smock. She pulled out a leather thong on which hung a small black amulet. She pulled it over her head and handed it to him. He looked at it. The amulet was crudely carved from some shiny black stone in the shape of a raven, wings folded as if it was standing on the ground. It was not much bigger than Edgar's thumbnail.

'It was my husband's,' she explained. 'I don't need it any more and he certainly doesn't.'

Edgar took the amulet and slipped the leather thong around his neck. It felt warm against his chest.

'Thank you… I don't even know your name,' he said.

'You may call me…' she paused and smiled cryptically. 'You may call me Mother.'

'Thank you, Mother.' Edgar gathered her into his arms and picked her up in a tight hug. After a moment he put her down again and she cupped his face in her bony hands. 'Go,' she said.

With a smile, Edgar turned and crept along the tunnel until he once again could see out across the forest floor. The horsemen had passed close to the entrance and were now disappearing into the wooded distance. Edgar crawled out into the open, making as little noise as possible. When he was sure the horsemen were out of sight, he set off at a leisurely pace in pursuit of them.

18

Return to Rapendun

Guthrum and Eric had greeted Edgar with shouts of joy. As he approached, Guthrum had at first drawn his sword but dropped it in amazement as Edgar jogged out of the undergrowth.

'Where have you been?' demanded Guthrum. 'We've searched these three days for you. We feared that you'd been captured by the Normans.'

Edgar laughed. 'No, not me. I fell in a ditch, banged my head. A passing traveller fed me and dressed my wound, see.' He held his hair back from his forehead, revealing the well-healed wound.

Guthrum looked at him askance. 'A traveller, out here?' he asked.

'There's more going on in these woods than we are aware of, Guthrum. It's enough that this good person fed and tended me and made me fit to return to your company.'

'Aye,' nodded Guthrum. 'Aye, my lord.'

Thegn

Eric jumped down from his horse.

'Up you get,' he said to Edgar, 'I'll walk.'

Edgar thanked him and climbed up into the horse's saddle. Although he would not admit it to his comrades, he still felt slightly weak from the head wound.

'Has the Paddock been evacuated yet?' he asked.

'Yes, that was all completed on the day you disappeared. I have to admit that Godwin is a very efficient organiser. He even organized search parties for you after you went missing. Seemed quite concerned, he did.'

'He's a good man. I've come to realize that. So where are we going?'

'We'll go to Alfweald's camp, it's about two miles beyond the Paddock. It's in deep, dense woodland. It's unlikely to be found except by sheer luck, and there's little we can do to defend against that.'

They rode on in silence for a short while, keeping their horses to walking pace in deference to Eric, who walked a few paces behind them.

'Do you want to tell me any more about this traveller?' ventured Guthrum.

'No. I don't think so. I reckon he must have been a hunter, maybe out to bag a deer or some grouse for his table. He had pain-relieving herbs and a lotion that he applied to my head. Some fresh water and the ability to make a small fire well hidden. He obviously knew the woods very well.'

'Any chance that he will give you away to the Normans? We saw what happened to Folcwine.'

'No chance at all. This was an entirely different kind of person. We will never see him again, and I suspect no one else will either.'

Guthrum gave him a puzzled look.

'I've said enough, Guthrum. The matter is closed.'
Guthrum nodded and said no more.

Two hours later, Guthrum led Edgar along a narrow path through dense undergrowth and a stand of closely packed birch trees. The light was fading and Edgar just caught sight of the glow of a covered fire before they broke through into a clearing. Around the edge of the clearing were tents, covered in undergrowth and looking like irregular bushes more than living quarters for men. As they entered the clearing, Alfweald stared at them and then stood up, barking in surprise. Edgar climbed off the horse, handing its reins back to Eric with a nod of thanks. He walked over to Alfweald, who grasped him by the forearms. His bushy grizzled beard twitched as his face broke into a warm smile.

'We thought you surely lost! Guthrum and Eric insisted on one last search. Thank God they did!' He hugged Edgar and led him back to the fire where they sat down and Alfweald poured mead for the four of them.

Alfweald demanded the story from Edgar, and Edgar repeated the tale much as he had told it to Guthrum on the journey back. His reticence about discussing his saviour elicited a sidelong glance from Alfweald, but he wisely let the matter lie.

Alfweald then related the details of the move out of the Paddock to Edgar. The Wildmen were now scattered far and wide, and a system of fast communication through repeating stations was being set up to keep everyone in touch with each other. Several small bands of Wildmen had been accepted into local villages and hamlets, working as labourers, but ever ready to spring into action if and when the call came. Others were setting up compact camps like the one they were now in, spread over many miles and far more difficult to find than the Paddock had been. In this way, Alfweald hoped to keep the fight with the Normans, who would fight back seemingly at thin air. An enemy they could neither see nor defend against.

Edgar hoped he was right, but quietly thought that from what he had seen, the Normans were very likely to take the fight to the innocent villagers and farmers of the area. It seemed to be a policy that had worked for them so far, so why should they stop?

He voiced these concerns to Alfweald, whose face crumpled in concern.

'You're right, of course. And yet I believe that such retaliation will harden our people's hearts even more against the Normans. Every farmer and villager will become one with us, will become Wildmen. The fight must never end until it ends in victory for us. Each of us would willingly give his life for the cause. The same will be true of the villagers and farmers. We will never give up.'

Lying awake in his tent that night, Edgar went over and over his conversation with Alfweald. The man was an inspirational leader, there was no doubt of that, and yet doubts were beginning to creep into Edgar's mind. Alfweald's insistence that Norman retributions against the innocent would accelerate the resistance process did not ring true with Edgar. These people who were being threatened were not warriors, but ordinary people. They were not trained in the way of the fighter. They had neither the physical nor the mental discipline. Their principal objective would be to stay alive and to keep their families alive. That would matter much more to them than some ideal of driving the Normans out and having the old order restored. After all, he thought, what difference does it make to the peasant in the field if his lord is English or Norman? Edgar thought it more likely that the peasants would soon see that it was English resistance that was the cause of their suffering, and if they sided with the Normans, there was more chance that life could get back to normal in the shortest possible time.

These thoughts made Edgar very uneasy, and he did not sleep well. One thing he decided just before dropping into a shallow, restless sleep, was that he and his men needed to get away from the Wildmen as soon as they could.

A few days later, Edgar and Guthrum sat in conference with Alfweald. Edgar had requested the conference the day before.

'So, Edgar, what do you wish to discuss with me?'

'Sir, when I travelled through Deorby on my way to find Godgifu, Thegn Godric was kind enough to offer me the service of four of his housecarls, one of whom has died in my service. Thegn Godric also offered me some words of advice. As my grandfather had just died and I had become Thegn of Rapendun, he reminded me that it was my principal duty as thegn to protect my people, those who till the land and spin the thread. At this difficult time, they must be looking to me for protection, and I have not been there for them.

'I wish to be released from your service so that I may return to fulfil my duties as thegn, and also to return Thegn Godric's housecarls.'

Alfweald nodded. 'I've thought for some time that you

were going to request that. If you are sure that you can do something for your people, Edgar, then of course you must go, and with my blessing. You have done more than your share for the Wildmen, you and your carls. Be aware though, that the world is different now. You may find that there is no place for you in it.'

'I must know that for myself. I cannot forget Thegn Godric's words. If there is anything I can do for my people, then I must be there for them.'

'Very well. I will release you and your men from my service. On your return, I must caution you to take the lesser lanes or remain in woodland where you can. Stay unseen. Armed English warriors will be attacked on sight. There are more of the thrice-cursed Normans every day, they are flooding into the country. If the worst does happen…' he paused. 'If you find you no longer have a home, you can always find one here with us.'

Edgar stood up. 'Thank you, sir. It's been an honour.'

He held his hand out to Alfweald. Alfweald took the proffered hand. 'For both of us,' he said graciously.

The following morning, Edgar, Guthrum, Eric, Halfdene, Sebbi, Osfrid, Hunwald and Alaric mounted their horses and rode out from the camp in single file. The Wildmen who lived in Alfweald's camp stood and watched as they left, each nodding or quietly clapping as they passed. Edgar felt a pang of regret as he walked his horse away from the Wildmen. He had come to the inescapable conclusion that Alfweald was wrong, and would ultimately lose his fight to regain England, but he had never experienced such comradeship as he had amongst the Wildmen. Despite this, he knew his decision was the right one. He had to think like a thegn now. He could happily have lived out his life amongst this disparate but highly disciplined community, and his carls would gladly have stayed with him. But his greater responsibilities called to him, and their call could not be ignored.

Soon the Wildmen encampment was lost behind them, and Edgar led them along the ephemeral trails that seemed like the king's highways to them now.

After a couple of hours, they reached the place where Edgar had fallen from his horse two weeks before. Edgar held up his arm to halt the column. He kicked his horse forwards, and next to a dense hazel bush he stopped, reached down and unhooked a bag from his saddle. The bag was filled with two large animal furs, four tunics, some leggings, a pair of child's shoes and a large quantity of vegetables. He dropped the bag onto the ground by the hazel and turned his horse to walk away.

Puzzled but unquestioning, his followers rode on in his wake. Only when they were three hundred yards away did they hear a faint cry from behind them.

'Thank you!'

Thegn Godric greeted them with bearish arms. He embraced Edgar tightly, squeezing the breath from his lungs.

'I note with some concern,' he began, 'that your wife is not with you.'

Edgar swallowed, the sense of loss welling once again from deep within him.

'No. She died before we could get to her.'

Godric exhaled loudly and stared at the floor between Edgar's feet.

Thegn

'I'm sorry. I hope she died well,' he said at last.

'She took some Normans with her, I believe.'

'Good, that is good,' Godric nodded his large, shaggy head in approval. 'That is something you can keep with you. Come, sit.'

As Edgar, the six carls and Alaric sat down on the benches, Godric called across the hall for ale to be brought.

'I see that one of my housecarls is also missing. Where is Enni?'

'I'm sorry, Godric. Enni died in my service. He also took some Normans with him.'

Godric's shoulders fell slightly. His face stilled. He looked away briefly and blinked. Then he nodded. 'Then Enni, too, died well, and tonight we will drink long and hard to the memory of his life. What of my other carls?' He indicated Sebbi, Hunwald and Osric with a casual jab of the fingers. 'Did they serve you well?'

'They served me as fully as any men could have. They have been steadfast and courageous. I could not have had finer or more loyal companions.'

Godric looked pleased. 'Then they shall have places of honour at tonight's feast. Will you be staying for that, Edgar?'

'We have ridden long and hard, and would appreciate your hospitality tonight, Godric. I thank you. My own hall lay in burned ruins when last I saw it. There will be much work to do when we get back.'

Guthrum cleared his throat, waiting for permission to address the two Thegns.

'Yes, Guthrum?' said Godric.

'What news is there of Norman movements in this area, Thegn Godric? Has there been much sign of them whilst we've been away?'

'Yes, yes indeed there has. Some small bands have passed through, and two days ago a party of maybe a hundred infantry and half a dozen horsemen were seen just to the south of here, heading north, though I don't know where they passed through. Maybe your area.'

'Perhaps we should return to Rapendun straight away, my lord. If such a large party passed through, there may be more for us to do than we thought.'

Edgar nodded, looking at Godric. Godric nodded swiftly.

'Guthrum always thinks clearly, Edgar. He's right, of course.'

At that moment, a serving maid placed a large flagon of ale on the table in front of them.

'Take some refreshment and then go. If you find that you need any help, send one of your men back to me and I'll send these three with another two dozen.'

'Thank you, Thegn Godric, your kindness to me has been unsurpassed. I am in your debt.'

'And don't think I won't be calling on that debt in my time of need, young Edgar.'

'I am eager to repay, sir.'

Edgar, Guthrum, Eric and Halfdene set off from Deorby at a canter. Alaric had gone on ahead, wanting to scout around on his own. He arranged to meet them either at Rapendun or somewhere on the road before they reached there. Edgar had gladly let him go ahead, feeling oddly that whatever happened to them on the road, Alaric would be aware of it, and most likely able to do something about it if necessary.

Thegn

Their horses had been carrying them all day and the previous day, and could not be pushed too hard. The countryside south of Deorby showed some signs of plundering, but thankfully no bodies were to be seen. Edgar began to hope that the Normans had passed through peaceably.

Halfdene was riding about a hundred yards ahead of the others, as vanguard. Edgar saw him pull up his horse and stop suddenly as they approached the tiny village of Osmundestun. He held up his arm, a signal that they should stay back, but did not give the signal to get away from the road. He slowly moved forward, and the others lost sight of him as he passed behind a clump of trees on the left-hand side of a shallow bend in the road. After a few minutes, he reappeared, riding swiftly back to the others. His face was white.

'Halfdene, what is it?' demanded Edgar.

'Osmundestun. It's gone. Burnt to the ground. There are bodies. It's all gone.'

'Come on,' ordered Edgar, and kicked his horse into a gallop.

Osmundestun had been a small collection of cottages and byres, a combined bakery and brewery at one end. Now nothing stood. Black, charred wood poked up from the ground where posts had held up walls and roofs. Scattered amongst the devastated buildings, the bodies of the residents lay, mutilated and trampled.

The four men climbed down from their horses and carefully inspected each body for signs of life. There were none. The injuries they had sustained were savage. Limbs had been hacked off, heads crushed and bodies eviscerated. The stench was overwhelming.

'Four, maybe five days,' said Guthrum.

'This must be the work of Godric's hundred footmen and six horsemen,' said Halfdene.

'We need to get back to Rapendun, organise a burial party to come out here,' said Edgar. 'Come on, there's nothing we can do here.'

The men remounted their horses and turned dismally back to the road. A cart lay overturned in the middle of the road, one of its wheels broken. They skirted round it and continued south.

Edgar turned round in his saddle to look back on the devastation one last time. This was another crime he swore he would avenge.

As he looked, he caught a glimpse of movement. He stopped his horse and stared. Yes, there it was, under the cart. He jumped off his horse and ran back to peer under the cart. He heard a faint whimper of fear. At the back of the cart was a young child, huddled into a corner, hands wrapped tightly round knees.

'Hello,' said Edgar.

There was no reply, just a small, strangled sob.

'It's alright. I won't hurt you. The bad men have gone.'

Guthrum, Eric and Halfdene arrived at Edgar's side.

'There's a child under here,' said Edgar.

'Want us to lift the cart?' asked Halfdene.

'No, not just yet.' He crouched down again and called to the child. 'It's safe to come out. We won't hurt you. We'll look after you. Are you hungry?'

'Kid must have been under here for days,' muttered Guthrum.

'My name is Edgar. What's yours?'

A shuffling noise came from under the cart. A thin

Thegn

voice, quiet and frightened, followed it. 'Edgar?'

'That's right, Edgar.'

'Master Edgar?' the voice was coloured with a trace of hope.

'That's right, I'm Master Edgar from Rapendun. Won't you come out?'

There was a little more shuffling and a hand reached out from under the cart. Edgar took it gently in his own. He held it for a moment, and then the rest of the child emerged, blinking in the light. It was a girl, maybe ten years old. Her yellow hair was matted and tangled. Her eyes never left the ground. Around her left wrist was a black shale bangle.

'I know you, don't I?' said Edgar. The girl said nothing. 'My grandfather, Thegn Wulfmaer gave you this bangle after the harvest feast last year, didn't he? It's…' he groped frantically for her name. 'It's Edda, isn't it?'

The little girl nodded her head, her eyes remaining fixed on the ground.

Edgar held out his hand to her again. 'Come with us, Edda. You can't stay here. We'll get you food and drink, and maybe something clean to wear. Would you like that?'

She nodded minutely, then cautiously took Edgar's hand. He walked her back to his horse. He climbed up, and Guthrum handed her up to him. He placed her on the saddle in front of himself and wrapped his cloak around her.

'You don't need to talk if you don't want to, Edda. Just hang on to my cloak, and I'll take you to where we can get some food.'

They set off south again, leaving the dismal remains of Osmundestun behind them.

Halfdene was again riding van, and as they approached

Rapendun, there was no repeat of the sights that had greeted them at Osmundestun. Edgar rode through the open gates of the palisade. The hall still stood roofless, and in a considerably worse state than when Edgar had last seen it. His grandfather's house stood at one end of the hall, still seemingly in good repair.

As they approached, the door of the house opened and a man stepped out.

'Master Edgar!' he exclaimed as Edgar dismounted in front of him. Edgar recognised him as one of his grandfather's administrators.

'We thought you surely dead, my lord,' said the man. Skalda, his name came back to Edgar.

'Not dead, Skalda, not yet. Let's get inside.'

Skalda led the four men into the house. Edda clung to Edgar's cloak. They sat.

Skalda looked skittish and frightened, his eyes darting between each of the four armed men in the house.

'I see you have made yourself at home in my house,' commented Edgar, looking at the trappings of another man's life around him.

'As I said, my lord, we thought you dead. There must still be some governance of the farms. We held a moot once we felt that you would not be coming back. I was elected headman. Others can verify that.'

'I don't doubt that they can. We must see to the rebuilding of the hall as soon as possible. It isn't appropriate for a thegn to be without a hall.'

Edgar's mention of his rank made Skalda stiffen momentarily.

'Yes, my lord.'

'You may have quarters in the hall once it is rebuilt.

Thegn

Until then you may return to your previous house.'

'My lord, it is gone. Burnt by the invaders.'

Edgar sighed. 'Then we will have to find you a billet elsewhere, won't we?'

They sat in silence for a few moments.

'Tell me how we're doing, Skalda.'

'We lost twelve men during the raid, my lord, including Thegn Wulfmaer. This has stretched our ability to work the fields, and some have fallen fallow this year. I have devised a plan of field rotation which should improve land usage next year. We have enough to feed our people, for now. The invaders are still demanding tax. Four times more than we paid to Edward-king. They have been back, not the same ones who came bringing death, but another kind. Bags of paper, inky fingers. They seek you, sir. They say you must pay for this land. They say that it now belongs to a king called William, and you must now lease it from him. The amount they demand is huge. We could not pay it.'

Edgar nodded. 'Thank you, Skalda, you have done well. You may sleep here until suitable accommodation is found for you.'

'Thank you, my lord.'

'Now please arrange for food and drink to be brought for myself, my housecarls and this child.'

Since Edgar had placed Edda in front of him on his saddle, she had fallen into silence. Her eyes stared into the distance and her face was etched with melancholy and pain. It was not a look that sat well on such a young face. Edgar tried to cajole her into speaking, but she simply didn't answer. It was as though she had withdrawn completely from the world and was no longer truly a part of it. Edgar hoped that she would return soon.

He looked away from the girl and at his carls.
'Where's Alaric?' he asked.

The following day, there was still no sign of Alaric, nor any word from him.

Edgar and Guthrum toured the area administered from Rapendun. Skalda had given an accurate description of the situation. Some fields were indeed fallow that had produced crops the previous year, but the choice of which fields to leave had been wise, the best fields were still producing crops. Edgar talked to many of the farmers to see how they were coping. The news was not good, but all seemed to think that the current crisis was survivable provided nothing else happened. There was great worry about the taxes, but many farmers expressed optimism now that the Thegn was back in control. More than one farmer asked Edgar about Skalda, and what his position now was within Rapendun's hierarchy. Edgar replied that for now, Skalda would continue to administer the estate, at least until Edgar was in a position to take control himself. Yet there was something more to these questions. A hidden undercurrent lurked beneath. Skalda was not well-liked.

Eric and Halfdene had inspected the remains of the hall. What they had found had not been encouraging.

'With the roof gone, the rain and cold has got into the walls and even the upright posts have begun to rot,' Halfdene reported to Edgar later that evening. 'I don't think we can salvage much. It will have to come down and be rebuilt.

'The benches and tables have gone, I don't know where, but there is nothing of value left within at all. The hangings are gone too.'

Edgar took in all the bad news with a stoical face.

'Has anyone seen Alfgaer?' he asked, referring to the priest who officiated at Rapendun's ancient church.

The housecarls glanced at one another. They all shook their heads.

'We need to find him. The people need a spiritual centre to their lives. For all the good it will do in reality, it will help to distract from the current hardships. Maybe Alfgaer can give them some answers from his Bible that I cannot.'

The housecarls exchanged glances.

'It will do tomorrow, lads. Come on, sit and dine with me.'

Edgar turned to Edda, who sat very close to him, in as much contact as she could. 'Edda, do you want to help the cooks and the serving girls like you used to?'

She looked up at him, just for a second, then cast her eyes downwards again. Edgar sighed and wrapped his arm around her thin shoulders.

'No word yet?' muttered Guthrum.

Edgar shook his head.

'Poor kid. Who knows what she's seen?' said Eric.

Changing the subject, Edgar said in a low voice, 'I'm becoming concerned about Skalda. He seems to have done a competent enough job administering the farms whilst we were away, but I sense that there is much unease about him amongst the people.'

'Nobody has a good word for him,' said Halfdene, forthrightly. 'No one will actually come out and say anything directly against him, but I think there is some fear of him. Problem is, many folk seem to think that we're in league with him somehow. They won't open up about whatever it is that they're in fear of.'

Halfdene fell silent as the door opened and a serving girl with a large plate of meat backed into the room, placed the meat on the table and left the way she had come in. Another girl followed with wooden plates and a jug of ale.

Once she had left, the men set about the plate of meat with their short seaxes, piling it onto the wooden plates. Edgar cut some slices of meat and put them on a plate for Edda, who sat in silence and picked at her food with her fingers.

'We need to get to the bottom of this affair with Skalda,' said Guthrum around a mouthful of food.

'Alright, then,' said Edgar. 'There's no need, as far as I can see, to suspect him of being anything other than overly officious, but I would like to know how he's been behaving. I want to know people's suspicions. I also want to know if he's been over-taxing the farms. Eric, Halfdene; I want you to go round tomorrow, on foot. Guthrum and I on horseback may have been a little intimidating. Leave your mail here and go in work clothes. You may get a more honest response like that.'

'You ask me,' said the field-worker, leaning on his spade, 'that Skalda, he's a bit too cosy with them invaders.'

He looked surreptitiously to left and right, to make sure that nobody had overheard him.

'What do you mean, "too cosy"?' asked Halfdene.

The man suddenly looked uncomfortable, turning quickly to look over his shoulder.

'I don't know as I should say,' he began, 'I didn't mean nothing by it.'

Halfdene held out his hand. In it was a shiny silver

penny. It glittered in the sunlight, and the man seemed transfixed by it. The stylized head of old Edward-king looked out at the man.

'Lord Edgar would know why his people are unhappy,' said Halfdene. 'If Skalda is causing problems, then he needs to know. Skalda, on the other hand, needs to know nothing. You see what I mean?' He held the penny between his forefinger and thumb and let it reflect the sunlight.

'Yes, sir. I see.'

'Good man, now find somewhere to put this and tell me what worries you about Skalda.'

Halfdene handed the penny to the labourer, who quickly placed it in a small scrip hanging from his belt.

'He's been walking round the villages and farms with some of the invaders. Not soldiers; well, there were a couple of bored-looking footmen with them, but he didn't talk to them. He was talking to the other fellows.'

'Which other fellows?'

'Looked like clerics. All dressed in dark clothes – expensive-looking, mind. Carried wooden boxes with them that they hung round their necks. There was paper in the boxes and the cleric-fellows were writing down everything Skalda said. He was showing them everything, and they were writing it down.'

'Why was that "too cosy"? Surely Skalda was just doing as these men had told him. He was responsible for the safety of the estate, and if he'd refused then there might have been trouble from the soldiers.'

'Wasn't that, sir,' the man rubbed his stubbly chin with a deeply soil-encrusted hand. 'He was laughing with them. He'd point at something, or someone, and say something and then they'd all have a good laugh. Like best mates, they were. It didn't seem right, what with Lord Wulfmaer being dead and Master Edgar missing. I mean it's not right, is it sir?'

Halfdene patted the man on the shoulder. 'Alright, you can get on with your work.'

He turned and walked away. Ahead of him stood a solitary oak tree by the side of the old north road. He had arranged to meet Eric there at noon, to compare notes and to eat their lunch. He could see that Eric was already there, sitting under the tree, leaning against its great, gnarled trunk.

Halfdene sat down beside him and drew a large chunk of bread from out of his shoulder bag. He tore it in half and gave half to Eric. He followed it with a lump of hard cheese. They sat in silence for a while, eating their lunch and letting the sun soak through their tunics and leggings.

Somewhere near to them, a bird was singing. Halfdene cocked his head towards the birdsong.

'Hear that?' he asked Eric.

'It's a bird,' said Eric, without interest.

'Little bit of bread and no cheeeese!' chanted Halfdene, to the same tune as the birdsong.

'What?'

'That's what my old dad used to say that bird was singing; "Little bit of bread and no cheeeese."'

The bird obligingly repeated its refrain.

Eric laughed. 'It does sound a bit like that,' he said. 'Who would pay attention to a thing like that?'

'My dad would. He noticed things.'

They fell into silence and finished their bread with cheese.

'So,' began Eric, wiping the last crumbs from his lips.

Thegn

'What have you found out about our man?'

Halfdene snorted. 'Not a lot. Several claim that he's been very tight with the Normans who've come through, which may well be true. Can't really blame him for that.'

'Same here. He's a bit of a weasel, but there doesn't seem anything really concrete that we can lay at his feet. Do you think there's anything else we can do here?'

'Shouldn't think so. Let's get back to Edgar and let him know what we've found.'

'Nothing.'

'Yeah, about that.'

Edgar shrugged his shoulders when Eric and Halfdene reported their findings back to him.

'We had to be sure,' he said, dismissing the subject. Edda poured a beaker of ale for each of the housecarls and then topped up Edgar's cup.

'Thank you, Edda,' muttered Edgar quietly. She bobbed a shallow curtsy and left the room in the direction of the kitchens.

Eric raised his eyebrows. 'She's coming round,' he said.

Edgar nodded. 'We had a long talk last night. Well, I did a lot of talking. She did a lot of staring at the floor, but I think she was listening. I still don't know what horrors she must have witnessed. She hasn't said anything about it, and I'm not sure she ever will. She's not said anything about her parents, either. I can only assume that they were amongst those killed at Osmundestun. Guthrum's out there today with a burial party. I sent a couple of men along with them who said that they would be able to recognise the dead, assuming they weren't too mangled. Fortunately, our priest turned up this morning. He's been away to the south, dealing with the spiritual needs of our neighbouring parish. Apparently, their priest died last month and no replacement has yet arrived. I sent Alfgaer after Guthrum, he should be there when the bodies are buried. Appropriate words and so on.'

As he spoke, Edgar's fingers found the small raven amulet around his neck. Its surface was worn and polished, and it brought to mind the old woman who had given it to him, and the herbally-induced dream that had prompted her to do so.

Eric seemed oblivious to the move, but Halfdene narrowed his eyes slightly, unsure yet what the significance could be. Was it just a piece of jewellery, or was it truly the pagan symbol it appeared to be? Halfdene blinked. No point in speculating; a man's beliefs were his own.

When Guthrum returned that evening, he brought Alfgaer in with him. 'The bodies are buried. There was a small consecrated plot of land close to Osmundestun, and we managed to fit them all in there, though we'll have to consider that plot closed for some time. There isn't room for anyone else. Alfgaer did the necessary.'

Edgar indicated for the two men to sit.

Alfgaer twitched in his seat, his eyes darting around the room.

'You seem uncomfortable, Alfgaer, are you unwell?'

'No, Mas… my lord. Not unwell.' He continued to fidget.

'Well, what is it, man?'

'Is… is Skalda here?'

Edgar nodded, 'Yes, he's in one of the other rooms, working on his crop rotation scheme.'

Thegn

Quickly, Alfgaer said, 'May we step outside, my lord? Maybe you would like to visit the grave of your grandfather?'

Edgar glanced at Guthrum, who looked slightly alarmed at the priest's discomfiture.

'Yes, that would be appropriate,' said Edgar.

The three men walked across the enclosure to the church. Alfgaer led them inside and to the east end of the building.

'I had him placed in the crypt, where the bones of the holy Saint Wystan lay. He lies also with the bones of Aethelbald-king and Wiglaf-king.

Alfgaer led them down a staircase to the left of the chancel. He took a candle from a sconce in the wall. The crypt was dark and smelled musty. In niches around the crypt lay funerary chests that held the mortal remains of the great Mercian kings. In the centre of the room were four columns, decorated in a simple spiral pattern, holding up the floor of the chancel above. The shadows danced fitfully in the flickering light of the candle. To one side of the spirally decorated columns, four floor slabs had clearly been moved recently and then replaced.

'Thegn Wulfmaer lies beneath these slabs. He is in good company, I think,' said Alfgaer.

Edgar crouched down and ran his fingers lightly over the slabs and mouthed a silent greeting to his dead grandfather.

Standing up again, he faced Alfgaer.

'What is this all about, Alfgaer? Why are you in fear of Skalda?'

'It is not him I fear, my lord,' replied Alfgaer in a low, urgent voice, 'but his friends.'

'Friends? What friends?'

'The Normans.'

'Why would Skalda be friends with the Normans?'

'He is ambitious, my lord. He believes the future lies with the Normans. He has given them full access to all the information we have about the estate. He has worked assiduously with the Norman clerks, to be sure that they are aware of the full worth of your holdings. I understand that whilst you were away from here, you were deemed to have abandoned your rights. You are not recognised by the new authority as thegn, and a new lord was to be appointed. For all I know, that appointment has already taken place. It depends on who bid the highest amount for it to the Norman Duke.'

Guthrum was growling under his breath, his face angry and grim in the dim, flickering candlelight.

'How came you by such knowledge?' demanded Edgar.

'The Bastard sailed here under a papal banner. The Pope in Rome blessed and approved the invasion, though I don't know why or how. The Normans assume that all priests are bound by that papal approval and that we are therefore bound also to do as the Normans require. I am seen as their ally. I have been with them when they discussed this matter with Skalda.'

'And what's in it for Skalda?'

'He has been promised the stewardship of this land. The new lord will likely be absent most of the time. The Bastard's barons are buying the rights to vast tracts of land. Rapendun is but a small plot to them. Skalda will effectively be thegn.'

'Just let me get at him!' exclaimed Guthrum.

'Then tell me, priest, why you are not bound by papal

Thegn

authority in this matter?'

'I am, my lord, but I am also English, and I feel a compelling loyalty to the memory of your grandfather,' his eyes slid to the recently replaced slabs. 'And therefore to you, too, my lord.'

'Is there then no hope for me, Alfgaer?'

'I am sorry, my lord. On my journeys south, I have seen how the takeover is handled. It involves many soldiers, and if the lawful thegn resists, it also involves much bloodshed and death.'

'Of the innocent, I presume?'

'Always, my lord.'

Guthrum looked in alarm at Edgar. 'Edgar, no,' he began, 'we can raise our fyrd, resist the invader.'

'No, Guthrum. We could raise twenty fyrdmen before Stanford. We lost four there, and two more since during Norman raids. We are down to fourteen housecarls. It's not enough, Guthrum. It's not nearly enough.'

'What of the men of the burwarran? They would stand with us.'

Edgar looked defeated. 'I will not ask them to do so, Guthrum, for we would not win. Those men would die needlessly, and their families would follow in Norman reprisals. We've seen it more than enough times already. Villages sacked; bodies left to rot in the sun. I will not allow that to happen here to my people. My last act as thegn will be the only one I can perform to keep them safe.'

Guthrum opened his mouth to argue some more, but Edgar stilled him with a hand.

'It is my duty, Guthrum. Remember the words of Thegn Godric; a thegn's first duty is to protect his people. The only way I can do that now is by not resisting the

Normans.'

Guthrum's face contorted in rage and sorrow.

'You must see that I am right, Guthrum.'

Guthrum stared at the floor, refusing to speak. His face was red with anger, and his eyes moist.

'Guthrum,' Edgar repeated his name, gently.

Slowly, Guthrum nodded. 'Yes, I see. You are right, my lord.'

'Come, then. We must make preparations. It seems that we are once again homeless.'

With a last look at his grandfather's grave, Edgar turned and headed back up the stairs into the church. Guthrum and Alfgaer followed.

At the top of the stairs, Edgar began striding towards the door.

'Before you go, my lord?' Alfgaer called.

'Yes, what?'

Alfgaer indicated the altar with his hands.

'What? Oh, yes, of course.' Edgar walked back and knelt in front of the altar, above the grave of his grandfather. Guthrum knelt beside him, and in a voice cracked with emotion, Alfgaer spoke words of blessing, invoking the name of Christ, and made the sign of the cross over Edgar's head.

Edgar and Guthrum rose and walked out of the church. As he reached the door, Edgar turned to Alfgaer. 'Thank you, Alfgaer. You have saved many lives today.'

Alfgaer watched the door close behind Edgar, and wondered why the young man had kept such a tight hold on his amulet during the blessing.

As they stepped out of the church into the cold, Edgar

Thegn

turned to Guthrum.

'Bring Skalda to me. I will be in the hall,' he nodded to the skeletal remains of his grandfather's mead hall.

'Aye,' nodded Guthrum and strode purposefully towards the Thegn's residence.

Edgar watched his retreating back, then turned to enter the hall. The great door had been removed, so Edgar walked straight through the gap in the stunted walls where it had once hung. Some of the wattle and daub wall remained, but only in places. The sections of wall were black and sagging. Edgar walked slowly through the wreckage, the carbonised debris crunching and shattering beneath his feet. He recalled the harvest feast, just a year before, when the world had been a more innocent place. In his mind's eye, he saw Alduin the bard making his lute weep musical tears as he sang of the death of good Oswald-king of Mercia. He saw Eric and Guthrum facing each other in the flyting, the insulting competition; he heard the roars of laughter and foot-stamping approval. He saw his grandfather place a shale bracelet in the hands of a tired young fair-haired girl, and he saw the girl turn in wonder to look at her proudly beaming father. He closed his eyes as he thought of what the future held for that little girl.

Guthrum ran back out of the residence and called to Edgar across the diminished walls. 'He's gone,' he said.

'Gone? Where?'

'I don't know. One of the women took him food at midday but left it outside his room. It's still there, untouched.'

Edgar sighed. He took one last look at the derelict hall and strode out, through a gap in the wall. Together, he and Guthrum returned to the house.

Edgar looked around him. There was nothing of his grandfather left in here now. The trappings were all those of a jumped-up farmer who had seen fit to step into the boots of a thegn.

'This is a comfortable house, is it not, Guthrum?'

Guthrum stiffened, uneasy at Edgar's calm, quiet tone. 'It is, my lord,' he replied.

'It has been a good home to my family, has it not?'

'It has, my lord.'

'It will make a fine home for Skalda, will it not?'

Guthrum paused, unwilling to give the reply. 'It… it will, my lord.'

'Get everyone out of the house, send the serving women back to their homes.'

'Yes, my lord.'

'Then burn it.'

'Yes, my lord.'

Guthrum wheeled and headed into the house to clear out any serving women and clerks who may have been in the house.

The fire crackled and roared into the afternoon sky. The heat felt strangely good on Edgar's face as he watched his family home being consumed by the voracious flames. He felt no sense of loss at the sight. His loss was already complete. There was a slight pleasure from knowing that all Skalda's worldly goods were deep within the fire. At a respectful distance, some of the locals had gathered and were staring at the fire. Some of the women were weeping. All stood in silence. They knew this was an ending. The more astute amongst them knew that the ending had come a year before.

Edgar turned at the sound of horses' hooves clattering into the courtyard. Eric and Halfdene pulled their horses up, their faces full of shock at the sight of the house in flames.

Halfdene pulled himself together first. 'Normans,' he said. 'It may be the troop Godric told us about – maybe a hundred foot and a dozen horse. Coming this way.'

Edgar nodded. 'And Skalda will be with them. I do hope he can persuade his new masters to pay for a new house for him, but I doubt it.'

'What of Alaric?' asked Guthrum.

'Alaric can take care of himself. We don't have time to wait for him. We need to go now.'

Guthrum sped off to retrieve horses for himself and Edgar. As they trotted into the courtyard, several of the ceorls ran forward to assist with the saddling.

Edgar climbed up onto his horse and as he did so, a child ran from the ranks of the gathered women. 'Edgar! No!'

Edgar looked down. A ceorl tried to catch her, but Edda sped round him to reach up to Edgar.

'Edgar! Please don't leave me! Please!' Tears were streaking down her cheeks as she tried to grab hold of Edgar's leg. Guthrum ran over to her and grabbed hold of her, holding her easily under one arm. He looked up at Edgar. The vision of Edda receiving her shale bangle once again flashed before Edgar's eyes. He looked down at the struggling, crying girl. He nodded to Guthrum and leaned over to help Edda up onto the saddle in front of him. She turned and buried her face in his chest, sobbing. He placed his hand gently on the back of her head and held her. Then with a nod to his comrades, the little band set off from Rapendun for the last time, along the north road.

The farmers who had gathered to watch the house burn stood aside respectfully, bowing their heads and pulling off their hats. The women stood and stared tearfully at them.

Edgar caught muttered phrases as his people bade him farewell for the last time.

'God bless you, Master Edgar.'

'Good luck, my lord.'

'Travel well, Edgar.'

Edgar rode on without looking back, Edda was sobbing enough for both of them.

19

Back on the Road

'Well, where to this time?' asked Eric as the horses carried them at a walking pace back up the north road. 'Are we going back to live with the Wildmen?'

Edgar shook his head. 'No, I don't think we'd do so well with them. Alfweald is a good man and a fine leader, but as our days there grew, I began to believe that his thinking had gone wrong. His actions are the exact opposite of what we are doing now. You all agree that leaving Rapendun, at least for now, is the right thing to do?'

They all muttered their agreement. None of them had wanted to bring a bloodbath on the people of Rapendun.

'Yet Alfweald will bring death and destruction to thousands by his actions. The only way we can regain what is ours is to organise a true resistance. That means a proper army, such as we had at Stanford when we forced the Norsemen to get out once and for all. Without a proper, disciplined army, we will never get back what we have lost.'

'How are we going to do that?' asked Eric.

'We're not. It will have to come from the earls, or from the king's thegns, or from whatever remains of the Witan. When the call comes, we'll be ready.'

'So what of us, now?'

Guthrum grunted. 'We follow Edgar, Eric. That's what we do.'

Eric remained silent.

'We head north,' said Edgar. 'But well north this time, far beyond the woods of the Wildmen. Into Northumbria, maybe to Bebbanburg.'

Halfdene whistled. 'Bebbanburg. There's a place of legends.'

'It's real enough, it will probably be the last place the Normans get to, maybe they never will, the Northumbrians are a tough bunch.'

'I thought we were tough,' muttered Halfdene.

They rode on in silence for some time, then Guthrum whispered hoarsely, 'Edgar.'

Edgar looked over at him and Guthrum looked pointedly at Edda, still clinging tightly to Edgar, but now apparently asleep.

Edgar nodded and mouthed 'I know. Later.'

Now every time Edgar closed his eyes, he saw not the burning house, not the ruin of the mead hall nor the body of his dead grandfather, but his imaginings of what Edda must have seen. Her mother and father being put to the sword by a merciless foreign soldier, whilst all around, her neighbours were being similarly slaughtered. Did Edda have brothers and sisters? Aunts, uncles, cousins, grandparents? Maybe she had seen them all massacred. How could he abandon her? She was the one amongst all his people for whom he could still possibly do something. It was his duty to protect her, and he would do that to the best of his ability. He would protect her with his life.

She stirred momentarily, whimpered a little and settled back into her fitful sleep. He placed his right arm protectively around her thin shoulders and held his horse's reins with just the left.

The journey north was mercifully uneventful. Although the ravages of the Normans were apparent to begin with, they grew less frequent as the party travelled further north. It was harvest time, and peasant farmers filled the fields, reaping and gathering. Usually too busy to be curious about travellers on the road, they seldom looked up from their onerous tasks.

They passed the occasional ox-cart, bringing huge bales of hay to be stored as cattle feed over the winter. The ceorl farmers nodded respectfully as Edgar and his housecarls passed them by. It was as if the Normans had never arrived. Edgar began to think that here, in fact, they had not. Yet he knew that it would only be a matter of time, a short time at that, before the Bastard's greed sent his murderous thugs north to grab what he claimed was rightfully his.

Three days travel took them at some distance past and beyond the woods of the Wildmen. They followed the same route as they had taken to Stanford the previous year, so their journey only took them into the very eastern edges of the great woodland, some way from the forest proper.

On the evening of the day when Guthrum declared that they must now be north of the vast forest, Edgar ordered them to stop on the banks of a deep, swift-flowing river.

The ground here was sandy by the river's edge, and small pebble beaches lined the bank. Willows drooped lazily into the water, their supple branches dragging along in the fast-flowing stream. The sun was nearing the horizon, and a chill was growing in the air. Autumn was taking a firm hold on the land, and the bleakness of winter was looming not far beyond. Eric and Halfdene collected wood for a fire while Guthrum, hunting bow in hand, ducked through a tatty hedge into a fallow field beyond. Ten minutes later he returned with two hares.

'You know, this stuff's much better if you leave it hanging for a while before cooking it,' said Edgar casually to Edda as they chewed on the roasted meat in the flickering light of the fire.

Edda looked at him and then at the meat in her hands. 'Doesn't it get smelly and horrible?' she said. Guthrum looked across at Edgar, who smiled slightly. It was the most she had said since they left Rapendun over a week before.

'No, not if you don't leave it too long. A week should do for a fellow like this, maybe a little longer in cold weather.'

She took another small nibble. 'Why?'

'The meat goes softer. It's not as tough as this if you leave it for a bit. You must have seen the birds and animals hanging up in the kitchens at Rapendun.'

She nodded. 'I wondered why they did that.'

They sat in companionable silence for a while until Guthrum cleared his throat. 'We will be approaching Eoforwic tomorrow by my reckoning. I think it might be a good idea if we avoided the town, turned east, headed for the coast. We may avoid parties of Normans for longer that way.'

Thegn

Edgar nodded his consent.

The land they travelled through now began to rise, and huge, hump-backed hills began to rear up ahead of them. Guthrum looked uneasily at the hills ahead and the gathering dark clouds on the horizon. It had got steadily colder over the past few days, and the skies were threatening rain.

'I don't much like the look of those fells ahead,' he said to Edgar. 'If we get caught in a heavy rainstorm, we could be in real trouble up there, worse if there's lightning.'

'I'll be honest with you, Guthrum, I'm not sure which way to go.'

'No, neither am I. May I suggest that we head east when we can, keep those hills on our left-hand side?'

'Stay on the low ground close to the coast? Yes, that makes sense. They do look threatening. God only knows what dangers may be lurking there.'

The road complied with their wishes, turning gently towards the north-east along a wide, shallow-bottomed valley. Scattered farmsteads dotted the area, with wide-open fields supporting a scant head of sheep. Arable crops grew too, but the crop seemed poor. There were no signs of a settlement for miles.

They travelled gradually eastwards until one cold, windy morning in mid-October, the last of the hills opened up before them and ahead lay the crinkly pewter vastness of the sea. Broken clouds flew swiftly overhead, allowing beams of sunlight to wheel and race among the peaks and troughs of the sea's surface.

Edda gasped and cried out, 'Edgar! What's that?' she

pointed at the sea.

'That is the sea, Edda. It's the edge of the land. The whole of Britain is surrounded by it. See, look,' he pointed off to her left. 'A ship!'

A small vessel was struggling against the wind a few hundred yards off the shore, its single square sail billowing and flapping in the wind.

'Merchant vessel,' said Guthrum, 'heading south.'

'Where's it come from?' asked Edda, her voice filled with awe.

'I don't know,' said Guthrum. 'Somewhere to the north, One of the ports in northern Northumbria perhaps, maybe even from the land of the Scots.'

'He's not having a nice time of it, is he?' asked Eric, watching the struggling vessel.

'He's doing fine,' replied Guthrum. 'It would take far heavier seas than this to cause serious trouble to that vessel, small though it is.'

'I don't ever want to go on one of those,' said Edda, seriously. 'It looks horrible.'

'Me too,' said Eric with a shudder. 'I've heard that people get very sick on boats and spend the whole of their journeys just throwing up.'

'You get used to it, apparently,' said Guthrum, 'though the only time I travelled on a boat, it was for a short journey and I didn't enjoy it. I wouldn't ever want to go on a sea voyage.'

'Well there's no need for anyone to go on a boat is there?' said Edgar, ruffling Edda's hair. 'We just need to find somewhere warm and comfortable to live, don't we?'

Edda nodded emphatically.

They rode on, taking a path that took them up along the

Thegn

tops of some precipitous looking cliffs, though the path itself was far enough back from the cliff edge for comfort.

Close to the highest point of the cliff, they spotted a farmstead maybe half a mile inland.

'I think it's time we learned where we are, and who's lord of this land,' said Edgar, and they turned off the path towards the farmstead.

As they approached, they saw some men herding a dozen or so cows out of a field towards a large barn.

Edgar rode up to them and one of the men approached him. He looked suspiciously at Edgar.

'Can I help you?' he asked, carefully, noting Edgar's fine cloak and sword.

'I'm looking for the lord of this land, can you tell me where I might find him?'

'That would be Thegn Sigesworth, sir. If you follow this road about another four miles north, you'll come to Bortone, that's where you'll find the Thegn's hall.'

He pointed towards a narrow track on the other side of the field.

Edgar thanked the man and indicated to the others that they should follow him. The track broadened out to become a passable road, and they followed it at a leisurely pace for another hour until they arrived at a compact settlement close to the banks of a clear, slow-moving stream. In the centre of the settlement was a stone-built chapel, and next to it a mead hall within a stockade of wooden posts. The gate was open and there did not appear to be any guards. Nevertheless, Edgar climbed down from his horse, leaving Edda alone in the saddle, and walked cautiously through the gate. The inner court was neat and tidy. A few chickens strutted and clucked to themselves, and a sleepy dog, obviously not on guard duty, cocked an ear at him and thumped his tail on the ground.

A door opened on a building to the side of the mead hall. A woman backed out, carrying a bucket of water in each hand. She turned and faced Edgar.

'Oh!' she exclaimed, and one of the buckets of water slopped over her skirts.

'I'm sorry,' called Edgar, holding up the palm of his hand to her, 'I didn't mean to startle you.'

The woman recovered. 'Who are you?' she demanded.

'My name is Edgar of Rapendun, I wish to speak with Thegn Sigesworth.'

She put down both the buckets and walked up to him. He could see that she was of middle age, powerfully built, with a lived-in face. Her hair, greying blonde, was pulled back severely from her face and fastened in a ponytail at the back.

'You'd better come with me, then,' she said, wiping her hands on the apron wrapped round her waist.

She started walking towards the mead hall, so Edgar followed. She turned her head round and said 'I'm Thingold, by the way. I'm the Thegn's wife.'

She pushed open the door in the mead hall and walked in. Edgar followed. It was dark and warm inside. A large fire burned low in the hearth at the centre of the room.

'Sigesworth?' she called. 'Sigesworth!'

A tall man stepped out from behind a partition wall at the far end of the hall. He held a goose-feather pen and had inky fingers.

'A visitor, Sigesworth. To see you.'

He stepped further out, looked down at the pen in his hand, and returned behind the partition before re-emerging

Thegn

without it. He absent-mindedly wiped his inky fingers on his already heavily marked tunic. His hair was neatly combed, and unfashionably short. His chin was covered with a neatly trimmed beard. His hair was not quite white, but soon would be.

'Hello?' he said, uncertainly.

'Thegn Sigesworth?'

'Yes?' he asked, warily.

'My name is Edgar. I'm Thegn of Rapendun in Mercia.'

Relief flashed across his face. 'Thank the gods for that! I was afraid you might be one of them Norman bastards, come for his money.'

'No, sir. Not me.'

'Well, come! Sit down and share a beaker of ale with me and tell me how things are in Mercia. Thinny, bring us some ale, will you, Love?'

Thingold clucked at him and disappeared out of the door.

They sat on a bench, worn shiny and smooth with age and use. Sigesworth looked drawn and worried.

'Have you had much trouble from the Normans, sir?' asked Edgar.

'No, not really. Other than a demand for a payment to lease my own land from the man who now calls himself king. I can't pay it. I have no idea what will happen to me and Thinny, but I know it won't be good.'

'I know it's no consolation, but it isn't only you. I've been unseated as thegn. Now my companions and I are looking for somewhere to settle for the winter.'

'Companions?'

'I have three housecarls and a young girl, orphaned by the Normans.'

Sigesworth made a non-committal grunt. 'You want to stay here?'

'If that is possible. We would of course work for our keep. If you can't help us, we'll be on our way.'

'Handy are they, these carls of yours?'

'As handy as they come, I would say.'

'Well, that's good. Strong men are always useful. Your men are willing to work for their keep, you say?'

'Of course.'

'And you, would you be willing to act as my housecarl, thegn or no?'

'I can hardly claim that title any longer. My hall is burned and my people are frankly safer without me.'

'How so?'

'The Normans wanted me out. They would not shy from killing every one of my people until I had nobody left to be thegn of.'

'Really? They would do that?'

'They are brutal, Thegn.'

The door opened, and Thingold brought in a large jug of ale and two beakers.

'Go and get your friends, bring them in for a warm and some ale. I'll have a look at them. Thinny, dear,' he looked up at his wife as she placed the ale on the table.

'More beakers,' she finished for him. She looked at Edgar. 'How many?' she asked.

'Four please, my lady.'

'Hah! Don't "my lady" me, young man. I'm nothing more than a scullion!'

She stomped out, and Sigesworth smiled fondly at her retreating back.

Edgar followed her out and into the courtyard. At the

Thegn

gate, he motioned his companions to come in. Edda managed to walk Edgar's horse in, and he smiled indulgently at her. 'We'll make a fine horseman of you yet, young Edda!'

She beamed proudly at his words of praise. He helped her down from the horse as the other three dismounted.

'I'll take care of the horses,' said Halfdene, beginning to remove the saddle from his horse.

'Very well. The rest of you come with me. Halfdene, follow on when you've finished.'

'Aye, Master Edgar.'

Back inside the mead hall, Guthrum and Eric sat beside Edgar on one side, whilst Edda sat on his other side. She sat close to him, making sure she was in contact all the time until Thingold came back in with another jug of ale.

'Who's this then?' she beamed.

'My lady Thingold, this is Edda of Osmundestun.'

Edda got to her feet and curtsied seriously to Thingold. 'How do you do, my lady?' she intoned solemnly.

Thingold clapped her hands with delight. 'What a precious one!' she declared. 'Come with me, my dear, let's leave these men to their boring talk.'

Edda looked at Edgar, and he nodded his approval. She and Thingold then left the mead hall hand in hand.

'The lady Thingold has a way with children, sir,' said Edgar.

'Ah, she always has had. We never had children of our own. She would have made a wonderful mother. What happened with her, Edgar? How is it that a girl child is travelling with four warriors such as yourselves?'

Edgar took a deep breath and related the whole story of the raid on Rapendun and the massacre at Osmundestun. Of how his grandfather was killed, of how his wife had died, of how Edda came to be travelling with them. He admitted that he felt a huge weight of responsibility for the girl.

'I was their thegn, and I was not there for them. I was not there for her, for her parents. They all died because I was not there. Edda is an orphan because I was not there. The weight of the guilt is crushing me. I have to atone for it by protecting that child with my life.'

Edgar did not include in his story the time they had spent with the Wildmen, nor the fact that he was, in the eyes of the Norman invader, a wanted murderer.

After he had finished, Sigesworth sat for a while staring at his cup. He looked at Eric and Guthrum and saw the truth of Edgar's story in their melancholy expressions. He took a deep draught of his ale and held his cup out to Edgar, who refilled it without comment.

'I have had little experience of these Normans,' he began. 'Apart from the tax demand, I've not heard anything of them. Your words fill me with fear. Fear for myself, my people and the whole kingdom. Yet also I feel pity. I feel your pain. There but for the grace of God go I. I fear that the wrath of the Norman will be on us here before we know it. Meanwhile, I would offer you sanctuary here with me and my people. I will take on your three carls as housecarls, they can work for their keep as they would in Rapendun. You, Edgar, if you will accept it, I will take on as my personal carl. I will respect your rank as thegn, but whilst you are here, you must also work for your keep, as must we all, including myself. If this is acceptable to you, then you may stay here as long as you like. God knows I could do with the help. What do you say?'

Edgar glanced up at Guthrum and Eric, who both nodded their assent.

'Thank you, Thegn Sigesworth, we accept your kind offer,' said Edgar.

20

Safety

December 1067 – January 1068

Edgar and the carls soon settled into a routine in Bortone. Thegn Sigesworth was a genial host and employer. Edgar worked side by side with the old Thegn, managing the estates and keeping the accounts in order.

Eric, Halfdene and Guthrum were set to work in the fields, repairing damaged field walls, digging a new well and repairing weather damage on buildings in the settlement, much as they would have done had they been at home in Rapendun.

The chill autumn soon turned to a bitterly cold winter. Snows fell heavily, and the carls found themselves walking through snowy fields searching for lost sheep, dragging them or carrying them back to one of the large shelters that were scattered throughout the countryside around Bortone. Edgar and his housecarls soon became an indispensable part

Thegn

of the workforce. Thegn Sigesworth held sway over a poor area by comparison to Rapendun. His arable land and livestock produced just a fraction of what could be produced further south. The soil here on the wild Northumbrian coast was thin and poor. Sigesworth had only three housecarls, two of whom, Agra and Gothric, were almost beyond their effective working days. The three of them were happy to share their labours with four younger and stronger men.

The third of Sigesworth's housecarls, a tough, short man called Cendred, suffered from agonising pain in his legs in cold weather. Despite his troubles, Cendred was out in the fields almost every day during that harsh winter, ensuring the safety of the animals under his care. When he returned to the mead hall after dark, Thingold would bathe his tortured legs in warm water and massage them with honey, whilst Cendred downed prodigious quantities of the Thegn's ale. His stout resolution and bravery in the face of such debility quickly earned him the respect and admiration of Edgar and his carls.

One evening, by the flickering fire of the mead hall, Guthrum broached the subject with Cendred.

'I've suffered with my legs since I was a young adult. I suppose I was about eighteen years old when they first caused me much pain, but even before then, I can't remember a time when I felt as comfortable as others do in cold weather. As a child, I couldn't play out with my friends on cold days. I was forced to remain by the fireside, helping my mother with household tasks. You can imagine the names I was called by my so-called friends.'

Guthrum nodded. 'Children can be the cruellest of all

of us. Did you suffer some injury as a child that might have caused you this problem?'

'Not that I can recall, and my mother never mentioned anything that happened to me as an infant. There are no scars that I can't explain, so I don't think it's the result of an injury. It seems to me very much like the painful aches that older people suffer from increasingly. It's just that they started very early for me and have therefore had longer to develop. Bugger it.'

He rubbed at his right thigh with both his hands. 'It's this bit that's causing me the most problems at the moment. It'll be better when the weather warms up.'

Despite his infirmity, Cendred was the senior of Sigesworth's housecarls, and in the absence of any children of the Thegn and his wife, had been named as successor to Sigesworth. Cendred himself was unmarried and had no children. Guthrum could not help reflecting that the future looked bleak for Bortone, even if the Normans did not steal it from its rightful owners.

It was on one of these grim, windswept days that a party of Norman militia arrived at the hall at Bortone. As usual, there were a few clerical types, backed up by about a dozen soldiers, mounted and carrying lances, and the long shields of the Norman cavalry, thin and pointed at the bottom, wide and rounded at the top.

One of the clerics called from the back of his horse.

'Sigesworth of Bortone, come forth to answer in the name of the King!'

Sigesworth was sitting with Edgar within the hall when he heard the call. He looked angrily round.

'How dare they address the Thegn in such a manner!'

he said angrily.

Edgar laid a hand on the old Thegn's arm.

'Please, Sigesworth. Please just go and answer them. Do as they ask. It will be much better for you and your people if you do not antagonise them.'

Sigesworth sighed. 'Very well, but only if they keep a civil tongue in their heads.'

'They won't. Please, for your people, for Thingold.'

Sigesworth stood and strode to the door. Edgar remained within. Although he had not told Sigesworth of his wanted status, he knew that by now his description would have been circulated to all the Norman tax-gatherers. Best to keep a low profile. Instead, he walked to the door of the hall and listened.

'I am Sigesworth, Thegn of Bortone,' he heard.

'Sigesworth of Bortone, your land tax has been calculated at four pounds of silver. In the name of the King, I am here to collect the payment in full or in part. Will you be paying in full or in part?'

Edgar could almost hear the old man bristle. He held his breath and silently willed Sigesworth to pay something, anything, to make the Normans go away, at least for now.

The silence grew. Edgar heard the clerics begin to mutter in their barbarian tongue. Then Sigesworth spoke.

'Today I can give you three hundred silver pennies.'

The cleric grunted. 'That is barely more than one pound. You owe far more than that.'

'I owe nothing!' cried Sigesworth.

Edgar tensed, looking across the hall to where his sword lay on the bench where he had been sitting.

'I am empowered by the King to collect this money from you. Failure to supply it will result in this land being leased from the King by someone who can afford it. The choice is yours.'

Another tense silence followed. Then in a quiet voice, Sigesworth answered.

'I will give you the three hundred pennies now. You can give them to your King in part payment of what he demands. Though know this; this land is mine by ancient right, granted to my ancestors by the kings of Northumbria.'

'All land is the King's,' replied the cleric wearily. This was clearly something he repeated many times a day. 'If you don't want to pay, or if you are not able to pay, then leave the land for someone who can. That is your choice. There is the third option, of course…'

Edgar heard the slithering sound of swords being drawn from their scabbards. This was obviously a well-rehearsed piece of theatre, but even so, Edgar ran quietly across the hall and carefully withdrew the Ulfberht blade from its scabbard before hurrying back to the door. As he reached the door, it opened inward, and Sigesworth entered, looking red in the face and visibly furious.

Edgar stood aside, keeping the door between him and the Normans outside. Sigesworth disappeared into his private rooms at the end of the hall and returned a few moments later holding a leather bag, tied at the top with a thong. He closed the door behind him as he walked out with the bag.

He heard the cleric dismount.

'Thank you, Thegn Sigesworth.' His voice was calmer now, as if a crisis point had been passed. It had; Edgar knew.

'Now, it is not that I don't trust you, but I must count out the coin.'

Edgar heard the chink of the coins in the bag and the

Thegn

slow and deliberate counting by the cleric.

'One, two, three, four…'

When he came to the end, he had counted three hundred and two pennies.

'Do you wish to pay three hundred and two pennies now, or do you want two pennies back?' he asked.

'Keep them,' said Sigesworth in clipped tones.

'As you wish.'

Edgar heard the cleric click his fingers twice. 'Receipt,' he ordered one of his assistants. 'Three hundred and two silver pennies from Thegn Sigesworth of Bortone. Dated today.'

There was some hurried scratching of a pen, followed by a ripping sound.

'Thank you, Thegn Sigesworth. I will be back in three months for the balance.'

Edgar listened carefully as the cleric climbed back onto his horse and breathed a sigh of relief when he heard the sound of hooves leaving the courtyard.

The door opened and Edgar stepped back, dropping the point of his sword to the ground. Sigesworth stepped in. His face was red with fury.

'Who do they think they are?' he demanded.

'They think that they are our new masters. I very much fear that they may be right, unless something is done very quickly.'

'What can be done?'

'Only a huge counterstrike would be effective, and with half the earls submitting to the Normans in the hope of retaining favour, and the other half squabbling amongst themselves, I'm afraid that the coordinated action that would be required cannot happen.'

Sigesworth's shoulders sagged. 'What am I to do, Edgar? How can I raise another...' he looked at the receipt in his hand '...six hundred and fifty-eight pence in three months?'

'You may not have to, maybe another part payment would keep them at bay.'

'Do you believe that?'

Edgar closed his eyes momentarily. He sighed.

'No, not really. The Normans are land-hungry. They are here for our land. They don't care about a paltry four pounds of silver. They want Bortone.'

Edgar walked back to the bench and replaced his sword in its scabbard.

'I have seen your accounts, Sigesworth. You could afford it.'

'Yes, but not all those figures are realised. I have enough money if I sell some of my belongings. I have a fine sword, a good quality helmet – two, in fact. That would help, but who would buy such things?'

'Could you not appeal to the Earl for help?'

Sigesworth laughed. 'Which earl? Morcar was deposed and replaced by one of Tostig's old toadies, a slimy little shit called Costig. Costig didn't last long, tax-gatherer for the Bastard as he was. He was killed by one of our own, Osulf of Bebbanburg. Osulf claimed the earldom for himself and for a short while we thought we might have a chance against the Normans, but the latest report I have heard, and I don't know if it's true or not, is that Osulf has been killed in a skirmish with some outlaws. If that's true, then I don't even know who's earl now.'

'I had no idea matters were so complicated.'

'Northumbrian politics has never been short of

Thegn

complications, Edgar. You'll come to learn this, I'm sure.'

'Well, meanwhile, we must all do what we can to ensure that the money is raised, one way or another.'

Sigesworth sighed heavily and sat down on the bench, pouring himself a beaker of thin ale.

'Thank you for your support, but I see little hope, lad.'

Two days later, the temperature rose for the first time in two months and the snows began to thaw a little. Spring had not yet arrived, but Edgar felt a change in the air that may have signified that the worst of the winter was now past.

As Edgar was taking the air shortly before his evening meal, three young boys came racing excitedly into the courtyard.

'Men, men!' they cried.

'What men?' called Edgar to them, running across the courtyard towards them.

'Sir, sir! There's a large party of men coming! All in armour and with banners! They're on big horses and there's a load of foot soldiers behind them.'

'Right, into the hall with you now. Come on, fast as you can.'

Edgar followed the boys into the hall where Sigesworth and his carls were sitting at their bench awaiting the arrival of their meal. Guthrum, Eric and Halfdene sat to the side of them, talking contentedly.

'What's this?' called Sigesworth at the three boys.

'Men coming sir!' said the largest lad.

'They've spotted an armed party coming this way. We should be prepared,' explained Edgar. The six carls immediately sprang to their feet, grabbing their mail shirts, which were never far away from them, and pulling them over their heads. Belts were buckled securely over the shirts, with swords and axes hanging from them. Edgar and Sigesworth ran to collect their mail and weapons.

Each man then pulled on his helmet, and the eight armed men stepped back out into the courtyard. The gate of the palisade was swiftly closed and the eight men took up positions on the palisade wall. Eric passed out the bows and quivers that he had grabbed as he left the hall.

They stood there in tense silence for about five minutes until the column of men appeared cresting the hill on which the palisade stood.

There were eight mounted men, and they were followed by two dozen foot soldiers. They made a splendid sight, with colourful banners fluttering above the horsemen, the riders themselves bedecked in fine, brightly polished mail and helmets, some sporting chain mail face guards, as did Edgar's.

The leader of the horsemen held up his arm and the column stopped. Then he rode forward alone, his black and golden banner streaming behind him. As he got closer, Edgar could see that he was very finely attired. His helmet was decorated with a boar on its crest, and the eyebrows were outlined in bright gold. He pulled up just out of arrow range and removed his helmet. Then he slowly and deliberately withdrew his sword and axe from their hangings and dropped them on the ground beside his horse. Holding his hands away from his sides, he urged his horse forward with a squeeze of his knees and approached the palisade gate. There he stopped, facing eight tightly drawn bows. He held up his hands.

'My name is Osfrith Edwinsson. Until recently I was

Thegn

thegn to Harold Godwinson-king. I seek shelter for myself, three other king's thegns, four thegns and our housecarls. We mean you no harm.'

'Four king's thegns?' called Edgar. 'Why do you not lie dead with Harold-king?'

'That is our shame, sir. We were all wounded at Senlac and had withdrawn from the battle when our King met his end. None of us were fit to return to the battle before it finished.'

'How have you evaded the Normans to get this far north?' demanded Sigesworth.

'We were unable to fight at the end of the battle at Senlac. That does not mean that we are unable to fight now. Our path north is littered with the corpses of the invading dogs. If you do not see fit to provide us with shelter, we will not trouble you. We will continue north. Though it grows dark and our foot soldiers grow weary. We have food aplenty to feed our men with, these lands are rich in game.'

'What do you think, Edgar?' muttered Sigesworth quietly.

'I think they are what he says. Who would pretend to be a king's thegn? A Norman?'

'You're right.' He raised his voice. 'Lower your weapons.' Immediately the arrows aimed at Osfrith were lowered.

'Osfrith Edwinsson, you are welcome in my hall.'

'I thank you, sir,' called the king's thegn. He turned his horse and returned to his men. One of the foot soldiers had gathered the Thegn's weapons and helmet and now held them up for his master to take.

Sigesworth led the men down from the palisade, unbarred the great wooden gate and swung it open.

The party walked into the courtyard. The boys who had first seen them stood staring in wonder. Rarely had they seen such magnificent looking warriors.

The eight thegns dismounted their horses and removed their helmets.

'Hallvindur,' called Osfrith.

A large foot soldier hurried forward.

'Sir!'

'Take a small detail and see to the horses. Join us in the hall when you're done.'

'Sir!' Hallvindur pointed at three men and they hurried forward to tend to the horses.

'You, boys,' called Sigesworth. 'Show these men where to take the horses.'

The three boys stepped forward, wide-eyed and eager to please.

Osfrith and his companions followed Sigesworth into the hall, with Edgar and the carls entering last. Once inside, they divested themselves of their mail and weapons and joined their guests at the table.

'Please be seated,' began Sigesworth, 'I am Sigesworth, Thegn of Bortone, you are welcome at my table.' He looked around, then called 'Thingold!'

His wife entered from the back door, took in the large party with a sweeping glance, rolled her eyes and left again.

'She'll be back in a minute,' said Sigesworth as he sat down. Sure enough, Thingold returned within moments with jugs of ale and fresh loaves and cheese.

The guests set about the bread and cheese with their seaxes, thanking Sigesworth and Thingold as they did.

In between mouthfuls of bread, Osfrith introduced his companions. Three more king's thegns – the kingdom's finest warriors – were his principal comrades. All had suffered badly at Senlac when the Bastard's army fought against the cream of the English nobility and warrior class. They had almost fought to a standstill, Osfrith explained, and then some Norman knights had feigned a retreat, and a section of the fyrd broke from its shield wall to pursue the knights down the hill. It had been a ruse, the shield wall was broken, not from without, but from within. The Normans had surged forward, and it was during this phase of the battle that the four king's thegns had suffered their injuries. Osfrith showed his badly hacked leg, a sword had sliced almost right through the thigh, leaving a deep, ugly scar. Even now his left leg was noticeably thinner than his right, and he walked with a pronounced limp. His companions also showed their scars and wounds. One had the lower half of his right arm missing, another showed the rippling scar across his belly where his mail shirt had been ripped open by a powerful swing from a double-headed battle axe.

'The girl who tended me had to push my guts back in with her bare hands,' he rubbed at the scar and grimaced. 'I think she left a finger ring in there.'

The third thegn displayed his wound, a straggling scar across the right side of his head. The scar ran high above his hairline, making a livid red path of shiny skin where no hair grew.

'Bloody great sword. Man on horse, big swing,' he said, his voice slurred, halting and indistinct.

'Thegn Alstan has not yet fully recovered the power of speech,' said Osfrith, kindly, 'yet his use of the axe in battle is still without par, and speaks more eloquently than many a man with no impediment.'

Alstan bowed slightly to Osfrith, gratitude in his eyes.

Edgar leaned over towards Osfrith. 'I see that you are all men of courage and honour, my lord, and I must apologise for my questioning why you do not lie dead with Harold-king.'

'No apology is needed…' he paused, giving Edgar opportunity to introduce himself.

'Edgar, Thegn of Rapendun, my lord,'

'Rapendun eh? Up here? Another thegn on the run?'

'So it would seem.'

'Anyway, no apology is necessary, Thegn Edgar. Your point was well made. As the King's personal housecarls we should be dead with him, and it is a matter of eternal shame that we are not. Despite my wound, I accompanied Ealdgyth Swan-neck as she trod through the slaughtered flower of England in search of Harold's body. No woman should have to go through that. We found a body eventually that Ealdgyth claimed was his. She pointed to certain marks on intimate areas of his body which she would know of, but not I. She was deeply distressed by the condition of the body. It had been so mutilated that I certainly did not recognise the man who was not only my King but also my friend. His…' Osfrith faltered. 'His manhood had been cut off. Ealdgyth went to the Bastard himself and tore a strip off him. I've always been impressed by the lady Ealdgyth, but standing in front of that big brute of a man and calling him a coward and a savage, she excelled herself. The fucker at least had the decency to look ashamed. I understand that he found out who had done that to Harold and had him executed.'

'What happened to the King's body?' asked Sigesworth.

'I don't know. We were not allowed to have it. The Bastard's men disposed of it somewhere. I suppose he didn't want to create a martyr's grave to inspire the English to resistance.'

'And the body the lady Ealdgyth identified was definitely Harold?'

'She said so. I don't know. I certainly didn't recognise the mangled mess.'

'Is there any chance,' Edgar said slowly and carefully, 'that Harold-king survived the battle?'

Osfrith looked thoughtfully at him. 'I have wondered the same. You are thinking that if the King did survive, then surely an effective resistance could be mustered under his Fighting Man banner. Yes, I too have thought that. But I doubt it will ever happen. I think it most likely that the King did die at Senlac, surrounded by those of his housecarls fortunate enough still to be with him. If he did not, then he would surely have been sorely wounded, perhaps beyond any hope of recovery. No, Edgar of Rapendun, you must not place your hopes there. We have lost the kingdom. A new age has begun, and I fear that we no longer have a place here.'

Edgar nodded sadly.

'I see you too bear the scars of battle. Will you not tell us of your deeds, Thegn Edgar?'

'Not so grand as yours, I think,' said Edgar modestly. 'I was at Stanford when Harold Godwinson-king defeated Harald Sigurdson-king. It was a Dane axe. The axeman must have been exhausted for it to have caused so little damage.'

Osfrith looked at Edgar's lumpy, scarred face, covered with shiny, red skin. He noted the signs of a shattered cheekbone and the damage to the area around the eye.

'I've known very few men to survive a blow from a Dane axe,' he said. 'It looks like you were fortunate to survive.'

'I had a very fine carer.'

Guthrum, Eric and Halfdene all grunted their assent.

'My carls were with me,' Edgar said, indicating the three men. 'I was found to be barely alive on the battlefield. I was taken back to a local village where I was tended to by a living angel.'

'Aye!' cried the three carls.

'You intrigue me,' said Osfrith.

'Her name was Godgifu, a gift from God indeed, though don't ask me which god.'

Osfrith raised an eyebrow but kept silent.

'Godgifu nursed me back to consciousness, and then back to health. By the time I returned to Rapendun, where my grandfather was thegn, she was my wife. Then the Normans came. They killed my grandfather and abducted my wife. By the time I discovered where she was being held, she had killed several Normans and taken her own life.'

A silence fell over the assembled men. Edgar gripped the handle of his seax tightly, the blood draining from his knuckles.

'Edgar, I'm sorry to have asked you to tell your tale. I'm all the sorrier to report that this kind of story is not uncommon these days. Please forgive me,' said Osfrith quietly.

Guthrum leaned over and gently took the seax from Edgar's hand. He turned to the assembled nobility of England.

'My lords,' he began. 'I am no thegn and have no right to address such exalted company as I find myself in, but I must speak.'

'This is Guthrum, Edgar's housecarl,' said Sigesworth.

'He bears listening to.'

Osfrith nodded his assent.

'I have served as a housecarl in Rapendun for twenty-five years. Firstly, for Thegn Wulfmaer, my lord Edgar's grandfather of blessed memory, and now for Edgar. Like you, my lord Osfrith, I counted my masters not only my thegns but also my friends. Thegn Edgar has suffered at the hands of the Normans as much as any man. His grandfather cruelly slain, his hall burned, his lands seized, his beloved wife seized and killed, for make no mistake, it was the Normans who killed the lady Godgifu, no matter that she herself was their instrument. Under his leadership, we have slaughtered more Normans than I can count. We have fought with the Wildmen of the woods, we have fought alone. Without Edgar, Eric, Halfdene and I would undoubtedly have been dead by now.'

'Aye!' cried Eric and Halfdene enthusiastically.

'He has saved us, and he has saved a young girl by the name of Edda, who I hope is currently working in the kitchens to bring us some more food.'

A laugh rose from Sigesworth and the carls.

'Might I beg your Lordships' indulgence to raise a cup of ale to my lord and my friend, Edgar, and to his wife, whom we all loved as sister or daughter, if not as wife?'

A rousing chorus of approval filled the hall, and all the gathered thegns, led by Osfrith Edwinsson stood and called 'To Edgar and Godgifu!'

They raised their cups and as a mark of respect downed the ale in them in a single swig.

Edgar acknowledged the compliment and patted Guthrum's shoulder in thanks.

When everyone sat down again, Edgar asked Osfrith,

'So what brings you this far north? Is there a chance of a fightback? Do you know of any plans?'

'I'm afraid not, Edgar. I wish it were otherwise, but my companions and I are leaving England. We intend to travel across to Denmark and find places for ourselves over there. I've heard that Sweyn Estrithson-king of Denmark pays well for experienced warriors. I think we shall be trying our luck at his court.'

'That makes me sad, my lord, that what is left of the flower of England is to be lost to us forever.'

'It is sad, Edgar, but what choice have we? I can see no possibility of a coordinated resistance to the Normans, my companions and I have all been ousted from our lands, as have you. Many of us, like you, have lost family and friends to the invaders. If we remain, we will be living on our wits, hunted like dogs. At least in Sweyn-king's court we will still have some dignity and some purpose in life.'

'And what if a proper resistance can be organised? What if the people rise up against the oppressor?'

'If that does happen, then I shall return with as many warriors as I can muster. Believe me, Edgar, I want nothing more than to see England returned to the English, and the Norman curs whipped out of the country for good, but I don't see it happening.'

'No. You're right, though I hate to admit it.'

'Yes, I'm right. We are right to leave.' He took a swig from his cup. 'You should consider coming with us.'

'Why would I leave?' asked Edgar, astonished.

'For exactly the same reasons that we're leaving. What is left for you here? Seriously?'

Edgar shook his head. 'I don't know. It doesn't feel right somehow.'

'It doesn't feel right to me, either, nor to any of us. It's just that we're a little short of options. Stay and live like a beggar, or be killed, or leave and stay alive with some dignity. Poor choice, but there it is.'

Edgar chewed on a lump of bread for a few moments. 'When do you plan to leave? Surely there won't be many ships crossing the sea in this weather?'

'No, we're going to head up to Bebbanburg, sell our services there until the ships start sailing again in the spring.'

Edgar nodded and chewed thoughtfully on his bread.

21

Decision

February – April 1068

Sigesworth sat in his private room in the hall, carefully counting out the coin which he kept in a locked box. He still had nowhere near enough to pay off the Norman tax-collector when he called next month.

He put the coins carefully away and locked the box with the little bronze key that hung on a leather thong round his neck. He put his elbows on the table and his face in his hands. There was no way that he could see of keeping his land. He had been thegn here for over thirty years, since the early death of his father. He knew nothing else. He was too old to join mercenary brigades like Osfrith Edwinsson and his companions had set off to do. Where would he go? Maybe the new Norman owner would allow Sigesworth to stay on as a manager? He didn't know, and fear started to gnaw at his belly.

Thingold walked through the door and saw her

husband in his despair. She walked over to him and held his head against her breast.

'What are we to do, Thingold?' he mumbled.

'I don't know, my love. You'll think of something. You always do.'

Spring had arrived slowly. Slightly warmer spells that promised better weather ahead had faltered and further snows had fallen. Eventually, six weeks behind its normal schedule, spring appeared to have arrived at last. Lambs had been born at the normal time, but the fierce weather had carried many of the newborns away. With losses amongst the older sheep as well, the Thegn's flock was looking sadly depleted. Resources were going to be strained this year.

Edgar called his carls to a meeting well away from the stockade, by an oak tree that had once been struck by lightning and now grew in a fantastical, twisted way. They sat with their backs to the trunk, their feet pointing outward across the fields.

'Things don't look so good here at the moment,' Edgar began.

'No, we've lost too many lambs to the snows. The crops are looking thin and weedy, too,' agreed Halfdene, who had helped with the ploughing through ground frozen hard. 'That doesn't surprise me though, and there's time yet for them to pick up.'

'The cows are doing well,' said Eric. 'We lost a couple during the final cold snap, but many are showing signs of being pregnant after we introduced the bull to the field.'

'Well, that's good,' said Edgar, 'but the fact is that the expected yield this year is well down on previous years. Sigesworth is going to have a hard time ensuring that everyone is properly fed. I think we have to face the fact that we're going to be more of a burden to Bortone this year than we are a help.'

There were mutters of agreement from the three carls.

'I think we have to face the fact that it's time for us to move on. I'm not sure where. Nowhere will have fared much better than Bortone after a winter like the one we've just had, but maybe if we find a larger community, better able to support itself than Bortone, then maybe we will fare better.'

The carls thought about Edgar's words for a moment, then Guthrum said. 'I'm loathed to move on. I've felt quite content here, but Edgar's words make sense. We can't impose ourselves any longer on Thegn Sigesworth's hospitality. I think we've acquitted ourselves well whilst we've been here, but from here on I fear, as Edgar says, we may become a burden.'

'Anyone got any different opinions?' asked Edgar.

Eric and Halfdene shook their heads.

'No? Right, I'll not inform Sigesworth of our decision yet, I'll wait until we've firmed up our plans a bit, then we can let him know where we're going to.'

Edgar stood up and the carls followed suit. As they walked across the field towards the road back to Bortone, a party of riders came into view round the corner.

'Shit!' said Guthrum.

'They've seen us. Gods, we're getting slack! Act like farmers.'

They continued walking to the road and arrived at the same time as the riders. Two clerics and four soldiers. The riders stopped and one of the clerics looked down on the four men. Dressed in their peasant smocks and not carrying any weapons, Edgar and his companions looked like common farmers and so should not arouse any suspicion.

Edgar pulled up his cloak's hood to hide his instantly recognisable features, a habit he had developed since he had learned that he was being hunted and his description had been circulated.

'You!' called the cleric.

'Me, sir?' said Guthrum, pointing at himself.

'You'll do. We are looking for a collection of hovels called Bortone. Where is it?' His English was heavily accented, but understandable.

'Oh, er, it's just along this road, sir, 'bout another two miles.'

The cleric looked satisfied and kicked at his horse to get it walking again.

'Hold,' said the other cleric, a slimmer man with thinning black hair, a long, knife-thin nose and dark eyes that were too close together. The first cleric stopped his horse again.

'You,' said the thin cleric, pointing at Edgar, who had been hanging back behind the three carls. 'Remove your hood.'

Edgar felt a rush of adrenalin course through him and a chill gripped his stomach.

'Me, sir?' he asked innocently.

'Yes, you! You're the only one with a hood, aren't you? Remove it at once.'

Edgar could sense the carls stiffening, preparing for a fight. Hands crept slightly closer to seaxes. He lifted his hands to his hood and slowly withdrew it from his head. The cleric recoiled.

'No wonder you keep that hidden. Drunken fighting no

doubt. You English are all the same. Filthy dogs. Ride on.'

The riders urged their horses forward.

The four men watched the riders receding into the distance.

'That was close,' said Eric.

'That was far too close,' replied Edgar. 'We'll have to be more careful in future. It's seemed so safe here that we're getting lax.'

'What do you think they wanted at Bortone?' asked Halfdene. 'The remainder of the tax isn't due for another month.'

'I think we should follow, but keep a healthy distance between us. We'll return to Bortone but not enter the palisade. I didn't like the way that shifty bugger was looking at me.'

They made their way cautiously back to Bortone. When they got close to the palisade, they kept buildings between themselves and it. They split up and each hid behind a house or barn, keeping an eye on the palisade entrance. After only a few minutes, the party of riders emerged and turned south, away from the settlement. Edgar and the carls walked into the stockade and into the hall.

'We saw the Normans,' said Edgar to Sigesworth. 'What did they want?'

Sigesworth sighed. 'More threats. I am to have no further "grace period" as they call it. I am to pay the full amount in fourteen days, or I will be evicted on the point of a sword.'

'I'm sorry, Sigesworth, I wish there was more that we could do.'

'I wish there was, too, but there isn't. I must make what

arrangements I can.'

Sigesworth turned sadly away from them and retired to his private room.

'Is there really nothing we can do?' asked Eric quietly. 'I mean, couldn't we fight them when they come?'

'Eric, don't be foolish,' snapped Guthrum. 'We are four, with Sigesworth's carls still only seven. They will come in force, and if by some miracle we did repel them, they would return in ever greater force, and take it out not only on us and the Thegn but also on the people who live here.'

Eric looked abashed. 'Sorry,' he said.

Sigesworth's mood deepened by the day. He fell into long silences, whilst Thingold fussed anxiously around him. Cendred spent more and more time with the Thegn as they struggled to hatch desperate plots to gain some money. All to no avail, and the deadline drew ever closer.

One night, after the Thegn and all the carls had eaten their meal, and as the ale was beginning to flow, Sigesworth hurried out of his private room, a look of shock and fear on his face.

'Edgar!' he called.

Edgar rose and hurried over to him. 'Sigesworth, what's wrong?' he asked, full of concern for the old man.

'Come with me,' replied Sigesworth and led Edgar back into his private room. Edgar gasped as he entered the room. In one corner, a man sat calmly on a stool.

'Alaric!' cried Edgar.

'You know this man?' demanded Sigesworth.

'Indeed I do. Thegn Sigesworth, this is Alaric. He's a spy, though I'm never quite sure for whom. He's been of great assistance to me in the past.'

'How did he get into my private chambers?' asked Sigesworth angrily.

Alaric rose from his stool. 'Your forgiveness, my lord. Walls and doors are for me less of an obstacle than for most men.'

'What do you mean by that?' asked Sigesworth.

'He's sneaky,' replied Edgar.

'Sneaky I am. It is good to see you again, my lord.' He rose and grasped Edgar by the hand.

'Where did you go, Alaric? We were supposed to meet at Rapendun.'

'I apologise, sir. Events took a turn that I had to follow. There was a large party of Normans about two miles to the south of Rapendun when I arrived there; the day before you did, I believe.'

'Yes, that's right. One of my grandfather's managers, a man called Skalda, who was supposed to be safeguarding the estates, was in league with them. We left when we heard they were approaching.'

'You did well, then. They were after your blood. They would probably have taken the whole town, too, if you had been there. As it was, bloodshed was minimal. For the Normans.'

Edgar closed his eyes and breathed deeply. 'I left in order to avoid bloodshed.'

'Bloodshed cannot be avoided where the Normans are concerned, sir. All we can do is try to lessen it. In that, you succeeded.'

'Were you there?'

'Yes, sir. I inveigled my way into the Norman party, citing myself as a former servant of Guillaume de Caen. Fortunately for me, the leader of the party was one of Baron de Barentin's men, and knew of de Caen. I informed him most sorrowfully of my former master's demise. The man seemed unconcerned about the fate of his colleague, but the story helped me to work my way in amongst them without suspicion. I thought I could be of more use there than on the run with you.'

'Good, Alaric, good.'

Sigesworth was looking mollified by Alaric's account of himself. 'You two carry on,' he said. 'I'll fetch ale.'

Sigesworth shut the door behind him and Alaric closed the gap between himself and Edgar.

He began speaking quietly and urgently. 'You have been spotted and recognised.'

Edgar cursed. 'The thin nosed cleric,' he spat.

'Yes, he's a crafty one. Face like a rat, mind as sharp as a razor. You wouldn't think it to look at him, but he's one of de Barentin's top advisers. The Baron himself is close by and has been told of the sighting. He's biding his time. He knows you're here or hereabouts, and he knows that the tax is to be collected here in just a few days. He will come himself, in force, and demand that you be handed over to him. Failing that, well, you know what the consequences will be.'

Edgar sat down and rubbed his chin.

'I have to get out of here. I'm putting everyone in danger again.'

'It's worse. I understand that de Barentin is going to announce a reward for your capture. Your potential enemies multiply around you, my lord.'

Edgar's shoulders sagged and he rubbed unconsciously at the scars on his face.

'What are my options, Alaric? I've already decided to

move on from Sigesworth's land. It's not wealthy and my men and I will soon be putting an unnecessary strain on their resources. I've considered moving further north, perhaps even to Bebbanburg itself. Do you have any information that might help?'

'I fear not, sir. The Normans' grip is as solid to the north as it is here. There are rumours of resistance, but little sign of a coordinated authority. I have heard that some thegns and former thegns, forgive me, maybe even many, are leaving England. Some have gone to Ireland, and good luck to them, but most are heading for the Norse lands.'

'I'm beginning to see that as a viable option. Out from under the Norman iron fist. At least until there is some sign of an organised resistance.'

'You have only days to decide your future, sir. The Baron will be here before a week is out, and by then your choices will be gone.'

'I see that. Will you wait here? I'll bring in Guthrum, Eric and Halfdene.'

'I cannot wait much longer, sir. I am expected back at de Barentin's headquarters. I will be reporting that your whereabouts are uncertain, but still within the area.'

'Can't you tell him that I've gone north?'

'That may precipitate an earlier raid on this place, in which case, you would be discovered anyway. If the Baron still believes that you are here, thinking yourself safe and undiscovered, he will bide his time.'

'Yes, I see. Very well, Alaric, we will be brief.'

Edgar opened the door of Sigesworth to find the old man behind the door with a jug in his hand.

He smiled at Edgar. 'Ale for your friend,' he said.

'Thank you,' said Edgar, taking the jug from him. 'May

we use your room a little longer?'

'Of course, just call me if you need anything.'

The three carls reacted in astonishment to see Alaric waiting for them in the Thegn's room. Between them, Edgar and Alaric relayed the information that Alaric had gathered, and the disturbing news that Edgar had been recognised and that de Barentin would be coming in force.

Guthrum was in no doubt. 'We must leave,' he said.

'Eric, Halfdene? What do you say?'

Eric replied for both of them. 'We'll follow you wherever you go.'

Edgar nodded and rubbed his scarred face again. After a moment, he had made his decision.

'Very well. I think we are all in agreement. We must arrange passage to the Norse lands. Where's the nearest port?'

Halfdene spoke up. 'There's a port at Bretlinton, and a market. Many merchant vessels dock there during the summer months, I'm told. The merchants will be starting to return now after the heavy winter seas. I'll make enquiries in the morning, see if I can gain passage for all of us, or failing that, just for Edgar, as it seems to me that he's the one in most peril from this de Barentin character. If we're not in his company then we'll probably be ignored, and we can join him later as passage becomes available.'

'Good, Halfdene. Though I hate to be seen to be fleeing, especially if I have to leave my most trusted companions behind.'

'Your choices are very limited, sir. I agree with Halfdene,' said Alaric.

'Everyone?' asked Edgar.

They all nodded and muttered their agreement.

'The matter is settled then. Halfdene, make what enquiries are necessary and if possible, book passage for all of us, including Edda.'

'Edda? My lord, are you sure? Would she not be better remaining here?'

'I think no one would be better remaining here. I won't leave her to the mercy of the Normans. We know what that'll mean. Edda is all that's left of my people of Rapendun, and I will not abandon her.'

Halfdene inclined his head in polite submission. 'As you will,' he said.

The following morning, Halfdene set off for Bretlinton. The day was bright and fresh, a light wind ruffled his horse's mane as he rode. The little town of Brctlinton was about six miles from Bortone, and Halfdene had the horse trot for most of the way.

He arrived around mid-morning and proceeded to the harbour, where the wooden jetties thrust out into the calm swell of the North Sea. Several boats were tied up to the moorings, and leaving his horse tied to a post on the seafront, he walked casually amongst the men unloading the cargo from the ships.

One was a wide, flat-bottomed boat, filled with boxes of some unidentified cargo.

A large man was directing the unloading. Local workers heaved the boxes onto their shoulders and scrabbled onto the jetty, taking the boxes into a warehouse where a stout bald man stood, checking a manifest and ticking items off as they were placed in the warehouse.

'Good morning to you,' called Halfdene to the man

Thegn

supervising the work on the ship.

'A' right,' replied the man non-committedly.

'I wonder if you can help me?' continued Halfdene.

'Mebbe,' grunted the man as he pointed to a crate and one of the labourers bent over to pick it up.

'Where have you come from?' asked Halfdene.

'Berewich,' replied the man. Berewich to Bebbanburg to here, back to Bebbanburg, back to Berewich,' recited the man.

'Do you know if there are any Norse merchants here?'

'I wouldne know,' he said. 'Talk to yon wee feller,' he pointed at the manifest ticker.

'Thank you, I will,' said Halfdene jauntily.

He walked back along the jetty but then spotted a sleek longship with an exquisitely carved horse's head at the prow. He turned towards it. The only person on board was a thin, sallow-faced youth who looked suspiciously at Halfdene as he approached.

'Morning,' said Halfdene to the youth.

'God dag,' replied the young man.

Halfdene switched to Danish. 'You're a Danish vessel?' he asked.

'We are,' said the young man, reluctantly.

'When are you sailing back home?'

'When the captain's done with his business.'

'What would that business be?' asked Halfdene patiently.

'Who are you?' demanded the youth.

'My name is Halfdene, I'm a housecarl.'

As he finished speaking, Halfdene felt a hard, cold point nestle in the small of his back.

'Is this man bothering you Orvar?' said a harsh voice in

Danish behind Halfdene.

'Wants to know the captain's business.'

'Does he now? Turn round, stranger, nice and slowly, then you won't get ripped.'

Halfdene held his arms away from his sides and turned to face the man with the harsh voice. The face did little to improve his impression. Wild, dirty grey hair and beard streamed from the man's head. His mouth was turned into a cruel smile. His face was crossed by a wicked scar, almost as severe as Edgar's, but the weapon that had made this scar had taken an eye. The single remaining eye glittered with malice.

'What do you want with knowing the captain's business?' he rasped.

'I don't really care what your captain's business might be, it's no concern of mine.'

'Then why ask?'

'I simply want to know how soon it will be before you're heading back to the Danish lands.'

'Trying to get rid of us so quickly? And we haven't even got to know each other properly yet.'

Halfdene sighed. 'Are you going to make this difficult?' he asked, tiredly.

'Not for me, son,' said the wild-haired man.

'Then tell me, when are you heading back?'

'No business of yours,' breathed the man. His putrid breath washed over Halfdene's face.

'I could make it my business,' said Halfdene, patting his tunic, under which a purse of coins chinked invitingly.

'Well now, that's different,' said the man. 'I'll have that.'

'You'll have some if you answer my questions.'

'That's not the deal, laddie,' snarled the man, pulling

back his sword ready to strike.

Halfdene feinted away from the man, his swing going wide. As he fell back, Halfdene pulled the extra-long seax from its scabbard and brought it point upwards under the man's chin. With his left hand, he grabbed hold of the man's sword wrist and forced the blade down until it scratched on the wooden pier.

'Drop the sword and live,' he hissed, pressing home his seax a little further.

The sword clattered onto the jetty. Halfdene maintained his hold on his opponent's wrist and swung him round so that Halfdene now stood behind him, the seax still pricking at the soft flesh under the man's chin.

'You're not very polite,' said Halfdene. 'Down you go.'

He pushed his knees hard into the back of the other man's knees, forcing him to the ground.

'Now, just answer me. When are you sailing back to the Danish lands?'

The man looked sullenly up at Halfdene. 'A few days,' he spat. 'Hah!' He looked down the jetty. 'Looks like your luck's up, boy!'

Halfdene looked towards the land end of the jetty. A group of men was walking towards them, drawing their swords as they came. At their head was a small, clean-shaven man in a close-fitting red tunic, bordered with fine braid. He held up his hand and his followers stopped.

'Hold!' he called.

Stepping forward towards Halfdene, the man spoke softly. 'Unhand my man, or it will not go well for you.'

Halfdene removed his seax from the man's throat and stepped back, smoothly replacing the seax in its scabbard.

'Rolki, pick up your sword and get on the ship.'

The rough man did as he was told.

'I take it you're the captain?' stated Halfdene.

'I am. Why were you assaulting my crewman?'

'I was defending myself. Your man had just stated his intention of robbing me.'

The captain's eyes flicked towards the youth on the ship, who nodded tightly.

A hand signal from the captain had his men resheathing their swords.

'Rolki can be a little enthusiastic at times. What business do you have here?'

'I was asking when you would be returning home.'

'And why would you want to know that?'

'I seek passage for four men and a girl child.'

'Let me guess. You're a thegn fleeing the Normans?'

'The reasons don't concern you. I can make it profitable for you.'

'Stormleaper is not a pleasure boat for fee-paying passengers,' said the captain, indicating his ship.

'I would have thought that any way of making a profit would be worth consideration.'

'You would have to make it very worth my time. And you would work your passage. Do you have experience with ships?'

'No.'

'I think you would probably get the hang of rowing fairly quickly if the need arose.'

'I dare say we would,' agreed Halfdene.

'And the girl?'

'She is but a child, she could not row.'

'How old?'

Halfdene did not like the direction the questions were

taking.

'Not old enough.' He placed his hand lightly on the handle of his seax to add weight to his words. 'But old enough for any man to die in the trying.'

The captain smiled. 'Very well. You agree to row and to pay?'

'You'll take all of us?'

'I will. The girl will be under my protection whilst on the ship. Present yourselves on the jetty before dawn in three days. Now, to the matter of the fare…'

Halfdene returned that afternoon with news of the passage he had arranged. The price had been steep, but affordable, and the fast, sleek ship offered their best chance of escaping quickly and unobtrusively.

'What was he like, this captain?' asked Edgar.

'Totally in control of his crew, I thought. He's small but must be tough to command such a crew. Very dapper. Shaved with neat hair and expensive clothes.'

'Nobleman?'

'I would say so.'

'Right. Well done, Halfdene. It seems we need just keep our heads down, or more specifically, my head down for three days and then we shall be away.'

'To what?' asked Eric.

'We'll know when we get there. When is life ever more certain than that?' replied Edgar.

'Might I suggest that you remain within the palisade until we're ready to go?' asked Guthrum. 'It would be well if de Barentin were not certain of your whereabouts. If he knows for sure that you are here, he will almost certainly post watchers to make sure you don't leave before he's ready to take you.'

'I think it's pretty certain that this place will be being watched in any event. Not just here, either, but the area all around. Our departure must be conducted with the utmost discretion. Alright, everybody, just three days. Do nothing to attract attention. Appear dull and slow-witted if approached by any Norman. Don't be riled by anything they say, just bow and say "Yes, sir", however much it catches in the throat. The last thing we want to do is draw attention to Bortone, it will make departure very difficult, if not impossible. Now, be about your tasks.'

22

Last Journey

The following morning, Edgar sat at the long table in the mead hall, deep in thought. He was devising and refining ways to get away from Bortone and to the port as quickly and discreetly as possible.

Sigesworth had not been present at the discussions about escape that he and the carls had held with Alaric, and had not been told about Halfdene's mission to the port at Bretlinton. Edgar had, however, decided that it was necessary to tell Sigesworth of their plans. Firstly, they owed it to him as he had been a generous host, and they all felt an affection for him and Thingold. Secondly, Sigesworth may be able to advise about routes that the four of them were unaware of. This final act of help from Sigesworth would be invaluable. Sigesworth had not, however, been present at the breakfast table and Edgar had not seen him afterwards either.

As he sat thinking, Edda wandered in from the back, a

broom held tightly in her hands. She began sweeping up the old rushes, which were grey and flattened.

'Edda, come and sit with me a while, we need to talk,' called Edgar.

Edda walked over with the broom held in one hand.

'Just for a short while, Master Edgar,' she chided, 'I must get on with my work.'

'Just a short while then. Well…' he stopped, short of words already. Edda looked at him inquisitively.

'How are you enjoying your stay here in Bortone?' he continued.

'I like it well enough, Master Edgar. I have plenty of work to do, and Lady Thingold is teaching me to weave. She's kind to me.'

'That's good. I'm glad you're happy.'

Edda's eyes narrowed. Young though she was, she was proving time and again that she had a wise head on her shoulders.

'Why, what's going to change?'

Edgar laughed a little, caught off-guard by Edda's insightful comment.

'You are a bright one, aren't you?' he asked. She simply stared back at him.

'Alright. You know that as far as the Normans are concerned, I'm a wanted man for killing an evil man called de Caen?'

'I know you had to kill someone to rescue some women whilst you were searching for the lady Godgifu.'

'That's right. Well, this particular man was a deputy to a powerful Norman lord called Roger de Barentin. And he hasn't taken too kindly to me killing him.'

She shrugged. 'This is a war. People get killed.'

'The Normans have chosen not to see it as a war. They have decided that they have God on their side and any opposition is treason and rebellion.'

'But God's on our side, isn't He?'

Edgar was reminded of the conversation he had had with Halfdene and Modbert on the road to Eoforwic over a year ago. How long ago it seemed, surely more than eighteen months? Once again, he found himself wondering what had happened to Modbert, and whether his old friend was still alive somewhere or if his bones lay whitening along with so many others on the field of Stanford. He forcefully brought himself back to the present.

'In any conflict, both sides believe God is with them,' he said.

'But how can you ever know for sure?'

'You can't, I'm afraid. That is why a man who absolutely knows that God is on his side is very dangerous. For in his own eyes he can do no wrong, no matter what he does, as all that he does is ordained as right and proper by God.'

'That's silly.'

'Yes, it is. The Normans have proved in spades how dangerous the righteous man can be.'

Edda shook her head as if to clear it of a fog.

'So, what did you want to tell me, then?'

He smiled at her and ruffled her flaxen hair. 'I've been seen by an agent of this de Barentin. He knows that I'm somewhere in this area, and he believes that I'm right here,' he pointed at the bench he was sitting on. 'He's right, of course. He plans to take me by force of arms within the next few days.'

Edda's eyes opened wide.

'Then we must leave,' she stood up as if she would lead

Edgar out of the hall and far away that very moment.

'We will be leaving. In three days.'

'Why wait so long? This man and his soldiers may be here any moment.'

'We have good reason to believe that he won't be here before we leave. We're waiting for three days because we've secured passage on a ship that will take us to the lands of the Danes, and it leaves in three days.'

Edda's hand flew to her mouth. 'Sailing on the sea?'

'Yes, that's the only way to get there.'

'How far is it?'

'Many miles. It will take us several days in the ship.'

'I've never been in a ship. I've only ever seen the sea during that time we travelled along the coast on our way here. It looked awful.'

'I've never been on a ship either, Edda. Don't worry about it, we'll be quite safe. It's a good ship with an experienced crew and a strong captain. We'll be fine.'

She looked worried. 'Don't you dare go without me!'

'If I was planning to do that, I wouldn't have told you all about it now, would I?'

'Suppose not.'

'Good. Now, not a word to anyone about this. It's a secret. The fewer people who know, the less chance that word about it can get back to de Barentin, and we'll slip away safely and easily.'

'Yes, Edgar, I understand.'

'Good girl. Now, be ready to go when we come for you. Back to your sweeping now. Oh, by the way, have you seen Thegn Sigesworth this morning?'

'No. Lady Thingold said he was up very early. She said he had to ride out to discuss some business with one of his neighbours to the south. She seemed quite pleased. She thinks that he might have some business that may help them with the tax, though she said that he wouldn't tell her what it was, something to do with the price of sheep.'

'That's good then. Thank you, off you go.'

Edda stood up without a further word and returned to her duties with a serious look on her face. If he was honest with himself, Edgar was also very worried about the sea voyage. Several days in an open boat on that terrifying, heaving water left a cold lump in the pit of his stomach, and a strong desire to rush to the privies.

Sigesworth returned to Bortone late that afternoon. He strode into the mead hall, where Edgar was in discussion with Guthrum about their forthcoming escape.

'Sigesworth,' called Edgar to him as he entered. 'Come and sit with us, there's much we need to discuss.'

'Oh?' said Sigesworth, pulling off his riding gloves and tossing them onto the table.

'I trust your business this morning was successful?'

'What? What do you mean?'

'Thingold believes you have a plan to raise some coin for the tax.'

'Oh, I see. Yes, yes indeed. I have been discussing a mutually beneficial venture with Thegn Ungeld in Chelc. We think it might just work, but I doubt that we have time to see it bear fruit.'

'I'm sorry.'

'Not your fault, lad. Now, what do you want to talk to me about?'

Edgar explained in outline the problems that faced him.

'You're a wanted man? For murder?' Sigesworth looked

shocked.

'It was not murder, my lord, it was a legitimate execution of a looter and kidnapper. No court in the land would find Edgar guilty of murder,' said Guthrum.

'No court *would* have found me guilty, Guthrum. The courts now will just be there to impose the Bastard's will. If tried today, I would be found guilty. So you see our problem, Sigesworth?'

'You must get away from here. I can't protect you from a company of Norman soldiers.'

'No, and we wouldn't expect you even to try. If I'm here when de Barentin arrives to collect his tax, then it will be bad for you and for all of Bortone. If I'm not here and you can claim complete ignorance of my existence, then at least you will be spared that particular piece of Norman wrath.'

'I see. There are seven days before the tax is due to be collected, though I wouldn't be surprised if the Norman bastards turned up early for it. You must go soon.'

'We leave the night after tomorrow. Passage has been secured on a Danish ship to take us away across the sea.'

'Good, very good. I take it that it will be sailing from Bretlinton?'

'That's right.'

'I'll travel to Bretlinton with you.'

'That isn't necessary, Sigesworth. Your help to us has already been beyond our ability to repay.'

'No, I insist. There's a much quieter route to the port town. It's slightly longer but it passes through woodlands and is hardly ever used. It was the main route when I was a boy, but we hacked out a more direct route about thirty years ago. That's the present road. That was when we had regular trade with the merchants from the ships, of course,'

Thegn

he said ruefully.

'Thank you, Sigesworth. That would be a great help.'

On their last night with Sigesworth and Thingold, Edgar, Guthrum, Eric and Halfdene were treated to the best feast that the household could manage. Three lambs had been slaughtered and a calf. Fresh bread was piled high, and dishes of beans and root vegetables steamed in front of the hungry men. Edda was called from her duties in the kitchen to sit with the Thegn and his wife as they entertained their guests for the last time.

The ale flowed freely, but Edgar had warned his men not to drink too deeply, as they would need their wits about them during their flight to the dock later that night. Sigesworth's housecarls were also present, but none of the local farmers were invited, as they would normally have been.

'We can't have tongues wagging after you've gone,' explained Sigesworth. 'That would reflect badly on us. Things are bad enough without us being punished for harbouring a fugitive.'

They feasted well into the night, then spent the next few hours talking with their hosts. At last, perhaps two hours past midnight, Edgar called his men to order. The talk subsided and all waited to hear what Edgar would say.

'The time has arrived. We must pack our meagre effects and leave Bortone, a place where I think we have all, for at least a short time, felt quite at home.'

Muttered agreements rose from his men.

'For that, we give our most heartfelt thanks to Thegn Sigesworth and Lady Thingold. Your kindness to us has been without par. We have no way to thank you, other than with our inadequate words. I just hope our labours in your fields have been more of a help than a hindrance.'

'Indeed they have!' cried Cendred, raising his cup of ale. The two other Bortone carls responded in like manner.

'But now is the time for us to take our leave of you. Our position in England is no longer tenable. We have fought for our lands, we have fought for our country and we have fought for our people, but we can fight no longer. It's time for us to leave England behind. We will be travelling to the lands of Sweyn Estrithson-king, where we hope to find gainful employment in the court, along, perhaps, with King's Thegn Osfrith and his colleagues.

'You will always be with us in our thoughts and in our hearts, as we find our new life, free from the Norman yoke. I hope that some day, it may be possible for us to return to these shores, and that we will find you all healthy and fat on the riches of your land.'

A cheer rose from Sigesworth and his housecarls.

Edgar stepped away from the table and bowed briefly to Sigesworth and Thingold. He walked over to the door of the hall, followed by his carls and Edda. There they pulled on their mail shirts and fastened their belts, hung with their axes, and pulled their helmets onto their heads. Edgar had insisted that they were all prepared for whatever may meet them along the road, for it was far from impossible that the Normans had been spying on them all along, and may attempt to stop them on the road. Fortunately, as they were to take the forgotten road revealed to them by Sigesworth, such an occurrence was far less likely.

To Edgar's surprise, Cendred and his two colleagues also pulled on their mail and joined them at the door. Sigesworth, too, donned the apparel of a warrior.

'You didn't think these three would let you go alone, did you?' Sigesworth asked.

They walked out of the door and found that during the night, an appreciable fog had formed. It was difficult to see all the way across the courtyard.

'Good,' said Edgar, looking around. 'This fog should muffle the sound of our passage and also help to hide us from view.'

Their horses had been saddled and prepared for the journey. A young lad from one of the outlying farms stood holding the horses' reins.

'Thank you, Radulf,' said Sigesworth, taking the reins from the boy. The young lad bowed and made a low murmuring sound.

'The lad is dumb. He could not speak of this even if he wanted to.' He pressed a silver penny into the lad's hand, at which the lad bowed again and made a more enthusiastic mewling noise.

The men climbed up onto their horses and pulled their mail shirts as comfortably as they could around them and straightened the dangling handles of their axes. Edgar took his sword from Guthrum, who had carried it out from the mead hall, and slipped the shoulder strap over his helmet so the sword lay by his left leg, just behind the axe. He leaned over and stretched out his arms to Edda, who lifted her arms into his. With a heave, he pulled her up onto the saddle in front of him.

'You're getting too heavy for this, girl,' grumbled Edgar. 'Lady Thingold has been feeding you too well.'

'Well then,' she replied tartly, 'you'll have to see to it that I get my own horse next time, won't you?'

'Impudent child!' grinned Edgar.

He looked around at his companions.

'Are we all ready?'

Receiving positive replies, he gently prodded his horse with his prick spurs and the animal started walking slowly towards the gate of the palisade.

It was still dark, though the glow from the sun's approach could be seen towards the eastern horizon, towards the sea. Still, it was feeble and faint in the fog. Edgar let Sigesworth and his carls lead the way, as they were far more familiar with the paths than he was, and could pick their way along them even in this twilit gloom. They walked their horses at a steady pace away from Bortone, until Sigesworth led them off the main road, along a hedge line. Edgar could just make out little specks of colour, flowers along the base of the hedge.

Birds were in full song by the time they followed the path into some woodlands. Here the ground became steep and Sigesworth slowed their pace. The growing twilight could not penetrate well here beneath the canopy of newly emerging leaves. The path continued downward alongside a gushing brook, which splashed and clattered over round, moss-covered boulders. Eventually, they emerged into a clearing, where the brook took a turning to the right and tumbled away from them. The path continued across the clearing, slightly uphill towards another stand of trees, somewhat more open than the woodlands they had just traversed. A slight lifting of the fog allowed Edgar to see right across the clearing. The sky was distinctly lighter now, the contrast of being under the open sky accentuating the increase in brightness. As Edgar watched, the fog rolled back across the clearing, making it impossible to see more than thirty yards or so in front of them.

'It's alright, I think I know where I'm going,' said Sigesworth, comfortingly. He guided his horse down the steep hill until they emerged from the woodland once again into another clearing.

'Let's pause a minute to regain our bearings,' said Sigesworth. It was a welcome suggestion. Edgar and his party all felt that they were travelling through the unknown, the mist making it unknowable. As they stood in silence and Sigesworth peered around him to confirm his knowledge of where he was, they could hear the faint sound of waves.

'I can hear the sea,' said Edda, quietly, not wishing to disturb the profound silence they found themselves in.

'Yes, not far now,' said Edgar.

'Ah, I see,' said Sigesworth confidently. 'This way.' He led them across the clearing and soon they joined a clearer path through scrubland dotted with gorse bushes. The path turned north and parallel to the shore, which from the sound of the waves was much closer now.

Ahead of them, Edgar saw some shadowy shapes moving quickly.

'What's that?' he asked.

The housecarls all strained to see what was ahead of them. A patch of thinner mist drifted past just at that moment, and Edgar saw the shapes resolve themselves into men.

Men with spears.

Normans.

They spread across the path, lowering their spears, pointing them towards the horsemen. A scuffling sound behind them confirmed that a second troop had closed in and that they were now trapped.

'How…?' Edgar stammered.

Around him, his housecarls and those of Sigesworth were drawing their axes from their belts.

'Cendred, Agra, Gothric, lower your weapons. This is not your fight,' said Sigesworth, a hard edge to his voice.

'What do you mean?' demanded Edgar.

'I'm sorry, Edgar.'

'You… you've betrayed us?'

Sigesworth looked sorrowfully at Edgar. He lowered his eyes, unable to look at the young Thegn.

'They said I could keep Bortone,' he said.

With that he wheeled his horse around and galloped back the way they had come, passing between the spearmen to their rear.

A voice called out from the mist behind the rank of soldiers ahead of them. 'Edgar of Rapendun! I want Edgar of Rapendun! Hand him over to me for trial and the rest of you can leave.'

'Bugger that,' muttered Eric.

Sigesworth's housecarls looked confused and distressed.

'Cendred…?' said Agra.

'The Thegn says we leave it.'

'But…'

'I know.'

'We can't…'

'I know.'

Cendred cleared his throat and shouted into the mist. 'If you want him, you'll have to come and get him!'

'You will all die, and Bortone will burn.'

'That remains to be seen.'

'Who speaks for you?' called Edgar.

'I am Roger, Baron de Barentin, and I speak for the

King.'

A slight thinning of the mist revealed the Baron with a smaller man beside him, presumably a translator, who was actually speaking.

'Not our king,' shouted back Halfdene.

De Barentin snapped an order and the spearmen began to advance.

'On my word,' said Edgar quietly. He took hold of Edda and lowered her from his horse. 'Fast and low,' he hissed at her. 'Hide.'

His Ulfberht sword slid from its scabbard. He noticed Edda, small and difficult to see in the fog, scamper away to his right. With luck, the Normans would not have seen her at all.

Edgar glanced round. The spearmen behind them were advancing cautiously. On Edgar's command, the riders formed a circle. At least they would be able to see all around them. Edgar admitted to himself that the situation did not look good.

'We'll have to take the battle to them,' whispered Guthrum. 'Otherwise they'll be on us from both sides at the same time.'

'Agreed,' said Edgar. 'The rear?'

Guthrum nodded and wheeled his horse round to face the spearmen behind them. Edgar followed, as did the other carls. With a shout, Edgar spurred his horse forward. He raised his sword, picked his mark and plunged towards the spearman. Each of his companions did the same. The spearmen, not expecting a full-frontal attack, faltered. One dropped his spear and turned to run.

His act served to confuse the other spearmen, and their spear tips wavered. They had no time in which to contemplate. In an instant, the English riders were on them, slashing downwards with swords and axes. Four Normans fell immediately. The riders broke through the rank and wheeled round to take on more. The spearmen had recovered from the shock and turned to face the oncoming riders. Spears were levelled and Gothric was unseated. He fell heavily to the ground, but sprang to his feet remarkably quickly, bringing his axe down on the spear that had toppled him. The spear shattered and the man holding it staggered back. He swiftly drew out his sword and swung it at Gothric, who deflected it with the haft of his axe. The hook of the blade caught round the sword, and with a powerful pull, Gothric yanked the sword out of the Norman's hand. As he grinned in victory and prepared to deliver a fatal blow to his opponent, another Norman to his left thrust his spear into Gothric's side. Gothric fell, his axe thudding into the ground beside his head.

Halfdene, arriving just too late, swung his axe down on the Norman who had just killed Gothric, splitting his helm in two, and smashing the skull within. A third spear jabbed towards Halfdene's face and he pulled back sharply to avoid it. The swift movement unbalanced him and he slid backwards from his horse. He hit the ground, and momentarily saw stars. Then his survival instinct took over, and he was on his feet and swinging his axe before he knew what he was doing. The third spearman pulled back as Halfdene's axe whistled past his face, but he did not see Cendred behind him. Cendred thrust his sword into the man's neck, just below the base of his helmet. Halfdene nodded his thanks and turned to face another Norman.

Edgar, Guthrum and Eric had dispatched their targets efficiently and now turned to face the other group of footmen. They were advancing quickly and were almost within spear reach of the riders. There were more of them than there were in the rear party.

Edgar caught sight of their leader, sitting on his horse, urging his men forward. He recognised the bulky shape of Roger de Barentin. Through the mist, Edgar noted a large man, tending to fat, as he remembered him from Rapendun. His features were hidden by his helmet, which sprouted long black feathers from its crown. His mail was well-fitting and the surcoat was a rich crimson, edged with gold braid. His shield was black with a red griffin painted on it. A shape danced round by de Barentin's horse's hooves. The dog growled at the sound of battle.

He had no more time to look at de Barentin, the soldiers were on him. He slashed with the sword, but his horse took a spear point deep in its chest and fell lifeless beneath him. He fell backwards, rolling away from the horse and the Normans. Guthrum immediately placed himself and his horse between Edgar and the Normans. Edgar stood and slapped Guthrum on the leg, letting him know that he was alright. The soldiers clustered around Eric and Guthrum, who hacked relentlessly at their attackers. Guthrum lost his horse quickly, it fell to a blow from a poleaxe. He slid elegantly off the horse as it fell, bringing his axe round in a mighty swing as he did so. The mail shirt of his horse's killer split under the heavy blow and the axe embedded itself in the man's chest. Guthrum brought his foot up and shoved the body off his axe.

Edgar glanced around. It was hopeless. There were too many Normans and too few of his own men. The Normans were going to win. He redoubled his efforts, swinging his sword with extra force. He killed two more Normans, stabbing at the unprotected parts of their faces.

As the second of these fell, another soldier stepped forward, already swinging his sword in a downward arc towards Edgar. Edgar stepped nimbly aside, deflecting the blow as well as he could from his awkward angle. The sword missed his head but glanced off his left shoulder. Edgar felt the collar-bone snap, and he involuntarily yelled in pain. The Norman in front of him grinned with satisfaction and began to bring his sword up again, but he stopped, suddenly. He looked confused and coughed, spraying blood into Edgar's face. Then he fell, a feathered arrow sticking out from between his shoulder blades.

More arrows were finding their mark in the backs of the Normans. Cendred and Agra, both now horseless, joined Edgar, having finished off the rearguard Normans.

The Normans were thrown into confusion, some turning to face whoever these new attackers were. Edgar stepped back from the fray and looked searchingly to find out who his new allies were. Marching forward behind the Normans was a wave of twenty warriors, swinging axes with such devastating efficiency that the Normans were losing men with every swing.

The Normans panicked and began to scatter. Roger de Barentin looked on in disbelief as his ambush party disintegrated in front of him. He was clearly not a stupid man and had recognised a defeat when he saw one. He turned his horse round and set off at a fast gallop from the scene of his humiliation. Arrows hissed through the air after him, but all missed. A second party of men stepped out from behind the trees ahead of Edgar. They all held powerful-looking bows, and sent more arrows futilely chasing after de Barentin.

'Quick!' shouted a voice. 'You must run, now!'

'Edgar!' shouted Halfdene. 'It's the ship's captain! Bloody hell!'

Edgar saw a short, well-dressed man gesticulating at him. The Normans were in despair now, having seen their leader abandon them. They also began to run.

'Edda!' cried Edgar, and to his relief, he saw a small bundle run out of the trees to his right and towards him. She ran into his arms, and he suppressed a cry of pain as his collar bones ground together as he hugged her. He lifted her up, relying almost entirely on his intact shoulder. Halfdene leaned down from his horse and pulled her onto the saddle in front of him.

'Come, now! They'll regroup quickly!' called the small man again.

Edgar, Guthrum, Cendred and Agra ran towards the man, whilst the still-mounted men circled round. They reached the cover of the trees ahead of them with their rescuers hard on their heels. Edgar paused and looked back at the field of battle, where Gothric still lay among several dead Normans. Halfdene crashed past him and into the trees, taking Edda to safety. Eric galloped a few yards behind. Suddenly Edgar saw Eric tense in his saddle. The wicked tip of a bodkin arrow had burst through the front of his throat. Blood gushed profusely from the wound.

'No!' screamed Guthrum, running back to help his friend.

'Guthrum!' yelled Edgar. He broke into a run, following Guthrum.

Ahead of them, Eric toppled slowly from his horse. From the loose and uncontrolled way he fell, Edgar feared the worst. Guthrum skidded to a halt next to where Eric lay, crashing to his knees. He held Eric's head in his hands.

'Eric! Eric!' he cried.

Edgar slid down onto his knees beside Guthrum. He looked down at Eric's face. His eyes were open but unseeing. The tip of the bodkin arrow stood out three inches from Eric's throat. The blood was no longer flowing.

'It's too late, Guthrum,' he said.

Tears were pouring down Guthrum's cheeks.

'Eric!' he called again.

Arrows began to thud into the ground around them.

'Guthrum, we must go now. We can't help him. He's gone.'

'No,' murmured Guthrum.

'Guthrum, now!' Edgar shouted. He pulled at Guthrum's arm with his uninjured one. More arrows were whistling past them now as the Normans began to regroup and attempt to snatch some small victory from their defeat.

Wordlessly, Guthrum got to his feet and he and Edgar, bent double, ran back towards the safety of the trees.

They trooped disconsolately down to the shoreline. The port was just quarter of a mile away. Edgar caught up with the ship's captain.

'Thank you,' he said, inadequately.

'You're welcome,' said the dapper little man. 'Loki,' he held out his hand.

'What?'

'My name. Loki.'

Edgar recalled the Norse myths that his grandfather had told him about when he was a child. Loki was a prankster, a wayward god, and killer of Baldur the Bright.

'An ill-starred name for such a welcome ally,' he said.

He took Loki's hand in his. 'Edgar,' he added.

'It's not my real name, but I like it.'

'Does it suit you?' asked Edgar.

Loki just smiled.

'I have to ask; why did you come to our aid? What's in it for you?'

'You would have me forgo the ridiculously overpriced fee that I negotiated for your passage?'

'I would say you've more than earned it today. But how did you know about any of this?'

'You'll see.'

They walked along the dockside to where Stormleaper, Loki's sleek ship, sat at a jetty. Standing next to the ship were two men, one a wild-haired, tough-looking character. The other was Alaric.

'Alaric!' said Edgar in surprise. 'What are you doing here?'

'I learned of de Barentin's plan two days ago.'

'Why didn't you tell me?' asked Edgar.

'I couldn't. Bortone was being carefully watched. If I'd gone in it would have been reported immediately. I'm sorry, I had no choice. I'd followed Halfdene to the docks and saw who he'd chosen to ferry you away. I made discreet enquiries and found that the choice was sound. When I learned of de Barentin's ambush, I came to Captain Loki and persuaded him to plan a counter-attack.'

'How on earth did you persuade him to do that?' asked Edgar, more astonished by the moment.

'I doubled his fee,' shrugged Alaric.

'From my money?'

'Indeed, my lord.'

'Besides,' said Loki, 'I bloody hate Normans. Your

friend didn't have to sell his proposition too hard; my men have been itching for a scrap with these officious bastards for months now.'

Alaric looked over the bedraggled party. 'You're a man down,' he said.

'We are. We are many men down.'

'Come,' said Loki. 'We must catch the tide. First, though,' he snapped his fingers and a crewman handed him a short woollen cloak. 'Your girl. She must wear this for the whole journey. She must pull the cowl up over her face and keep it there until we make land at the other end.'

'What?' said Edgar. 'Why?'

'It is bad luck for a female to be on board a ship. Being young, if she keeps her head covered, the daughters of Aegir may not recognise that she is female, and may let us cross the waves unmolested.'

'What?

'No hood, no passage. Just do it.'

Edgar turned to Edda. 'Do what the Captain says, Edda. Keep the cloak on and the hood up all the time until we arrive at the Danish port.'

Edda nodded and took the cloak without complaint. She pulled it on and put the hood over her face, holding it closed at her chin.

'All aboard!' called one of Loki's men.

Halfdene handed the reins of his horse to Cendred.

'What will you do?' asked Halfdene.

Cendred exchanged a look with Agra. 'We will return to Bortone. Our Thegn has acted dishonourably, but he is an old man and desperate. And he is our friend. I apologise for his behaviour. It is out of character for him. I am deeply sorry for the loss of your friend.'

Thegn

'And I for yours,' replied Halfdene. They shook hands and Halfdene followed Guthrum onto the ship. Edgar picked Edda up and passed her to Loki.

As the crew of the ship put their backs and shoulders to the great oars, the ship slipped gently away from the jetty and out towards the open sea. Guthrum sat unmoving and silent at the prow of the ship, his face an immobile and unreadable mask.

Edgar stood at the rear of the ship, hanging on to the tall, carved stern, staring back at his homeland as it slipped quietly and irrevocably into the mist.

Historical Note

The Battle of Stamford Bridge took place on 25th September 1066. The invading Norwegian forces had won a crushing victory against the northern earls Edwin and Morcar at Fulford on 20th September and had received the surrender of York.

King Harold II Godwinson's forced march north and then a few days later south again are the stuff of legend, but nonetheless real and remarkable for that. His opponent at Stamford Bridge, Harald III Sigurdson, King of Norway, is the man later called Harald Hardrada. The epithet 'Hardrada' means 'hard ruler', with overtones of 'tyrant'. It is not a name that was ever used, for obvious reasons, during the King's lifetime and was only coined some years after his death.

There is some disagreement amongst scholars about what was present at Stamford Bridge at the time of the battle. There is a wide, stony ford at the site of the present town (hence the name 'Stanford'). Recently, a Roman settlement has been discovered just to the south of Stamford Bridge, and if there had been a bridge over the river in the eleventh century, then it may have been there. The present bridge at Stamford dates to 1727 but does replace an earlier structure.

With the large, easily crossable ford, and the possibility that there was no bridge, the story of the lone swordsman (or axeman in some versions) on the bridge is probably apocryphal. Even if a lone swordsman did block the bridge, then surely an English archer could have stepped up to the mark. It is such a good story, though, with its themes of courage, determination, pluck and trickery, that it deserves a retelling.

The battle resulted in a resounding victory for the English. Harald Sigurdson and Tostig Godwinson both perished, as did most of the Viking host. The Battle of Stamford Bridge traditionally marks the end of the Viking Age in England, even though more Scandinavian invasions were to follow.

Nineteen days later, King Harold Godwinson lay dead on the field at Senlac.

The Norman advance across England was one of the most brutal periods in English history. The flower of the English aristocracy had been cut down in three battles in close succession. Duke William's claim to the throne of England was very tenuous. It is possible that Edward the Confessor promised the throne to him at some point (Edward had been reared in the Norman court), but any similar promise made by Harold Godwinson (who was effectively William's prisoner at the time that the alleged oath was made) would almost certainly have been made under duress and thus would not be binding.

In the absence of an effective English leadership, resistance movements appeared all over England. Some resistance leaders are known to us, Edgar the Atheling, Eadric the Wild and Hereward (the epithet 'the Wake' is a later excrescence). There will have been many others. These groups are mentioned in contemporary Norman chronicles as *silvatici*, or forest-dwellers.

There remains the intriguing possibility that the early development of tales of such heroic outlaws as Robin Hood owe their inception to the silvatici, or Wildmen.

During the writing of this book, I spent much time visiting the sites mentioned, a very enjoyable part of the writing process during which I made many new friends.

Edgar's home of Rapendun is now Repton, in Derbyshire. The church in this story still stands there to this day, and the crypt where St Wystan and a couple of Mercian kings were buried can be visited, though the saint and the kings were removed long ago.

Edda's home of Osmundestun, now Osmaston, although mentioned in the Domesday Book, reveals nothing of its thousand-year history to the casual visitor.

York is worth a visit at any time, and you can follow the Roman road (now marked by the A166) from there through Gate Helmsley (Elmeslac) to Stamford Bridge, a pleasant little town in which to while away a few hours. If you go there, seek out the stony ford itself.

The tiny village of Skirpenbeck lies just two miles to the north-east of Stamford Bridge and contains a moated manor and a church with elements dating back to before the Conquest.

The settlement of Bortone, where Edgar and his

companions stayed with Thegn Sigesworth and Lady Thingold, is now called Burton Agnes. I took great pleasure in my visit there, not just because my paternal grandparents were called Bert and Agnes, but because next to the huge and impressive Elizabethan stately home Burton Agnes Hall, stands the Norman manor house, possibly on the footprint of the earlier Anglo-Saxon thegnly hall owned by Sigesworth himself.

Gazetteer

Eleventh-century place names used in the book and their modern equivalent.

Bebbanburg	Bamburgh, Northumberland
Berewich	Berwick upon Tweed, Northumberland
Bretlinton	Bridlington, Yorkshire
Bortone	Burton Agnes, Yorkshire
Burtone	Burton upon Trent, Staffordshire
Cestrefeld	Chesterfield, Derbyshire
Chelc	Great Kelk, Yorkshire
Deorby	Derby, Derbyshire
Donecastre	Doncaster, Yorkshire
Elmeslac	Gate Helmsley, Yorkshire
Eoforwic	York, Yorkshire
Heldernesse	Holderness, Yorkshire
Hildeston	Fictional
Hochenale	Hucknall, Nottinghamshire
Lincolia	Lincoln, Lincolnshire
Lundenburg	London. One of several names for London, this was current in the eleventh century.
Mammesfeld	Mansfield, Nottinghamshire
Osmundestun	Osmaston, Derbyshire
Rapendun	Repton, Derbyshire
Redford	Radford, Nottingham
Richale	Riccall, Yorkshire
Scardeburg	Scarborough, Yorkshire

Scarpenbec	Skirpenbeck, Yorkshire
Senlac	Location of the Battle of Hastings. The name by which the English called this place is not known, but the Anglo-Saxon Chronicle refers to it as 'the place of the hoary apple tree'. By the early twelfth century, it was being referred to as Senlac.
Snotingeham	Nottingham, Nottinghamshire
Stanford	Stamford Bridge, Yorkshire
Tatecastre	Tadcaster, Yorkshire
Tilsdene	Fictional
Warwic	Warwick, Warwickshire
Westmynster	Westminster
Willeton	Willington, Derbyshire
Windeham	Fictional

About the Author

Patrick Maloney had diverse jobs before settling down as a writer: court assistant, computer programmer, systems analyst and actor. He is an active volunteer archaeologist and, amongst other sites, has excavated at the 1066 battlefield at Fulford. He lives in Lancashire with his wife, Toni.

Acknowledgements

Special thanks to Mum, Dad, Toni, Dee, Karl and Alan, my beta-readers. To Bill Rogers and Christopher John Payne, both of whom have provided invaluable help and advice. To the members of the Battle of Stamford Bridge Heritage Society for their hospitality and friendship during the excellent 950th anniversary celebrations of the battle in 2016. To the late Tom Wyles for his tour of the Stamford Bridge battlefield and unfortunately brief friendship. To Chas Jones for his very informative tour of the Fulford battle site, and for the opportunity to dig there. To Vladimir Shvachko for his beautiful artwork and to Ken Leeder for his brilliant cover design. Also to Theo Moorfield, for the outstanding website.

www.ThegnEdgar.com

Thegn Edgar will return in

THE LOST LAND

Printed in Poland
by Amazon Fulfillment
Poland Sp. z o.o., Wrocław